W9-CBG-106

THE LUDWIG CONSPIRACY

The LUDWIG CONSPIRACY

A historical thriller

OLIVER PÖTZSCH

Houghton Mifflin Harcourt
Boston New York
2013

PAPL DISCARDED

Text copyright © 2011 by Ullstein Buchverlage GmbH, Berlin
Maps copyright © Peter Balm, Berlin, Germany
English translation copyright © 2013 Anthea Bell

All rights reserved

For information about permission to reproduce selections from this book,
write to Permissions, Houghton Mifflin Harcourt Publishing Company,
215 Park Avenue South, New York, New York 10003.

The Ludwig Conspiracy was first published in 2011
by Ullstein Taschenbuch Verlag as *Die Ludwig Verschwörung*.
Translated from German by Anthea Bell.
First published in English by Houghton Mifflin Harcourt in 2013.

www.hmhbooks.com

Library of Congress Cataloging-in-Publication Data is available.
ISBN 978-0-547-74010-2

Book design by Victoria Hartman

Printed in the United States of America
DOC 10 9 8 7 6 5 4 3 2 1

For my father

History is the lie that is commonly agreed upon.

— VOLTAIRE

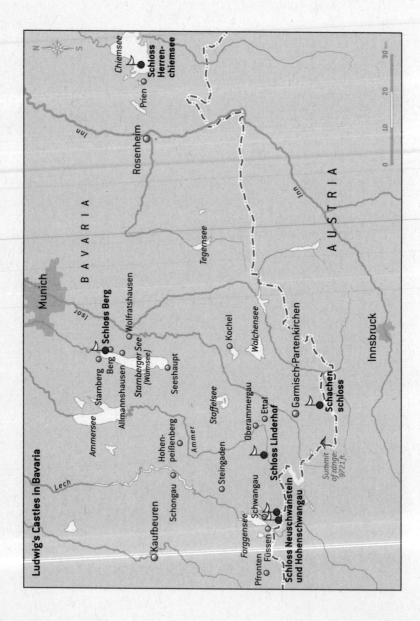

Ludwig's Castles in Bavaria

N

0 10 20 30 km

BAVARIA

AUSTRIA

Munich

Isar

Rosenheim

Inn

Prien

Chiemsee

Schloss Herrenchiemsee

Schloss Berg

Wolfratshausen

Tegernsee

Starnberg
Berg
Allmannshausen

Starnberger See
(Würmsee)

Ammersee

Seeshaupt

Kochel

Walchensee

Staffelsee

Garmisch-Partenkirchen

Schachen schloss

Hohenpeißenberg

Ammer

Oberammergau

Ettal

Schloss Linderhof

Steingaden

Schongau

Kaufbeuren

Lech

Forggensee

Schwangau

Füssen

Pfronten

Schloss Neuschwänstein und Hohenschwangau

Summit of range: 9721 ft.

Innsbruck

Inn

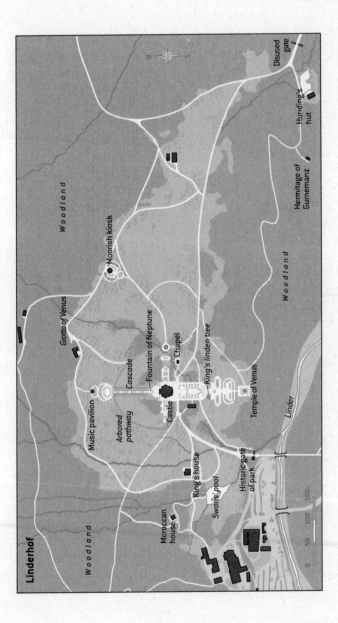

Linderhof

Woodland

Woodland

Woodland

Woodland

Grotto of Venus

Moorish kiosk

Music pavilion

Arbored pathway

Cascade

Fountain of Neptune

Chapel

Castle

King's linden tree

Temple of Venus

King's house

Swans' pool

Historic gate of park

Moroccan house

Hermitage of Gurnemanz

Hunding's hut

Disused gate

Linder

0   50   100   150

Herrenchiemsee

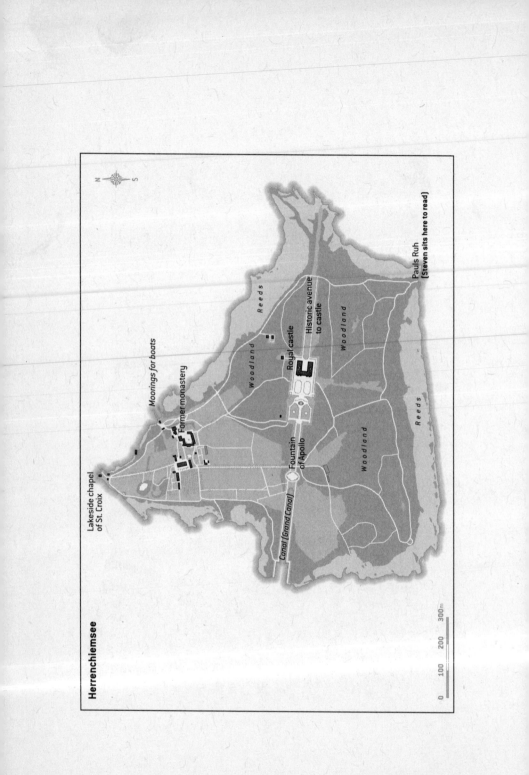

Lakeside chapel
of St. Croix

Moorings for boats

Former monastery

Reeds

Woodland

Woodland

Royal castle

Historic avenue
to castle

Woodland

Pauls Ruh
[Steven sits here to read]

Reeds

Fountain
of Apollo

Woodland

Canal [Grand Canal]

N

S

0   100   200   300m

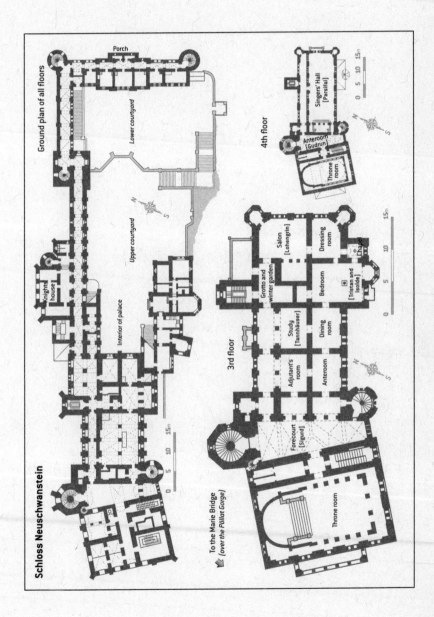

Schloss Neuschwanstein

Ground plan of all floors

Porch

Lower courtyard

Upper courtyard

Knights' house

Interior of palace

0 5 10 15m

To the Marie Bridge
[over the Pöllat Gorge]

3rd floor

Grotto and winter garden

Salon [Lohengrin]

Dressing room

Study [Tannhäuser]

Bedroom

[Tristan and Isolde]

Chapel

Adjutant's room

Dining room

Anteroom

Forecourt [Sigurd]

Throne room

0 5 10 15m

4th floor

Singers' Hall [Parsifal]

Anteroom [Gudrun]

Throne room

0 5 10 15m

Dramatis Personae of the Historical Characters

Ludwig II, king of Bavaria

Professor Dr. Bernhard von Gudden, doctor specializing in insanity

Dr. Max Schleiss von Loewenfeld, royal physician

Theodor Marot, his medical assistant (not recorded in history)

Alfred, Count Eckbrecht von Dürckheim-Montmartin, adjutant to the king

Richard Hornig, equerry and constant companion of the king

Hermann von Kaulbach, painter

Maria, maidservant to Ludwig II (not recorded in history)

Johann, Baron von Lutz, president of the Bavarian Council of Ministers

Maximilian Karl Theodor, Count von Holnstein, Master of the Royal Stables

Carl von Strelitz, Prussian agent (not recorded in history)

Other Historical Characters

King Maximilian II, father of Ludwig II

Marie Friederike of Prussia, mother of Ludwig II

Otto I, Ludwig's deranged younger brother, later king

Prince Luitpold, uncle of Ludwig II, later prince regent

Empress Sisi (Elisabeth) of Austria, cousin and confidante of
Ludwig II

Prince Otto von Bismarck, chancellor of the German Empire

Richard Wagner, composer

A Few Introductory Words

On the night between 13 and 14 June 1886, the bodies of two men were found drifting in the shallows of Lake Starnberg. Both were among the most famous personages of their time: Dr. Bernhard von Gudden, a psychiatrist known all over Europe, and King Ludwig II of Bavaria, sometimes known today as the Fairy-tale King, or Swan King, or simply "Mad King Ludwig." Ludwig was born in 1845 and ascended the throne in 1864. He commissioned two castles and a palace—Schloss Neuschwanstein (imitated by Walt Disney for his company's logo and symbol of Disney World), Schloss Linderhof, and Herrenchiemsee (an imitation of Versailles). He was a crucial patron of the composer Richard Wagner, and a Roman Catholic who struggled with his homosexuality. His death remains a mystery.

An investigating committee, convened at short notice, concluded that the king, who had been deposed only three days earlier on the grounds of insanity, had strangled his doctor and then committed suicide in the water.

That is the official version.

PROLOGUE

Somewhere near Munich, October 2010

THE KING TOOK OUT a cell phone and stared at the text message, while Professor Paul Liebermann, lying at the royal feet, spat out blood and spruce needles.

The message appeared to annoy The Royal Highness. The king raised an eyebrow and sighed regretfully, as if disappointed with a small child. Then the king dug the toe of one boot into the man on the ground, to make sure that he was not, at this very moment, choking to death. Paul Liebermann moaned, then coughed out a few more spruce needles. Everything around him was shrouded in fog, a mystic landscape where a few dead spruce trees rose to the overcast night sky.

"I . . . I really don't know what you want from me," the professor gasped, turning over on his back with a groan. "There must be some mistake . . . a terrible mistake."

"Terrible. Yes, indeed," the king murmured. "I am extremely displeased."

The Royal Highness was wearing a suit of the best English tweed, with a red silk cravat and a white fur coat. The hem of the coat was spattered with blood.

My blood, Liebermann thought. *And a lot of it. It makes that coat look like ermine. Could it actually be?*

He couldn't tell for certain, because his left eye was swollen and completely closed while his right eye was encrusted with blood. His glasses lay twisted and broken somewhere in the undergrowth; he had lost his hat and walking stick already, in the car on the way here; and remains of moldering spruce needles still stuck to his gums. The two thugs had stuffed his mouth with them until he was almost choking on the stuff. In addition, the effects of the injection hadn't worn off yet.

They had seized him only a few steps from the secondhand bookshop. When he heard the car, he knew he had to act. He had hidden the book and hurried out so as not to give away the man in the shop. After only a little prick, he had collapsed into the arms of the two powerful men beside him. They pushed him into the car. He had lost consciousness after a few seconds, only to come back to his senses in this wood, among mushrooms and withered bramble bushes. In the distance, he could hear the faint droning of cars; otherwise, only the cawing of a few crows broke the silence of fall.

They had been hitting Liebermann over and over again for the last two hours, in the stomach, in the face, between the legs. Meanwhile, twilight had fallen over the wood. The king and the thugs were only dark shadows against an even darker background.

Looking at it now, it really does seem to have something to do with Ludwig. What irony! Who could have guessed?

The fact that Liebermann had not said anything yet was due partly to his inborn obstinacy, but also partly to his history. During his tenure as a professor at Jena University, Paul Liebermann had been an outspoken critic of the East German system. When that landed him in Bautzen prison for two years, things happened that still made him cry out in his sleep. He had learned how to take a beating. And he would sooner bite off his tongue than tell these people where the hiding place was.

The secret of the book had been kept for more than a hundred years. He mustn't give it away. Not now, when their goal was finally within reach.

The injection had felled him like a hammer blow. He could still remember the deserted street in the Westend district, and the car that had looked so like an old Wartburg. But the hours after that were a nightmarish blur. Even events before the injection seemed curiously vague. Liebermann's last concrete memory was of his breakfast muesli, the last of which he had brought up some time ago on the woodland floor.

"Want us to work him over some more?" asked one of the two thugs, whom Liebermann saw through the mist, along with the king. "I know a few more tricks from the camp. They'd be sure to make him talk."

"I suppose it's pointless." Shrugging, the king put the cell phone away somewhere in the folds of the ermine fur coat and stared at Liebermann. "This man is stubborn as a mule. And I do so hate violence. Apparently the search of his hotel room didn't turn up anything either. Gawain and Tristan turned the whole place upside down. If only I knew . . ."

The king fell silent, eyes wandering over the woodland floor, which was covered with leaves and countless scraps of paper. In the middle of them, Liebermann lay like a broken doll, twisted and bound, a piece of paper smeared with soil tickling his nose. The letters on it swam before his eyes. Only after some time did they begin to make sense. It seemed to be a line of poetry.

Don't you see the Erl-King, father dear?

In spite of his condition, the former professor of modern history smiled. The Romantic period had always been his hobbyhorse, and Goethe's "The Erl-King," a ballad in the form of a dialogue between a father and his dying son, who is about to be taken from earthly life by the Erl-King, was his favorite poem. Nothing from any other ballad, he thought, so expressed the longing to die and dissolve into the natural world as those lines. Now Liebermann himself was facing the Erl-King.

O lovely child, come play with me . . .

"*Mon Dieu!*"

The king kicked the damp woodland floor with the toe of a boot, sending foliage and scraps of paper flying into the air. The white fur coat flapped in the cold October wind, making the king look like a fat monstrous swan.

"Where the hell is the bloody book?" the king hissed. "We were so close, and now this. Nothing but damn poems!" The king grimaced and slowly breathed in and out. "Still, I shouldn't have torn it up. If anything in this world lasts, it's art. Only art is timeless. Why didn't you stop me?"

This last remark was for the two thugs, who awkwardly rubbed their bloodstained fingers.

"It . . . it all happened so fast, Excellency," one of them muttered. "You were holding that book of poetry, and . . ."

"Ah, *arrêtez!*"

The king made a dismissive gesture, and then winced, as if afflicted with a terrible migraine. After a long moment, and with no advance warning, the king kicked the professor in the stomach.

"What did you do with the book?" the royal shouted. "What did you do with it? It's mine. All mine!"

Liebermann spat blood and needles, and a few scraps of paper. Groaning, he curled up in the fetal position to protect himself from further kicks, but luckily none came.

Liebermann wasn't sure whether he could take any more pain. Maybe he would give the secret away after all?

Stand fast! The royal line is at stake.

Humming quietly, The Royal Highness knelt down in front of Liebermann and let soil and scraps of paper run through those aristocratic fingers.

"Nature and art," the king murmured. "What could be more beautiful? We must remember the old myths when those two things were still one. A twilight of the gods lies ahead. Away with false idols . . ."

Suddenly the king stopped, staring at a scrap of paper. Then the royal began to giggle.

"Of course," the king spluttered, hand over mouth like a little girl. "The same wrapping paper, it's only the book that's different. You . . . you idiot halfwits!" The king had shouted those last words, waving the scrap of paper in front of the noses of the two thugs. "*This* is where you ought to have been looking. *Merde*. I'll have your eyes put out, all of you!"

The king stopped, eyes glazing over. Walking over to Liebermann and leaning over him, The Royal Highness leisurely took out a small, old-fashioned pistol from beneath the fur coat. Its butt looked like a bird's head.

"Crafty old man," the king whispered. "You bourgeois are all the same—you just love to intrigue. And your plan almost worked. But this gave you away."

Giggling again, the king held a grubby piece of paper in front of the eye that wasn't swollen shut. Once more, it was some time before the letters came together to make any sense. They seemed to be the imprint from a stamp, a kind of *ex libris*, using old-fashioned script. On the paper, the professor made out a name and address.

STEVEN LUKAS, ANTIQUARIAN BOOKSELLER
Rare and valuable books of the
seventeenth to nineteenth centuries
Prices on application

Suddenly a shrill bell rang in Liebermann's mind. He must not endanger the man in the bookshop. If he did, then all was lost.

"Listen," he stammered. "I . . . I can get the book for you. Give me an hour, and then I'll . . ."

But the king suddenly seemed to have lost all interest in him.

"My dear Professor," the king said softly, "thank you for your readiness to cooperate. But you will understand that your survival would stand in the way of my noble aims. At least you are dying in a good cause."

The Excellency held the pistol against the forehead of the distinguished Professor Paul Liebermann and pulled the trigger. White matter from Liebermann's brain spurted out over the woodland floor, covering spruce needles and parts of Goethe's "Erl-King" poem.

"And now to go and pick up my property at last," the king hissed, stalking away through the wood, bearing erect as if inspecting an invisible parade.

The professor's empty eyes stared up at a nocturnal October sky where a few crows were circling.

THE LUDWIG CONSPIRACY

· 1 ·

Steven Lukas sat at the scratched old mahogany desk in his antiquarian bookshop in Munich's Westend district and watched the water in his teapot slowly turn brown. The aromatic fragrance of bergamot and orange peel rose to his nostrils. He gave the tea infuser another minute, then took it out and placed it carefully on a saucer beside a couple of large disintegrating tomes.

As a small cloud of vapor rose from the teacup, the bookseller let his eyes wander around his small domain. He very much hoped not to be disturbed for the next few hours. Outside, the dull gray of an October afternoon reigned, plunging the little shop, which was full of nooks and crannies, into dim twilight. The bookshelves up to the ceiling cast shadows like mighty trees; in the back part of the shop, beside the door leading to the stockroom and the large archive in the cellar, stood a 1950s brass lamp, casting warm yellow light on the desk. The place smelled of tea, leather, and old paper. The only sound was the ticking of an old nineteenth-century grandfather clock that Steven had bought in better times at a Munich antiques fair.

Steven sighed with pleasure and turned to the book on top of the stack to his right. This leather-bound folio volume was his latest acquisition. Carefully, he opened the discolored brown cover and began reverently leafing through it. Before him lay one of the early editions of the Grimms' *Tales*, dating from 1837. The illustrations of giants, dwarves, bold princes and soulful princesses were smudged here and there, and some of the pages had been torn, but even so, the folio volume was in very good condition. Steven guessed that it would be worth five thousand euros, if not more. He had found it at an estate sale in the upmarket Bogenhausen district of Munich, along with a few crates of other books from the attic of an old lady who had recently died, and he had pressed three hundred-euro bills into the hand of her startled nephew. A Philistine—the nephew had taken the money, not even wondering what was special about the book. Obviously paper meant something to him only when it had denominations printed on it.

Steven smiled as he spooned brown sugar into his tea. Buying that book had been a real stroke of luck. In theory, it would allow him to pay the rent on the shop for the next six months. In reality, he knew he wouldn't be able to part with the Grimm. Old books were like a drug to Steven; the mere smell of yellowing paper made him feel weak. He loved the rustle of the pages, the firm feel of painted parchment or printed handmade paper between his fingertips. It was a sense of happiness that had accompanied him since childhood, and the feeling couldn't be compared to anything else.

Dreamily, the bookseller leafed through the Grimm, admiring the hand-colored engravings. How many generations had held this book in their hands? How many grandfathers had read its stories to their grandchildren? Steven stirred his tea and immersed himself in a world of castles, wolves, witches, and good fairies. He had been born in the United States, in Massachusetts, where people still thought of Germany as a country of dark forests, castles, and the romantic banks of the Rhine. As a child, little Steven had liked the idea of that, but grown-up Steven had discovered that the Germans cared more about expressways and shopping malls than dark, mysterious legends. The old, fairy-tale Germany existed only in the dreams of American and Japanese tourists these days.

And in books.

The shrill sound of the doorbell stirred him from his thoughts. Annoyed, Steven looked up and then sighed. Obviously it wasn't going to be as peaceful a weekend as he'd hoped.

"Frau Schultheiss," he murmured, sipping his tea. "To what do I owe the honor?"

An elderly lady with a pinched expression and combed-back hair had marched into the shop as if she owned it. Now she took off the sunglasses that she wore in spite of the fall rain outside. Small, icy gray eyes flashed at the bookseller, but she at least tried to produce a smile.

"You know exactly what I'm here about, Herr Lukas. I thought we could talk about your price. My husband can come up with another two thousand euros if you—"

"Frau Schultheiss," Steven interrupted, pointing to the walls of shelves overflowing with books, old Jugendstil journals, and framed engravings. "This place is like my home. Would *you* move out of your nice apartment just because someone offered you a few thousand euros?"

Frau Schultheiss looked disparagingly at the once-valuable but now-scratched cherrywood shelves. The varnish had peeled off here and there. Dust had settled on them, and they sagged in places under the weight of the books. In the corridor, a few crates stacked unsteadily on top of one another held newly acquired treasures waiting to be put on display. Steven's unwelcome visitor, still with that iron smile, shrugged her shoulders.

"This is not an apartment but, if I may say so, a rather untidy bookshop."

"Not just a bookshop, an *antiquarian* bookshop," Steven corrected her. "If you know the difference."

Frau Schultheiss frowned. "Very well, then, an antiquarian bookshop. But not living quarters, anyway. Or if it is, not in a state that I would care to live in." She stopped, as if realizing that this was not the cleverest way to conduct negotiations.

"Herr Lukas," she went on, more mildly, "when did you last sell anything? Two weeks ago? A month ago? The Westend is not a district for bookshops these days. Maybe it was once. But now people in this part of town want to buy shoes and clothes, and then drink a nice *latte macchiato*. The fashion boutique I'm planning, with an integrated café and lounge, would fit in here just perfectly. And I don't understand how you, as an American . . ."

"My father was American, Frau Schultheiss," Steven said. "I've told you that a thousand times. I'm as German as you or Chancellor Merkel. Anyway, what, in your opinion, should an American be doing? Selling hamburgers and donuts?"

"You misunderstand me," Frau Schultheiss said. "I only meant . . ."

"If you're interested in eighteenth-century engravings or literature from the Enlightenment, you're welcome to look around," Steven said brusquely. "Otherwise I'll ask you to please leave."

Frau Schultheiss compressed her lips, which were thin enough anyway, then turned without a word and went out. A last chime of the doorbell, and Steven was alone again.

The bookseller took another sip of his tea, which by now was getting unpleasantly cool. Frau Schultheiss just wouldn't let it be! She'd already offered him eight thousand euros to give notice to his landlord, old Seitzinger, and leave the premises available for her boutique. Kurt Seitzinger used to have his joinery workshop in these rooms, but he had retired twenty years ago. At the time, just as Steven finished studying literature at the Ludwig Maximilian University of Munich, he had been entranced by the shop at once; he still thought he could smell the wood, the wood shavings, and the glue. He had never regretted his decision to open his antiquarian bookshop in the Westend district. But that had been at a time when it was still a genuine working-class district with a high proportion of foreigners and students among its inhabitants; now boutiques, trendy bars, sushi takeouts, and hairdressing salons were shooting up like colorful toadstools. The Westend was hip, and his antiquarian bookshop seemed to belong to a forgotten epoch. Even the way Steven dressed seemed old-fashioned compared to the people living here. Other men of his age wore tight-fitting sweatshirts printed with hip logos or band names, paired with sneakers and baseball caps. Steven preferred tweed and corduroy, combining them in suits that, together with his graying, neatly combed hair and reading glasses, made him look like an impoverished British country gentleman. In a Scottish castle, he would look like the rightful heir; here, he sometimes felt twenty years older than he really was. Only a few months earlier, he had quietly celebrated his fortieth birthday. He didn't fit in with his times. He preferred the company of very old books to that of most people, and on most days, he was perfectly happy if the store remained empty of customers.

Sighing, Steven rose from his mahogany desk and wandered around the little shop into which he had put so much of his heart— and so much of his money—for twenty years. Lovingly, he stroked the spines of individual books, straightening one here or there, putting copies gone astray back in their proper places. Finally he began emptying the crates from the estate of the old lady in Bogenhausen and putting the books in the few open spaces on the shelves. Among the books he had bought were an 1888 Baedeker travel guide to Belgium, an eighteenth-century work on chess, and Shelton's standard work on shorthand, *Tachygraphy*, in one of the later editions—treasures, all of them. Whether he would ever sell them was another question.

On one point at least Frau Schultheiss was right: business was going badly, in fact very badly. Not that it had ever really gone well, but until now Steven hadn't minded that so long as he could rummage around in flea markets, libraries, and other antiquarian bookshops to his heart's content. But now the once-handsome inheritance left by his parents was exhausted, and he had to turn his mind to one of the least edifying aspects of human existence: earning money.

When people did come into the shop, most of them were just passersby who didn't want to wait out in the rain for the next bus, or who hoped to buy a cheap Perry Rhodan or the latest Dan Brown.

Not to mention drunks visiting Oktoberfest and looking for a public toilet.

The distinguished old gentleman with glasses and an ivory walking stick that morning, however, had been different. He had shown a great deal of interest in Steven's life in the antiquarian book trade, and he had asked him many questions about an early copy of the diaries of Samuel Pepys. Experts considered particularly valuable the rare work that Steven had acquired only recently.

But knowledgeable as he was, the man had seemed to Steven slightly distracted—indeed, almost as if he were being hunted. His hands had been nervously clutching a package done up with gray wrapping paper and string, obviously a fairly large book. When Steven mentioned it to him, the man just smiled and whispered something that made no sense.

The royal line is at stake . . .

He had also been intrigued by the stranger's nervous glances. Several times, the man had looked through the display window as if expecting something to happen. When Steven went into the stockroom behind the shop for a few minutes to fetch the Pepys diaries, he came back to find that the old gentleman had simply disappeared without so much as a goodbye.

The memory made Steven smile.

Oddballs and old fools, he thought. *No one else comes into my shop anymore. If I don't watch out, I'll be turning into an oddball myself. Maybe I already am?*

He went on clearing the crate, distributing books around the appropriate shelves by subject, climbing up a narrow ladder again and again, and humming the theme of Schubert's *Death and the Maiden*.

Suddenly he stopped.

Level with his head, in between an old, leather-bound Bible and an antique edition of Molière's works, there was a large tome, almost as wide as a man's hand, that he had never seen before. He took the book off the shelf and saw, to his surprise, that what looked like a folio volume wasn't paper at all, but was made of cherrywood glued together. Only the back, made to look like the spine of a book, was leather. The fake book seemed to be one of those camouflaged containers in which, back in the old days, good, respectable middle-class citizens used to hide their bottles of liquor or their cigars in the family library. Steven was reminded of the kind of small treasure chest where little boys sometimes kept their marbles, penknives, and Lego figurines. Surely he'd had a very similar little box for his treasures when he was a child.

Feeling curious, he opened the little box and suddenly sensed an odd tingling that he couldn't explain. Briefly, everything went dark before his eyes, and he almost fell off the ladder. It was as if a misty hand were reaching out to touch him. Then he had himself back under control. Only an acrid, almost burning taste was left clinging to his palate.

What the hell was that? Some kind of aroma that I don't tolerate? The smell of some varnish or something? Or have I turned allergic to something, just like that?

Carefully, Steven climbed down the last few rungs and looked inside the box. It was lined with dark fabric and had a musty smell. Inside, there were a few faded photographs and a lock of black hair tied with a silk ribbon—as well as a handsomely designed little book. Bound in blue velvet, adorned with ivory ornamentation, it looked like an enchanted book of spells. Steven traced the outline of a knight with a sword who seemed to be riding on a swan, stroked the blue velvet of the binding, and ran his fingertips over the intarsia work of white flowers and leaves. When he blew into the little treasure chest, a cloud of dust flew up; the smell of it made him dizzy again.

Once again, he felt a misty hand reach out for him; he closed his eyes and opened them again. His throat was suddenly dry, as if he'd been up all night drinking. Steven shook himself and tried to concentrate.

Don't be silly; pull yourself together. It's only an old box, that's all.

The photos were the first thing he saw. They seemed to have been taken in the last third of the nineteenth century, and in matte gray colors and various positions they showed a young man of about thirty sitting on an adjustable wooden stool. Beside him stood an older, rather portly gentleman, wearing a black coat; in some of the pictures his left hand was resting almost caressingly on the younger man's shoulder. He looked like a kindly giant. Did the dry lock of hair in the little box come from one of the men? They both had dark hair, anyway.

Thoughtfully, Steven put the pictures and the lock of hair back in the container, then focused again on the book with its valuable ivory intarsia work. When he began turning the pages, he stopped short in surprise. The fine handmade paper was covered not with letters and words, but with curious scribbles and hieroglyphics, like some kind of secret code. Could this really be an old book of magic spells? Steven's heart beat faster. He knew that amazing sums were offered for *grimoires,* as such things were called. Self-styled "white witches" and others with a yen for esotericism competed to get their hands on them. The title page, however, did seem to be legible. Frowning, Steven took out his reading glasses and inspected the faded writing.

Memoirs of Theodor Marot, Assistant to Dr. Max Schleiss von Loewenfeld.

Steven rubbed his eyes. He had never seen either the book or its container before. Or had he? A strange sense of familiarity passed through him. For the life of him, though, he couldn't remember how the little box came to be in his possession. It hadn't been part of the estate left by the old lady from Bogenhausen; he would certainly have noticed such an unusual item. And he had been through all his purchases from flea markets over the last few weeks, classifying them one by one and keeping a written record. So how did this little treasure chest come to be in his shop?

He picked up the photographs again. Suddenly he was sure he'd seen a picture of the gigantic older man in them somewhere before. He hadn't looked quite so portly, but the gentle eyes, the beard, and the full head of black hair were the same. He made a genuinely imposing, almost regal impression.

Suddenly Steven stopped dead.

Was it possible?

Thoughtfully, he tapped one of the photographs. Carrying the little box, he hurried into the stockroom behind the shop, where the books from flea markets and estate sales that he had already classified lay in stacks, waiting to be sorted and placed on the crowded shelves. He rummaged busily around in the cartons, in search of a book that he had bought quite cheaply when he found it only a few days before at a stall in the Munich Olympiad Park, among trashy novels and wartime stories. At last he found it at the bottom of the third carton that he searched.

The book, which was falling apart, was a treatise on the royal house of Bavaria written early in the twentieth century. It featured a whole series of heroic paintings of members of the Wittelsbach dynasty, beginning with Maximilian I Joseph, and ending with Ludwig III, the last king of Bavaria, who had to abdicate at the end of the First World War in his senile old age. Steven leafed quickly through the book until he found the right picture at last. There it was! A handsome young man with black hair looked out of it at him. He had no beard yet, but he had the same hairstyle and the faraway look that was in his eyes until the time of his mysterious death. He wore a blue coat with a white ermine cloak over it.

Steven smiled. No doubt about it, the portly giant in the photograph was none other than King Ludwig II, the Fairy-tale King. He must have been one of the best-known of all Germans, and his youthful portrait adorned beer mugs, T-shirts, and postcards all over Germany.

Steven compared the painting in the book with the photograph in his hand. Judging by the king's appearance, the photo must have been taken in his later years. But there was no question—the little box really did contain photographs of the world-famous Bavarian monarch, probably taken shortly before his death. Maybe even still unpublished? Steven knew that in certain circles, one could ask a high price for such things. All of a sudden the rent problem seemed to retreat into the distance.

At that moment, the bell at the front of the shop announced another visitor coming in.

Irritated, Steven put the book and the photographs back in the little box and placed it on a shelf. Then he left the stockroom and went back into the shop. Couldn't he ever be left in peace? It was seven in the evening already. Who on earth could want to buy something from him so near to closing time? Or was it Frau Schultheiss again with another offer?

"We're really closed," he began brusquely. "If you'd like to come back tomorrow morning . . ."

As he took a closer look at the man, he knew at once that this wasn't one of the usual Perry Rhodan customers. The stranger was around sixty, with sparse gray hair, an old-fashioned pair of pince-nez perched on his nose, and he wore a suit in the Bavarian style of the kind favored by elderly gentlemen from the country complete with lederhosen. He was tall and thin, with a high forehead; his whole bearing suggested that he wasn't used to having his authority questioned.

"I won't take up much of your time, I promise you," the man said in a gruff voice, inspecting Steven through his pince-nez. "My interest is only in very *special* literature."

A slight shudder ran through Steven. "What kind of literature do you mean?" he asked, smiling faintly. "If you're looking for typical Bavarian writers like Ludwig Thoma or Oskar Maria Graf, then—"

"I am interested in eyewitness accounts from the time of King Ludwig the Second," the stranger interrupted. "Do you have anything of that nature, Herr . . . ?"

"Lukas. Steven Lukas."

Steven bravely went on smiling, but he was feeling uneasier with every moment spent under the other man's gaze. The newcomer seemed to be scrutinizing him closely, as if he didn't trust him for some reason. Then he looked hard at the bookshelves. He was obviously searching them for something.

Eyewitness accounts from the time of King Ludwig II . . .

Steven forced himself to appear calm, showing nothing on the surface. But his mind was working furiously. Could this really be just coincidence, or did the stranger know about the photographs? Had he come to get hold of the little treasure chest?

"You hesitate," the man said, examining him curiously through his pince-nez. "You do have something."

"No, I'm sorry. I don't. But if you'd like to give me your contact information, I'll be happy to let you know if I get hold of anything."

Steven had come to this decision in a fraction of a second. He didn't trust the stranger; the man's whole demeanor unsettled him. It reminded him of the self-satisfied manner of certain Bavarian politicians who were used to getting their way no matter what.

But you won't get anything from me.

"Are you quite sure you have nothing of that nature?" the man in the Bavarian suit asked again.

"Perfectly sure. If I can have your telephone number . . ."

The tall stranger gave him a thin-lipped smile. "That won't be necessary. We'll come back to you." He nodded a goodbye and then went out. Darkness had fallen.

Steven felt as if an icy wind had entered the shop, covering all the books with hoarfrost. Shivering, he went over to the window, but the man had already disappeared.

Fine rain was pattering against the panes.

AFTER A WHILE, Steven shook his head and chuckled quietly to himself. What on earth was the matter with him? First that odd dizziness when he had found the little box, and now this. He wasn't usually so easily scared. What was more, he'd had far worse customers in his shop. A couple of years ago, a drunk had thrown up in his display during Oktoberfest. And unsavory characters in Bavarian-style suits were all over Munich, not just in upmarket Maximilianstrasse.

After looking out at the street one last time, the streetlamps casting dim light on its wet surface, he went back into the stockroom and took the little box off the shelf. Briefly, he was overcome by the fear that its contents could suddenly have disappeared, as if by magic. But when he opened the container, it was still all there: the faded photographs, the lock of black hair, the book bound in blue velvet and decorated with carved ivory . . .

All at once he felt extremely tired and just as hungry. It struck him that he hadn't eaten anything since breakfast. All the excitement over the Grimms' *Tales*, followed by Frau Schultheiss and the stranger, had made him forget any hunger pangs, but now they announced themselves forcefully. Steven decided to stop work for the day and indulge in a large plateful of farfalle primavera and a bottle of wine at home. While the pasta was cooking, he'd take a closer look at that strange diary and the photographs. If the pictures were really genuine, they would create a small sensation. Steven knew, from hearsay, of a number of people who would pay good money for photographs like that. If he had to decide whether to use the illustrated Grimm or the photos to pay the rent, he would opt for the photographs.

With his mind at rest again, he put the little wooden box in his shabby brown leather briefcase, put on his wool coat, left the shop, and locked up behind him. The wind and rain immediately blew in his face; the light drizzle had turned heavy. Steven put up the hood of his wool coat and marched away. It wasn't far to his apartment in the Schlachthof district of Munich, but it was no pleasure walking through this rain. Countless office workers with umbrellas and waterproof ponchos hurried past him as they emerged from the complex of office buildings that had only recently been built on the old site where trade fairs used to be held; the new supermarkets were teeming with late customers, hastily making their evening purchases and disappearing into the multistory parking lots with frozen pizzas and boxes of sushi.

Only a few streets farther on, everything was noticeably quieter. Ahead of and below Steven lay the Theresienwiese, the open space where Oktoberfest was held. Now, just after the end of that annual event, it spread out before him, deserted and desolate. The giant wheel and a few of the festival tents hadn't been entirely dismantled yet, and they rose like metal skeletons on the flat, asphalted grounds. From up where Steven was, the silent rides and boarded-up snack booths could have been abandoned buildings in a ghost town.

In spite of the many puddles, Steven decided to cut across the Theresienwiese on his way home. It would cut short the walk through the rain by a good ten minutes. He turned right, where a white temple with a statue of Bavaria rose. The bronze statue, almost sixty-five feet tall, with a lion and a wreath of oak leaves, always reminded Steven slightly of the American Statue of Liberty. A homeless man had spread out a few layers of newspaper in one corner of the temple, right under the bust of King Ludwig I. He was lying on them and babbling to himself. Otherwise, silence reigned, a silence that seemed curiously alien to Steven after the noise of the city.

He cautiously climbed down the broad, slippery steps of the temple. A loose balloon, whirled up by the wind, flew past him and finally disappeared in the darkness. There was a smell of spilled beer and garbage. In this weather, there seemed to be no other pedestrians out and about on the broad space, covered as it was with puddles.

When Steven was about halfway across the Theresienwiese, he suddenly heard a sound behind him. It sounded like a soft, hoarse voice calling.

He spun around in alarm and saw three figures standing there, right under the statue of Bavaria. They wore dark capes and hoods that made them look like black-robed Ku Klux Klan members. All three hooded men held burning torches that flickered wildly in the wind. Steven closed his eyes and then opened them again, but the figures were still there.

Very odd. It's not Halloween yet.

And the figures were obviously too large to be kids. They made Steven think more of trained thugs in monastic habits. Once again he felt the same strange fear that had come over him earlier, in the shop.

He turned to look ahead and went hesitantly on. But after a few feet, he quickened his pace, and soon he was running. Behind him, he could hear footsteps in the pouring rain.

The men were following him.

Looking briefly behind him, Steven saw three red dots in the darkness, bouncing up and down, slowly but inexorably coming closer. Were these men really after him? Could it be because of that strange little treasure chest? Heart thudding, Steven ran on. He tasted the metallic tang of blood in his mouth.

He hurried across the deserted Theresienwiese. In the dark, it looked like a huge black lake threatening to swallow him up. To his right and left, alleyways opened up, leading to empty beer tents, and in front of them switchback tracks reared up like the bones of a dinosaur. The opposite side of the plaza, bordered by shining streetlamps, seemed endlessly far away; behind every one of the abandoned snack bars, in every niche, behind every caravan, Steven thought he saw a hooded figure scurrying by.

He stepped into a puddle, tripped over the raised edge of a manhole cover, and fell flat in cold, shallow water. The briefcase slipped from his hands. As he frantically groped for it, he could hear footsteps coming up behind him. They were distinctly closer now; he heard the sound of shoes slapping down on the wet asphalt. Where was the damn briefcase? Something crunched very close, as if someone had stepped on the pieces of a broken beer stein, and then there was a snort and a cough. Something deep inside Steven told him that he mustn't lose the briefcase, not under any circumstances, even if he didn't know why.

At last his hand felt familiar leather, caught between a couple of garbage bags left lying around. Steven seized the bag, got to his feet, gasping for breath, and ran on until, at last, he reached the safety of the light from the streetlamps. Still breathless, the bookseller stumbled past a few stunted linden trees, and then finally reached the Bavaria Ring on the other side of the Oktoberfest site.

When he turned around once more, the men and their torches had disappeared. Car horns were honking, a set of traffic lights changed to green, passersby pushed busily past him.

He was back in the bustling city.

Who or what in the world had that been?

Steven was trembling all over. Until now, he had always felt very safe in Germany's most beautiful and expensive city. Finding that someone had intended to rob him in the city center itself, and indeed not just someone but several weird characters in monastic habits, suddenly made him see Munich with new eyes. All at once the narrow streets of the residential area where he lived, the flickering streetlamps, and the tall old buildings that had been spared by the war seemed to him strange and uncanny.

ANOTHER FIFTEEN MINUTES, and Steven was finally back at his apartment building in Ehrengutstrasse.

He leaned against the front door, briefly closed his eyes, and listened to the familiar sounds of his home—the distant ringing of trolley bells, the horns of cars, the laughter of the many people out drinking in the local bars. In the middle of the night or very early in the morning, before dawn, Steven sometimes heard the mooing of cattle and calves and the squealing of pigs on their last journey to the slaughterhouses from which the district took its name. Now and then there was even a smell of blood in the air. All the same, he couldn't imagine living anywhere else in the city. Here in the Isarvorstadt area, with the old South Cemetery, the winding alleyways, and the magnificent bridges across the nearby river, Steven thought he could still sense the spirit of past centuries—a Munich that now existed only in a few corners of the city.

The kind of Munich that this man Theodor Marot would have known, he suddenly thought. *Is what he wrote in that little book so valuable that I'm being followed already by whoever wants it?*

Tired and still shivering, Steven climbed the many well-worn stairs to the top floor of the building. Only when he had closed the door of his apartment behind him did he notice that his pants were torn and that he was bleeding in several places. His hands were dirty, the wool coat was as wet as a dishcloth, and his briefcase was damp and spattered with mud.

He decided to drink his first glass of wine before the pasta was ready.

· 2 ·

A GOOD HOUR AND THREE-QUARTERS of a bottle later, Steven Lukas, showered and in clean clothes, was sitting on his beloved old shabby leather sofa in his attic apartment. Outside, rain beat against the window, and the wind blew more strongly. Steven could see the light of the Munich Olympiad tower through the drops on the pane, while the red brick buildings of the Schlachthof district were discernible only in outline.

As usual, he had had to start by clearing a dozen or so books off the cushions. The coffee table was overflowing with empty teacups, the remains of sandwiches, and newspapers from the last few days with the pages coming apart. In contrast to his bookshop, Steven's apartment had no sense of order. Sunday the cleaning lady would come and disparage his way of life once again. It was a ritual for fat Joanna to preach to him, in her Polish accent, about the dangers of a bachelor existence.

Steven's last real relationship had been four years ago, and by now he was used to thinking of books as better partners than women.

Steven closed his eyes and enjoyed Brahms's Second Piano Concerto in B-flat major as the music came softly over his old Philips record player. The nearly empty bottle of Montepulciano stood in front of him. By now he had calmed down a bit. Probably there was some perfectly simple explanation for the incident on the Theresienweise. The hooded figures were most likely teenagers out to scare any passersby they happened to meet. And he had run away like a headless chicken. The kids were probably still laughing themselves silly over the old fool in the muddy puddle.

Steven shook his head at his own cowardice, then turned to the book in code from the little treasure chest. Fortunately, neither the box nor its contents had been damaged when he fell over. As Steven ran his fingers over the cover with its ivory carvings, he again felt that vague sense of having seen the little book somewhere before. It was like a faded picture from a long-forgotten time. But when he searched his memory, he could find nothing—only a slight dizziness, and a strange, bitter smell as if something had been left burning.

By this time he was sure that the curious hieroglyphics were some kind of secret writing, but no matter how hard he thought about it, he couldn't work out just what it was. It was true that in the course of his life as an antiquarian bookseller, he had once read a treatise about nineteenth-century cryptology, but as far as he could remember, it was generally a case of exchanging certain written characters for others, with numbers also playing a part at times. The signs in front of him, however, were more reminiscent of those old Germanic runes that made no sense at first glance. Steven put on his glasses and looked more closely at the first signs.

What on earth was that supposed to be? A child's scribble? Very occasionally, conventional characters, all of them capitals, appeared among the signs, but they didn't form actual words. They were as much of a mystery to Steven as the runes. He leafed through the book, counting at least five of these sequences of uppercase letters distributed through the early pages, and more farther on. The first three were the following:

VZLMCTLJT
NECAALAJ
FHRT

Steven drank some more wine and looked again at the title page, while outside the rain continued to patter against the windowpanes.

Memoirs of Theodor Marot, Assistant to Dr. Max Schleiss von Loewenfeld.

He decided to ignore the mysterious inscriptions inside the book for now, went over to his desk, and opened the laptop. It started with a hum. Once it was up and running, he typed the name *Theodor Marot* into a search engine, but all he found was an Austrian swimming club and a site selling construction equipment in Canada. He was much more successful with Max Schleiss von Loewenfeld; the search engine came up with about two hundred hits. When Steven clicked on the first of them, his heart began to beat considerably faster.

The websites informed him that Dr. Schleiss von Loewenfeld had been King Ludwig II's personal physician, and before that had treated Ludwig's father, King Maximilian II. According to a scholarly blog that Steven found, Loewenfeld had been considered one of the best Bavarian doctors of his time. He bore the title of privy counselor to the king, and he died at the end of the nineteenth century at almost ninety years old, rich and respected. A black-and-white photograph showed an elderly gentleman with nickel-framed glasses and a thoughtful expression, his coat neatly buttoned up, holding a top hat. His striking beard was reminiscent of Abraham Lincoln.

Steven put one of the photos from the box beside his shimmering laptop. Like all the other pictures, it had obviously been taken in a studio. There were dummy columns in the background, and a curtain cord. The young man seated beside the king wore a well-cut suit, his dark hair combed to one side; he had attractive, soft features that made him look almost girlish. By now Steven was convinced that the young man in the picture was none other than the royal physician's assistant.

Hello, Theodor Marot, pleased to meet you. What story do you have to tell? Are your memoirs so explosive that you had to write them in secret code? Or so . . . delicate?

Thoughtfully, Steven picked up the lock of hair lying beside the photographs in the little wooden treasure chest with its black cloth lining. The hair tied with a ribbon must have been raven black long ago.

As black as the king's hair.

Steven finished his wine and put the journal, the photographs, and the lock of hair back in the box. Then he opened another bottle to help his thinking along.

It looked very much as if the contents of the little box were worth far more than he had first thought.

His headache the next morning told Steven that the Montepulciano had been a bit stronger than he was used to. Eyes closed, it took him some time to locate the radio alarm clock that was cheerfully playing Mozart's *Eine kleine Nachtmusik*. With a well-aimed swing of his hand, Steven killed Wolfgang Amadeus stone dead, sat up groaning, and ran a hand through his untidy gray hair. There were some days when you felt that you were forty with particular clarity.

The little wooden box was still standing beside his bed on the desk. It had spent the night in his dreams. He vaguely remembered a gigantic royal cloak that threatened to smother him. Men in black hoods had also been there, prodding him with red-hot fingers.

Steven rubbed the sleep out of his eyes, stood up, and limped into the kitchen, where the dirty dishes of the last few days were stacked. He carefully picked an antique edition of the satirical magazine *Simplicissimus* off the table and blew a few croissant crumbs off the front page. This copy of the journal had appeared just before the First World War and deserved better than to get jam on it. Humming quietly to himself, the bookseller filled the espresso jug to the top with freshly ground coffee and twiddled the knob of the radio until he found a classical music concert. The music soothed him instantly. His knees were still sore, and someone was knocking against his forehead from inside his skull, but at least the memories of his bad dreams had gone away. Steven massaged his temples and listened to the deep notes of a cello, while he thoughtfully sipped his heavily sweetened espresso. Yesterday's events—first the visit of that guy in the Bavarian-style costume, then the hooded men—had upset his stomach. And then, of course, there was the little treasure chest itself, with its sensational contents. Only why had the mere sight of it shaken him so badly?

Well, he'd take a closer look at it all back in the shop. If this man Marot really had taken a royal secret to his grave, Steven would make a few phone calls, earn good money, and then, so far as he was concerned, Frau Schultheiss could go and open her boutique in the downmarket Hasenbergl district. As an expert on the literary history of Bavaria, Steven knew that rumors of King Ludwig II's homosexuality had come up time and again. To him, it made no difference one way or the other, but he was sure that plenty of newspapers would come up with a large sum of money for actual evidence—money that could pay the rent on his shop for a good long while.

After a long, hot, almost boiling shower, he put on a new brown corduroy suit, with a white shirt and a tweed bow tie, put the little treasure chest back in his leather briefcase, and set off for the Westend district. The rain clouds had disappeared overnight, the leaves on the chestnut trees in the beer gardens were red and yellow, and the people coming toward him had friendly expressions on their faces. As Steven strolled over the Theresienwiese, populated this morning by cyclists and pedestrians, it was hard to imagine that a few teenagers wearing hoods had scared him so badly here only a few hours ago. The almost summery warmth and the mild sunlight helped to banish his headache, and his mood improved with every step he took. It was one of those mornings that herald a very pleasant day.

But even as Steven was still more than fifty yards away from his antiquarian bookshop, he guessed that, on the contrary, this was going to be one of the lousiest days of his whole year.

A SMALL GROUP of curious onlookers stood in front of a pile of broken glass that had once been the display window of his shop. A few books lay out in the street, looking like limp, dead flies, their leather bindings splayed. Pages of parchment had been torn out and were splashed with mud. But that was nothing compared to the chaos that Steven saw when he looked through the broken window into the bookshop itself.

It looked as if a medium-sized and very specific earthquake had wreaked havoc in there.

One of the tall bookshelves had fallen over, and books, maps, engravings, and folio volumes covered the floor like a sea of paper. Steven saw the eighteenth-century book on chess that he had only just bought; someone had slit the leather spine lengthwise. A dirty footprint left by a boot adorned the dramas of Molière; other books had come apart entirely, and their pages were crumpled or torn out. A gust of wind whirled a few ragged pages up in the air like withered leaves. The mahogany table in the backroom of the shop was the only piece of furniture still in place. The scene was so appalling, so unreal, that Steven stood there for a long time as if turned to stone, staring into his shop. It was the thought of a single book that brought him back to life.

Oh God, not the Grimm. Not the *Grimms' Children's and Household Tales.*

Taking no notice of the onlookers, he stumbled to the door and unlocked it. He tried to make his way into the shop but was prevented by the pile of books pressing against the inside of the door. For a while the people outside watched, spellbound, as Steven fought a desperate battle against a mass of printed paper and parchment. He continued these useless efforts until someone placed a hand on his shoulder.

"Is this your shop?"

The female police officer in front of him was still young, maybe in her midtwenties, and she looked genuinely concerned. Her older male colleague was waiting, with a bored expression, in the police car parked at the curb with its blue light switched on.

As Steven nodded silently, the police officer went on calmly. "We'll have to investigate this break-in, although it looks more like a few young hooligans out to make trouble than anything else."

Or like Frau Schultheiss, who just can't wait to open her fashion boutique, thought Steven.

Would she really go that far? Had she hired a few thugs to hurry things along and make sure Steven moved out?

He was so deep in thought that at first he failed to hear the police officer's next question.

"Can you tell us if there's anything missing?" she repeated gently. "Money? Valuable items?" She took out a notepad.

Steven looked at the chaotic muddle of torn, dirty, soiled, and slashed books, and heard himself laugh quietly.

"Sorry, silly question," said the young woman sympathetically. "We'll just record details of the scene and report back to police HQ, and then you'll probably want to start cleaning up."

She patted him on the shoulder, then went over, notepad in hand, to her colleague, who was dispersing the crowd of onlookers in a loud, official voice.

Steven said nothing, just went on staring at his wrecked shop. He corrected his earlier impression: this was not just the lousiest day of the year; it looked more like one of the lousiest days of his entire life.

· 3 ·

"ARE YOU OPEN?"

Steven paused his tidying up, and looked at the broken pane of the display window, which he had sketchily and temporarily mended with sticky tape. It was evening, and an unpleasantly cold wind whistled through the cracks and kept sending torn pages flying about.

The face of a young woman peeked through the network of black strips of tape. She had dark hair and was wearing a bright green headscarf and a pair of black-framed 1950s sunglasses that made her look remarkably like Audrey Hepburn. Steven had always admired that delicately built movie star, but right now he simply was not in the mood to make polite conversation to anyone, not even her double.

"Closed for now," he growled, and went on putting any books still intact back on the shelves. A heap of torn copies on the counter had grown larger and larger over the last few hours. Actually, the damage had turned out to be not quite as disastrous as Steven had feared at first—but it was certainly bad enough to be depressing. The restoration of old books was very expensive. Steven knew that he would never be able to scrape together the money to have approximately forty damaged volumes restored to their original condition. At least the Grimm had survived. He had found it lying under an overturned bookshelf, slightly crumpled, but otherwise unharmed.

"Stock-taking?" the woman asked curiously, pointing to the pile of books that he hadn't looked at yet.

Steven sighed. "If you really want to know, someone broke in. And I'm just trying to get my ruined shop back into some kind of order. Thanks for asking. Goodbye."

"Oh," Audrey Hepburn said. After a moment, she asked, "Was anything stolen?"

"I really don't know what business that is of yours."

His tone was far harsher than he had intended, but he was worn out. Hours of dealing with damaged books had hit him harder than he liked to admit. Curiously enough, as far as he could tell, only one book was actually missing. It was a volume of German ballads that had not been especially valuable. Perhaps he just hadn't found it yet. Which was why he had said at the precinct house that afternoon that nothing was missing. The duty officer told him in friendly but detached tones that they would be looking into the crime committed by a person or persons unknown, and sent him back to his shop, where he had been clearing up and brooding ever since.

Over the next few hours, Steven had kept wondering who could be behind the mysterious break-in. He didn't really think Frau Schultheiss was capable of hiring someone to trash the place. Maybe her husband, though? And then, of course, there was yesterday evening's stranger in the Bavarian-style suit. What was it he had said before leaving?

We'll come back to you.

Whom had he meant by *we*? The same people who had turned his shop upside down? Searching for something that was still, apparently, in his possession? Were these people after the little treasure chest?

I am interested in eyewitness accounts from the time of King Ludwig the Second. Do you have anything of that nature?

Steven sneezed as the dust he had raised went up his nose. When he had blown his nose thoroughly, he looked up. The woman was still standing outside the broken display window, smiling like a diva.

"Gesundheit."

In spite of the circumstances, Steven couldn't help grinning. "Sorry I snapped at you like that, but all this"—he pointed to the pile of wrecked and damaged books and loose pages on the table—"has been a bit too much for me."

Audrey Hepburn nodded. "No need to apologize. I just have one very simple question, and then I'll be off." She took something out of her purse, which was bright green like her headscarf, and handed it to Steven through the open doorway. "Do you know this man?" she asked seriously. "He's my uncle. Did he by any chance visit your shop?"

Steven looked at the photo and gave a start. No doubt about it, it was the elderly man who had been in the bookshop yesterday—the man with the bundle done up in wrapping paper and the hunted look in his eyes who had disappeared so suddenly. It was not a good picture, but all the same it was easy to recognize the amiable old gentleman with the gray blazer and the nickel-framed glasses.

Steven nodded and gave the photo back to the woman. "Yes, in fact he was here yesterday morning," he said. "We talked a bit, and then he left."

"About what?" The young woman's voice suddenly had a hard edge. "What did you talk about?"

"Oh, this and that. Mainly literature. He was interested in the diaries of Samuel Pepys, and . . ."

"You didn't by any chance talk about King Ludwig the Second?"

Steven froze. He straightened up and gave the young woman with the black sunglasses a dark look. "Listen, if you have anything to do with the guy who turned up here yesterday evening, then . . ."

"What guy?"

"The guy who asked me the same thing. If I have any books about King Ludwig the Second."

"Who asked you that?"

At that moment Steven saw something flash behind the woman's back; it was a brief flicker behind the side window of a black Chrysler just pulling up to the deserted sidewalk. Two powerful-looking men in dark green tracksuit jackets got out and slowly came toward the bookshop in the twilight. When the woman saw them, her face behind her sunglasses suddenly went white as a sheet. She came into the shop and looked around the still-untidy room in a harried way. "Can you lock the door?" she whispered.

"Er . . . that wouldn't be much use." Steven pointed to the broken glass. "The window's done for. And anyway, what . . ."

"For God's sweet sake, do it! And quickly." The woman's voice was nothing like Audrey Hepburn's in *Breakfast at Tiffany's* now. Only at this point did he catch the faint touch of a Berlin accent in it. "Lock the door, then help me push that bookcase in front of the window. That ought to hold them up for a little while, anyway." She was already tugging at the bookcase, while Steven, in total confusion, locked the door.

"I'm afraid you owe me an explanation," he said. "Did those men do something to you? Are they after you?"

"Not after me, you idiot. They're after *you*. Now, push this hard, will you?"

Too baffled to say anything, Steven helped her push the bookcase over to the broken window. Only a moment later someone was hammering at the door.

"Herr Lukas," called a deep, hoarse voice. "We know you're in there. Don't be stupid. We won't hurt you. We just want to have a little talk. You have something that belongs to us. Unfortunately, we didn't find it last night. Herr Lukas, can you hear me?" The voice sounded like it was running out of patience. "We're ready to pay you a hefty sum for the book. How much do you want? Ten thousand? Twenty thousand?"

Steven was about to say something, but the woman beside him put a finger to her lips.

"Do you have it?" she whispered.

"Have what?"

"You know what I mean. Do you have it?"

Steven hesitated for a moment and then nodded. "I . . . I think so," he said. "In my briefcase on the table. Although I don't know—"

"Is there a back way out?" the woman interrupted.

Steven pointed to the bookshelves on the back wall. "There's a little door beside the toilet, out into the backyard. Do you really think that . . ."

Just then the man's deep voice spoke up again outside. "Listen, Herr Lukas, we can always do it another way. Last time we only searched your shop. Next time we'll burn it. All that paper—what do you bet it'll burn so bright that they can see for miles around? So how about it? Think of the money you can earn. *One* . . ."

"We have to get out of here," the woman beside him hissed. "And don't forget your briefcase."

"*Two* . . ."

Steven swore quietly. He didn't get the impression that the men out there were joking. If he gave them the little treasure chest, they would presumably leave him alone. And they'd also just offered him twenty thousand euros. Twenty thousand! That would pay the rent until the Easter after next, maybe even longer. He wouldn't need customers. He could keep his own company in the shop. His eyes went to the briefcase on the table.

"*Two and a half* . . ."

"Don't do it," the woman whispered, obviously reading his thoughts. "You don't think they'll just hand you a few euro bills and let you go, do you? They killed my uncle, and they'll do the same to you. Faster than you can say *Principal Decree of the Imperial Diet*, my antiquarian friend."

Steven looked nervously at the barricaded display window. He could see the outlines of two broad-shouldered figures on the other side of it. One of them took a small black object that looked suspiciously like a pistol from under his jacket.

"*Three!*"

"For crying out loud, what have I gotten myself mixed up with here?"

Steven snatched up his briefcase and ran for the back door with the unknown woman. At the same time, he heard the bookcases along the wall fall to the floor with a crash behind him, and someone climbed through the wrecked window.

They're going to torch my books. My beautiful books.

Audrey Hepburn hauled him out into the backyard, which was full of garbage cans, bicycles, and old junk, and surrounded by the high walls of buildings. An old neighbor stared curiously down at them over the geraniums in his window box. Bavarian folk music came from a radio nearby. To their left was the wall, as tall as a man, between his and the neighboring property. A paper-recycling bin overflowing with newspapers stood beside it.

"This way," the strange woman called, hurrying toward the wall.

With catlike agility, she hauled herself up onto the bin, climbed the wall, and the next moment she had disappeared. Hesitating, Steven looked around. When he heard footsteps coming, he heaved himself up on the recycling bin, too, cursing. A brief glance over the wall showed him another yard beyond it, with a broad entrance leading into the street. It was at least six feet to the ground.

"Come on, jump," the woman urged him. She was already on her way out of the yard. "They're right behind us."

Steven could hear shouting behind him now. He closed his eyes, then spread his arms wide, jumped down to the asphalt of the yard next door, stumbled, and ran to the exit, clutching his briefcase close to his body. When he was finally out in the street, the woman closed the double doors after him with a metallic clatter. Next moment there was loud hammering at the doors inside the yard.

"We'll take my car." The strange woman ran out into the street. "It's just around the corner. I only hope you don't suffer from claustrophobia."

She made for a yellow Mini Cooper, and opened the door. Then she took off her dark glasses for the first time. The green scarf had slipped back, revealing a sternly pinned-up chignon. Steven put her age at somewhere in her late twenties.

She really does look like Audrey Hepburn, he thought. *Or Eva Marie Saint in* North by Northwest. *Only I'm no Cary Grant.*

"Get in. I'll take you to my place. You'll be safe there." The stranger's eyes twinkled at Steven. "Don't worry, I don't bite. Unlike those guys behind us."

"Only if you promise to tell me what all this is about," Steven said breathlessly.

"I promise. But first we've got to get out of here."

He could still hear the furious hammering on the door in the backyard. Audrey Hepburn slammed the car door, turned the ignition key, and stepped on the gas.

Steven had had no idea how fast you could drive a Mini Cooper.

· 4 ·

THEY RACED ACROSS A BUSY square, past a couple of fruit and snack stalls, and then, accompanied by loud honking, turned right onto the Mittlerer Ring. Audrey Hepburn overtook a silver Audi and then stepped on the gas so suddenly that Steven was briefly pressed back in his seat.

This is all a bad dream, he thought. *Just a bad dream. I'll wake up in my bed any second now, with a few volumes of poetry and a book by Gabriel García Márquez beside me. I'll brush my teeth, go into my shop . . .*

"Are they following us?"

The voice of the brunette stranger beside him brought him back to reality.

"What?" he asked, dazed. Only now did he realize that the bag with the little treasure chest in it was on his lap.

"I asked if they're following us. Those guys in the black Chrysler."

Steven turned around and looked through the rear window at the traffic behind them. Now, at about seven in the evening, a lot of people were on their way home from work, so the streets were crowded. He didn't see a Chrysler among the mass of cars blinking their indicators, pulling into and out of traffic.

"I think we've shaken them off." The bookseller looked straight ahead again, until finally he began to feel unwell.

"Right. We'll go back to my place, and then . . ."

"And then nothing. It's about time you finally dropped all this mystery," Steven interrupted. "Just tell me straight out what's going on here. Or I'm getting out of the car right now and taking the bag with me, understand?"

"What, doing ninety on the Mittlerer Ring? Okay, have fun."

Steven sighed. Once again he noticed the touch of a Berlin accent in the woman's voice, sounding rather unusual here in Munich, the capital of Bavaria.

"Look, seriously," he said, emphatically calm now. "Don't you think we're a little too old for this childishness?"

"You may be. I'm not." The stranger switched down into third gear to get past some lights just as they turned red. "But you're right. Too much blood has been spilled to call it childish."

"Blood? What do you . . . ?"

Without slowing down, she reached into the glove compartment and brought out a crumpled newspaper, which she handed to Steven without comment. He saw that it was the day's evening edition.

"Take a look at page twelve. The story at the top of the page."

Steven leafed through the paper until he found the place she meant. His pulse instantly sped up. In the middle of the page of newsprint, he saw the slightly blurred picture of a man he knew. It was the likable old man with the gray bundle, who had come to his shop yesterday. A screaming headline in bold twenty-point type leaped out at him.

HORRIFIC DEATH IN THE FOREST
University professor tortured and murdered
Police face a mystery

Steven swiftly skimmed the report, which emphasized the sensational aspects. Its vigorous phrasing told him that sixty-seven-year-old Professor Paul Liebermann of Jena University had died a horrific death. He had been found the previous evening in a forested area just outside Munich with his head shot to pieces. Before his death, the retired history professor had been drugged, abducted, and tortured. His body had been discovered lying among torn-up pages of a book; further inquiries were being pursued. The police expected to find evidence regarding the remarkable murder weapon. More would follow in tomorrow's edition. Then there were a few lines about Professor Liebermann's career, and a couple of risqué assumptions associating him with the red-light district.

"It was a Derringer," the woman suddenly said.

Steven gave a start and looked up from the newspaper. "What?"

"The murder weapon. I've kept my ears pricked. Two .44 caliber rimfire cartridge cases were found at the scene. That kind of cartridge is out of use these days. However, ammunition like that was very common in the nineteenth century, in small ornamented pistols but most of all in the American Derringer. A pretty toy. But Abraham Lincoln was shot with a Derringer just like that."

Steven frowned. "You mean the murder victim was killed by a weapon that doesn't exist today?"

"Or by someone who shouldn't be alive today," the strange woman replied, and turned into a side street, tires squealing. "Which at least narrows down the suspects."

"How do you know all this?" Steven asked suspiciously. "You said you were the niece of the professor who came to see me yesterday, but you sound more like a police officer."

"Wait until we reach my place. I'll explain it all to you then."

In silence, they joined the evening traffic that took them down Ludwigstrasse, with its imposing white buildings, to the upmarket Schwabing district of Munich. They passed boutiques, discotheques, trendy bars with the first nocturnal revelers already gathering outside, talking noisily with one another or shouting into their phones. Their journey ended at a quiet side street near the large park of the English Garden.

Audrey Hepburn parked her Mini in a gap so narrow that Steven suspected he wouldn't even have been able to fit his bicycle into it. With the newspaper in hand, she climbed out and walked toward a low-built, old-fashioned little house with a tiny front garden. Among the modern buildings with their expanses of glass, it looked as if it had fallen out of another time. There was a bronze plate with elaborate lettering beside the door. Steven glanced at it and then looked in surprise at the woman in the black sunglasses.

"Dr. Sara Lengfeld. Art Detection," he murmured. "Are you really a detective?"

"First and foremost I'm a qualified art historian," she replied, holding the door open for him. "And let's get one thing clear right away: my work is deadly boring. I look through art catalogs as thick as your arm, I surf the Internet, I talk on the phone until there's steam coming out of my ears, and now and then, for a change, I get to go to an exhibition of enormous old paintings where the museum curator eyes me suspiciously over his shoulder." Her lips narrowed. "So you can forget all the private-eye nonsense you know from movies and books. And anyway, in this case, I think of myself more as a niece than a detective."

Without another word, she walked into the little house. Steven followed her, looking around in surprise. The building was much larger inside than it appeared from the outside. On the walls of a softly lit corridor painted a pale orange hung prints by German Expressionists side by side works by Toulouse-Lautrec and modern photographs of nudes. Passing a hallway on his right, Steven saw a small kitchen, and beyond that a bedroom. A door on the left led into a well-lit office that seemed to take up almost half of the first floor. Here, too, there were countless paintings and sculptures illuminated by small halogen lights, giving the room, which had a ceiling almost nine feet high, the look of an exclusive art gallery.

"What is all this?" Steven asked. "The Museum of Modern Art?"

"God, no, only my office." The young woman smiled. "I know, the rubber plant is missing. But the view makes up for that."

Steven looked appreciatively out of the large panoramic window, with its view of bushes, trees, and the English Garden beyond. The woman really did have good taste, even if it wasn't entirely in line with his own. In the middle of the office stood a showy kidney-shaped table from the fifties, piled high with art catalogs, file folders, empty Chinese food containers, and dirty coffee cups. A computer covered with yellow Post-it notes was enthroned among the mess.

"Sorry, I haven't gotten around to tidying up yet," Sara Lengfeld said. She cleared a few brochures and art books off the broad leather sofa before sinking down on it with a weary sigh. "It's been a busy few days."

Steven sat down beside her and briefly admired her long legs, one crossed over the other. She wore comfortable shoes. Sara had taken off her bright green rain cape and her scarf; her sunglasses stuck in her brunette hair like an extra pair of eyes. She had on jeans and a close-fitting woolen pullover that came down over her hips. Only after some delay did Steven remember why he was there.

"The dead man in the newspaper," he began hesitantly. "Is he really your uncle?"

She nodded. "My mother's older brother. We lost touch a long time ago. Until very recently, the last time I saw him he was reading *Pinocchio* to me." She smiled wanly. "I'm something of a loner, you see. It runs in the family. Maybe it comes with my work as well."

"And what exactly do you do?" Steven inquired.

"I look for lost art. Stolen works, art that was looted, paintings thought to have disappeared years ago. Every year six billion dollars' worth of art is stolen, but most of it turns up again eventually. At auctions, in galleries and museums, in private collections." Getting to her feet, she tossed Steven one of the big catalogs on the table. "It's my job to find those paintings. That earns me a percentage of their real value—and usually a volley of furious insults from the supposed owners," she added with a grin. "See, the people who have the paintings generally have no idea that they're stolen. When I go into a gallery, the curator makes the sign of the cross three times and puts a laxative in my prosecco."

Steven put the catalog aside and looked around. "Obviously a lucrative job. But what does it have to do with your uncle?"

At once Sara was serious again. "How about if I see what's in that bag of yours first?"

Carefully, Steven handed her the little treasure chest. She opened it and took a quick look at the photographs and the lock of black hair. Then, lost in thought, she leafed through the yellowed pages of the notebook. Almost reverently, she ran her fingers over the velvet binding with the ivory decoration.

"So it's really true," she murmured at last.

"True?" Steven asked. "What's true?"

The art detective went on staring at the book, as if trying to recognize something in it. Only after a long while did she look up again.

"Uncle Paul had a rather unusual hobby. He collected literature about King Ludwig the Second, especially literature to do with his death. As he saw it, Ludwig's murder was the greatest unsolved crime in German history."

"Murder?" Steven said skeptically. "I've heard speculation, but . . ."

"Herr Lukas," Sara interrupted, "what exactly do you know about King Ludwig the Second?"

Steven shrugged. "He was a cranky Bavarian king who slowly lost himself in a dream world, built some fairy-tale castles, and was finally certified insane and deposed. Soon after that, he died in a way that's unexplained to this day."

"A rather abbreviated account, but generally speaking correct. Though you could say that Ludwig the Second wasn't just any Bavarian king. He was *the* Bavarian king. At least as far as his popularity was concerned." Sara took one of the black-and-white photographs out of the little chest and held it in front of Steven's nose. He noticed that the art detective had painted her fingernails green.

"There's no other German monarch as well-known as this man," she said, smiling. "The perfect mirror to reflect our hopes and imagination. A dreamer who actually had the money to put those dreams into practice."

"But politically he . . ." Steven began to object.

"Was a total failure. Yes, I know." The art historian sighed. "If we judged Ludwig the Second solely by his political achievements, no one would give a damn about him now. But what are politics compared to the fairy-tale castle that you see at the beginning of every Disney movie? And then there was his death."

"What do you mean?"

"Well, mysteries are always intriguing," she replied, carefully returning the photograph to the little chest. "I'm sure you have your own ideas about his death."

"My own ideas? All I know is the official version," Steven said. "As best I remember, after he was declared insane and deposed, the king was taken to Berg Castle on Lake Starnberg. While he was there, he gave his psychiatrist the slip. The psychiatrist ran after him and finally caught up with him on the banks of the lake. They fought and Ludwig drowned the doctor, then committed suicide in the lake."

"In waist-high water?"

Steven frowned. "What do you mean?"

"The water King Ludwig is supposed to have drowned himself in would have only come up to his waist," the art detective replied. "Ludwig was an excellent swimmer. Not to mention that no water was found in his lungs."

"You mean . . ."

"I don't mean anything at all," Sara went on. "I'm just stating the facts. And those are only a couple of the inconsistencies surrounding Ludwig's death. They all nurture his legend. Did you know that the doctors who came to the scene weren't allowed to examine the two bodies? And that the pocket watch belonging to the psychiatrist— Bernard von Gudden—didn't stop until an hour later than the king's? Then a bunch of witnesses either died in strange ways, or went missing, or suddenly became rich overnight. And, and, and . . ." She waved the subject away. "Whole libraries could be filled with the books that have been written about the strange events of the thirteenth of June 1886."

"I had no idea that qualified art historians went in for conspiracy theories," Steven said. "Clearly, you've inherited a taste for your uncle's unusual hobby. But I guess that would suit a detective."

Sara gave him an icy stare from her gray eyes. "Herr Lukas, if you take me for a fool, you're mistaken. I do indeed specialize in nineteenth-century art, but aside from that, I couldn't care less how Ludwig the Second died. As far as I'm concerned, he could have drowned in a cream pie, heavily made up and wearing high heels. What I do care about is my uncle's death. And that's what it's all about here, right?"

"Sorry," Steven murmured. "That was really tactless of me."

Sara waved his apology aside. "That's okay." She took out a crumpled pack of menthol cigarettes and lit herself one. Only when she had twice inhaled deeply did she go on.

"Over the last few years, Uncle Paul discovered the Internet. That's presumably how he heard about a small auction near Nuremberg. An apartment was being cleared, and this curious object was one of the pieces on sale." She picked up the wooden box and gently rattled it. "Paul was more interested in the diary than the box, because of the name of the man who kept it, Theodor Marot."

"Assistant to the king's personal physician, Max Schleiss von Loewenfeld," Steven put in.

She nodded. "Marot was an ambitious young man from Strasbourg. He'd been working in the surgical hospital in Munich since 1872. That was probably where Loewenfeld got to know him and appointed him his assistant." She drew deeply on her cigarette again. The smell of burned tobacco and menthol made Steven feel dizzy. And he couldn't take his eyes off Sara's green-painted fingernails.

"What makes Marot so interesting for research into Ludwig," Sara went on, "is that Loewenfeld's assistant was not only ambitious and clever; he was also extremely handsome. A genuine French dandy with a weak spot for fine art. Ludwig must have fallen for him. Anyway, he appears in the king's letters over and over after 1875.

Some of the chronicles even call him Ludwig's favorite playmate. And . . ." She paused for dramatic effect, smiling. "Marot was with him in Schloss Berg until the end. There were several witnesses who say that after Ludwig's death, Marot claimed it was murder."

Steven gave a low whistle. "When I saw the old photos and the lock of hair, my first thought was that it showed that the king had some kind of homosexual relationship," he murmured. "But if I understand what you're saying, there's far more than that in the diary. Your uncle really believed that it could solve the mystery about Ludwig the Second?"

"He certainly hoped so," Sara replied. "He bought the chest with the book in it for a few hundred euros in an Internet auction. But when he finally got the package, he realized that the diary had been written in some kind of secret code that he couldn't read. So he came to Munich to ask for my help." She ground out her cigarette so energetically that Steven feared she might push it right through the ashtray.

"As an art historian, I know a couple people involved with that kind of thing," she went on. "But it turned out there was someone else after the book. I'd arranged to meet my uncle yesterday, but he didn't show up. First, I tried calling him on his cell phone. Finally, I went to his hotel this afternoon, and all hell had broken loose there. Police, a forensic unit, the works. I called a friend in the state investigation bureau, and he told me what had happened." Lost in thought, she lit another cigarette and stared at a painting of a stack of brightly colored rectangles on the opposite wall. "I never knew Uncle Paul really well, but that threw me for a loop," she murmured at last. "Tortured and executed just for some damn book."

"Can I ask how you found me?" Steven asked hesitantly.

A thin smile appeared on Sara's lips. "Once the police left, I went back to the hotel," she explained. "I knew that even though Uncle Paul didn't own a laptop, he liked to surf the Net for old books. And sure enough, the guy at reception remembered an elderly gentleman who'd been using the hotel computer the previous afternoon. So I checked the history, and guess what popped up? Your secondhand bookshop. In connection with none other than Samuel Pepys."

"You know about Pepys?" Steven asked, surprised.

Sara cast him a mocking glance. "Herr Lukas, I'm a qualified art historian. The fact that I do some detective work on the side doesn't mean I'm some thick-headed Philistine."

Steven smiled. He liked this woman's style, even if he still couldn't really get a handle on her.

"Pepys," he summed up, "kept a diary in the seventeenth century that gives an unparalleled view of life in England in the early modern period. So the professor was looking at my website for it. I guess that was why he came to my bookshop. But then why did he leave the box there?"

"Maybe he knew that he was being followed," Sara said. "Someone was close on his heels. He came to your shop and . . ."

"And exchanged his book for one of mine." Steven snapped his fingers. "That must be it. A collection of German ballads was missing from my shelves after he left. Not bad thinking on your uncle's part."

Sara rubbed her eyes; they were reddened by weariness and the smoke from her cigarette. Her mascara was running, but she didn't seem to notice. "It didn't do him any good," she whispered. "They caught him, tortured him, and killed him. And somewhere along the line he must also have given up your name, so now the same people are after you. And it seems pretty clear that these guys won't pull their punches."

Steven shook his head. "All this because of a book that *might* explain the death of a king from a hundred and something years ago? That's absurd!"

"Believe me, I know the collectors' scene. Some of them would feed their own mothers to piranhas for a rare-enough work."

"I'm afraid it wasn't the first time they tried getting at me," Steven replied after a pause.

The art detective frowned. "What do you mean?"

Steven told her about the odd stranger in the traditional Bavarian suit, and the subsequent mysterious encounter on the Theresienwiese.

"The men were wearing black hoods?" Sara asked. Suddenly she was very agitated. Her face went paler.

Steven nodded. "Black hoods, and they were carrying torches. Why? Do you know who they were?"

With her cigarette in the corner of her mouth, Sara Lengfeld went over to the computer and clicked away for a few minutes. She beckoned to Steven to come and look at something on the screen.

"I don't know if I'm right," Sara said, pointing to the monitor. "You'd better look at this for yourself."

Steven stared at the computer. He saw three figures in black capes and pointed hoods standing in front of a wooden cross sticking up from a shallow lake surrounded by reeds. Each of them held two burning torches making the shape of an X. Their eyes were narrow slits.

The bookseller held his breath. The men who had been following him on the Theresienwiese yesterday had looked just like that.

"If *those* were the men," Sara Lengfeld said, stubbing her second cigarette out in a coffee cup, "then we've really got a problem on our hands."

· 5 ·

THE KING WAS CROSSING a lake that reflected green and blue light. Stalactites hung from the roof like frozen tentacles. Frescoes of angry knights covered the rocky walls, their swords raised in battle, their mouths open in a soundless cry.

The boat silently glided in toward the bank where two paladins were waiting. With their dark green tracksuit jackets and precise crewcuts, they looked like travelers from some bizarre future in this underground world.

"Well? Erec, Bors?" the king said over a rendition of Richard Wagner's "Ride of the Valkyries" that boomed through the grotto from sinfully expensive Dolby loudspeakers hidden in the rock. "Have you found what I'm waiting for so eagerly?"

"It . . . it's not easy, Your Excellency," began the taller of the two men, whom the king had addressed as Erec. "We turned the whole place upside down, but the book wasn't there."

"It wasn't there?" the king said quietly. "What does that mean? Did you question that bookseller?"

"We couldn't during the day," said Bors, the other bodyguard, a wiry little man with pockmarks and a squashed boxer's nose. "The police were all over because of the break-in. But we paid the guy a visit in the evening. We're more or less sure he had the book with him then."

"*Had?*"

"Well, yes." Bors looked nervously up at the roof, as if afraid that one of the stalactites might break off and skewer him. Which was a manner of death preferable to what he faced if that damn book didn't turn up soon. "He . . . he was there with some woman, no idea who she was," he continued, stammering. "They made off together, I guess with the book. We took a couple of photos of her when she was standing outside the bookshop. They talked for a few minutes and . . ."

"Of course we checked where this Lukas lives right away," Erec chimed in. "We searched the whole place, but there was nothing there. Not the guy, not the woman, not the book."

"And where are they now?" The king's voice was still low, but it took on a threatening undertone that the henchmen knew only too well.

"We left men watching his apartment and the bookshop," Erec murmured, his broad shoulders drooping like injured wings. "Gareth, Ywain, and Tristan. He can't get away from us. Sooner or later he has to turn up."

The king adjusted the royal signet ring and blinked very slowly. Little beads of sweat ran down the foreheads of the two bodyguards. The grotto was as hot as a sauna. To reach this place they had had to pass two security barriers. They had descended into the depths in an elevator, then hurried through the throne room with its mighty Bohemian glass chandeliers, and passed countless windows that looked out on a painted scene of a mountainous landscape in bright daylight. Neither of the men could have said how much their boss's eccentric hobby had cost to date. Behind the king's back, they sometimes joked about The Royal Highness's crazy notions, which had recently been getting even crazier. But no matter how deranged the king was, they took care that none of their comments ever reached the royal ears. The pay was too good for that.

And the king was far too unpredictable.

"That . . . is not good," The Excellency murmered after a few minutes of silence. "Not good. We were so close to it, so close. And now this!"

The last words were a shout, the sound of the king's voice echoing around the grotto. But seconds later, the king was composed again.

"I want you to do everything possible to find this antiquarian bookseller," The Royal Highness whispered. "Everything. I'm sure he has the book in his possession. I can *feel* it. If anyone solves the riddle, all is lost."

One of the gorillas muttered something unintelligible. The king raised an eyebrow.

"What did you say?"

"I'm just wondering what we're supposed to do if this guy takes the book to the police. Not that I think he will, but well, if he did, then we would have a problem."

"We would indeed." The Excellency breathed slowly and deeply, eyes closed, as if suffering from a migraine. "That would most definitely be a problem. One hell of a problem."

Suddenly the king's expression brightened, and giggles filled the room.

"But I think I know how to solve it."

The king outlined a plan to the two paladins, who nodded along enthusiastically. Once finished, the king steered the boat out into the water again, and it glided back to the middle of the lake, where it slowly turned in a circle, bathed in blue and red light.

· 6 ·

Wᴏ . . . ᴡʜᴏ ᴀʀᴇ ᴛʜᴏsᴇ guys?" Steven asked, staring at the screen in front of him. The three figures in hooded capes, carrying torches, looked as if they came from another time. Images of burning pyres passed through the bookseller's mind, of priests flagellating themselves, of monasteries enveloped in mist. He could almost hear the somber polyphonic chant of monks.

"Them?" Sara tapped the monitor as if it would bring the strange figures to life. "Cowled Men. Members of a secret order that's been around since Ludwig's death. They preceded the casket at his funeral. They operate in the underground, and for a hundred years they've been trying to prove that their beloved Fairy-tale King was murdered. Sounds loopy, but it's true." The art historian clicked her way through a couple of websites about the hooded figures. "The Cowled Men are everywhere they think there's danger of someone casting aspersions on the name of Ludwig the Second. At theatrical performances, musicals about Ludwig, major anniversaries . . . A few years ago they even tried to open the king's casket, to no avail."

Confused, Steven shook his head. "Are you kidding me? A gang of lunatics in black hooded capes. That's absurd."

"Absurd or not, the Cowled Men come from all over and all types of people. Garbagemen, artists, university lecturers, civil servants. It's thought they have connections very high up in the Bavarian government."

"Hang on a second," Steven interjected. "Are you trying to tell me there's a Bavarian secret society that's been around for a hundred and twenty-five years, operating underground, with connections to the highest levels of government? It sounds more like some crazy Freemason conspiracy theory."

"You know, Herr Lukas, the Illuminati themselves started in Bavaria. As a Berliner, I can tell you the Bavarians are surly little mountain people who have always been a little different from the rest of the world."

"If you say so," Steven said. "But why would these Cowled Men be interested in getting their hands on that little box? If your uncle had decoded the book and published it, then that would prove Ludwig was murdered, and the Order would have what it wanted."

Sara dropped to the sofa again. "These Cowled Men are about as conservative as they come. They're only slightly to the left of Genghis Khan. Remember that theory that Theodor Marot could have had a relationship with the king? What do you think would happen in Bavaria if something like that came to light? The beloved Fairy-tale King turns out to be an old queen who likes cute boys? It would be scandalous." She took off her ballet flats, aimed, and threw them on top of a crushed pizza box in the corner of the room. "Believe me, the Cowled Men will do anything they can to get hold of that book. And they won't publish what's in it until they've removed any reference to that particular suspicion."

"Then you genuinely think these Cowled Men murdered your uncle?" Steven asked.

Sitting cross-legged on the sofa, her head raised, Sara stared straight ahead. "Think about it," she finally replied. "They have a strong motive, and they're definitely after that book. Your encounter with them on the Theresienweise proves that. And I'm sure that guy in the lederhosen is one of them."

Sighing, Steven picked up the yellowing notebook again and

leafed through it. "That doesn't change the fact that the book was written in code. Nothing but odd signs, and now and then a jumble of capital letters. If I only knew . . ."

Suddenly he stopped dead.

"What is it?" asked Sara.

"The book your uncle was asking me about," Steven began thoughtfully. "The diaries of Samuel Pepys . . ."

"What about them?"

"As far as I know, they were written in a kind of code, too. An early seventeenth-century variety of shorthand."

Sara frowned. "What about it?"

"I bought the book online," Steven said, "but I haven't looked inside it yet. I may be wrong, but . . ."

He went over to the computer and typed *Pepys* into Search. It took him some time, but at last Steven found the right site. His heart leaped.

"I was right," he said. "See for yourself."

Sara jumped off the sofa and padded over to the bookseller. Together, they stared at the screen. A cryptic script flickered on the monitor, consisting mainly of flourishes, lines, and dots. Only a few recognizable English words stood out.

The art detective whistled softly through her teeth. It was the same coded script the king's assistant had used in his diary.

"Shelton's shorthand from the seventeenth century," Steven said. "Samuel Pepys used it in his diary to keep all his affairs secret from his wife. It wasn't decoded until two hundred years later. Your uncle must have guessed something and came to me to check his suspicions." He shook his head. "Who'd have expected a little French assistant doctor to write his diary in an antiquated secret code?"

"Theodor Marot studied history as well as medicine in Strasbourg," Sara said. "He obviously qualified with distinction. Nice work!" She patted Steven on the shoulder. "The competitor progresses to the next round of the game. Although that brings us to another problem: how are we going to decipher the damn thing?"

Steven clicked back two pages. "It says here that Shelton wrote a manual for his shorthand in 1635. It's called *Tachygraphy*. That's ancient Greek—it means 'fast writing,' and . . ."

"Okay, Professor, I don't need a lesson in ancient Greek—I need one in stenography," Sara interrupted him impatiently. "So what about that manual?"

"You ought to let me finish what I'm saying, dear Ms. Art Detective," Steven said. "I was about to tell you that not only do I have Pepys's diaries in my stockroom, but I recently acquired a copy of *Tachygraphy*. A very rare book." He tapped his forehead. "Nothing like keeping a good inventory in your head."

Thoughtfully, Sara took a third menthol cigarette out of her crumpled pack.

"My compliments, Herr Lukas," she replied dryly. "Through to yet another round of the game. At this rate, you might yet be the champion. But to do that, the two of us have something else to do first."

"And that is?"

Sara's face disappeared behind a cloud of white menthol-scented smoke. "We have to get over to your stockroom as fast as possible to fetch that book. Before the Cowled Men take it into their heads to rummage around there some more."

· 7 ·

WHEN THEY REACHED THE WESTEND district, it was well after midnight. Most of the trendy pubs, sushi bars, and cafeterias had closed, and there wasn't much going on in the streets. A few cars searched for one of the rare parking spots; otherwise, the place was deserted. The drone of Turkish music reached their ears from somewhere. If TV sets hadn't been flickering like strobe lighting behind several windows, one might have thought it was a dead city.

Steven wasn't sure just how deeply he should get involved. From what Sara said, the men who were after the diary would kill for it without a second thought. They had tortured a man to death over it already. On the other hand, the discovery of Marot's diary was a real coup, any antiquarian bookseller's dream. If it was really written in Shelton's coded script, and they could decode it, and if it gave information about the death of Ludwig II, all Steven's financial worries would be over, not to mention the publicity he would get. *Der Spiegel, Stern, Focus*—they'd all be writing about his discovery.

But suppose it's a forgery?

The forged Hitler diaries sprang to Steven's mind. They had plunged *Stern* magazine into the greatest scandal in German media history. He decided to be wary, for safety's sake, but the diary held an almost magical attraction for him.

It's like a drug. Since I first leafed through it, I've been obsessed with it . . .

By now they had turned into Gollierstrasse and were driving slowly past his bookshop. To Steven's great relief, he saw that the men had not made good on their threat. His shop had not been burned down, but in the dark, with its display window smashed, it looked desolate and uninviting. The little place that had dominated his life for so long didn't seem to be his anymore; it was like a diseased part of a body that had been cut off.

"We'd better go through the backyard," Sara whispered. "If those guys are still watching the shop, they'll be in front."

Steven nodded. As they slowly passed in the car, his gaze lingered on the black hole that had once been his display window. For a moment he thought he saw movement in the darkness of the shop. Were the Cowled Men in there? Or maybe some kind of vandals? The bookseller blinked and looked harder into the shop. But he must have been mistaken. Nothing. No movement, no sound, just a broken window.

Sara brought him down to earth. "What's the matter?" she hissed. "Seeing ghosts? Come on."

She parked the car in a dimly lit side street and got out. Steven followed her, turning up the collar of his flimsy corduroy jacket. In their frantic escape, he had left his coat and cashmere scarf in the bookshop, taking only his briefcase with him. That, with its precious contents, had stayed behind in Sara's office. Shivering, he went with her to the street behind the shop, where the gate barred their way into the yard.

"Shit!" the art detective cursed. "Now what?"

"Leave it to me."

Steven pressed one of the many bells beside a list of names and kept his finger on it. After a minute, a sleepy voice with a strong Bavarian accent came through the speaker.

"Christ almighty! If this is supposed to be a joke, then . . ."

"Herr Stiebner," Steven interrupted. "It's me, Herr Lukas from the bookshop. I forgot my key. Would you be kind enough to let me in?"

"Oh well . . ." There was a buzz, and the gate opened with a click. "You owe me a beer for this," the voice grumbled.

"A whole case, Herr Stiebner. Genuine König Ludwig dark beer."

Steven showed the art detective into the interior courtyard, which was overgrown with Virginia creeper. The back door of his shop was still open. The men obviously hadn't taken the trouble to close it during the chase.

"My main stockroom is down in the cellar," Steven whispered. "Through the door on the right."

They entered the building and turned down a steep staircase leading downward.

"How many books do you store down there?" Sara asked quietly.

"About three thousand."

"*Three th—*"

"Don't worry," Steven reassured her. "They're all neatly classified. It won't take us long, and then . . ."

Sara pressed his hand. "Did you hear that?"

The bookseller went quiet. He could hear a slight dragging sound coming from the cellar. Suddenly there was a hoarse scream, then gasping from at least two men, and what sounded like a large bookcase falling over.

"What the hell is that?" Steven said, ducking low on the narrow stairway. "Sounds like a fight going on down there."

There was another scream, but it soon turned to spluttering, gurgling sounds.

"Wrong. It sounds like someone being murdered," Sara said. "Come on!"

They hurried down the stairs and came to a door standing ajar and leading into a dark room. Two shadowy figures wrestled with each other; he could make out the outlines of wooden racks that had been pushed over, as well as a couple of iron bars as long as a man's arm. Steven intended to eventually use them to build a new set of shelves.

Frantically, Steven felt for the light switch to the left of the doorway. But when at last he found it and pressed it, no light came on. After clicking it on and off several times, he gave up, cursing, and stormed into the cellar. He could see the two figures more clearly now. A powerful, broad-shouldered man was forcing the other one to the floor. He was clasping his victim's throat and throttling him. The legs of the smaller man thrashed wildly back and forth. Steven thought his movements were getting weaker.

"Stop!" Sara shouted, right beside him. "Stop it right now!" But the powerful man ignored her and tightened his grip on his adversary's throat. Sara grabbed him by the shoulder and pulled. When she did, the man took a pistol out of the inside pocket of his jacket and aimed it at her. He looked ready to pull the trigger.

For a moment, time seemed to stand still. Steven saw nothing but the small black pistol and Sara with her hands held protectively in front of her face. Instinctively, he snatched up one of the iron bars and rushed toward the two of them. Raising the heavy bar high in the air and uttering a hoarse cry, he brought it crashing down on the man's head.

There was a sound like an overripe pumpkin falling to the ground.

The man toppled, twitched a little, and then lay still, his fingers still clutching the pistol.

My God, what have I done? Steven thought. *What on earth have I done?*

The bar dropped from his hands and rolled away behind a bookcase. For a moment there was an unnatural silence. Steven was hesitantly approaching the lifeless body when the second man suddenly jumped up and shoved him aside. The bookseller stumbled back over a bookshelf and fell to the floor.

"Hey!" Sara shouted, but the stranger pushed her away with his elbow and ran upstairs. Steven caught a brief glimpse of a black hooded sweatshirt with some kind of slogan on it, and then the man was gone.

"Put the light on, for Christ's sake," Sara gasped. She clutched her right side; obviously the stranger had hit her harder than it had looked. Steven made his way out of the stockroom, groping about until he finally found the fuse box on the back wall of the corridor. Running his hand over the switches, he could tell that they were all pressed down. He clicked them up, there was a brief crackle, and then the corridor was suddenly bathed in bright light.

"Someone's been at the fuse box . . ." he began. But Sara was already speaking, her voice low and strangely husky.

"Forget the damn fuse box. Take a look at this."

Steven went back into the cellar, now brightly lit, and saw a chaotic scene: overturned bookshelves, crates, books with pages torn out. Among them lay the powerful stranger with the pistol. Only now, in the light, could the bookseller see him properly. He was a giant, almost six feet tall, in jeans, work boots, and a dark green tracksuit jacket. A pool of red blood had formed around his fashionably shaved skull. It was quickly spreading and had almost reached the nearest books. The man's eyes stared at the ceiling like two blue glass marbles.

"My God, he's dead," Steven said, kneeling over the lifeless body. His corduroy pants were soaking up blood, but he didn't notice. "I killed him. I've killed a man."

Sara came closer and cautiously touched the body with the toe of one of her ballet flats. The art detective, pale and trembling, was still clutching her stomach where the man had driven his elbow into it as he ran away.

"It's one of those thugs who was after us a few hours ago, no doubt about it," she said to herself. "But then who was the other one?"

She hesitated, then bent down to the dead man and, firmly compressing her lips, searched his pockets. At last, using just her fingertips, she pulled a wallet from his tracksuit jacket.

Sara held the opened wallet up to her eyes and peered at it. "His ID says his name is Bernd Reiser. Ever heard of him?"

Steven shook his head. Without much hope, he pressed his fingertips to the man's carotid artery, but there was no pulse. His own pulse raced; he was incapable of rational thought. Meanwhile, Sara seemed to have regained her composure. Secretly, the bookseller admired how coolly she searched the dead body, although at the same time it made him wonder.

What is this woman? Art detective? More like a female Philip Marlowe . . .

"A man might think you've done something like this before," he said. "Part of standard art detective training, is it? Robbing dead bodies?"

"Not that it's any business of yours," Sara replied without looking up, "but you can assume that I have a certain amount of experience."

"As an *art* detective? But . . ."

"Well, what have we here?" Sara drew out a small pendant from under the dead man's T-shirt. Engraved on it was the image of a golden swan, wings outspread. Under it there was an ornate inscription.

"*Tmeicos Ettal*," she said thoughtfully, letting the pendant on its chain swing in front of Steven like a hypnotist's pendulum. "I wonder what that means? It's not in any language I know. Could it . . ."

"Never mind that," Steven snapped. "There's a dead man here. And I killed him."

"He was about to kill someone else." After a moment's hesitation, Sara put the amulet in her pocket. "And he was aiming a gun at me. Don't forget that."

Steven was still staring at the corpse and the pool of blood, which by now had grown to a fairly large puddle. Finally he stood up and turned to the door. "Anyway, we have to call the police." He turned to Sara. "Could I use your phone? Mine's somewhere up in the office."

The art detective brought out a black smartphone. At the sight of its splintered display, she cursed.

"Shit, this won't be any good except to throw at someone." She pressed a couple of keys, but in vain. "Must have been smashed when I fell. Great—and it cost me three hundred euros."

"We can go up to my office and call from there," Steven suggested. "The best thing will be if we . . ."

"And what are you planning to tell the police?" Sara asked sharply. "That you were looking for a seventeenth-century book about deciphering secret writing, and you just happened to kill the Hulk here with an iron bar in the process?"

"It was self-defense. You said so yourself. He was going to kill that other guy."

Sara looked around and shrugged. "What other guy? I don't see anyone else here."

"But . . ."

"Herr Lukas," she said in a mollifying tone, "this story is complicated enough as it is. What were the two of us doing down here in your stockroom so late at night? Who was the man who ran away? What does it all have to do with that book? Trust me, I know the cops. They aren't just going to pat us on the back and let us go. They'll take us into custody, and then the questioning will start." She took a deep breath before going on. "I'll tell you what we're going to do. We'll wipe your fingerprints off that iron bar, we'll go home like good little kids, and we'll act as if we were never here. And tomorrow some neighbor will discover the break-in and an unfortunate thief who got killed fighting over the loot. What do you think of that?"

Steven stared at the art detective incredulously. Her ruthlessness was troubling him more and more.

"You want me to sneak away like a criminal?" he asked, baffled.

Sara's eyebrows shot up. "Could you cut the drama? I'm only trying to help you. Both of us."

Steven massaged his temples. Once again, his eyes traveled over the corpse lying in the bright red puddle of blood. The sight was surreal among the white pages of the books.

Like spilled red ink, he thought. *Or melted red sealing wax. Blood sticking to my fingers.*

He took a deep breath. "Okay," he said quietly. "We'll play it your way. I have enough problems right now, anyway. I don't need a horde of suspicious police officers after me."

"Glad to hear it. Believe me, you'll thank me yet."

Sara knelt down, her face briefly contorting in a painful grimace. She peered behind the bookshelves until at last she found the bloodstained iron bar. Fishing the murder weapon out from between two crates, she carefully wiped it down with a handkerchief.

"Here we are." Sara gingerly placed the bar beside the body, stopped for a moment and finally took the pistol from the giant's lifeless fingers. With a practiced hand, she secured the trigger-guard and put the gun in her jacket pocket.

"I have a feeling we may be able to use this," she said, turning back to Steven. "Now let's go look for that decoding book."

As if in a trance, the bookseller nodded. He had entirely forgotten what they were really here for. At last he clambered cautiously over the puddle of blood, to rummage around in the back part of his archive, where he stored scientific books from the seventeenth and eighteenth centuries. His hands shook; he thought every little sound was someone on the stairs—maybe the other intruder? He imagined that the dead man might rise from the floor any moment like a zombie and strangle him with his strong hands.

"Damn it, how long is this going to take?" Sara asked. "That hoodie character may call the police himself, and then we're screwed."

"I . . . just one second . . ."

Steven went along the rows of books arranged alphabetically by their authors' last names. At last he found Shelton's *Tachygraphy* on the top-right shelf of a bookcase. It was an inconspicuous, fat volume with a leather binding. He took it out and stowed it under his cord jacket as if he were shoplifting it.

"Finally. Now let's get out of here," Sara said, already on her way up the stairs. "We can say a prayer for Hulk in the car, okay?"

A GOOD HOUR later, clad only in sweatpants and a washed-out woolen sweater, Steven sat in Sara's office, sipping a cup of black tea.

The art detective had convinced him that his own apartment wasn't safe at the moment. If the men in tracksuit jackets had found his bookshop, they'd have no difficulty in tracking down his home address as well. Steven was too worked up to sleep anyway; the past twenty-four hours had completely upended his life. So, gritting his teeth, he had agreed to stop off at Sara's office, even if only for a cup of tea and some clean clothes.

Steven bit his lip. He couldn't get the body in his bookshop out of his head. Even though it had been in self-defense, he had killed a man, and this woman who called herself an art detective carried on as if nothing had happened. It was true that Sara was affected to some extent—she had already put back her second whisky—but all things considered, she seemed to take the incident in the cellar pretty much in her stride. Who was this woman really?

Realizing he was staring at her, Sara smiled at him and pointed behind her. "I guess I'd better make us something to eat," she said. "My mother always said the world looks different when you have something inside you. Not that it was true, but that could have been just my mother's terrible cooking."

"How can you think about eating right now?" Steven asked indignantly. "I just killed someone! Is that all part of a day's work for you?"

"I assure you, it isn't." Sara cocked her head and looked at him thoughtfully. "But it could be that my skin's rather thicker than yours. Where I grew up, violence was the order of the day."

"Let me guess," said Steven sarcastically. "New York's Bronx? Soweto in Johannesburg?"

Sara grinned. "The Wedding district of Berlin. Ever been in that part of the city? One-third immigrants, one-third unemployed. If you never got a bloody nose, no one wanted to play with you. The best entertainment was when the police raided some junkie's apartment. We used to find used syringes in the sandbox in the playground near where we lived." She drew in the air as if smoking an invisible cigarette. "That guy down in your stockroom looked just like one of the dealers who were always kicking us kids off the swings."

Steven nodded thoughtfully. "I assume your parents weren't much help?"

"My parents?" Sara laughed under her breath. Abstractedly, she examined her green-painted nails. "I helped my parents, not the other way around. Ever had to get your mother, drunk as a skunk and babbling, into bed and then undressed?"

"I . . . I'm afraid I can't say I have, no," Steven muttered. "Not an experience I've ever had." He hesitated for a moment before going on. "But couldn't your uncle do anything? I mean, he was a university professor. You'd think he . . ."

"You didn't know my mother," Sara said roughly. "Uncle Paul did all he could, but if people like that are going to drink, then they will, and if you give them money, they won't buy clothes for their kids; they'll buy cheap booze." She rose to her feet abruptly. "Now, excuse me, please. The kitchen calls."

Steven watched Sara disappear into the kitchen. He couldn't understand this woman. She seemed to be surrounded by invisible armor. Whenever he tried to be friendly, she retreated. It was as if Sara was a magnet, attracting him briefly and then pushing him away again.

Sighing, Steven turned back to the leather-bound volume of Shelton's *Tachygraphy* on the table in front of him. It was not the original edition but a revised version from 1842. Luckily, it would serve its purpose just as well as the original work, maybe even better. Steven had already leafed through it. The text was in an old-fashioned English that the bookseller knew from other books of that period. But he had problems with the curious scribbles that Shelton had established as shorthand in England in the seventeenth century.

Steven knew a little about stenography. At university he had attended lectures on Johann Gabelsberger, whose nineteenth-century shorthand system was at the root of modern German shorthand. But Shelton's signs were different, reminiscent of the scribblings of a five-year-old.

Steven sighed and took another sip of his strong tea. It would probably be some time yet before he was in a position to decipher Marot's diary. And what the curious sequences of capital letters that appeared on a number of pages might mean was a complete mystery to him.

"Sandwiches?" Sara came out of the kitchen with a tray full of them. She was smiling now. "I went all out with the mustard sauce. Not that that means much with me."

Repulsed, Steven shook his head. The consistency of the grainy sauce dripping from the salmon sandwiches reminded him of the blood on his stockroom floor. "Thanks, that's very kind of you," he murmured. "But somehow I've lost my appetite in these last few hours. I hope your decision not to call the police was really right."

"Oh, it was. Definitely." With a sandwich oozing sauce in her hand, the art detective gestured at the book in front of Steven, a volume nearly two hundred years old. "Getting anywhere yet?"

Steven instinctively pushed Shelton's *Tachygraphy* a little farther to the right. "Mind that sauce," he said. "This isn't some tabloid."

"Sorry." Smiling, Sara put the plate down. "I was forgetting that you have such an erotic relationship with books."

"I just don't like it when they get mustard all over them," Steven replied. "Apart from which I wouldn't want to get grease spots on these distinguished garments." He pointed to his T-shirt and the old jogging pants that hung loose around his thighs. "Belonged to you once, did they?"

"You'd better be joking." Sara's eyebrows shot up in indignation. "Who do you think I am, Miss Piggy? My last ex left them here. I guess he was a bit larger than you." She shrugged. "His stuff has been waiting in my old clothes collection ever since. Somehow I find it harder to part with them than with their owners."

Steven smiled. "Not particularly easy to be in a relationship with you?"

"Let's just say I'm high maintenance," Sara said. "I'm not about to cuddle up to someone on the sofa while he watches Formula One. Plus, most men don't like their girlfriends to be smarter than they are." Grinning, she let her eyes go to the T-shirt Steven was wearing, which was adorned with the logo of some grunge band. "I'll admit that David was quite cute, but a time comes when you want to talk to your boyfriend about something other than surfing, trendy clubs, and house music."

"Well, you don't have to worry about that with me," Steven said, raising one hand as if taking an oath. "I can't surf, I don't know any trendy clubs, and I can't stand house music. And no doorman would ever let me in in *this* getup anyway."

Suddenly he thought of his bloodstained corduroys, now in a garbage bin in the hallway, and all at once he was serious again.

"That guy in the tracksuit jacket," Steven said. "Bernd Reiser . . . what could he have been looking for in my bookshop?"

"I assume he was posted there to lie in wait in case you came back," Sara said. "First thing tomorrow I'm going to check up on that inscription, *Tmeicos Ettal*, and the swan on the amulet. There's something not quite right about it. It looks more like something a twelve-year-old girl would wear, not some bruiser." She reached eagerly for another sandwich. "But it's the other guy who bothers me more. I'd been thinking it was only the thugs we know who are after the book. But obviously there are other interested parties."

"You think the man in the black hooded sweater was already down in my stockroom looking for the book, and Reiser took him by surprise?" Steven asked.

Sara shrugged her shoulders and bit into her salmon sandwich, sending out a spray of sauce. "Or the other way around," she said with her mouth full. "In any case, there are obviously several people who'd like to get hold of your little box and the book inside it."

"Or else the man in the hoodie was a perfectly normal burglar who saw the smashed display window and took the opportunity to come in," Steven suggested.

"A thief with a weakness for Rilke and Flaubert? I don't know about that." Sara swallowed her mouthful and pointed to the old book on stenography. "One way or another, we're a step ahead of those guys. Unlike them, we know how to decipher the notes made by our friend Theodor Marot."

"*We* don't know anything yet." Steven wearily rubbed his red-rimmed eyes. "First of all *I* have to make my way through three hundred pages of stuff about tachygraphy. Ask me again in a few hours."

"Are you sure you don't want to get some sleep first?"

"I'm far too worked up to sleep." The bookseller pushed the comfortable leather chair over to the table and opened the book to the first page. "And you've made me very curious."

"Okay." Sara went over to the leather sofa and threw a thin woolen rug over herself. "Just wake me up when you know who the murderer is."

She yawned, stretched, and closed her eyes. Steven hadn't even heard that last remark because he was so immersed in the introduction to Shelton's shorthand. He soon realized that it wasn't as difficult as he had assumed. While it would be weeks before he could write Shelton's shorthand fluently, he was able to decipher it surprisingly quickly. The signs were repeated; many words were simply abbreviated or a single sign stood for them. Steven realized that he hadn't completely forgotten the stenography lectures he'd attended at university. After two hours, he decided to attempt deciphering Marot's notes. He would simply regard the notebook as an exercise to be solved. Later, he could go back to the strange sequences of capital letters that began occurring on the second page.

The bookseller opened the diary, and once again that sense of familiarity immediately came over him, together with an unfounded fear. His throat constricted, and he felt slightly nauseated. What was it about this book? Was it magic in some way? Or was he simply seeing ghosts?

Laboriously, he tackled word after word. At first he had to consult *Tachygraphy* constantly, but as time went on he got faster and faster. He worked his way through the lines like a scythe cutting through tall grass. When he couldn't entirely decipher certain sentences, he tried to reconstruct the sense of them. Word by word, paragraph by paragraph, Steven wrote it all out in a notebook on Sara's desk, mingling his own style with the old-fashioned expressions of the assistant physician.

For the next few hours Steven was entirely immersed in the world of Theodor Marot. Before his mind's eye, horse-drawn cabs rattled along narrow, dirty alleyways, gentlemen in tails and overcoats raised their top hats in civil greeting, women in corsets and full skirts swayed in time to the music of a Johann Strauss waltz. Steven saw fairy-tale castles, festive banquets, shimmering grottoes; he heard the shrill giggling of a melancholic king and the resounding music of Richard Wagner; he breathed in the aroma of thousands of candles burning in a ballroom; he tasted Bordeaux a hundred and fifty years old.

But above all, Steven sensed that this well-worn little notebook was in the process of telling him an extraordinary story—a mystery that only a small and select circle had known before; a secret written from the heart of the royal physician's assistant, as if he were making a confession.

The bookseller thought he could still see Theodor Marot's fears behind the lines of text, like traces of blood not quite washed out of a white vest.

· 8 ·

QECSOQNZO

*M*y name is Theodor Marot. I am assistant to the royal physician, Dr. Max Schleiss von Loewenfeld, and one of the king's true friends, of whom His Majesty had far too few. We tried to save him, but we failed. Tears fall on these pages, like sand shaken to blot the ink, but even they cannot undo the fact that the king is dead and his enemies are victorious. May these notes help to bring the truth to light, painful as it is.

As I write this, the great men of the land are gathering for the funeral banquet in the royal residence, where they will fall, like carrion crows, on oxtail soup, saddle of veal, and roast venison. They will wipe their greasy mouths and congratulate one another over coffee on the success of their intrigues. For the king is dead, and he has taken his secret with him to the grave. Only we few know what really happened, and if the ministers should ever learn this, we must all fear a shot delivered without warning. Not until the last of us has followed Ludwig to the grave can they be sure that no word of what happened will reach the general public, that they can go on ruling the country undisturbed. Their puppet, the prince regent, is sent off hunting and hiking while these gentlemen play politics on the grand scale.

They laid the king to rest in the church of St. Michael in Munich on Saturday, two days ago. Although Dr. Loewenfeld is presumably a filthy traitor in the eyes of the ministers of state, we were both permitted to accompany the funeral procession, together with the other doctors. It was probably a final favor, before they force Loewenfeld to retire on the grounds of his age, and leave me free for anyone to gun down.

Briennerstrasse, that magnificent street, was so full of people that day that the hearse, drawn by eight black horses, could hardly make any progress. Many wept, all the shops were closed, and black banners hung from the windows, whipping back and forth in a stormy wind. It was as if, on that day, the people of Munich wanted to give their king all the love that they had withheld from him for the decades of his life. But it was too late now.

What would Ludwig have said if he had been watching it all, as the military men goose-stepped ahead of his casket in their gold-trimmed uniforms? If he had seen all the sycophantic courtiers, civil servants, and lackeys drawn up in rank and file in the funeral procession, faces sad and frowning while inwardly they rejoiced? At that moment I almost wished that the two dozen black-clad Cowled Men would turn on the whole pack of them with their fiery torches, but they walked in silence at the head of the procession, muffled in their ghostly robes, with the king's coat of arms on their breasts, and the crossbones as a sign of death.

When the casket was carried out of the Residence Palace, the sun briefly broke through the clouds in a last greeting. The people of Munich glanced up at the sky as if Ludwig might wave to them once more from on high. The king had just been laid in his final resting place in the crypt of St. Michael's when bright lightning struck with such a loud peal of thunder that people fell to their knees, covering their ears with their hands. Many saw it as a sign that Ludwig is still among us, and already there are rumors that he has withdrawn to the depths of the Natternberg near Deggendorf, and will return someday to sit in judgment of his murderers.

But I know that will never happen. The king is dead.

NECAALAI

Sitting down now to describe the events of the last few months, leading to Ludwig's terrible end, I will begin with his final birthday celebration in August 1885. It was his fortieth. If we had guessed that no other birthday would follow, we would have shed tears and gone on our knees to the king, begging him to see reason at last. As it was, we put up with his whims and joined in his little games, in which each of us had an established part to play.

Ludwig was celebrating his birthday, as he did almost every year, in his hunting lodge on the heights of Schachen in the massive Wetterstein mountain range. The local peasants had lit bonfires on the peaks, so that we were surrounded by a wreath of fire with the wooden hunting lodge at its center. The king had invited only a few of his faithful friends there with him, including his adjutant, Alfred Count Eckbrecht von Dürckheim-Montmartin; the postilion, Karl Hesselschwerdt; and my humble self.

Since I had risen to the post of Loewenfeld's assistant more than ten years before, the king had frequently invited me to keep him company. We often stayed up until the small hours of the morning, discussing the French court theater, or the poems of Schiller, as well as that remarkable writer Edgar Allan Poe, whom Ludwig loved more than any other contemporary author. I may say that I had become a genuine friend of the king's in those years. And although his whims and posturing often seemed to me like the games of a boy of twelve, he was my king. There was no one else like this poetic, melancholy, pugnacious man on the earthly globe. An artist as head of state—what other country can claim as much for itself?

On the night of 24 August, we were sitting up late on the upper floor of the Schachen lodge, in what was known as the Turkish Room. A few years earlier, Ludwig had had this room designed in the style of Moorish palaces. A fountain played, splashing gently; soft, richly ornamented carpets covered the floor, and the walls were decorated with gilded carvings and bright stained-glass windows. Wearing kaftans, we leaned back on cushions and divans, smoking hookah pipes and sipping mocha from tiny cups as thin as parchment. Servants fanned us with peacock feathers, and the music of a shawm came from somewhere.

I was by now used to such spectacles staged by our king, so I was not surprised when he sat up on his cushion, placid as a portly Buddha, and offered me his pipe.

"Dearest Mahmoud, my grand vizier and most loyal of my Mussulmen," he said, turning to me with a grave expression, "you are too high-strung. Here, inhale some of this delicious tobacco. It will help you to dream a dream out of the *Thousand and One Nights*."

Smiling, I took the pipe and inhaled deeply. It was not a rare occurrence for the king to address us by historical names, or names of his own invention. In the last few years I had already been Gawain, Gunther, Faithful Eckhart, and Colbert, the French minister. Why not a grand vizier for a change? Through the smoke, I looked at Ludwig's expansive figure and tried to recall him in his prime.

It was some time since the king had been the well-built warrior who had had all the women at his feet in the first years of his reign. It was true, at almost six feet tall he was still a giant, but by now he weighed well over two hundred pounds. His face was pale and bloated, his eyes cloudy, his mouth fallen in and near toothless. I could smell his fetid breath from where I sat. The brightly colored Turkish costume that he wore in the Schachen hunting lodge did not conceal the fact that Ludwig was more and more letting himself go to seed. Only his hair was unchanged, still as thick and black as it had been when he ascended to the throne more than twenty years ago.

But what alarmed all of us most were the sometimes deluded, sometimes dreamy moods that came over him with increasing frequency. He was a king of the moonlight who made night his day and lived in his own fairy-tale world. Even we, his faithful friends, could get through to him less and less often.

Beside me, Count Dürckheim shifted restlessly on his cushion. Like the rest of us, the usually dashing adjutant with his neatly twirled mustache was wearing a loose silk caftan. Dürckheim hated these masquerades, but he knew that at such moments he could get much farther with his king than in any official meetings.

"Your Majesty, we have to talk," he began in a serious tone. "I went through the items on your civil list again yesterday. Your debts now amount to almost fourteen million marks, and I think that the building of your castles . . ."

"Dürckheim, how many more times do I have to tell you that I don't want to hear this tiresome financial drivel on my birthday?" the king snapped at him, and he closed the book of Turkish poetry that he had been about to go on reading. "It's bad enough to have you pestering me with it in Munich. We'll continue building the castles— that's settled. They are the expression of my very being—without them I would not be king." Suddenly his lips were narrow as two straight lines. "My father, my grandfather, they were all allowed to build such castles," he hissed. "It's only my own ministers who act in such a way. On my honor, Dürckheim, if those gentlemen don't grant me more money, I'll blow Hohenschwangau sky-high. I won't endure the shame of it any longer. Money must be forthcoming, never mind how, understand? Have you *understood?*"

Ludwig almost screamed those last words. Embarrassed, we all looked at the floor. The king's financial difficulties had increased and multiplied in those last few years. The building of the new castle of Hohenschwangau (known as Neuschwanstein by the peasants), the castles of Herrenchiemsee and Linderhof, as well as a whole series of other projects, swallowed up huge sums of money. The king had only a restricted budget available, the civil list, as it was known, and he had more than exhausted that. By now he was in debt to several crafts-men, and the council of ministers was pressing him to discontinue the building works. In vain—Ludwig designed palaces the way little boys build castles out of sand or snow. One after another, a fairy-tale world in which he took refuge to be the kind of king he imagined himself. He was Arthur, and we were his knights of the Round Table; we were brave Germanic warriors—or, alternatively, as now, we were Saracens rattling our sabers and smoking our water pipes.

After a moment's silence, Dürckheim began again, low-voiced. His mustache was trembling, but he tried to sound composed. "Your Majesty, the ministers will not put up with this much longer. I am afraid that an attempted assassination . . ."

"An assassination? By my ministers? Dürckheim, don't be ridiculous." Ludwig laughed so hard that his belly bounced up and down under the Turkish costume like a pig's inflated bladder. "That corrupt band of civil servants is capable, at the most, of spoiling my dinner. An assassination attempt? More likely by the anarchists, if anyone." Suddenly he was serious again. "Apart from that, I've been asking you for years to get a bodyguard together for me. True knights of the Grail who would go to their deaths for me. And what has come of that, pray?"

"There aren't many left who can be trusted," murmured Dürckheim. "I've heard news that Bismarck—"

"That's enough of such gossip." The king pointed to Hesselschwerdt, the postilion who had risen to become a kind of second adjutant in the past year. I considered the little turncoat a hypocritical lickspittle, but unfortunately Ludwig had fallen for him hook, line, and sinker.

"Our good Hesselschwerdt will solicit money from abroad next week. England, Venice, Genoa—isn't that so, Hesselschwerdt?"

The skinny postilion, who looked even more ridiculous than usual in his Turkish garb, nodded obsequiously. "Very good, Your Majesty," he said. "Always at your service."

Ludwig let himself drop back again. "And now let us go on celebrating my birthday," he purred like a fat, contented cat. "I've found a wonderful fairy tale here. I would like to read it aloud to the best of my ability. *Compris?*"

A LITTLE LATER Dürckheim and I were standing out on the balcony of the hunting lodge. In silence we looked at the many bonfires slowly going out around us. Although it was August, an icy wind blew over the mountain.

"What in God's name did you mean when you spoke of an assassination attempt just now?" I asked at last. "You mentioned Bismarck. Do you really think that—"

"Shhh." Dürckheim put a finger to his lips. "Even here on Schachen I don't know who's still to be trusted. That postilion, Hesselschwerdt, plays whatever tune the king wants to hear. Damn lackey!" He kicked the balcony, while the king's monotonous voice droned on inside. Ludwig had reached his third fairy tale.

"But you're right," he said at last. "I did find out something that makes me uneasy. I know a few people in the Ministry of the Interior. It's rumored that one of Bismarck's men will soon be coming to Munich. None other than Carl von Strelitz, an agent whom the chancellor has employed in"—he drew a finger briefly across his throat—"in, well, rather delicate affairs. Von Strelitz has already worked for many different powers. He is regarded as one of the best spies in Europe, and one of the deadliest."

My heart missed a beat. "You really think that the chancellor of the German Empire plans to have Ludwig *killed?*" I asked in a hoarse voice. "Why?"

Count Dürckheim was speaking so quietly now that I could hardly hear what he said. "Do you remember the king's last furious outburst against the Prussians?" he asked. "When he said he'd sooner let the Austrians have his kingdom than stay in the German Empire under the heel of the Hohenzollerns?"

Diffidently, I nodded. It was a fact: Ludwig had never forgotten that early in his reign he had lost the war against Prussia, and therefore had to fight against France in 1870 on the side of the Hohenzollerns he despised. The German Confederation had won the war, and King Wilhelm of Prussia, who as it happened was a distant relation of Ludwig, had put on airs as German Emperor ever since. Ludwig had made several attempts to hand over his crown to the Austrians and simply abdicate.

"Bismarck has had enough," Dürckheim went on quietly. "If Bavaria leaves the Empire, his dream of a German fatherland is over. For some time the imperial chancellor has been thinking of installing Ludwig's uncle Luitpold as ruler of Bavaria. But, of course, the present king is in the way . . ."

His last words lingered menacingly in the air. I began to shiver under my thin caftan.

"But perhaps von Strelitz is only coming to assess the situation in Munich," whispered Dürckheim. "Whatever happens, we must be on our guard."

"What do you suggest?"

The count looked at me thoughtfully for a moment. Finally he asked, "Would you trust yourself to keep this man Strelitz under observation?"

I felt all the color draining from my face. "But I'm not a police officer, a detective of any kind. I'm only a doctor. I hardly think . . ."

"Theodor, I beg you!" Dürckheim had never before addressed me by my Christian name. "There's no one else I can trust! The Ministry of the Interior turned away from the king long ago, and even the police may have been infiltrated. We have to find out what Bismarck has in mind, and before Ludwig's enemies do." A smile showed on his face for a moment. "What's more, as an unknown assistant doctor, you have a considerable advantage. No one will suspect you of being a Bavarian agent on a secret mission."

"Oh, wonderful," I whispered. "And how do you expect me to proceed?"

He briefly outlined his plan, while, inside, the king recited an

Ottoman poem from the last century. Several of the servants had already begun snoring quietly beneath their turbans.

IIEAPQRX

Two weeks later, I stood in a lightweight black overcoat, with a top hat and a riding whip, at Munich Central Rail Station, waiting for the four o'clock afternoon train. Count Dürckheim had found out from his informants in the Ministry of the Interior that von Strelitz would be staying in Munich under the name of Alfons Schmidt. The Ministry had assured the special Prussian envoy that a horse-drawn cab and driver would be sent for him. It couldn't have been easy for Dürckheim to find out which cab company had been commissioned to supply them. But once he had done it, fifty marks had been enough for him to change the cabby for someone of his own choice.

Me.

Little beads of sweat prickled on my forehead, and not because of the sultry September day. I was expecting police officers to run toward me any moment and take me into custody in my cheap disguise. But nothing like that happened. The four P.M. train came into the station, whistling and puffing, the doors were opened, and out poured busy travelers from Berlin, Augsburg, and Nuremberg. Most of them were middle-aged men in rigid bowler hats, with the gold chains of their watches dangling from their fashionable double-breasted suits. There were also a few women among the passengers; they wore elaborate hats and full-skirted dresses with bustles, and they twirled parasols between their fingers as thin, badly shaved porters took care of their mountains of baggage.

I recognized Strelitz by his lean figure, tall top hat, and neatly shaped side-whiskers. Count Dürckheim had shown me a photograph of the Prussian agent the day before. He carried a small traveling bag in one hand and a walking stick in the other. His overcoat billowed in the smoke of the locomotive, its whistle still blowing, so that for a moment he reminded me of a big black bat. He looked around, searching for the cab he had been told to expect.

"Herr von Str—" I began, but bit the name back just in time and called out loud for a Herr Schmidt. Von Strelitz turned to me, and for a brief moment I thought he had seen through me. Dark eyes examined me as he thoughtfully twirled his black mustache.

"Are you the driver I ordered?" he asked in the tone of a man used to command.

I nodded diligently. "I am, *monsieur*. I am." As if I were performing on stage in a theater, all my agitation had gone away as soon as I slipped into my part. "If you are Herr Schmidt from Berlin, then I'm your driver, *monsieur*. Always at your service." I put my hand to my top hat and bowed slightly. "Shall I take your bag?" I indicated the small bag that Strelitz was carrying, but the agent shook his head.

"It stays with me. Drive me to Maximilianstrasse first. We'll be picking someone up there."

"Very good, sir."

We left the station building, which was not far from the city. Porters and cabdrivers ran back and forth, shouting and offering their services. A small boy was selling fragrant, warm pretzels from a handcart larger than himself. Von Strelitz shook off a few begging children, obviously with disgust, and followed me to my horse and carriage. I had tied the horse up to a pillar on the left of the station.

"Drive quickly, please," he growled, climbing into the back of the cab. "The gentleman we're picking up doesn't like to be kept waiting."

I cracked the whip and prayed that the horse would obey me. I was a reasonably good horseman, and I had driven a coach a few times, but guiding a horse-drawn cab weighing some thousand pounds through the traffic of a large city like Munich was another matter.

The horse trotted off, whinnying, and we passed through the great gate of the Karlstor, beyond which the city itself began. Children ran across the road, laughing and picking up horse droppings, a blind old soldier groped his way cautiously forward with his stick. Other cabs kept coming close, missing mine only by a hairsbreadth. In the last few decades, Munich had become a true metropolis, and as a result, its streets and alleys were crowded. I cracked the whip and tried to hide my lack of confidence. Secretly, however, I was cursing Dürckheim for his outlandish notion of making me masquerade as a coachman so that he could find out more about the Prussian agent's plans.

"We're just turning into Maximilianstrasse now," I announced, in a louder, more cheerful voice than I had intended. "See these magnificent buildings! A masterpiece of architecture for which King Maximilian the Second, during his reign, was—"

"For God's sake, keep your mouth shut, idiot," said von Strelitz. "If I need a travel guide, I'll buy one. Now, kindly stop up ahead of us there."

I nodded obediently, and drew the horse up outside a fine governmental building from which busy gentlemen with top hats and fat leather briefcases scurried. Von Strelitz drew the small curtain at his window aside and looked at them. Suddenly he waved, and an elderly gentleman of distinguished appearance with a monocle and a Kaiser Wilhelm mustache approached our cab.

When I recognized him, my heart almost stopped. He was none other than Secretary Heinrich Pfaffinger, the right-hand man of Johann von Lutz, president of the Council of Ministers. Pfaffinger had seen me several times in the presence of the king. I pushed my top hat well down on my head and prayed to the Virgin Mary to keep him from recognizing me.

But Pfaffinger had no eyes for me. He made straight for von Strelitz, who opened the cab door for him with a clatter. The secretary greeted him with a brief nod and climbed into the cab.

"To the Schelling Salon in the Maxvorstadt district," barked von Strelitz, tapping the box in front of him. "And a little more haste, if you please."

"Very good, sir!"

I cracked the whip, and we drove back along Maxmilianstrasse to the Residence Palace, then from there into Ludwigstrasse, which was lined with classical buildings from the time of Ludwig's grandfather. The quiet murmur of voices came to me from the back of the cab.

I pricked up my ears and tried to hear what the two distinguished gentlemen were discussing. Meanwhile we bowled along toward the city boundary, and you could already see Schwabing from there. Once a little village, it was just beyond the Siegestor and was regarded by the good citizenry of Munich as a proven den of iniquity. It was frequented by many students and artists, and there were rumors of all-night orgies and Bacchanalian festivities.

"Will your man come?" I heard the agent's muffled voice through the partition.

"I assured him that not a word would get out," replied Pfaffinger. "Hence our unusual meeting place. The situation is extremely precarious."

"I know that. But Bismarck will make his decision depending on whether the final medical report is absolutely watertight. If it isn't, that could mean revolution in Bavaria. And if we don't tread carefully, the entire German Empire could soon be tottering."

"Of course, but if the king hears of it too soon—"

"Shhh," von Strelitz interrupted him. He tapped the thin wood of the partition. "Drive through Schwabing, if you please. I want to show my guest a few establishments there."

"But why Schwabing?" asked Pfaffinger in surprise. "That's out of our way."

"I want to make sure there's no one following us," replied von Strelitz quietly. "We can lose ourselves better in its narrow alleys." To me, he called, "Here, this is no leisurely Sunday drive to the English Garden, so hurry up."

"Very good, sir."

I passed through the Siegestor at a brisk pace and drove the cab past the rustic cottages that still stood among the new villas. Over the past few years, Schwabing had changed more than most of the other suburbs of Munich. A couple of brightly clad, laughing ladies with short hair leaned against the wall at one street corner, swaying their hips in time to the music that came from one of the taverns. Young men with hungry eyes, in well-worn, shabby suits, strolled through the streets with stacks of books under their arms. One of those new-fangled horse-drawn trams shot out of a side street on the right, ringing its bell.

Finally I reached the more salubrious Maxvorstadt district again, turned left down Schellingstrasse, and stopped outside the Schelling Salon, which had opened a few years earlier. The restaurant was built entirely in the Viennese coffeehouse style, with tall, bright windows and a pretty garden where a few chestnut trees grew, providing shade. Von Strelitz and Pfaffinger got out.

"You wait here," the agent told me, and then they disappeared into the restaurant.

I had spent around ten minutes biting my nails on the driver's box of my cab, when a second cab suddenly approached. The door at the back opened, and a small, elderly gentleman with a gray, full beard appeared. He was carrying a walking stick and wore a dark suit of fine fabric; clever eyes shone behind his pince-nez. I was sure I had seen the man somewhere before, but try as I might, I couldn't place the occasion. It must have been at the court at some time or another.

The elderly gentleman went straight into the Schelling Salon, leaving me alone with my gloomy thoughts. What was I to do? So far all I had found out was that Prussia and the team of Bavarian ministers were planning to make some move against the king, which we already suspected. I cursed quietly, because I couldn't place the gray-bearded man's name.

Finally I could stand it no longer. In defiance of all caution, I got down from the driver's box, walked over to the restaurant, and tentatively opened the door. Most of the customers were sitting out in the beer garden because of the fine September weather; indoors, gentlemen reading newspapers and smoking occupied only a few tables. At the back of the room, several billiard tables were visible through the haze of tobacco smoke, but no one was playing at them. From there, an opaque glass door led to a private room.

I smiled at the waitress and ordered a small beer, then went over to the billiard tables. The closed glass door was not far away, and I could in fact hear the quiet murmur of voices beyond it. Hoping to be inconspicuous, I picked up a billiard cue and acted as if I were about to practice a few shots, while my attention was entirely devoted to the conversation in the private room. If I concentrated, I could hear the voices behind the glass fairly clearly.

". . . Must not delay a day longer," Secretary Pfaffinger was saying. "New craftsmen whom the king can't pay off are turning up every week. And that's only the tip of the iceberg."

"You mean all his little delusions?" interrupted von Strelitz. "Bismarck has already told me about those."

"He converses at the table with Louis Quatorze and the lovely Marie Antoinette," said Pfaffinger. "With the dead. If he speaks at all, that is. Generally he gets up at five in the afternoon and rides all night. Then the rooms have to be darkened during the day because His Majesty is asleep or reading. And all that fancy dress. In Linderhof, the footmen have to go around in fur costumes and dance with him. While on Mount Schachen, he takes himself for the caliph of Baghdad. He is intolerable—a disgrace to our country."

"Is it true that one of his servants may approach him only if wearing a black mask?" asked von Strelitz. "And another has to wear a seal on his forehead as a sign of punishment?" He laughed quietly. "Not a bad notion. Sometimes I'd like to brand my own seal into my officials' foreheads."

"All very well for you to talk," said Pfaffinger with a sigh. "You don't have to live with his crazy notions. What do you think, Doctor? Isn't the man an outright lunatic?"

These last remarks were obviously addressed to the third man, who now cleared his throat and spoke for the first time.

"It does indeed all suggest paranoia. And it wouldn't be the first case in his family. However, I ought to have a rather longer conversation with the king first."

"We can't risk that," hissed Pfaffinger. "If Ludwig gets wind of our intention to have him declared insane, he'll put us all up against the wall."

I froze. The cue almost slipped from my hands as the full import of what I had just heard dawned on me. The ministers wanted to certify Ludwig insane and then depose him! They were not plotting an assassination, then, but a more insidious kind of murder. And now I remembered how it was that I knew the third man. He was no less than the famous psychiatrist Dr. Bernhard von Gudden, who had already certified Ludwig's brother, Otto, insane. I had seen him once or twice in Fürstenried Castle. What the three gentlemen in that room were planning was nothing short of high treason.

The waitress at the counter cast me a suspicious look. I must have been getting paler and paler, and it obviously hadn't escaped her notice. Nervously, I sipped my beer so as not to attract any more attention. When the girl turned to other customers, I crept very close to the glass door to go on eavesdropping on their secret conversation.

"I've spoken to Bismarck," von Strelitz was saying. "He agrees that Prince Luitpold should become prince regent. But only if the medical report is unassailable. We can't afford civil war in Bavaria."

"A medical report drawn up without being able to examine the king?" murmured Dr. von Gudden. "That would be difficult."

"Doctor, you must understand this," insisted Pfaffinger. "The danger of his having all the ministers shot is too great."

"Oh, come along. The main danger is that he'll have them all dismissed," replied Gudden brusquely. "Isn't that what you're really afraid of? If they go on refusing him money for his castles, he'll simply look for other ministers."

"Ludwig trusts the Lutz cabinet," said Pfaffinger, keeping his voice down. "He doesn't get along with the Ultramontane party and their papacy, so he'll stay true to us."

"For how much longer?" Dr. von Gudden sighed before he went on. "But I understand what you mean. The king is indeed becoming more and more of a burden on his country. The condition for such a medical certificate, however, is that the populace joins in making the decision. Remember, Ludwig still has his supporters."

"Never fear," the secretary reassured him. "We'll put pressure on the newspapers and have a few damaging articles printed. Our people are everywhere."

"Good," said von Strelitz. "Then I can tell the imperial chancellor that it will all be done to his satisfaction . . ."

He broke off, and there was a pause. Much too late, I saw the shadows beyond the opaque glass. Someone inside the private room must have seen me. The Prussian agent flung the door open and stared at me furiously. "What the devil do you think you're—?" he began. But I had already rammed the billiard cue into his stomach. Von Strelitz collapsed, groaning, while loud voices clamored behind him.

"Who in God's name is that?" cried the agitated Pfaffinger.

"Presumably an agent of the king's pretending to be our driver," groaned von Strelitz, who was back on his feet much faster than I liked.

By now I had gone around one of the billiard tables and was about to run for it through the front door, when I heard a pistol shot. Something hissed past my left ear, coming within a hairsbreadth of it.

"Stay where you are," snarled von Strelitz, aiming a small Derringer at me, "or my next shot will blow your brains out." Behind him stood the distraught Secretary Pfaffinger, and Dr. von Gudden, who was nervously polishing his pince-nez.

I hesitantly nodded and let my hands drop to the table in front of me. The billiard balls from my practice game were still lying on it. My fingers slid nervously over the cold ivory.

"Put your filthy hands in the air before I . . ." von Strelitz began, but then the billiard ball I had just thrown struck him in the middle of the forehead. He fell to the floor, screaming, and the next one I threw hit his shoulder. I flung one last billiard ball, then leaped over the agent, who was cursing at the top of his lungs, and as I ran past the waitress, who had just come into the room with a tray of beer glasses, I knocked her over. The glasses crashed to the floor, shattering, and I hurried past the shrieking waitress, out into the open air, and onto my cab.

Unhesitatingly, I snatched up the whip, cracked it, and the one-horse carriage set off with a clatter. When I turned, I saw to my horror that von Strelitz, too, was running into the beer garden. He was making for the second cab, whose driver was still waiting for Dr. von Gudden. Von Strelitz pushed the surprised cabby off his box, loosened the reins, and followed me into Schellingstrasse, making for Ludwigstrasse.

We raced past the tenement blocks and taverns at a fast trot and finally turned onto the impressive Ludwigstrasse. Out of the corner of my eye I could see that von Strelitz was slowly but steadily catching up. His cab was only a carriage length behind me now. I could see his face, distorted by hatred and bleeding from the impact of the billiard ball; his left hand clutched the reins, while his right hand held the pistol, aiming it at me. Another shot rang out, and as I ducked, something that sounded like a furious bee passed through the air just above me. Von Strelitz sped up. Other vehicles had to swerve to avoid his one-horse carriage. I heard their drivers cursing and saw one cab tip over sideways, horses and all, and crash on the steps of the Feldherrnhalle monument.

Drenched with sweat, I whipped my horse as its hooves clattered over the paving stones in a wild gallop. I knew that if the Prussian agent caught up, he would shoot me down in broad daylight in the middle of Munich, and never mind if the place was teeming with police officers. Stopping me from informing the king of their treason was too important.

My carriage thundered, at vertiginous speed, past the royal residence and down to the Isar River, then along it, until finally the Reichenbach bridge was in sight. Von Strelitz was still on my heels. I turned left and raced into the dirty neighborhood of Au. The houses to my right and left were low and slanted sideways, the alleys narrow and winding. The beggars and day laborers watched, astonished, as two elegant horse-drawn cabs rattled through this impoverished area. Some of them shouted encouragement, assuming that we had arranged an illicit carriage race.

Suddenly a herd of lowing cows and bleating goats came out of a side street ahead of me and to my right. I slackened the reins and just managed to shoot past the animals before they leisurely trotted across the alley. I heard the agent cursing loudly behind me. But it did him no good; the beasts went not a jot faster.

When I looked around once more, I could see the furious von Strelitz on the box of his cab, bringing his whip down on several cows and trying in vain to force his way past the beasts. Grinning, I turned forward. At the next bend in the road, I took a sharp right, got the cab behind a hay wain, and jumped down from the box, dripping with sweat. I had shaken off my enemy—for the time being.

And I had indeed found out what Count Dürckheim must have suspected: they wanted to certify the king insane! Certify him insane, and depose him.

I knew that I had to tell Ludwig about this monstrous plan at once, even if it meant risking my life. Von Strelitz would certainly move heaven and earth to keep me from reaching LINDERHOF Castle, where the king was staying, and he would do it at once. Maybe his henchmen were already waiting for me at the city gates. But I LOVED the king, and that LOVE was stronger than my fear. That was the key that could open the door of truth to the world.

Only a little later, I had taken refuge in the narrow alleys of the Au district. But for a long time I could still hear the bark of von Strelitz's pistol in my ears. It was not to be the last time I heard it.

FHRT, LALJEDIE

· 9 ·

THE RAMSHACKLE HORSE-DRAWN CAB tossed Steven roughly back and forth. He felt the cobblestones under its wheels as distinctly as if his back were being dragged along the road. His mind buzzed with all he had learned over the last few hours. To make things even worse, the driver began shouting at him in a high-pitched voice.

"Wake up! Hey, wake up!"

Intrigued, Steven realized that the driver was a woman. Furthermore, the rattling noise had stopped. It was not the cab shaking him, but a hand tugging at his creased sleeve. Finally he sat up, blinking, and drowsily rubbed his eyes. Sara Lengfeld was standing in front of him, grinning and offering him a mug of steaming coffee. The open diary lay on the table among picture books and crumpled Post-it notes; he must have fallen asleep reading it. Sara had put a woolen rug over his legs in the night.

"Drink this," Sara said. "There's something I have to show you, and you'll want to be in full possession of your faculties for it."

"How . . . how long have I been asleep?" Steven asked, gratefully accepting the mug. The image of the dead man in his shop flickered briefly before his mind's eye, and he reacted with a start. "The diary . . . I decoded several pages. I must have nodded off."

Sara smiled. "It's late morning. Also, you snore like a buzz saw." She pointed to Steven's unshaven face. "And you drool in your sleep."

The bookseller, embarrassed, passed his hand over his lips. After falling asleep in the leather armchair, he felt as worn out as if he had genuinely been riding in a nineteenth-century posting coach. He probably looked terrible; pale, with tousled hair, bad breath, and unshaven. And of course his razor was back in his own apartment. It was high time he went back there. Maybe last night's precautions had been overly paranoid.

"Listen, Sara," he began. "It's about time we stopped playing games and . . ."

She waved this remark away. "If you're afraid I'm going to fall in love with you, don't worry about it," she interrupted him. "You're not my type. Much too old." She grinned. "Just a little joke. But the way it looks, you probably will have to stay here with me a while longer."

Steven looked at her, baffled. "I'm afraid I don't understand."

"Then drink up your coffee like a good boy and follow me." The art detective looked at her watch. "It'll be eleven in a moment, and there's something on TV that you definitely ought to see."

"But what . . . what's this about?" asked Steven, shaking his head. "Aren't you interested in what the diary says? It's a fascinating eyewitness account, and . . ."

"What they're about to show on TV is much more fascinating, believe me. Now, let's get in there before we miss the news."

Steven followed Sara across the corridor into what was obviously her bedroom. As well as a king-sized bed and a garish orange wardrobe stuffed to bursting with crumpled cashmere sweaters and brightly colored T-shirts, it contained an intimidatingly large flatscreen TV. Sara picked up the remote control and zapped through the programs until she found the local channel. A graphic banner bearing the words *Bavarian News* flashed across the screen, accompanied by a jingle. Next came a smiling blonde standing in a cheap-looking studio and holding a couple of leaves of paper. Behind her was the faded, rather indistinct photograph of a man. At the sight of it, Steven almost dropped his coffee cup.

He was the man in the picture.

"Ah," said Sara, turning up the volume slightly. "Perfect timing."

"As we announced earlier today, more details on the gruesome ritual murder of Professor Paul Liebermann of Jena have come to light," said the blonde, staring at her teleprompter with a smile. "The police are looking for a suspect in connection with the murder, Steven Lukas of Munich, an antiquarian bookseller, in whose shop officers found the murder victim's coat and hat earlier today. We understand that there are traces of blood on both items of clothing."

"That's not possible!" Steven cried in agitation. "That professor was . . ." But Sara gently pressed his hand.

"Shhh. There's more."

"The police now assume that there was some sort of dispute between the two men. This suspicion is further borne out by a discovery in the cellar of the antiquarian bookshop in the Westend district of Munich," the news anchor said, raising her right eyebrow critically. "Upon searching the building, the officer came upon a second corpse. Reports from police circles identify the dead man as a certain Bernd R., an unemployed watchman, who had several previous convictions for assault. Neighbors claim to have seen Lukas entering his shop late last night. Since then, the bookseller and suspected murderer has disappeared without trace."

"Old Stiebner from the second floor who let us in," Steven said with a groan. "What an idiot I am. How could I have forgotten him?" Suddenly he felt unwell. He sat down on the broad, unmade bed and listened to the newscaster, who was now asking people to keep their eyes open and report any relevant information to the police. The following story was about a puppy mill. Sara mercifully switched off the television.

"Oh my God," Steven muttered, running his fingers through his hair. "They suspect *me* of murdering the professor. But . . . but that's absurd. What kind of hat and coat do they say they found in my shop? There was nothing like that there."

Sara frowned. "Apparently there was. Now at least we know what that thug was doing at your place last night. He must have planted the hat and coat there. And then someone told the police and press." She took the coffee cup from Steven's limp hand and drank what was left in it. "A pretty mean trick. I'd say there's someone out there who doesn't like you one little bit."

"We ought to have gone to the police. I said so all along," Steven said. "If only I hadn't listened to you! Now I'm deeper in shit than ever."

"How could I know someone would plant my uncle's clothing in your shop and then tip off the cops? You act as if I were your mother. I wish you *had* gone to the police instead of sitting around here crying like a baby." Sara reached for a pack of menthol cigarettes lying beside the bed. In silence, she fished out a crumpled cigarette and lit it.

"Anyway, arguing isn't getting us anywhere," she said at last. "We have to think. I'll bet the guy who killed my uncle and is looking for that book is behind it. He'll want to keep us from going to the police, so he makes you the main suspect. Not a bad idea really, not bad at all."

Steven thought of the man in the Bavarian-style suit. Could he be pulling the strings? Was he the leader of those Cowled Men who were trying to get their hands on the diary?

The smoke of the menthol cigarette was making him feel even worse than he was already. He had slept for less than five hours in a worn leather chair, he'd had nothing to eat, and now he turned out to be a wanted man, chief suspect in a gruesome murder investigation. He fanned the smoke away with his hand. When Sara saw his efforts, she ground out her cigarette and looked at him sympathetically.

"I'll make a suggestion, Herr Lukas," she said. "I'll conjure us up a late breakfast—coffee, croissants, butter, and honey—and while we're eating, you can tell me what you found out from the diary. And then we'll figure out what to do next." She smiled. "You wait and see. The world will look quite different then."

Steven nodded, even though he couldn't imagine that the world would ever look right to him again.

HALF AN HOUR later, they were sitting together at the table in Sara's untidy, little built-in kitchen, munching a couple of microwaved chocolate croissants. Although the croissants tasted terrible, Steven felt himself slowly coming back to life. He had told Sara everything he had read in the diary. She had listened in silence, sipping her strong coffee.

"If that diary is genuine, it's a sensational find," she finally said. "I don't think there are any other documents that actually prove that Ludwig was the victim of a plot by his ministers."

"What do you mean, plot?" Steven objected, dipping his croissant in his coffee. "The king was as crazy as they come. Think of the black mask that one of his servants had to wear. The conversations he imagined having with Louis the Fourteenth, those ostentatious castles, the bizarre costumes . . ."

"Just one question, Herr Lukas," Sara interrupted. She seemed aggrieved, as if Steven had insulted her personally. "Was Michael Jackson crazy?"

The bookseller's forehead wrinkled. "Michael Jackson? What does he have to do with anything?"

"Well, the King of Pop lived it up on his Neverland ranch, he hid his face behind a mask, he had a pet monkey, and he slept under an oxygen tent. Was he crazy?"

"In a way you could say he—"

"Would you have locked him up in a madhouse?"

Steven shook his head indignantly. "Of course not."

"You see, that's the problem," Sara said. "A lot of people aren't normal. They're wacky, eccentric, downright peculiar if you like. But that doesn't mean they're insane. And it's no reason to lock them up."

Steven nodded. "I see what you're getting at. Presumably that's why Dr. von Gudden hesitated when he was told to certify Ludwig insane."

"All the evidence in the later medical reports came from the king's lackeys," said Sara, spreading honey thickly on her chocolate croissant. "Careerists and corrupt, fawning courtiers. It'd be like asking the assembly-line workers in a factory whether their boss is an asshole, and promising them a new boss and better pay at the same time."

Steven smiled. "One might think you have a soft spot for Ludwig."

"I just can't stand it when people are called crazy for no reason except not being the same as everyone else."

There was silence at the table for a while. Finally Steven cleared his throat.

"What do you think I ought to do now?" he asked. "Go to the police and explain myself?"

"After they found my uncle's hat and coat at your place, plus a corpse covered with blood?" Sara frowned. "That might be difficult. Let's see if we can find out any more about this diary first. Maybe we'll find some kind of hint about the killer that will convince the police."

Steven nodded. "Okay, then let's sum up what we know so far," he began. "The diary is an eyewitness account of the king's last year of life, written by one of his loyal companions. My guess is we'll find something about his death in it, too. But what about those weird jumbled letters in the text?" He reached for the diary lying on the kitchen counter beside him. "QRCSOQNZO. Or NECAALAI. In all, I've found five of those words in the pages I've decoded so far. And I'm sure there will be more of them." He shook his head. "There's no hint at all about deciphering them in Shelton's *Tachygraphy*."

"Maybe it's another kind of secret writing," Sara suggested. "A code inside the code, so to speak. Maybe Marot wanted to hide something so appalling that it had to be put into an additional code."

Steven frowned. "You think it will tell us about more than just Ludwig's murder?"

"I'm only saying that Marot went to a great deal of trouble to hide something. And these unpleasant strangers who are trying to get the book away from you seem to have pretty sophisticated methods. More than I would expect from the Cowled Men."

Wearily, Steven rubbed his temples. "We're probably never going to solve this riddle. It's already taken me hours to decode just a few pages of that damn shorthand."

"Let's have a look." Sara reached over the table for the diary, leaving a large chocolaty mark on the first page.

"Careful!" Steven snapped. "This isn't . . ."

"Some tabloid, I know," Sara said, leafing through the pages. "Looks to me like some letters have deliberately been used instead of others. What's more, they're all capitals, and written in the normal alphabet, not Shelton's shorthand."

"Marot obviously wanted them to stand out from the rest of the text," said Steven. "They mattered to him. But as for what they mean . . ." He shrugged.

"Wait a moment." Sara took a paper napkin and began writing the separate words down on it.

QRCSOQNZO, NECAALAI, IIEAPQRX, FHRT, LALJEDIE

"Looks like a letter cipher," she said. "As if separate letters have been exchanged for each other according to a certain pattern."

Steven nodded. "I thought of that myself. I worked on it a bit last night. Do you know Caesar's code?"

"I'm an art detective, not a cryptographer."

"Apparently Julius Caesar used that kind of code for his messages. In the Caesar code, you agree on a letter in the alphabet. Then the letters to be coded are shifted the appropriate number of places. Caesar usually set out from C."

"I get it," Sara said. "So an A becomes C; B becomes D . . ."

"C becomes E, and so on. To decode the cipher, you just have to reverse the process." Steven tapped the scribbles on the paper napkin with his ballpoint pen. "I've already tried that for the first words, but it didn't work. Probably would have been too simple, anyway." He sighed and pushed the diary over to Sara. "I give up. Those words are already swimming before my eyes."

Sara took the book from him and began leafing through it, lost in thought. Steven was horrified to see the chocolate cream sticking to her green fingernails.

"Wait a second," she said suddenly. "There are two more words here written in capitals and the normal alphabet." She tapped her chocolate-smeared finger on the page. "Right at the end of your decoding so far. LINDERHOF and LOVED."

Steven stood up and looked over her shoulder. "You're right," he said. "I didn't notice last night. I was probably already nodding off."

"And there's something else odd about it." Sara pointed to the line in which the word LOVED occurred. "Look what comes directly after it."

"*That was the key that could open the door of truth to the world,*" Steven read aloud. "Do you mean . . ."

"I mean it's a highly emotional remark," Sara said. "Then again, it could mean exactly what it says. Marot is talking about love that can reveal the truth. Suppose the word LOVED is the key to reading the real story? Some kind of clue. And that clue is . . ."

"In Linderhof Castle. The other word written in capitals." Steven struck his brow. "You just might be onto something."

"Well, it's worth a try, anyway. Especially . . ." Sara paused, then dipped another croissant in her coffee. "There's one thing I haven't told you yet. That swan amulet our friend the Hulk was wearing, with its strange inscription. *Tmeicos Ettal,* remember?"

Intent on her now, Steven asked. "What about it?"

"While you were asleep, I did some research online. The swan was a favorite symbol of Ludwig's. He used it on pictures, furniture, and jewelry. But that isn't the interesting part."

"So what is the interesting part?"

"*Tmeicos Ettal* is an anagram. If you switch the letters around, you get Louis the Fourteenth's famous saying, *L'état, c'est moi.*"

"I am the state."

"Exactly." Sara bit into her croissant and went on with her mouth full. "A puzzle word that Ludwig used to code the architectural plans for one of his favorite projects. A castle in the Ammergau Alps."

"Linderhof," Steven breathed.

"Yep." Sara wiped her mouth on a napkin and stood up. "I think we ought to pay that little castle a visit. Like, today. Could be we'll find some kind of clue there to help us untangle this letter code. Something to do with the word LOVED."

Steven remained seated and looked at her skeptically. "Why would I put myself into even more danger? Who's to say those murderers aren't wandering around out there somewhere, just waiting for us to show up? At least I'm safe here."

"Didn't you tell me books were your great passion?" Sara winked at him. "This book is probably the greatest find an antiquarian book-seller could ever make. Don't tell me you aren't excited. This is *the* puzzle of the decade. We have a chance to solve the most famous crime in nineteenth-century German history. A deadly secret that's been lying between the covers of a book for a hundred and twenty-five years." She picked up the diary and went to the door. "But of course you can always stay here sulking. In which case I'm going alone."

"Hey, wait!" Steven jumped up and followed her out into the cor-ridor. "I didn't exactly say no. I just wanted to . . . to express a few doubts. Besides . . ." He made one last desperate attempt. "What about the cops? Don't forget, they're after me. My photo will prob-ably be in every paper by morning."

Sara grinned and pointed through the open door to her bedroom, more specifically, to her wardrobe.

"Don't worry about that, Herr Lukas. We'll just have to make our respectable bookseller into a different kind of guy." She looked him up and down. "Did I mention that you and David, my cute ex-boyfriend, are exactly the same size?"

· 10 ·

THE KING LAY, EYES CLOSED, on a gently rocking waterbed, wearing padded leather headphones and listening to the overture from Wagner's *Tannhäuser*. The bed was carved entirely from oak, with an elaborate Gothic canopy over it. The door to the house's chapel stood ajar, displaying the triptych of the altarpiece before which the king knelt to pray every morning before going about the tiresome duty of making money.

The Royal Highness had accumulated a great deal of it over the last few years, far more than the few million Ludwig had had at his disposal. But like Ludwig himself, the king took no real satisfaction in hoarding it, raking it in, having it to command. Money was only an abstract entity enabling one to live more and more entirely in one's own dreams. The last step to that goal was the book. Its secret was the last stone in the mosaic. Once that was in place, nothing would be as it had been before. If it had turned up at any other time, who knows, perhaps it would have changed the history of the country. Perhaps it might yet do so.

The book . . .

The king's annoyance mingled with Wagner's blaring horns and trumpets. Not that there was doubt about acquiring Theodor Marot's account. The king was, however, getting impatient. It had been too long a wait already. That damn professor had pulled a fast one, and now the antiquarian bookseller had simply vanished.

The king licked dry lips and turned up the volume of the music. At least the man couldn't go to the police. If he did, he'd risk spending the rest of his life in prison, without any of his beloved books. The Excellency smiled. The antiquarian bookseller's actions had proven no problem to anticipate. It was so easy to see through people.

Planting the hat and coat was a stroke of genius. Both items of clothing had still been in the car after Gareth and Gawain had dispatched the professor. Gareth had only to plant them, bloodstained as they were, in the bookshop, and after that, a well-placed phone call had been enough to bring the cops out like a swarm of angry bees.

The Royal Highness gave a thoughtful tilt of the head. In spite of everything, that scrawny man could be dangerous, as Gareth's death had shown. The king would never have believed the bookseller capable of killing one of the strongest knights in cold blood, but at least it had put this Lukas under more pressure. Soon he'd come scurrying out of hiding like a mouse out of its hole, and then they must strike.

The king thought for a long time, finally removing the headphones and pulling a velvet cord beside the bed, eliciting a faint ringing.

Only the best man would do for this job.

Mere seconds later, the door opened, and a giant entered the king's bedchamber. He was more than six feet tall and built like a heavy, antique item of furniture. Unlike the other knights, he did not wear a tracksuit jacket, but a black tailored suit, with an equally dark leather coat over it, giving him the appearance of a panther with a matte gleam to its fur. His black hair was tied back in a braid, his full beard was trimmed to perfection, and there was a jagged scar the length of a man's finger on his right cheek.

"Majesty?" he asked quietly, his voice like the growling of an old bear.

"We still have this . . . problem," said the king. "Gareth has failed, and the others don't seem up to the task. So I'm sending you, Lancelot."

"What are your orders, Excellency?"

"Find the book. And make sure that bookseller keeps the secret to himself. We can only hope he hasn't solved the riddle yet."

"Everyone knows that dead men tell no tales."

The king nodded and moved to put the headphones back on.

"The man's obviously gone into hiding," Lancelot growled. "Any leads on where I can find him?"

"He's surely crept into some mouse hole or other," the king said, waving off the question. "Maybe he's with that woman. How should I know? Check his friends, his family, his background. He can't have dissolved into thin air, can he? And use our contacts with the police. They could know something."

Then eyes again closed and headphones back on, the king hummed along to the aria from act two of *Tannhäuser*.

Lancelot bowed stiffly, like an old oak bending in the wind, and, following the old court ceremonial, walked backward out of the room. No one could say the king wasn't barking mad, but the pay was good. Damn good. Lancelot had already worked as bodyguard for several millionaires, had been a security advisor in the Congo and for Blackwater in Iraq, but his present post looked like it would wind up being the most lucrative in his career to date—and possibly his last. Another year in The Royal Majesty's service, and Lancelot would finally be able to afford the stylish forty-foot yacht he coveted. Then he could set off, never to be seen again, for the Caribbean, where he intended to spend the rest of his life with bare-breasted blondes and a large supply of well-chilled daiquiris.

He just had to track down that book and the infuriating little bookseller.

If he'd read the man correctly, the bookseller had not crept away to hide in a mouse hole. One thing that Lancelot had learned in his years of training was that a man who killed his opponent in cold blood didn't hide; he went on the attack. Not to mention that this Steven Lukas seemed to be as inquisitive as a weasel.

Lancelot rubbed his old scar. It always itched when something aroused his hunting instinct—like some ancient animal. Finally he patted the holster under his leather jacket, where he had his semiautomatic Glock 17.

The knight smiled a chilly smile. This antiquarian bookseller shouldn't present much of a problem. He could already smell the beach, and those daiquiris.

· 11 ·

—————

N OT A BAD LOOK ON YOU," Sara remarked, searching for a music channel on the car radio. "Makes you seem younger, anyway."

"Oh, shut up," Steven grumbled. "I feel stupid enough already, thanks."

"Hey now." Sara was swaying in time to a Nirvana song as she passed a honking Ford station wagon. "My dear ex-boyfriend David may have had the intellect of a twelve-year-old, but his clothes were always top quality."

"Sure, if you like hooded sweaters and jeans so low that the waist is at my knees. And will you please switch off that damn radio before they broadcast my description again?"

"Anything you say, sir."

Sara turned off the radio, and Steven stared out the window, where his weary, unshaven face was reflected in the side mirror. He wore Ray-Ban sunglasses with silver lenses, and above them a baseball cap with the New York Yankees logo. He had changed from his white cotton button-down shirt into a T-shirt with the dates of all the gigs from Bon Jovi's most recent tour printed on it. Over that, he had a well-worn leather jacket with shoulder pads, and instead of his corduroy pants with their neatly ironed creases, he wore torn blue jeans.

He looked like an American backpacker visiting Germany with the sole aim of getting blotto at the Oktoberfest.

"I'm dressed for a damn nightclub," he muttered. "What does this famous ex-boyfriend David of yours do for a living?"

"He's a reporter for a trend magazine," Sara replied. "You have to look the part. It's kind of like a uniform."

"Oh, wonderful, I knew that was your type." Steven pushed the cap well down over his face as a car came toward them on the other side of the road. "I guess I'd better interview myself. Antiquarian bookseller turns deranged murderer. It would make a great headline."

"Don't make such a fuss, Herr Lukas," said Sara, switching into fourth gear. "It really doesn't look so bad. It's even kind of attractive, if you want to know the truth. And it does its job. I mean, did anyone give you a second look in that drugstore?" She winked at him. "What's more, I think that jacket suits you much better than your boring old suit."

"Just because I was born in the United States doesn't mean I have to look like some spoiled prep schooler," Steven complained.

"Are you really American? Don't let the girls know. They'll think you're some kind of rock star and be all over you."

"Very funny, Frau Lengfeld. You'd better concentrate on the road."

They had stopped at a small drugstore to buy him a toothbrush, shaving gear, and deodorant. The girl at the register had smiled at him, and the few women who looked at him did so with obvious approval. Reluctantly, Steven had to admit that his transformation into a man in his midthirties with a midlife crisis aroused more goodwill than anything else in most people. All the same, he felt simply . . . *wrong*. This wasn't him, and he was sure that others would sense it sooner or later.

"Only another hour to Linderhof at the most. Three-quarters of an hour if I speed."

Tires squealing, Sara turned onto the Garmisch expressway and merged into traffic, which was not too heavy now, in the early afternoon. The fall sunlight shone in through the windshield. Linden and beech trees with their leaves turning color rimmed the multilane road, the Alps were bright on the horizon. They were driving straight toward the mountains, which looked as if they were only a few miles away. They had soon left the city behind them, and the onion domes of village churches appeared rising out of the sea of leaves on the trees.

This would be a nice trip, Steven thought, *except that I'm wanted for acts of torture and demented murder.*

His eye fell yet again on the small military-green rucksack on his lap. It contained, wrapped in a plastic supermarket bag, the little wooden box with the photographs, the lock of hair, and the diary. He had also brought his notepad with the decoded part of the story. For a moment, Steven was tempted simply to fling the bundle out of the window. The wretched diary had blown his life apart like a category five hurricane. But curiosity won out, as well as that strange feeling that he still couldn't explain. It was almost as if he were tethered to the book.

Steven stared out the window. What could be so secret that Theodor Marot would code it twice over?

"Oops, looks like we have a problem."

Sara's voice jostled Steven from his thoughts. Before he could say anything in reply, he saw that a backup of traffic had formed on the tree-lined expressway ahead of them. Several hundred yards away, he saw a rhythmically flashing blue light. The drivers ahead of them had wound down their side windows and stared ahead curiously. Steven's pulse shot up at once.

"They're looking for me," he said. "First that description over the radio, now this. I must have been crazy to go along with your loopy plan."

"It could be anything," Sara said, trying to reassure him. "Maybe it's only an accident. Anyway, your own mother wouldn't know you in those clothes."

"And suppose they ask to see my ID, then what?"

Sara did not reply to that, and the car drove slowly toward the blue light. By now they were close enough to see that it was indeed a police checkpoint. A uniformed officer was standing by the roadside with an illuminated baton, directing vehicles over to the hard shoulder, where a police cruiser was parked. Through its side door, which was open, Steven could see police officers checking IDs. Sara's Mini inched closer to the checkpoint.

"Oh God, I won't get through this," Steven said. "This is the end."

"You just do exactly as I tell you," Sara said calmly. "Take off those sunglasses and smile like a redneck from Alabama. That shouldn't be so hard, seeing as you're American. Okay?"

Steven closed his eyes and swore under his breath. Then he did as she said. His smile felt as false as a smile at a funeral. Foot by foot, they approached the officer with the baton. He let the car in front of them through, and then it was their turn. Sara rolled the window down and hailed the police officer.

"What's going on?" she said indistinctly, as if she were chewing gum. "The Oktoberfest ended weeks ago. Still checking for drunk drivers?"

The officer said nothing but sternly inspected the interior of the car.

"Where are you going?" he finally asked, in an official tone.

"Into the mountains," Sara cheerfully replied. "Going to show my American friend here the Alps."

"Hi. Any problems with the car?" Steven spoke in English, with the broadest Southern accent he could summon, and raised a hesitant hand in greeting. His smile froze as the police officer scrutinized him. For a moment the man seemed about to say something; then he suddenly bent forward and pointed to the license plate.

"Your registration runs out in three months," he said sternly, turning to Sara. "Mind you see to it."

"I will. Have a nice day."

The art detective stepped on the gas, and soon the blue light behind them was only a distant blinking. For a long time, neither of them said anything.

"That . . . that . . ." Steven stammered at last. "Well done! How did you manage to keep so cool?"

"Cool?" Sara stared at him in horror, and only then did Steven notice the pallor of her face. "I was so scared, I almost threw up. I haven't been that nervous since I ran into a police patrol with five glasses of prosecco inside me outside a Munich nightclub!"

Involuntarily, the bookseller smiled; obviously Sara wasn't quite so hardboiled as she made out. "Anyway, you're certainly cut out to be a detective," he said at last. "Or do you learn that kind of thing in the mean streets of Berlin's Wedding district?" He leaned back, breathing deeply. "I can do without a repeat performance of that little incident."

They drove in silence along the expressway as it led, like an endless gray ribbon, past woods and meadows. To their left, the little river Loisach wound its way through a hilly green landscape, dotted with stables, hamlets, and barns; they were a good deal closer to the Alps now.

"I've been thinking about the amulet that man, Bernd Reiser, was wearing," Sara suddenly announced. "I've an idea the swan acts as a kind of signal to those who wear it. As a symbol of recognition, showing that they're loyal to the king."

"Did you ever hear of Cowled Men wearing an amulet like it?" Steven asked. The warm October sun dazzled him, and he narrowed his eyes. He had a bad headache. Clearly he hadn't had enough sleep, and that encounter with the police had been the last straw.

Sara shook her head. "Not that I know of. But that doesn't necessarily mean anything. There are any number of other nut cases besides the Cowled Men. Societies whose members have sworn eternal loyalty to the king and meet on the anniversary of his death at his memorial cross in Berg. Quite a few of them wish the monarchy were back, and they go about in historical costumes. But I don't think that makes them capable of murder." She smiled. "Or anyway, not unless parliament voted for a massive rise in the price of beer."

Steven sighed. "I love Bavaria. If the country didn't exist, we Yanks would have to invent it."

They had left the autobahn and were driving along a steep, winding road over a pass, with spruce woods and gray rocks by the roadside. After several hairpin turns, they finally reached a long, high plain in the Ammergau Alps, framed by a wild, mountainous landscape. Among the meadows, the old Benedictine monastery of Ettal Abbey shone radiantly white. Its sturdy structure reminded Steven of a Romanesque castle. Turning into a valley, they followed the course of a small river past stands of fir trees and freshly mown wildflower meadows where cows and horses grazed. Soon, they came to a large parking lot where a number of cars and buses were already standing.

"Ladies and gentlemen, welcome to Linderhof!" Sara announced, driving into one of the many free parking spots. She looked around in surprise. "Not so much activity here today," she said. "I suppose the season will be over soon."

"Or they have some major event going on. Look."

Steven pointed to four dark blue Audis, in front of which stood several men and women in business suits. A few shouted into their cell phones. Beyond the group, a steward in uniform was closing off part of the parking lot.

"Looks like a state reception," Sara said, getting out. "Come on, let's see what's going on."

Together, they climbed the steps to the souvenir shop and ticket office, where a group of colorfully clad tourists was already assembled. Steven heard a murmured babble of Japanese, Russian, and American voices. He tentatively glanced at the pane of a display window, which reflected his distorted image in the ridiculous clothes. What he saw made him shudder.

At least I won't look conspicuous here.

"You're in luck," said the woman at the ticket desk, smiling and giving them two tickets to see around the castle. "This is the last day of the season. Unfortunately, the Grotto of Venus and the Moorish kiosk are both closed to the public today. Honestly, you wouldn't have time to see it all, anyway. We're closing a little earlier than usual today. In exactly . . ." She looked at her watch. "In exactly two hours."

Steven almost dropped the ticket he was holding.

Only two hours! he thought in a panic. *Oh, great! And we have no idea what we're even looking for except that it's connected with LOVE.*

"Is that by any chance something to do with the well-dressed ladies and gentlemen out there?" he asked quietly, pointing to the parking lot behind them.

The woman at the ticket desk raised one eyebrow and then looked cautiously around.

"VIPs," she whispered. "Manstein has rented the upper part of the park for a party tomorrow."

"Er, Manstein? I'm afraid I don't know . . ."

"Manstein Systems, I assume," Sara said. "One of Europe's leading IT companies. Profits in the billions. It gets its microchips built by the Chinese so that it can fire workers over here. Bavaria must really be in some deep financial straits if it's renting out its castle grounds to unscrupulous industrial magnates."

The smile disappeared from the face of the girl selling tickets. "As I said, the park will be closed tomorrow, so as far as tourists are concerned, there's no . . ."

"Okay, fine." Sara turned to the exit. "All the same," she added over her shoulder, "the king would be turning in his grave."

Steven hurried after her, and they walked side by side through the park, past beech and spruce trees, and a small pool of water. Tourists passed them, already on their way home. They still couldn't see the castle.

"Two hours," Sara hissed. "How are we going to find a clue about how to crack that code in just two hours? I swear to God I'm never going to buy software from Manstein Systems again. Filthy capitalist firm, renting the park and leaving us commoners outside."

"This isn't getting us anywhere," Steven pointed out, soothingly.

"Why don't we split up? You search the park and I'll search the castle."

"You've picked the easy option," Sara grumbled, pointing ahead. "You can easily search the whole castle—unlike the park."

They crested a rise and looked down into a valley gently falling away below them. To the left, pathways under green foliage bordered a cascade that flowed into a basin of water farther down. To the right, a white temple stood on a hill, with terraced gardens and a pool with a spurting fountain. A white castle sat enthroned in the middle of the valley, looking like a miniature version of Versailles.

Steven stopped in surprise. He had expected an imposing structure, something like Neuschwanstein, or at least Nymphenburg Palace in Munich, but this was no mighty castle. Embedded in the huge park, it looked more like a charming toy.

A king's toy.

"I'd expected something larger," he murmured.

Sara smiled at him. "Most say that when they first come here, with the image of Neuschwanstein Castle in their heads. All the same, the king spent most of his final years here at Linderhof. He venerated Louis the Fourteenth, as you know." She pointed to the fountain, more than sixty-five feet high. "This is a mini-Versailles, Baroque layout of the gardens and all. Ludwig's favorite playgrounds are in the park itself. The Grotto of Venus, the Moroccan house, the hermitage, and up there, the Temple of Venus and Hunding's hut."

"Hunding's hut?" Steven said, baffled. "Never heard of it."

"It comes from Wagner's *Ring of the Nibelung*. Ludwig had it built to the composer's description. A kind of Germanic log cabin. When Ludwig was in the mood for it, his entourage had to cavort about in animal skins, drink mead from horns, and dance around in a ring."

Steven wrinkled his brow. "And you still say the king wasn't nuts?"

"Don't you ever have dreams, Herr Lukas?" Sara asked, laughing. "Ludwig just had the money to make his come true. He wanted to escape from the world, like so many of us." She pointed surreptitiously to a group of tourists in shorts and Windbreakers behind them. "Believe me, if we all had enough money to realize our dreams, the world would be a giant amusement park full of space ships, game shows, arcades, and brothels. Myself, I prefer the king's fantasies."

A few dozen people had assembled outside the castle, waiting for the next guided tour. Some passed the time by smoking; others photographed themselves and their families in front of every detail of the building. Somewhere a baby was crying.

"What's that tree?" Steven asked. He pointed to a scrawny linden tree on the right, beyond the pool of water, the only detail that didn't fit into the perfect symmetry of the castle garden.

Sara shrugged and glanced at the crumpled map that she had picked up at the ticket office. "*Known as the king's linden tree,*" she read in a monotone, "*it grew here long before the castle was built.* Blah, blah, blah. Time's wasting." She pointed to the crowd in front of the entrance. "The pack is getting restless. We'll do as you suggested. I'll look around the park, and you go on one of those guided tours of the castle. Enjoy!" She winked at him again and then disappeared down one of the paths under the arbors.

Sighing, Steven joined the line of overweight American tourists whose accent told him they came from Texas. A man pressed his chewing gum onto the castle wall, and then the procession slowly started moving.

· 12 ·

An hour and a half later, Steven was no wiser than before.

The rooms inside the castle were, in fact, impressive. That didn't alter the fact that he still didn't have the faintest idea of what he should be looking for. He had taken three successive guided tours with commentaries in English, in German, and finally in Dutch. He had memorized every detail of those rooms. When he finally asked the tour guide about the name of Marot, she only responded with an annoyed shrug. By now, word had obviously gone around that this American tourist with the baseball cap and leather jacket was an incorrigible Ludwig fan. Steven consoled himself by thinking that he was probably not the only one around. The tour guides had certainly encountered worse.

He stood alone in the ostentatious entrance hall, right in front of an equestrian statue of Louis XIV. On the ceiling above him, one of the Sun King's favorite sayings was prominently displayed between two frescoes showing chubby little cherubs.

Inferior to no one, Steven translated silently to himself. *The very opposite of how I feel right now.*

The bookseller looked around the hall but found no hint of how to solve the problem of the cipher. However, one thing struck him: the entire castle was a tribute to Greco-Roman antiquity on one hand, and the French baroque on the other. It was full of portraits of French noblemen. There was a hall of mirrors like the Sun King's, and a four-poster bed with a canopy as tall as a high-diving board. Most amusing of all was the dining room with the famous dumb-waiter in the middle of it. It consisted of a flap through which the dining table, already set, could be brought up into the middle of the royal chamber by means of an ingenious mechanism. Steven imagined the king sitting up at night on his own, dining there with mirrors and lighted candles reflecting to infinity all around him.

And after that he lies on the Moroccan divan, smoking his chibouk, that long-stemmed Turkish pipe, or he rolls about on bearskins in a wooden hut while his servants have to perform, dressed as ancient German tribesmen for his benefit. Sorry, Frau Lengfeld, but the man was way out of his mind.

Steven was so deep in thought that he didn't immediately notice the art detective's light touch.

"Well, find out anything?" she asked encouragingly.

Gloomily, Steven shook his head. "No Marot, and nothing remotely like a clue."

Sara sighed. "Same here. I ran around the park until I was worn out. Hunding's hut, the Temple of Venus, the hermitage, the chapel, the Fountain of Neptune . . . This whole park is a damn labyrinth. And the upper part has already been closed to visitors. I guess this whole venture was doomed to fail all along. Sorry."

She went out, lit herself a cigarette, and dropped wearily onto a park bench. "If we at least knew what we ought to be looking for. A sequence of numbers, a sentence, a picture. But at random like this? All we know is that the clue has something to do with the word LOVE."

"I was thinking about that just now," Steven said. "The Caesar code—the one I told you about at breakfast this morning—obviously wasn't Marot's chosen cipher. But there's a considerably more complicated one. It's known as the Vigenère cipher. If I remember correctly, it was rather popular in the mid-nineteenth century, so Marot would have known it." Steven closed his eyes to concentrate. "In the

Vigenère cipher, a *different* shift value is used for each of the letters to be coded, arising from the respective letters of the keyword. That avoids code letters appearing with too much frequency and giving away which letters they represent."

Sara groaned. "This is beyond me."

"It's very simple, really. Look at this." Steven broke a twig off one of the bushes near the castle and started writing in the gravel. After a minute he had two words, one above the other.

RIDDLE
LUDWIG

"Now, let's suppose the word we want to write in code is RIDDLE. And our keyword is LUDWIG," Steven began. "L is the twelfth letter of the alphabet, so the R of RIDDLE moves twelve letters forward, and it becomes . . ." He thought for a moment before writing down another letter. "It becomes C. The next letter in RIDDLE is I, so count out another twelve letters from C and it becomes U. Then D becomes G, the next D becomes S, and so on." He scribbled a few more letters in the gravel and looked at the result with satisfaction.

PUZZLE
LUDWIG
AOCVTK

"Well, it certainly looks as jumbled as the sequences of letters in Marot's diary," Sara said. "So you could be right. All we need is the right keyword."

"LOVE, maybe?" Steven suggested.

"Possibly. But I'd say that's too obvious. It must be some other word, one that . . . well, that sort of symbolizes love."

"Symbolizes?" the bookseller asked. "What's that supposed to mean? There are thousands of—"

Suddenly he stopped. Sara looked at him in surprise.

"What is it?"

"I think I really do know a word like that," Steven said, and pointed to the white temple on the hill in front of them. "Didn't you say that's the Temple of Venus? And there's a Grotto of Venus somewhere around. This place is full of statues of Venus, and I saw a couple of paintings of Venus in the castle itself."

"The goddess of love," Sara said. "Why didn't I think of her myself?"

Steven grinned. "Maybe because you don't know enough about the subject?"

"Very funny, Herr Lukas. Let's see if we're on the right track with VENUS as the keyword, and never mind the wisecracks. If you're right, I'll prove you wrong with a kiss."

"I think you need something called a Vigenère square for decoding words." Steven tried to remember. "With a bit of thought, and a good sharp pencil, I guess we—"

"Are you nuts?" The art detective giggled so loudly that several tourists turned to look at them. "What are computer programs for? I'm sure we'll find a website to do it for us." With a last glance at the Temple of Venus, she turned toward the park's exit. "I suggest we get a room over in the hotel and make ourselves comfortable in the lobby."

"Suppose they don't have a computer there?"

Sara Lengfeld looked at the bookseller with a mixture of pity and horror. "Oh, Herr Lukas, Herr Lukas," she murmured. "Sometimes I really think you're living in the wrong century."

THE HOTEL WAS slightly run-down and old-fashioned, as if its best days were long behind it. An elderly waiter moved through the first-floor restaurant, where there were not many guests. Yellowed photographs of Bavarian landscapes hung in the stairwell. Somewhere someone was playing a zither. However, the hotel did have a computer in the lobby, if not the latest model. At the hotel bar, Sara ordered a martini, which was too warm, and then she began tapping away at the keyboard, while Steven watched her curiously.

"It says here that Blaise de Vigenère was a sixteenth-century French diplomat who wrote several books on cryptography," she said as she stared with concentration at the scratched screen. "The cipher named after him was regarded as impossible to decode for a long time, until it was finally cracked, first by a British mathematician and then by a Prussian officer in 1863. Today of course it's simpler. Voilà!" Sara leaned back with satisfaction, pointing to a table on the monitor. "Here's a program we can use to crack Monsieur Vigenère's cipher."

"Let's try it with LOVED first," Steven suggested. "Just to be on the safe side. It says there you need five letters in the keyword."

Sara nodded, then typed the first coded word from Marot's diary, QRCSOQNZO, into the computer. In the "Key" field she typed LOVED. After only a few seconds they had the solution.

Input	QRCSOQNZO
Key	LOVED
Output	BFXWRBBUS

"Well, that obviously didn't work," Sara said, disappointed. "It would have been too simple, I suppose. Now let's try VENUS."

She carefully typed in the five characters, but all she got back was another tangle of nonsensical letters.

"Shit. Maybe I typed something in wrong." Sara tried again, but with the same result.

"Try APHRODITE," Steven said. But again the result was nonsense words, and it was the same with AMOR, EROS, HEART, and a dozen other love-related words.

Sara sipped her martini silently, while Steven racked his brain for more possible keywords. "Damn," he finally exclaimed. "And I was sure I was on the right track with the Vigenère cipher."

"You could still be, and it's just that we don't have the right word yet," Sara said. "I don't think we ought to give up."

She looked at some leaflets she had picked up in the ticket office, which described the Fairy-tale King's other castles. "At least this is the smallest of the castles that Ludwig built," she said. "I guess we can be glad we don't have to search Herrenchiemsee or Neuschwanstein."

Sighing, the bookseller got off the hotel sofa. "I guess there's nothing I can do but decode a few more pages of the diary," he said wearily. "After all, by the last point I reached, our friend Theodor hadn't arrived at Linderhof. Maybe Marot's account will put us on the track of the right word yet." He nodded, suddenly determined. "I'd better start right away. Did you reserve me a room?"

"Well, as it happens, I have good news and bad news for you." Sara drained her warm martini and nibbled the olive. "Yes, I did manage to get a room, which wasn't easy, because Manstein Systems has booked almost the entire hotel. And no, it's not a room for you; it's a room for both of us. It's up in the attic and was really meant for the hotel staff. I'm afraid there was nothing else free. I just hope you don't snore as much as you did last night."

THE ROOM WAS about the size of a walk-in closet. It contained a double bed that took up most of the space, a television set, and a wobbly table at which Steven sat hunched over the diary on a chair that was much too low. A dusty bedside lamp was the only source of light. If he looked out the window, he could just make out the mountains on the other side of the valley in the evening twilight. They cast shadows that reached out to the hotel like long fingers. In another few minutes, Linderhof would be in darkness.

The bookseller had taken out the diary and his notepad, and he was now staring in the lamplight at the twining shorthand, which looked to him much more familiar this time. Where had he stopped?

For a long time I could still hear the bark of von Strelitz's pistol in my ears. It was not to be the last time I heard it . . .

Steven tried to concentrate, in spite of the long, tiring day. Sara had seen to it that there was a plate of ham sandwiches and a bottle of red wine within reach, but he didn't have much of an appetite. Absently, he let his eyes wander over the worn bedspread beside him, an empty bag of chips, and finally Sara, who was following some kind of soap opera on TV, listening to the sound through headphones, while she leafed through the castle brochures.

Women and multitasking, I'll never understand how they do it . . .

"That's garbage you're watching," Steven finally said. The faint murmur of conversation from the headphones was getting on his nerves. The falling darkness made him nervous; it reminded him of the dark cellar of his shop where he had killed a man only the night before. Steven felt he had to talk to someone, even if that someone was a chips-munching creature staring at a TV set with blank interest.

"Surfing instructors, barbecues, big-breasted blondes," he grumbled, pointing to the TV screen. "What subject did you study?"

"What?" Sara took the headphones off. "Are you talking to me?" When she saw his glare of annoyance, she involuntarily had to smile.

"Men don't understand," she replied dryly. "We need this sort of thing to put us into a trancelike state that enables us to reach a condition of higher consciousness." She winked. "Anyway, this *garbage* is from your native land. Let's have a little more patriotism from you, Herr Lukas."

"If that's America, then I'm glad my parents came back to Germany when I was a child."

"Back to Germany?" Sara frowned.

"We have German roots." Steven sipped the hotel's house red and twisted his mouth. The burgundy, as he expected, was not good, but all the same it gave him a pleasant sense of repletion. It felt good to talk; it had been so long since he had told anyone about the past. The events of the last few days had brought memories of his childhood back to his mind.

No silence, he thought. *Silence brings back memories. Silence and dark-*

ness. Like being in my bed as a child when footsteps creaked along the corridor.

"My grandfather emigrated during the Nazi period," he began hesitantly. "But my father, his son, could never entirely rid himself of feeling that he was German. As an adult, he came back here with his family." He smiled wearily. "My mother was a German student he met at Boston University, where he was her lecturer in English Literature."

Sara's right eyebrow shot up. "I assume he read her Shakespeare at home. So a weakness for books runs in your family?"

"Books and a sense of being German," Steven said. "Sometimes I feel more German than the Brothers Grimm." He hesitated a moment before going on. "And where do *you* feel at home, Frau Lengfeld? On the Internet or in Berlin's Wedding district?"

Sara laughed. "Nowhere, I'm afraid. No one's proud of coming from Wedding. You feel proud of leaving it behind."

"And you do that best with TV and the Internet?" Steven inquired.

"Well, they're both windows to other worlds," Sara said. "If you only have comics and a Snow White book to read as a child at home, the Internet offers fantastic possibilities." She put her headphones back on. "Now, go on reading, Mr. Grimm. For a shy bookworm, you're very inquisitive."

Steven couldn't stay annoyed. Sometimes the bristly, outspoken art detective beside him seemed like a being from another world. All the same, he found himself liking her more and more. It had been a long time since he'd been so closely involved with another person for such an extended period. Most of the time he lived with his books and parchments, glad to be left alone. Sara was right to say he could come from another century. Sometimes he felt like an outcast, a scholar from a distant age not yet ruled by cell phones, computers, and text messaging.

With a tingling sense of excitement and anticipation, the bookseller turned to the coded notes. As he leafed through the pages, flecked with age, he once again felt the familiar slight dizziness. But his fear of silence had gone, giving way to a quiet longing. In Steven's eyes, the past really was more colorful and exciting than the gray twenty-first century.

Especially the past of Theodor Marot.

· 13 ·

FALKHQR

On that September evening of the year 1885, in some dark corner of the Munich suburb of Au, I found myself in greater difficulties than ever before in my life. The king must be warned at once! I was sure that as soon as he discovered the ministers' intentions, he would come to Munich by the fastest possible route to confront his enemies.

The power of the bureaucracy had grown apace over the last few years. Ludwig himself had played a part in that by avoiding the capital city of Bavaria, which he regarded as a stinking sewer. It was years since he had been in Munich, and he took no interest at all in politics. So his ministers concocted their own plans, placing only treaties and other such documents that needed the royal signature before the king, and in other respects determining the fate of the country on their own. They were the real monarchs; Ludwig was no more than a shadow king living in his own world of dreams.

What could I do? I was sure that von Strelitz already had the rail stations and telegraph offices watched. My one chance of reaching the king, therefore, was a fast horse. I stole back to the cab and unharnessed the exhausted nag. But I soon realized that I would never get back to Linderhof on this lame horse. I needed another, faster mount—but where would I find one? With my head bent so as not to attract attention, I went through the streets with the lame horse, under the eyes of the hungry, dirty inhabitants of that part of the city.

The poorest of the poor lived in the Au district. Like ghosts shunning the light of day, the houses huddled low by the steep wall of the valley of the Isar River. Many of them were no more than tiny hostelries where the families of day laborers lived, sometimes ten to a single room. The millstream of the Au flowed sluggishly past; refuse and dead rats drifted in its clouded waters. A gray cloud of smoke from the wood stoves of the houses and the countless coal-burning furnaces of the factories hung over the whole district.

After a while, I found an inn that did not look quite as dilapidated as the others. It was called Lilienbräu and lay close to the millstream. The small windows were smeared with soot, but the enamel inn sign looked new. The noise of drinkers came out of the taproom now that it was early evening, and a few people were bawling out a song to the music of an untuned fiddle.

I tied up my nag to a hook and entered the inn. A dozen eyes turned at once to stare at me suspiciously, and conversations and the song died away. I was looking into the faces of debilitated factory workers, drinking away their meager wages here before staggering home to their hungry families.

"A fine gentleman, eh?" growled a sturdy, bald man in a dirty leather apron, obviously a driver for a brewery. "Don't he like it no more up there in the city, or what brings him here?"

Laughter broke out. I looked down at my black overcoat, slightly torn now. I had lost my top hat during the wild pursuit, but all the same the workmen realized at once that I came from a higher social class.

"I'm a cabby, no fine gentleman," I said. "My horse is lame, and I need . . ."

"Better take Hartinger's donkey," crowed one of the men. "You won't find nothing better, not here in the Au, you won't!"

Once again the men roared with laugher. Some of them banged their tankards heavily on the scratched tables, but soon their fleeting interest in me was gone. I was about to go out again and look for another inn when an elderly gray-haired man, who had been standing at the bar in silence, turned to me, bowing and scraping. He wore a shabby black tailcoat and a battered bowler hat, and there was an impertinent glint in his eye.

"Could be I might have a hoss for the gennelman," he growled, drawing on a stumpy cigar. "Could be, could be. Wouldn't come cheap, though."

"As I mentioned before, I'm a cabdriver, and . . ."

"Huh!" The man spat into a bowl on the bar counter. "You don't fool me, my young dandy! I been a cabby myself, and you talk like the nobs, not like us. So what'll you pay?"

I decided not to let myself in for any more argument and brought a few coins from my coat pocket.

The old cabby chuckled. "That all you got? Guess you could buy a calf and ride away on that."

"I'm afraid I have no more at the moment. You can have the horse that's tied up outside."

He peered through the window, then took a deep puff on his cigarillo and enveloped me in smoke. "That one outside the door?" His chuckle gave way to a severe fit of coughing that shook his whole body. Very likely he was in the early stages of consumption. "That jade's no good to no one but the knacker," he finally croaked. "Won't do no business that way."

Reluctantly, I decided to let him into at least part of my plan. Unobtrusively, I opened my shirt and showed the ragged, sick man the golden amulet with the likeness of Ludwig that hung around my neck. On the back of it was a white swan with the royal seal. Ludwig himself had given it to me as a sign of his trust. Only a select few owned such a pendant.

"Very well," I whispered. "No, I am not a cabdriver. I am here on the king's business. And I need a horse—a fast one. The king will reward you more than generously later."

"On the king's business, eh?" The old man's eyes glittered as he examined the golden amulet with the ivory intarsia work. "Even if that's the truth, the king's stark raving mad, ain't got no money left. Even the sparrows on the rooftops whistle that. So what'll Herr Huber, like we call Ludwig in the taverns, what'll Herr Huber pay me with, then?"

"Your king has money, believe me." I tried to look important. But I was seething with anger inside. I knew that jokes about crazy "Herr Huber" with his empty coffers were current among the regulars at any tavern. Nonetheless, I always felt indignant when I heard such comments.

"I'll make you another offer," said the old cabby now, pointing to the amulet. "You give me that old nag and this pretty thing, and we're square. The king can look in and thank me personally, for all I care." He offered me his dirty paw and grinned like a wolf. Suddenly a small revolver appeared in his other hand. "Or you can hand the amulet over now," he growled, suppressing another fit of coughing with difficulty. "Shake on it, then, young dandy—before I regret my generosity."

HALF AN HOUR later I was sitting on a saddled horse that, contrary to my expectations, was not the worst mount in the world. His black coat gleamed, his tail was clean and combed, and he pranced on the spot as if to race all the way to Seville with me.

The old cabby had told me that he had won the horse in a race, but I could tell that he was lying through his teeth. More than likely the old rascal had stolen the horse and was glad to sell him quick and at a good price. Thus it was all the more important for me to leave the city as quickly as possible. Otherwise I would be wanted not only as the king's agent, but as a horse thief as well. At least by some hard bargaining I had induced the old man to throw his revolver into the deal. I had a foreboding that I would end up needing the little gun sooner or later.

I let the reins drop, and the horse galloped through the narrow streets of the Au district swift as an arrow. When I turned to look back once more, I saw the old cabby grinning as he waved me goodbye in the gathering dusk. He had driven the bargain of his life.

RIJKHQR, EIVOEDITP

I soon left the stinking suburbs of Munich behind. I rode south through the wooded valley of the Isar, with the river on my right, making for the Alps. By now it was full night, and I was alone on my way along the moonlit country roads. The monotonous beat of the horse's hooves made me feel tired; my eyes kept closing. I turned off into a little thicket to sleep for a few hours.

By the time day dawned, I had nearly reached Kochel. From there, it was only half a day's ride to Linderhof. All the same, I decided to stop and rest in that little town. My horse and I urgently needed to break our journey. In addition, I was sure that von Strelitz had the roads to the castle watched. If I were to succeed in reaching the king, I was more likely to do it under cover of darkness.

I spent the whole day dozing in the flea-infested bed provided by a small inn, woken abruptly again and again by nightmares in which the Prussian agent held his Derringer to my temple and pulled the trigger. More than once the thought of the ministers' diabolical intrigue passed through my mind. They couldn't simply depose the king from office. In fact the opposite was more likely; they must know that His Majesty could dismiss them at any time. But if they declared him insane, he would no longer be considered capable of ruling, and Prince Luitpold, Ludwig's uncle, would automatically move up a place in the succession to the throne. However, for that the ministers needed an incontestable expert opinion, preferably from one of the most famous psychiatrists in the German Empire: Dr. Bernhard von

Gudden, royal medical officer and director of the Upper Bavarian Hospital for the Insane. The plan was watertight.

The well-known psychiatrist had already treated Prince Otto, Ludwig's pitiable younger brother. Otto was severely demented and spent his monotonous days wailing and giggling in Fürstenried Castle. An aunt of Ludwig was also considered insane. Years earlier she had liked to claim that she had swallowed a glass keyboard. Heaven knows, the Wittelsbachs were not an easy family to understand. But for all his eccentricity, all his fantastic notions, Ludwig was not deranged! The sole aim of the ministers' intrigue was to oust an increasingly refractory king obsessed by his architectural plans and replace him with a willing marionette.

That evening I fortified myself with half a loaf of bread, butter, and bacon, mounted my horse, and rode along the Loisach River toward Garmisch. In the darkness of night, I finally climbed to the high pass of the Ettal Saddle and galloped past Ettal Monastery. From here, I realized, I must proceed carefully. The road to Linderhof was a narrow one; to the left and right of it lay woods and marshy meadows that I dared not cross on horseback. In von Strelitz's place, this was exactly where I would have laid an ambush.

Only a few miles to the castle, I was beginning to think myself safe, when branches suddenly snapped to my left. The next moment a loud explosion rang out. I dropped off my horse, rolled away, and crawled into the thicket beside the ditch at the side of the road. I saw a figure hurry out of the wood. The moonlight was bright enough for me to recognize him at once. It was indeed von Strelitz, in his dark coat looking even more like a large bat by night than he did during the day. He held the still-smoking pistol in his hand as he looked searchingly in all directions. But what alarmed me more was the sight of the men with him.

They were four police officers.

Not hired murderers, not Prussian agents, they were instead four good, honest Bavarian officers, clad in green uniforms, who now drew their own pistols and scanned the roadside with them. A cold shudder ran down my back. How far did the power of the ministers reach if even the police were now involved in the attempt to topple Ludwig? These men had certainly been told a false story, probably by von Strelitz, to the effect that I was a murderous anarchist plotting against the king. Nonetheless, my hair stood on end to think that Bavarian officers could so easily be won over to the side of evil.

While the police officers searched the bushes on the other side of the road, von Strelitz approached my hiding place with his firearm at the ready. He was only five paces from me now, and coming slowly closer. In the wan moonlight, I could see the gleam in his eyes; I almost felt that he could smell me. I cautiously fumbled with my coat, trying to get out my own revolver, but I quickly realized that the slightest sound would give me away at once. Finally I abandoned the attempt and prepared to attack.

Von Strelitz was only two paces away when I launched myself at him, like a dark nightmare, yelling at the top of my voice. As I had hoped, the agent swerved aside, and his shot went wide. I turned around and, darting sideways, ran for a little copse of fir trees where I hoped to find at least temporary shelter. Behind me, I heard angry cries, followed by shots. But as if by some miracle, they all missed me.

At last I reached the trees, which were gnarled by wind and weather, and plunged into the darkness of the wood. Birds flew up with hoarse cries, and I soon realized that I had fallen into a trap. The little wood was more of a spinney, a tiny overgrown island surrounded by flat, marshy terrain. The police officers and von Strelitz circled around the group of trees, dividing up at regular intervals. From the cracking sounds in the undergrowth, I realized that they were approaching me in a star-shaped formation. They wanted to drive me out of my hiding place like an old boar.

I thought quickly and decided on a strategy of forward flight. When I heard stealthy footsteps very close, I drew my revolver, leaped out from the cover of a fallen tree, and fired without hesitating.

Von Strelitz stood in front of me.

For a split second, time stood still. I saw the Prussian agent gasping as he clutched his right shoulder, and his own gun fell to the ground with a dull thud. He swayed, fell, and with two fast strides, I was past him and away.

Without another thought, I ran for the distant outskirts of the wood. Beyond them, a gray and seemingly endless expanse of meadowland lay in the moonlight. It was obvious that out there the police officers would be able to pick me off like a rabbit, but I was also in a trap if I stayed in the wood. What ought I to do? Surrender? Von Strelitz would probably give orders for my immediate execution, so that no one would hear about the ministers' plot. And suppose the agent himself was dead? Then the officers would very likely take instant revenge by shooting me down. I raced across the meadow, expecting a death-dealing bullet in my back at any second.

At that moment a miracle happened.

Only a little way from me, I suddenly saw my horse. He was grazing calmly and peacefully, illuminated by the moonlight like a unicorn in a fairy landscape. He raised his head when he sensed me on the outskirts of the wood.

I took a deep breath and then ran as I had never run before in my life. I could hear shouting and gunfire behind me. However, I took no notice but swung myself up on the horse and dug my heels into his sides. The horse reared up, whinnying, and then raced away over the marshy fields.

The cries behind me died down, and soon I was on the road again. Without looking back, I galloped on and on, until at last a narrow stone bridge appeared before me.

The bridge to Linderhof.

I thundered over it and stopped at the wall around the castle park. Inside it, I could see the Temple of Venus shimmering white on a hill. The castle lay beyond it. I had nearly reached my destination, but at this time of night the iron gate was locked. Jumping off my horse, I shook the bars of the gate frantically.

"Hey there!" I cried, hoarse after my headlong flight. "Open the gate at once! In the name of the king!"

Suddenly I heard the hoofbeats of a galloping horse behind me. They were quickly coming closer. Once again I tugged at the barred gate and shouted for the gatekeeper. At last I caught the sound of dragging footsteps and the clink of a key.

"Coming, in the devil's name, just coming!" growled a voice inside the gate. "It's four in the morning—wait a moment, will you?"

At that moment a gigantic figure appeared on the bridge, a monster from a shadowy world. It took me a moment to recognize it as a mounted man with his coattails fluttering in the wind like two great wings.

Von Strelitz.

He had bound up his upper arm and shoulder as best he might with a piece of cloth. Sitting erect on his gray horse, he held his pistol in his left hand, aiming it at me, his face distorted with hatred and pain. Open-mouthed, incapable even of fear and unable to move, I stared into the muzzle of the pistol, expecting to see a jet of fire hiss out of it at any moment.

But it never came.

Squealing, the barred gate opened. Holding my horse's reins, I reeled through the narrow opening into the park, stumbled, and fell almost fainting into the tall grass. There was a loud bang; I couldn't have said whether it was the pistol being fired or the gate closing behind me. Then at last everything went black before my eyes. I smelled fallen leaves and felt my horse licking my face.

I was safe. For the time being, anyway.

XOIMLQI

A little later, although still out of breath, I had calmed down enough to hurry after the baffled gatekeeper toward the castle. In the moonlight, with its shimmering white statues and latticework ornamentation, it looked to me like an elf-king's palace. Two peacocks made of valuable Sèvres porcelain stood to the right and left of the entrance.

They announced, as I knew from earlier visits, that the king was in residence.

As I strode toward the building, past the flowering gardens on the terrace and the sparkling fountain in its basin, old Johann from Berchtesgaden, one of the simple old-style Bavarian servants whom Ludwig liked to have around him, came to meet me.

"Why, Herr Marot!" he cried in surprise. "God in heaven, what happened to you?"

"Never mind that now," I panted. "I must speak to the king at once! It's a matter of life and death."

Johann nodded obediently and pointed to the hill behind us. "His Majesty is in the Grotto of Venus. May I take you there?"

I shook my head. "No, thank you, I can get there by myself."

Making my way along dark paths under canopies of foliage over the terraces behind the castle, I finally reached the music pavilion. From here it was not far to the Grotto of Venus, Ludwig's favorite spot.

In the darkness that was at its deepest now, just before morning twilight, I could see a narrow strip of light not far away. When I approached, I saw rocks piled on top of one another, and a stone door standing slightly ajar, like the entrance to a magical cavern. Only when I knocked on it cautiously did I realize that it was only a thin layer of cement. Blue light shone through the gap, and I heard the gentle lapping of waves breaking on a shallow bank.

Hesitantly, I opened the imitation rock door and stepped into the grotto.

The magnificent sight of it made me forget my fears for a moment. It was as if I had entered a world so far from all the noise, stink, and busy activity of our modern times that I felt safe, as if held in the earth mother's lap. After going down a long, narrow passage lined with rocky niches, I finally came to an artificial cave bathed in blue light. Stalactites and plaster garlands of brightly colored flowers hung from the ceiling, and I heard the sound of a waterfall to the right. A small, sparkling lake lay in the middle of the grotto, and two swans with their heads raised swam past me. Farther on, a gilded boat shaped like a huge seashell rocked on the shining surface of the water.

The king was sitting in the boat, with his eyes closed.

I had been here once before with Ludwig, a favor that he bestowed on only a few of his subjects. All the same, a shiver ran down my spine when I saw him there. I was reminded of Emperor Barbarossa, asleep in the Kyffhäuser mountain until the day when danger would threaten the German Empire. But now danger threatened the king himself, and it was for me to warn him.

I cleared my throat tactfully, and Ludwig opened his eyes. A slight smile spread over his face.

"Ah, Theodor," he said, indicating for me to join him in the boat. "Did Munich upset your digestion so much that you hope to be cured in Linderhof? I'm glad to see you here. You bring light into my dismal thoughts."

I stepped into the rocking boat and sat down opposite Ludwig. He looked bloated, and pale as a newt that spends all its life in the dark. Yet he still had that dignity and charm that had always distinguished him as king. Out of the corner of my eye, I saw a painting of a scene from Wagner's *Tannhäuser* on the back wall; I could make out its details only indistinctly in the blue light. It showed a knight in a dark cavern. Little angels hovered around him, while beautiful women moved in a round dance. The man in the picture looked exhausted and happy at the same time.

"Majesty," I began quietly, "I fear that I do not bring good news. You are in danger. Your ministers want you declared insane. They are in touch with the psychiatrist Dr. Bernhard von Gudden. He is to give an expert opinion that will describe you as unfit to rule the country."

In a few hasty words, I told him about Dürckheim's suspicions, my masquerade as a cabdriver, and my headlong flight. Gradually the smile disappeared from Ludwig's face, and for a long time he said nothing.

"How certain is this?" he asked at last.

I breathed a sigh of relief. You never knew how Ludwig would react, but he seemed to be taking the matter seriously.

"As I said, I myself overheard the conversation between Secretary Pfaffinger, Dr. von Gudden, and a Prussian agent."

"A Prussian agent?" said the king quietly. "But Bismarck has always assured me that . . ."

"The chancellor will always do what he thinks serves the interests of the German Empire," I interrupted. "And the Bavarian ministers must have been suggesting to him that you cannot continue to rule this country."

"Not continue to rule the country?" Ludwig's voice was suddenly cold as ice. "Merely because I do not rule Bavaria in a way that happens to please those gentlemen? I have had to lead the country into two wars. Wherever you look, there's saber rattling. The German Empire is too powerful to work any longer. Those damn Prussians and their lust for power." He angrily sat up in the boat, making it sway as his weight shifted. "They'll take us into another war that will burn this world to rubble and ashes. Where are the old ideals? The old ideas of kingship? Find me an island, Theodor. Some island where I can be the king I wish to be."

I closed my eyes, praying that Ludwig would remain reasonable. Recently he had spoken enthusiastically, multiple times, of leaving Bavaria. He had even commissioned several of his employees to seek out some distant land—which they were happy to do, as it sent them on luxurious travels. Unfortunately, the king's moods changed like the wind. He could write down-to-earth letters and give sensible orders, and the next moment threaten a lackey with deportation for life, or hold a conversation with the bust of Marie Antoinette.

"You must go to Munich and show yourself to the people," I begged him. "If you make only a gesture of approach to the people, they will take you to their hearts again as they did in the past. And that will destroy the ministers' plan. No one will believe that medical report if you show how reasonable you are."

"So I'm to prove that I am not crazy?" asked the king. "How ironic. Do *you* think me . . . deranged, like my brother, Otto?"

"No, Majesty. On my honor, I think you like to dream, and you are more sensitive than most people, but not deranged."

Ludwig was smiling again. "Sensitive." He relished the word like a sweet plum. "I think you are correct there. Thank you, Marot. You have always been one of those dearest to me. I value your honesty." He carefully steered the boat to the bank and climbed ponderously out. "Now, come with me. I want to show you something that will take your breath away."

As we left the grotto, the blue light inside it changed to a shade of red.

XOIMLQI

We walked over to the castle as the first light of dawn showed in the east. I followed the king in silence until we were on the dark forecourt.

Early as it was, there were already some servants there, carrying a small table decorated with intarsia work, two chairs, and a silver tray laden with all kinds of delicacies on it. In surprise, I realized that they were approaching the tall old linden tree that stood not far from the basin of the fountain. When I looked at the trunk, I saw that roughly halfway up it was a platform to which a simple wooden ladder led. The servants now hauled the furniture and the tray up to this airy terrace with a block and tackle, and they arranged it all as if the table were not sixteen feet up in the air, but in the royal dining room.

"My supper shall be your breakfast today, Marot," said Ludwig, pointing with a smile to the platform. "Be so kind as to keep me company in my linden tree. I have the finest bedchamber in the world up there."

The wooden ladder creaked alarmingly as His Majesty and I

climbed it. I clung to the rungs and tried not to look down. As so often, I had to shake my head over Ludwig's eccentric notions. A king in a tree house! No doubt the servants were already gossiping about this latest whim.

But once I was finally up on the platform, the view before me almost brought tears to my eyes.

The Alps surrounded us, like mighty giants of rock, with the soft green of the forests at their feet. The park with its castle, the pavilions, the Temple of Venus, and the chapel lay below us like a child's toy landscape. At that very moment, the sun rose behind the mountains in the east, bathing the scene in a warm, almost unreal light. In the shady canopy above our heads, the linden leaves rustled quietly.

"Help yourself, Marot. You must be hungry after that ride." The king had already taken his place on his chair and was serving himself from a dish of fragrant and particularly tender roast veal. But I couldn't take my eyes off the magnificent landscape. As if at a secret signal, a mighty jet of water suddenly rose from the middle of the fountain below us, and a cool spray wafted up to me.

"Out here in the mountains, far from the city, I am the king I would like to be," said Ludwig, wiping his fleshy lips with his napkin. "A law of nature, like the sun and the moon. Do you understand now why I can't go back to Munich?"

"Majesty, times have changed," I told him "You are not Arthur in Camelot, but the king of Bavaria. Laws have to be signed . . ."

"Let the ministers bring their paperwork on pilgrimage here to Linderhof!" Ludwig interrupted me, pointing to the landscape around us. "What is real and what is false, Theodor? The dirty city of Munich with its intriguing and politicking, or this fairy-tale world? The people still love their king here, and here I am not a marionette."

"You need not be a marionette if you . . ." I began. But suddenly the words dried up in my mouth. Down below us, a boy, laughing, approached. Beside him was a young woman, wearing a plain bodice and linen skirt with an apron, such as the simple women of these parts

often wear on festive days. Her black hair hung loose, fluttering behind her in the wind. The girl's face was radiant; her whole appearance seemed designed to drive my gloomy mood away, like the sun
dispersing the mists of a cold, damp morning. In his loud, cheerful
voice, the child beside her was spurring her on to run a race with him.

"Marot, what's the matter?" I heard my king's voice behind me.
"Does the view up here take your breath away?"

Dazed, I shook my head and sat down opposite Ludwig. "It's nothing, Majesty. Probably only the long ride." Surreptitiously, I looked
down and tried to catch another glimpse of the unknown girl, but she
had already disappeared from my field of vision. Only her laughter
rose to me, clear as a bell.

"Do you hear that?" said Ludwig, heaping another portion of
steaming roast veal on a porcelain plate with a pattern of swans. "That
laughter is music to my ears! Not the music of Wagner, perhaps, but
more beautiful, in any event, than the whistling of locomotives and
the ringing of bells in those newfangled horse-drawn streetcars in the
city."

"The . . . the young woman down there," I asked tentatively, trying
to show as little interest as possible. "Is she a governess?"

Ludwig laughed, almost choking on a mouthful of veal.
"Governess? Oh God, no! That's Maria from Oberammergau.
Daughter of a peasant woodcarver." A smile played around his lips. "I
like to have her near me. She keeps me company, helps a little in the
kitchen, and tells me what the people are thinking. You see, Marot, I
am not indifferent to the world."

"If you are not indifferent to the world, Majesty, then promise that
you will come to Munich."

"What liberties do you think you can take, Marot?" he snapped. "I
do not have to promise you anything. Who do you think you are?"

I humbly bowed my head. "Majesty, it is only because . . ."

"Be silent, before I regret bringing you up here at all!"

Without another word the king rose to his feet. His chair fell over with a crash, and Ludwig climbed down the ladder to the ground. He did not deign to favor me with another glance and disappeared into the castle.

I struck my forehead and cursed myself for my thoughtlessness. Ludwig was well-known for cultivating an almost fraternal relationship with his social inferiors, but it could change into icy coldness from one moment to the next. I ought to have known! Instead, I had been incautious and endangered my mission. I dared not think what Count Dürckheim would say when I told him about my faux pas. Now how was I going to convince the king that he must go to Munich?

Gritting my teeth, I made my way down the ladder hand over hand, wondering how I could mollify Ludwig. My game of hide-and-seek, my flight—perhaps it had all been for nothing.

"Don't be downcast," said a clear voice behind me suddenly. "Sometimes the king is like an angry child. His tantrums are like storms. They come suddenly, but they disappear again just as fast."

Startled, I turned around and found myself looking straight into the face of the black-haired girl whose looks had taken my breath away. Now, at close quarters, the young woman seemed if anything even more beautiful than she had appeared from the platform in the tree.

"Oh . . . I didn't know . . ." I stammered. She shook her head, laughing.

"I couldn't help hearing your quarrel. Think nothing of it. You got off lightly; the king has been known to push other men into the fountain from up here."

I smiled, while I went on surreptitiously looking at her.

"You seem to know His Majesty well. Does he allow you an audience, ma'am?"

Her clear, bell-like laughter rang out again, and my heart beat faster. "Never mind the formality, sir," she said, chuckling. "I am only the daughter of a simple peasant woodcarver from Oberammergau." Suddenly her voice was grave, and a small frown of annoyance appeared on her brow. "But you are right, I do know the king well. Better, anyway, than many a minister, state secretary, or councilor. To you, coming from Munich, Ludwig is only a dreamer, am I right? A wayward oddity who won't do what you all tell him." She pointed to the forests stretching up into the mountains behind the castle. "But ask the common people here in the Graswangtal, and they will tell you a different story. The king talks to us, asks how we are. And when one of his grooms has a birthday, he serves him a festive meal with his own hands."

I said nothing but looked in admiration at the young woman who had spoken with so much feeling. Her face was fine-featured, with high cheekbones and clever eyes that hardly suited a maidservant. But for the simple linen skirt and apron that she wore, I would have taken her for a court lady, or a merchant's daughter. Her whole appearance had something playfully ladylike about it; she had a natural elegance lacking in most of the ladies of high social standing whom I knew.

"The king was right to be angry with me just now," I said at last, hesitantly. "I was a fool. Perhaps it would be a good thing if someone were to take me to task more often."

"Well, don't expect me to do it. Two scamps are quite enough for me." Her eyes twinkled at me, and I felt a slight shiver down my back all of a sudden. This girl could reduce me to the state of a naïve, stammering peasant with her glances alone.

"Two . . . er, scamps?"

"Well, the king and the naughty little boy shooting sparrows out of the trees there."

She pointed to a group of bushes from which a flock of birds, twittering angrily, was just flying up. A little boy of about six, with unruly black curls and wearing short lederhosen, was running after them with a slingshot, shouting. It was the boy I had seen from the platform.

"Is that your child?" I asked, and looked at her in surprise. She seemed so young that I would never have thought the boy might be her own. When she nodded, I felt a sharp pang deep inside me.

"Leopold," she said quietly, and a shadow came over her face. "He will be six next summer. He's the apple of my eye, even if I sometimes curse him to the devil."

We were walking together toward the basin of the fountain, which was still sending a powerful jet of water up into the air. Tiny drops moistened my face and formed a misty veil with a rainbow in it above our heads. The girl had now bent down to pick a bunch of flowers. A little way off, the boy was aiming his slingshot at a couple of crows who had come down to settle on the head of a Greek statue of Diana.

"Your boy does indeed seem to be a real scamp," I said only half seriously. "I expect his father has to read him a lecture pretty often. Where is his papa, by the way?"

The girl went on picking marguerite daisies, bellflowers, and red poppies in silence. Only after a few moments did she turn to me, shaking her head sadly.

"Leopold has never had a father. The king was kind enough to take us in."

"I . . . I'm sorry about that," I replied, at the same time ashamed of myself for feeling something like relief. "An accident?"

"No, it's only that . . . Leo, get down from there at once!"

She had called the last words to the boy, who was now trying to balance on the rim of the fountain. She looked at me, and at least she was smiling again now.

"I'll have to go and save my little scamp's life again. I'm pleased to have made your acquaintance, sir. May I ask the gentleman's name?"

"Marot," I stammered. "Theodor Marot. I am assistant to the royal physician."

"Marot." She put her head on one side and blinked into the sun. "A handsome name and a handsome man to bear it." She took her leave of me with a little curtsey and a slight glint of mockery in her eyes. "My name is Maria. Always at your service, sir."

Then she turned and ran toward the rim of the fountain opposite.

"Maria is . . . is a beautiful name, too," I murmured, and waved to her, but she already had hold of her little boy, and they had disappeared into the bushes.

Still dazed, and weary after two days of riding, I let myself slide down the trunk of the linden tree to the ground, from where I stared up at the white Temple of Venus.

"*Maria*," I whispered.

All my anger, my bad luck, the quarrel with Ludwig, were forgotten. I closed my eyes and abandoned myself to pleasant daydreams, in which Maria ran through the meadow with me as she had just been running with her child. A veil came down over my consciousness, and I had to admit to myself that, against all the dictates of reason, I had fallen head over heels in love.

I really cannot have been of sound mind, because the next thing I did was distinctly childish—and it would cost me my king's favor if he were ever to hear of it. I took my knife out of my pocket and began to carve that day's date and the name of the clever black-haired girl into the bark of the king's linden tree.

MARIA 10.9.1885

When I had finished, I ran my forefinger over the letters and softly whispered her name. How was I to guess, at the time, that this girl would determine the fate of so many of us long after our deaths?

RLLKH, XEXMNPE, NACTAPE

· 14 ·

A KNOCK ON THE DOOR WOKE Steven. Alarmed, he sat up in bed abruptly and for a moment didn't know where he was.

The Cowled Men! The thought shot through his mind. *They're coming to get the book!*

"Who . . . who's there?" he croaked.

"Housekeeping," a gentle voice fluted. "I'll come back later."

Drowsily, Steven groped for his watch beside the bed. It said nine thirty. At the same moment he remembered where he was, and why he was there. The memory did not improve his temper very much.

Good morning, Herr Lukas. We have the police downstairs. They want you for torture and murder. There are also a couple of gentlemen in black hooded robes who want a word with you. Would you like orange juice for breakfast?

He had gone on working on the diary until late into the night, finally going to bed around two in the morning. By then Sara was fast asleep, with the headphones still over her ears, while on the TV screen busty women silently promised carnal pleasures.

Sara . . .

Steven looked to his right, but the other side of the bed was empty. He stretched and rubbed his eyes. The art detective was probably down in the breakfast room by now. Finally he went into the bathroom and spread shaving cream on his face, humming while contemplating Marot's experiences at Linderhof. The transliteration of Shelton's shorthand had not brought anything conclusive to light. There had been eight new words in cipher in those passages, but no clue to the means of decoding them. All the same, Marot had mentioned the Grotto of Venus.

Venus . . .

Could a clue perhaps be hidden *in* the grotto? But how was Steven to check, when the grotto was closed to visitors?

After he had shaved carefully, Steven put on the torn pants again, with the printed T-shirt, and leather jacket. He put the notebook containing the decoded diary pages away in his inside pocket, then set off down to the almost-empty breakfast room. Two of the hotel staff were hanging garlands and lanterns for some kind of party. Yesterday's elderly waiter was shuffling around the room, looking morose and pouring coffee from a large pot. To his surprise, Steven saw that Sara wasn't there yet. He asked in the lobby, where he was told that the lady had driven away at eight that morning. No, she hadn't left any message.

Thoroughly bewildered, Steven sat down at a table and sipped the black coffee, which was far too bitter. Where could Sara be? Why hadn't she told him where she was going? Once again, he had a feeling that the art detective was hiding something from him. He remembered how calmly Sara had searched the body of that hit man in his bookshop. What had she said at the time?

Why don't you just assume I have a certain amount of experience . . .

Steven quickly skimmed through the local paper, until on one of the back pages he found a headline that ruined his appetite.

BOOKSELLER MURDER SUSPECT:
THE SEARCH GOES ON

The story under it didn't contain much news; it simply reiterated that a certain Steven Lukas had disappeared, and the police were still in the dark. Steven sighed and put the paper down in revulsion. At least they'd refrained from printing a photo of him this time. He got to his feet, deciding to follow up his suspicions of the Grotto of Venus, even without Sara.

Outside the hotel, the October sky was gray and cloudy, and with only a thin T-shirt under the leather jacket, Steven immediately began shivering. A notice on the nearby entrance to the park announced, as he expected, that the castle and the upper part of the grounds were closed; otherwise, however, there seemed to be free access. The bookseller passed the wrought-iron gate and walked through the little wood, which was surrounded by bushes. He met only a few tourists at this early hour, and soon he was on his own among the tall trees. A curious squirrel scurried past his feet, and somewhere he heard the cawing of a crow. Morning mist lay over the hedges and arbors, from which brightly colored leaves fell to the ground.

Steven left the little pond and walked east until a red and white plastic tape barred his way. Beyond it he saw several limousines outside the castle, and the shrill laughter of women reached his ears. Half a dozen domestic staff were setting up little cocktail tables.

Nice place for a party, Steven thought. *And in this outfit, I could pass for an invited guest, maybe a rock star.*

"Hey, you! What are you doing here?"

A powerfully built steward in a gray suit was coming toward him. A walkie-talkie at his side was chirping.

"I'm . . . er . . . going for a walk," Steven replied. "Is that forbidden?"

"So long as you stay this side of the barrier, it's okay," growled the man. "There's a private event here today."

"Manstein, yes, I know." Steven nodded and pointed up at the Grotto of Venus. "Listen, couldn't I take a little look all the same?"

"Forget it," the steward said. "Better find somewhere else to go for a walk." His walkie-talkie squawked, and he turned abruptly away as he muttered unintelligibly into it.

Steven waited for the man to be out of sight, and then he turned around. He walked back the way he had come, until a narrow path turned off into the wood to the right. There was another tape barrier here, too, with a notice in red lettering dangling on it.

NO ENTRY. PRIVATE FUNCTION.

Rather undecided, Steven stopped in front of it, but there was no steward to be seen.

What the hell, he thought. *It's not like they're going to shoot me.*

After looking carefully around once more, he slipped under the tape and climbed the steep path that led to the upper part of the park. He heard laughter and the occasional car engine in the distance, but apart from that, it was quiet among the beech, spruce, and linden trees.

Another shady path branched off to the right, leading Steven to a small mound of rocks. Past it was a door-shaped stone slab with a keyhole. Knocking gently, he sensed a hollow space behind the slab.

The entrance to the Grotto of Venus.

Should he just go in? Once again Steven looked around, but apart from a few curious squirrels, he couldn't see a soul. He took a deep breath and pushed the stone slab.

At the same moment, the revolving door concealed in the rock opened in front of him, and a woman in her midforties with short gray hair came out.

"Can I help you?" she asked sharply, inspecting Steven as if he were a piece of garbage.

The bookseller was so surprised that at first he was at a loss for words. Only after what felt like an eternity did he finally get his mouth open. "I . . . I only wanted to see the grotto," he stammered.

"Forget it. It's closed today." The gray-haired woman folded her arms and looked challengingly at him. Her close-fitting pantsuit and lack of makeup gave her an austere, masculine appearance.

"Oh, how stupid," Steven said. "Now what am I going to tell my boss when I come home without a story?"

"Story?" The stranger, probably another steward herself, raised her right eyebrow. Apart from that, her attitude had not thawed one bit.

"Er . . . I'm Greg Landsdale from the *Wisconsin News.*" Following a sudden inspiration, Steven brought out his crumpled notepad and a pencil, and bowed to her slightly. "I'm writing a story for our readers in Milwaukee about Ludwig's fairy-tale castles. Neuschwanstein, Herrenchiemsee, Linderhof . . . A great many people locally are descended from German immigrants who are interested in that kind of thing. Oh man . . . I fly back to the States tomorrow, and my boss said I absolutely had to visit the Grotto of Venus or he'd have my head."

Steven spoke with a strong American accent, trying to sound like a provincial Milwaukee reporter who had studied German for a few semesters. He had remembered, just in time, that David, Sara's ex-boyfriend, had traveled in these clothes as a magazine journalist. Steven gave the woman a beaming all-American smile—*the world belongs to me*—while sweat dripped into the collar of his leather jacket.

"Just a little look?" he asked, twinkling at her. "The United States of America will be grateful to you."

The woman eyed him suspiciously, and then without a word went back inside the cave. Unsure what to do, the bookseller was lingering at the entrance when he heard the woman's voice come out of the grotto, with a slight echo.

"Well, come on then. Hurry up before I change my mind."

Steven breathed a sigh of relief. The woman hadn't even asked to see his press pass. He followed her into the cave, which at first was only a narrow passage with a few niches in the rock, but broadened into a large hall. It was all exactly as it had been described in Marot's diary. The shell-shaped golden boat rocked gently on the lake. Beyond it, at the back of the cave, was the painting from Wagner's opera *Tannhäuser*, and in front of the painting there was a small stage made of artificial stone. Only the lighting, the swell of the waves, and the swans were missing.

"It . . . it's *magnificent!*" Steven cried enthusiastically as he looked around desperately for any sign left by Marot.

"It is indeed. A magnificent illusion, and a masterpiece of technology," said the woman, pointing to the stalactites hanging from the roof. "All that is only linen sprayed with cement. There was a machine to make artificial waves, and a device to project a rainbow. The lighting installation responsible for the red and blue light in the grotto was driven by twenty-four dynamos."

"Dynamos? Lighting installation?" Steven was intrigued. "I thought the king lived in the nineteenth century?"

"And was well ahead of his time," the woman said. "Neuschwanstein Castle has one of the first telephones, the moon-lamp of his sleigh was battery-powered, and he even planned to build a flying machine. Ludwig tried to unite technology and nature into a single whole."

"You obviously know a lot about it," Steven said, smiling. "Is it a hobby or your profession?"

The woman's lips narrowed in a thin smile. "My vocation, if you like. Only those who know the roots of technology can see its future."

"I'm afraid I don't entirely understand," the bookseller replied. "Are you responsible for maintaining this grotto?"

At this the woman genuinely laughed, a soft, gurgling sound like a babbling brook. "Not entirely; my business is with computers." She gave him a small bow. "Luise Manstein of Manstein Systems."

Steven nearly dropped his notepad. "You . . . you're Herr . . . I mean Frau Manstein?" he stammered. Only now did he register the fact that the middle-aged lady's suit was perfectly cut, and she was wearing an expensive perfume. "But I thought . . ."

"That I would be a man." The head of Manstein Systems nodded. "Women in leading positions always have to contend with that prejudice. The fact is that my dear husband died more than ten years ago. I have been running the company since then, and I think I may say that I do it well." She gave Steven a sharp look. "Our revenue has increased by almost fifty percent in that time, and we have expanded considerably."

"Forgive me, I didn't . . ."

Luise Manstein waved this away. "Forget it. I don't have much time. As you probably know, I have planned a private birthday party for today. Part of it will take place in here, too. So if there's anything else you want to know, please hurry up."

Steven industriously brought out his pencil and concentrated on where Theodor Marot might have hidden a clue. In his mind he went through everything that the assistant doctor had written about the grotto.

The king's favorite spot . . . the boat like a huge seashell . . . the red and blue light . . . the painting from Tannhäuser . . .

The bookseller started. Sure enough, Marot had written at some length about the picture. Could there be something hidden in it? Maybe hinting at a theme that would get him and Sara farther forward? Some legendary figure, relating to the subject of love, that they had forgotten? A name of some kind?

"Er . . . the painting over there?" He pointed to the large canvas, which showed a handsome man enchanted by the scene and surrounded by half-naked women and cherubs. "What does it mean?"

"Interesting that you ask about that in particular," Luise said. "It is known as *Tannhäuser with Lady Venus* and illustrates the first act of Wagner's famous opera. The knight Tannhäuser visits the pagan goddess and stays in her cave." She pointed to the stalactites under the roof. "This hall is intended to be Venus's Cave, and at the same time it is modeled on the Blue Grotto of Capri. Ludwig took refuge here from the modern world when he found it too menacing." She looked at Steven, who was busily pretending to make notes as she talked. "How about yourself, Mr. Landsdale? Don't you, too, sometimes feel that the present day is threatening?"

More than you can begin to imagine, Steven thought.

"Not really," he replied. "And Ludwig himself was obviously inconsistent if he wanted to live in an old-fashioned fairy tale, but at the same time he had Siemens dynamos clattering away here."

"As I said, it's a matter of uniting the new and the old." Luise

Manstein abruptly turned to the way out of the cave. "But now we really must go. I have a good deal to do before this evening."

Steven hurried after her. "But I still have so many questions to ask."

And what's more, damn it, I still have no idea where I ought to be looking, or what for.

At the exit from the grotto, the industrialist stopped and locked the door in the rock behind them with a large, rusty key. Then she gave Steven a long, searching look.

"Did you know that Ludwig gave an interview to a newspaper only once in his life?" she suddenly asked. "It was with an American journalist, and they talked about Edgar Allan Poe. So don't underestimate King Ludwig. In certain areas he was way ahead of his time." She hesitated for a moment, and then her hard face relaxed and she smiled almost girlishly. "I'll tell you something, Mr. Landsdale: I like you. Come to my little party this evening, will you? Maybe we'll have a chance to talk some more." She handed him two gleaming golden plastic tickets. "This is your security pass. And another for a companion in case you'd like to bring one. It's been a pleasure meeting you."

Without another word, she went away along the path and soon disappeared among the trees.

SARA LENGFELD TURNED up about midday.

Her lemon yellow Mini Cooper pulled up, brakes shrieking, on the hotel forecourt as Steven, sitting in the restaurant, was leafing through Marot's notes yet again. When he looked through the restaurant window and saw Sara coming, he hurried to meet her.

"Where in heaven's name have you been?" he asked. "I was worried about you!"

Sara, a broad grin on her face, held up a thin white box about the size of a lady's purse.

"I've been shopping in Garmisch. A MacBook Pro with a 500-gigabyte hard disk and one of those superfast Intel Core 17 processors. I've always wanted one of those."

"And you had to go off to buy it now?"

"Herr Lukas, just because you're still writing with a quill pen doesn't mean I have to do the same. Someone wrecked my smartphone in your basement, remember? And this will make our search a whole lot easier. I've already downloaded a pair of deciphering programs, and if we want to surf the Net, we don't have to go to the hotel lobby anymore. How about a word of thanks for a change?"

"Thank you, Frau Lengfeld."

"You couldn't manage to make it a tad chillier, maybe, Mr. Freeze?"

Steven took Sara aside and gripped her hard by the shoulders. "Listen," he whispered, "I really don't have time for this nonsense right now. Marot's account indicates that there could be a clue in the Grotto of Venus. I was there early this morning, although . . ."

Sara looked at him in surprise. "You were there? I thought it was closed."

"Believe it or not, Frau Lengfeld, I can do quite a lot with my quill pen."

Steven filled her in about his meeting with Luise Manstein in the Grotto of Venus. He ended by telling her about the invitation.

"You want me to go to some party for a bunch of pompous idiots given by Manstein Systems?" she asked. "Warm prosecco, small talk, boring, boring, boring . . . Christ, as if I didn't get that all year round at gallery openings."

"Then I'm sure you can manage it one more time." Steven looked at her hard. "Don't you understand? This may be our last chance to search the grotto. So pull yourself together." He raised an admonitory forefinger. "You were the one who wanted me to get involved, remember? 'The greatest coup an antiquarian bookseller can land'— those were your words. So don't let me down now."

Sara sighed, then suddenly turned and walked to her car.

"Hey, where are you going?" Steven called after her.

"Where do you think? Back to Garmisch." Wrinkling her nose, she held up the hem of her green wool skirt. "You don't suppose I'm going to some hoity-toity party with you in this getup, do you?"

· 15 ·

THE PARTY THAT EVENING OUTDID all expectations. Steven and Sara stood beside a statue, a little way apart from the other guests, and from that vantage point watched the high society of Bavaria celebrating with champagne and caviar. A heated marquee had been put up outside the castle, with a small string orchestra in Baroque costumes and wigs playing Vivaldi's *Four Seasons*. Although it was nearly mid-October, many of the guests, adorned with Venetian masks, were only lightly clad as they strolled in the park, which looked like a bright fairy-tale land lit by torches and candles. Butlers in frock coats served canapés and glasses of bubbling champagne; farther off, a magician with his face painted white held onlookers spellbound with a top hat and a rabbit. Women stalked around the arbors and gardens in their cocktail dresses like exotic jungle birds, accompanied by gentlemen in classic double-breasted suits whose every gesture spoke of power and authority. Carriages drawn by teams of four horses took the guests over to the nearby hotel, where the party would continue.

With a sour expression, Sara sipped from her glass and then poured out the contents on the gravel path. "You'd think they could lay on a better champagne for such a fancy party," she grumbled. "And the salmon rolls taste like cotton batting."

"Oh, stop complaining. We're not here to eat and drink," Steven said. "Just enjoy the atmosphere a bit."

Unobtrusively, he looked down at himself. He wore a black suit with a shirt and bow tie, all of which he had bought with the last of his cash as he shopped with Sara. He felt properly dressed for the first time in days. Only the glittering silver mask over his eyes bothered him, but he had finally let Sara persuade him to wear it. After all, it was perfectly possible that one of the guests would have seen his photograph on TV or in a newspaper. He wasn't so conspicuous among all the other masked guests. The diary was safely locked in their hotel room's safe.

The art detective, too, wore a Venetian mask with her dress. After much deliberation, she had opted for a red evening dress cut very low in the back, a Prada jacket, and high-heeled shoes with pointed toes. Considering that the art detective had made such a fuss about going to the party, she had spent quite a lot on her outfit. All the same, he thought it had been worth it.

If she didn't have such a sharp tongue, it would be easy to fall in love with her, he thought. *But no doubt I'd have to be at least ten years younger to have any chance.*

"There's some kind of Wagner event going on in the grotto," Steven said, dismissing his thoughts. "But when it's over we can go and have a look around."

The art detective nodded abstractedly and went on watching the guests, frowning. You know, Manstein Systems have actually booked Mario Baldoni for the Wagner event."

"*The* Baldoni?"

"Yep, the world-famous tenor. He's singing right now in the seashell boat, in front of about thirty people. Wouldn't surprise me if they've also hired a couple of genuine nymphs for the lake. Oh, and look over there."

She pointed to a tall, stout man in a noticeably ill-fitting suit, approaching Luise Manstein. The industrialist wore a close-fitting gray jacket and skirt, with a sparkling ring on one finger. When she recognized the man, she smiled, and offered him her hand to kiss.

"Well, at least we now know why the lady there is throwing herself a party," Sara said. "The interior minister of Bavaria himself has done her the honor of attending. Now they can negotiate the next party donation over champagne and caramel mousse."

"Why are you always so negative?" Steven asked crossly. "I've made inquiries, and the money coming in here is used exclusively to restore the castle."

"Sure, and I'm Mother Teresa."

Sighing, Steven gave up and ate his salmon canapé. He had to admit that Sara was right; the little roll really did taste like cotton batting spread with mayonnaise. He put his plate down and watched Luise Manstein talking to the interior minister. She had not given Steven so much as a glance since the party began. Only when the minister had left her, with a bow, did her eyes chance to fall on Steven. Her lips twisted in an ironic smile as she raised her glass to him.

"Ah, our American journalist," she called cheerfully. "I almost failed to recognize you with that mask on. Are you enjoying my birthday party?"

"It's . . . more than spectacular," Steven replied hesitantly. "I thought only movie stars threw parties like this."

Smiling, Luise Manstein came a few steps closer to him. "Parties are always theatrical performances as well, don't you agree? Think of Ludwig—I'm sure he'd have enjoyed this one. After all, his whole life was nothing but an ostentatious spectacle."

"I admit I've never thought of it like that."

"Well, you should. That explains much of his bizarre behavior, interpreted by posterity as derangement. It's all a question of perspective." The industrialist looked attentively at Steven. "Have we already met somewhere? You seem familiar to me somehow."

"Sorry, no." Steven shook his head, hoping desperately that she didn't read the local papers. "Not that I know of."

"Well, be that as it may—if you'll excuse me now, I have a couple of important guests to welcome."

Luise Manstein turned away with something like a wink, and Sara audibly spat out her prosecco. "More than spectacular! Wow, you certainly buttered her up. If you ask me, the old trout wants to get you into bed." She went on in a falsetto. "'Have we already met some-wheeeere?' What a laugh!"

"That's nonsense. It's known as civility, Frau Lengfeld. A word that obviously isn't part of your vocabulary." Steven bit grimly into his smoked salmon canapé. He would have liked a little more conversation with Luise Manstein. Her brusque way of leaving just now annoyed him more than he wanted to show Sara.

Suddenly applause came from their right, where the magician had just taken two white doves out of his top hat. In his black tailcoat and with his face painted white, he looked like a music hall artiste from an earlier century. Steven caught himself thinking again, how he would have liked to live at that time. A time without laptops, cell phones, PowerPoint presentations. A world where the gentlemen still wore top hats and tailcoats, like that magician with his white face.

The magician . . .

Something about him intrigued Steven, and he looked again, more closely. At that very moment the stranger with the top hat turned his head, and their eyes met. The magician's face was white with makeup; his eyebrows, eyelids, and lips gleamed moist and black. This, together with his tailcoat and hat, gave him the uncanny appearance of a human being who had turned into a scarecrow.

Steven started with surprise. He knew the man.

He didn't know where, but he was sure that he had seen him before.

"Sara," he whispered in a dry voice. "The magician over there. I think I've met him already."

Sara, looking bored, shrugged. "At the circus, maybe?"

"No, no. Somewhere different. I think he's watching us."

"Are you sure?"

Steven nodded and went on looking at the thin, heavily made-up stranger, who was now bringing a long red scarf out of his hat. "Just about sure."

"Then we'd better find out what he wants as quickly as possible," Sara whispered. "I tell you what, we'll go walking in the park and see if he follows us. Maybe then we'll find out more about what he wants."

She took Steven's sleeve, and together they strolled toward the fountain from which a huge jet of water shot up at regular intervals. There were not many people here now. Steven looked around, but the magician had disappeared behind the marquee. The sound of Vivaldi's *Four Seasons* drifted softly down to them.

"Maybe I was wrong," said Steven thoughtfully, taking a deep breath. "I'm getting paranoid."

"Don't let it bother you," Sara said. "That sometimes happens with advancing age."

"Very funny, Frau Lengfeld. Very funny indeed. He was staring at me, though. I'm sure of it."

"Herr Lukas, if I took everyone who stared at me for a potential criminal, all I'd think about would be running away. Maybe he just thinks you look cute in your Silver Surfer mask, hmm?"

"For God's sake, can't you keep your big mouth shut for once?"

Angrily, Steven tore his mask off and marched through the park toward the Temple of Venus. He wanted to be alone. The whole situation was too much for him; he wasn't used to this kind of life. Three days ago his greatest adventure had been getting his hands on a complete *Grimms' Fairy Tales*, and now he was being menaced at every turn by Cowled Men and magicians with their faces painted white. If he didn't take care, he'd end up as crazy as Ludwig himself, rocking on the water in a shell-shaped boat and breakfasting in the treetops.

This whole diary was pure farce. Presumably Theodor Marot had just scribbled any random letters to lend a touch of mystery to what he was writing. The way it looked right now, the book threatened to become a slushy romance, anyway. Vows of love carved in the trunk of a linden tree! It was the opposite of what Steven had hoped for from the diary. Romantic confessions of an academic late bloomer.

The linden tree . . .

In his fury the bookseller had marched on without looking right or left, and now he faced the mighty tree. Its leaves rustled gently in the wind. He looked up at the tall trunk and tried to imagine Marot eating there with the king more than a hundred years ago, meeting Maria, and finally carving her name in the bark of the tree.

A glimmer of an idea surfaced in his mind. Could the name possibly still be there? Or had Marot simply invented the whole love story? Steven went closer to the tree trunk. The floodlights from the marquee were so bright that they cast a faint light on the tree, far away from them as it was. The bookseller walked around the linden tree, brushing away a few cobwebs and a handful of dry leaves clinging to the bark. Suddenly, at chest height, his fingers passed over notches forming separate letters and figures. They were weatherworn and had grown together, but even after nearly three human lifespans they were still legible.

MARIA 10.9.1885

The sudden realization struck Steven like a blow.

SARA WATCHED STEVEN disappear into the dark of the terraced garden and shook her head.

Men could be so touchy. She had often irritated the opposite sex with her remarks. Usually her occasional lovers couldn't cope with the fact that she had a quicker mind and wasn't going to do as they said. It had been like that with her last boyfriend, David. The relationship had lasted just six months; then she had found his empty phrases increasingly getting on her nerves—and he himself, in a brief moment of acumen, had correctly interpreted her silence, her tight smile, and her raised eyebrows, and had disappeared from her life. By now David was probably drifting around some London club or other, making eyes at silly floozies and playing house music.

Steven was different. He was clever, well-read, and obviously didn't feel it was a problem if she took the lead now and then. But she felt as if he came from another planet. Even more: if women were from Venus and men were from Mars, then Steven came from Pluto, if not from the faraway Horsehead Nebula.

Which made him very interesting.

Smiling, she turned away and went back to the castle. The unworldly bookseller would soon calm down again. Meanwhile, she could look around on her own for once without his company. Sara looked at her watch. The aria sung by the famous tenor, who must surely be wickedly expensive to hire, would be over by now. So it couldn't hurt to pay the Grotto of Venus a visit.

She took off her mask and her high-heeled shoes, which were already giving her blisters, and, carrying them, set off on the way to the upper part of the park. As soon as she rounded the corner of the castle, she was completely alone. A carpet of violet and blood-red flowers spread out around her, while ahead a stern statue of Neptune with his trident looked down at her. He stood in the middle of a fountain fed by a splashing waterfall that cascaded down from the slope above. To the right and left of the waterfall, pathways roofed by foliage led up to the Grotto of Venus.

Sara took the left-hand path, which had a shimmering white statue of a woman watching over it. Immediately it was pitch-dark all around her. She was briefly tempted to turn back and look for an easier path. But then she decided to trust her other four senses and simply go on. She heard gravel crunching beneath her feet. There was a last hint of summer in the air. After a while, her eyes became accustomed enough to the darkness for her to make out at least outlines close at hand. Leaves brushed her face; faint moonlight shone through the branches.

It must already have looked like this here more than a hundred years ago, she thought with sudden nostalgia. *I could almost expect to see the king himself turning the next corner.*

Suddenly Sara heard footsteps on the gravel behind her.

"Is there anyone there?" she asked hesitantly, but there was no reply.

She waited for a minute but sensed nothing unusual. When she finally went on, all was peaceful at first. But then she heard the crunch of footsteps again.

"Herr Lukas!" Sara called. "This isn't funny! I really would have expected better from you. Just because I said you were getting on in years, you don't have to sulk like a little kid. So just you listen to . . ."

Sara stopped as the footsteps behind her suddenly sped up. They were coming up the leafy path straight toward her. Now she could make out a gigantic figure about sixteen feet away. Even blacker than the surrounding darkness, the figure was a bear of a man, with broad shoulders and a long coat, from which he now produced something that looked like a small piece of cloth.

The next moment the giant was upon her.

Sara fell to the ground, buried under the colossus. She breathed in the pungent smell of his leather coat and tried to escape from under the man. But it was as if a rock were lying on top of her. Something hard pressed against her thigh.

My God, he's going to rape me! Here I am at a glittering millionaires' party with the interior minister of Bavaria, and this guy wants to rape me. I don't believe it.

She tried to scream, but the giant pressed his hairy hand down on her mouth.

"Where's the book?" she heard him growl. His voice was surprisingly melodious; Sara was reminded of a sonorous radio announcer. "The book, you slut! You know what I'm talking about."

Sara froze. She was finding it difficult to swallow. This wasn't a rape; it was an attack! Although she doubted whether that improved her situation much. Probably the opposite.

"I . . . I don't know what you're talking about at all," she gasped. "I don't know anything about any . . ."

The man hit her hard in the face. She felt warm blood running over her lips. Sara whimpered and was instantly ashamed of herself.

"All right, all right, I'll tell you!" The words came out of her mouth like a croak. "The secondhand bookseller has it. He's over there at the old hermitage!" It was a feeble evasion, but the man swallowed it. All the same, he hit her again in the pit of the stomach, so hard that she almost vomited.

"What are you two doing here?" he growled. "What's in that book to make you go poking around this place? What's hidden here?"

"I . . . I swear I don't know. There was an indication, but . . . but we've been looking for it since yesterday and we've found nothing. If anything was hidden, it must be somewhere else."

"If you're lying to me, I'll break every bone in your body. Understand? Every single bone!"

Sara nodded, and she felt tears and blood running down her cheeks. She remembered that the late Bernd Reiser's pistol was in her case back at the hotel. Stupidly, she had decided not to take it to the party with her—a mistake that she now regretted with all her heart.

"And now we're just dropping off to sleep," growled the bear, and now his voice sounded quite gentle again. "Shut your eyes and breathe deep. Here comes the sandman."

A white handkerchief with a slightly sweet smell appeared in front of Sara's face. She felt her senses failing her; all at once the world around her was like a wall of white rubber.

Chloroform! It's chloroform!

Sara reared up. At the last moment, she managed to turn her head aside. She dug her hands into the gravel and tried to crawl away, but the giant's hands took her in their viselike grasp and hauled her inexorably back. Her fingers scraped over the gravel like the tines of a rake; one by one, Sara's green-painted nails broke.

Suddenly she felt a hard, smooth object between her fingers. It took her several precious seconds to work out that it was one of her high-heeled shoes. She had dropped it when the man attacked.

Without a second thought, she took firm hold of the shoe and hit out behind her at random. She felt the sharp heel, which was only about the diameter of a penny, meet resistance and finally go through something soft.

There was a slippery sound, and then a hollow scream.

The hands let go of her, and Sara scrabbled out from under the giant like a lame beetle. When she frantically looked around, she saw the man with his hands to his face, writhing in pain. Blood flowed out between his fingers; he was groaning. Finally he turned and looked at her.

Sara uttered a low scream.

For the first time, she could see his face. It was as if a childhood nightmare had come into the park to take her away. Before her, in the darkness of the leafy path, she saw the grotesque face of a wicked medieval knight. The stranger had a small, neatly trimmed beard, a scar on his right cheek, and long black hair plaited into a braid. His left eye flashed with hatred.

His right eye was a black hole.

My God, I've put out his eye with the heel of my shoe.

"You bitch! I'll send you to hell for this!"

The giant straightened up, bellowing. With his one eye, he looked like an angry Cyclops. Sara didn't stop to think but plunged into the foliage at the side of the leafy path. Twigs and leaves brushed her face; she felt for a moment as if long, sticky arms were trying to hold her back, and then, finally, she was out on the other side.

Sara staggered into the sheltering darkness of the park, while she could still hear the cyclops roaring behind her. She almost thought she could sense the eyes of the shining white statues on her back, all those marble nymphs, dryads, and gods watching over Linderhof like guardian spirits.

They seemed to be following her flight with amusement.

MARIA 10.9.1885

Steven Lukas rubbed his eyes, and stared again at the letters carved into the trunk of the tree. The bark had grown, trying to obliterate the wounds made to it more than a century ago, but the word could still be made out easily.

MARIA . . . Was that possible?

Suddenly it all made sense. The love story in Marot's diary, the name in the linden tree, the capital letters. This must be the keyword! And he would almost have overlooked it. Not VENUS, not AMOR or EROS, but simply MARIA was the word that would decode the problem capitals in Marot's text. In fact the clue had been contained in the first word, LINDERHOF; a linden tree in which the name of Marot's secret love was carved forever. What was it that Marot had written at the end of the last chapter?

How was I to guess, at the time, that this girl would determine the fate of so many of us long after our deaths?

Steven looked around, searching. He must find Sara and tell her about his discovery. She would be able to try out his assumption with her new laptop. Then at last they would . . .

Suddenly Steven stopped, intuitively sensing that he was under observation. Very slowly, he turned his head until he was looking back in the direction of the party.

Beyond the basin of the fountain, about twenty yards away, stood the magician.

He had a torch in his hand and waved it to Steven. His top hat was gone, so that Steven saw only the hair smoothed down with gel and the high forehead where the white makeup suddenly stopped. Now the man held the torch directly in front of his face. He was smiling, and his white teeth shone in the flickering light. All at once Steven knew where he had seen him before. He had talked to him once, and it had not been a pleasant conversation. Steven remembered the man's words clearly.

I am interested in eyewitness accounts from the time of King Ludwig the Second. Do you have anything of that nature?

The magician standing by the side of the fountain was none other than the man in the traditional Bavarian suit—the man who had asked about the book in his shop, and who was presumably the leader of the Cowled Men. Now he was gesticulating as if to demand Steven's attention, and the next moment he had a black cloth in his hand.

Damn it all, it's not a cloth; it's . . .

The magician waved the hood back and forth like the severed head of a man on the block. The hood was like those worn by the Cowled Men.

In panic, Steven turned and ran up the garden terraces planted with colorful flowers to the Temple of Venus. As he reached the top, bathed in sweat, the magician still stood down by the fountain, waving—a tiny dot in the bright moonlight.

SARA RACED THROUGH the dark grounds of the castle toward the lights of the marquee. In front of her, not a hundred yards away, people were laughing, talking to one another, listening to Vivaldi. None of them, obviously, had noticed a fight taking place very close to them. When the art detective finally reached the lights, she stopped for the first time and looked around her.

The colossus had disappeared; the nightmare seemed to be over.

Sara took a deep breath and adjusted her dress, which was torn at the back and on one side. Her face and arms were scratched and dirty from the leaves, gravel, and earth; several of her fingernails were broken. Her stomach still hurt from the heavy blow it had suffered, but otherwise she seemed to be intact. All the same, she couldn't stop shivering.

I've put a man's eye out. I'll never forget that noise.

She stared across at the other party guests and wondered what to do. Alert the stewards at this Manstein Systems party? Call the police? There would certainly be questions; she would have to explain who she was and what she was doing there. Sooner or later the officers would ask about her companion, they would find out about Steven, and that would be the end of her search.

Once again her eyes wandered over the male guests, most of them in black, with their masks, cigars, and champagne glasses. Where the hell was Steven? She couldn't see him near the fountain, and there was no sign of him on the castle forecourt either. Sara could only hope that he hadn't run into another of those fanatics. She had to find him and then get out of there as fast as possible, with or without the keyword.

The keyword!

She felt a panicked surge of heat as she remembered that the diary was still in the safe in their hotel room. It wouldn't be long before that crazy knight or one of his henchmen began wondering where Sara and Steven had actually spent the last night. And the colossus didn't give the impression of a man who would find that a hotel safe presented him with insuperable difficulties.

After scrutinizing the terrain one last time, Sara hurried to the waiting coaches and had herself chauffeured to the hotel. The building's facade was adorned all over with little colored lights that cast warm light over the forecourt. Both inside and outside, guests were partying to the sound of loud laughter. Sara saw the corpulent and obviously tipsy tenor at the hotel bar with a couple of giggling blondes; older couples moved in time with a Strauss waltz in the blue and white breakfast room. Crowded with all the guests in their festive clothes, the hotel that had seemed so sleepy yesterday seemed to radiate an uncanny brightness.

Sara hurried up the stairs and stopped briefly at the door to their room. She put her ear to the thin wood but heard no suspicious noise on the other side. Finally she quietly unlocked the door, pushed down the handle, and swung the door inward without a sound.

The room was empty.

Relieved, Sara went to the safe in the wall directly beyond the door. She opened it and took out the diary; before setting out, they had hidden the little treasure chest, her laptop, and Steven's notes under the mattress. Once again she listened intently in case anyone was coming upstairs. The sound of music and laughter rose from the ground floor, but otherwise all was quiet.

Sara flung the book, the little chest, and everything else in her small case, along with her few items of clothing. To be on the safe side, she put the late Bernd Reiser's pistol in her purse. Then she quietly zipped up the case and turned back to the door, where she almost collided with a man in the dark. She uttered a hoarse scream before breathing a sigh of relief.

It was Steven Lukas.

"We have to talk, Frau Lengfeld," the bookseller gasped, his voice cracking. "The Cowled Men were lying in wait for us. It was the magician. And now I know what the keyword is. It's . . ."

"Wonderful. You can tell me all about it in the car. Now, come on."

Steven looked at her in surprise. "But why . . . ?"

"Because there's a knight six feet tall trying to steal the journal, and I've put out one of his eyes, that's why." Sara was already running downstairs with her case. "I'll tell you all the rest on the drive. Come on, for heaven's sake."

Steven followed her. They forged a way through the dancing, laughing hotel guests in the foyer, hurried across the forecourt, and at last they sat, exhausted, in Sara's Mini Cooper. For a few seconds there was nothing to be heard but their breathing and the soft sound of a waltz. The hotel stood among the forest like a gigantic Christmas tree decorated with thousands of ornaments; only a few yards behind it, all was pitch-dark.

"So you've cracked the code?" Sara finally asked, starting the engine. She put the car into first gear with shaking fingers. "Great. Now we can finally say goodbye to this castle with its deranged inhabitants—one-eyed giants, magicians, fat tenors . . . Talk about a degenerate society."

Tires squealing, the Mini rounded the corner of the hotel building.

HALF AN HOUR later, the car was driving steadily through the darkness of the Ammergau Alps, and Sara was on her third menthol. The fir trees stood like silent giants on the sides of the road, and few cars came the other way toward them. The only sound was the quiet humming of the engine.

They had told each other what had happened to them in the park, and Steven had also told her his theory about the keyword. The art detective had switched places with Steven and was now in the passenger seat with the new MacBook on her lap, the monitor shimmering with a ghostly effect in the night. She felt cold. The memory of the giant on the leafy pathway sent shivers down her spine.

"And you're sure the magician was that guy in Bavarian costume who came into your shop?" Sara asked yet again.

Steven nodded as he drove through the dense forest. "One hundred percent sure. He's the leader of the Cowled Men. When I ran, he showed me his hood."

"But why would he do that?"

"How do I know? To scare me? To let us know that they're after us?"

Sara sighed. "That knight certainly scared *me*. I guess he's something like a watchdog for those lunatics, and it's his job to get hold of the book for them."

"But suppose he has nothing to do with the Cowled Men at all?" Steven suggested. "Remember those two guys in the cellar of my shop? We still don't know who they were. And you said yourself you wouldn't really expect such crimes from the Cowled Men. Suppose it only *seems* to be about the death of Ludwig the Second? Suppose that's just a front? I'm beginning to feel that there's something much bigger at stake."

"Like what?"

They both fell silent as the Mini rolled on through the clear, starlit night with its quiet hum.

"Let's think about something nicer," said Sara at last. "For instance, your theory about the keyword." With a couple of rapid clicks at her MacBook she opened the decoding program she'd downloaded. "MARIA, then," she murmured. "Why not?"

"It's the keyword. I know it," Steven said, trying to concentrate at the same time on the dark road ahead of him. "Everything points to MARIA. Of course, that assumes that the journal really is using the Vigenère code."

"And if it isn't?"

"Then I abandon the book and go to the police. My nerves can't take any more. This is the last try—right or wrong."

Sara laughed quietly. "I'm afraid it's too late to turn back now, Herr Lukas. Those men don't look like they'd give up so easily. Even if the police believed you—we've already found out too much, and these other guys don't like it. Think what they did to my uncle."

"Are you suggesting that my only options are spending the rest of my life on the run or dying painfully by torture?" Steven asked wearily.

"Not if we move faster than our pursuers. If we solve the mystery, we may find out who's behind it." Sara tried to smile. "Now, let's see what dear Maria's dirty little secrets are."

She drew deeply one last time on her menthol cigarette, threw the stub out of the window, and tapped letter after letter into her laptop.

"The first coded word was QRCSOQNZO," she said, lost in thought.

"We've known that for ages. Don't pile on the tension like that."

"Hold your horses," Sara said. "My MacBook may have four processors with two point six gigahertz each, but I have to do the typing myself. That takes . . ."

She stopped, staring at the word on the screen.

"What is it?" Steven's voice almost broke. "Was I right? Is MARIA the keyword? Come on, say something!"

Sara nodded as she gazed at the screen. "Bingo, Herr Lukas," she whispered. "Looks like we get to play another round of the game. Which doesn't mean that we'll be any the wiser."

"What do you mean?" Steven asked, baffled.

"See for yourself."

The bookseller cast the screen a quick look as he drove. The next moment he almost drove the Mini down a steep slope. He wrenched the wheel around just in time.

Input	QRCSOQNZO
Output	ERLKOENIG

"ERLKOENIG?" Steven shook his head, puzzled.

"A ballad by Goethe about a father, his sick child, and the Erl-King," Sara said. The laptop had slid off her knees. Grimacing with pain, she rubbed her elbow. "And please keep your eyes on the road."

"I know who the Erl-King is, Frau Lengfeld. But what, for heaven's sake, does the title of a poem, however famous, tell us?"

Sara shrugged. "*You're* the antiquarian bookseller. My line is art, not interpreting the boring poems you have to read in school." She picked her laptop up from the dark footwell where the screen was still shimmering away. "Thank God this thing is shock-proof."

"Try the other words."

Sara typed the next coded words into the computer and finally leaned back. "Oh, wonderful," she muttered. "BELSAZAR, THAL, ZAUBERIN, LORELEI, WINSPERG, FLUCH, RING, SIEGERICH, TAUCHER, FISCHER, LEGENDE, BALLADE . . . Can you make sense of any of that?"

"'Belsazar,' 'Lorelei,' 'Taucher' . . . They're all titles of German ballads," Steven said after a little hesitation. "'Belshazzar,' 'Lorelei,' 'The Diver.' Then 'Fisherman,' *'Der Fischer,'* 'The Angler,' as far as I know, it's by Goethe, too, and *'Fluch,'* 'curse,' may refer to Ludwig Uhland's ballad 'The Singer's Curse,' *'Des Sängers Fluch.'* But what's the point of it all?" He struck the wheel angrily, raising a plaintive little toot from the horn. "Damn it, I'm beginning to think that Marot was simply having a joke with the whole book."

"He goes to a lot of time and trouble for a joke." Sara whistled quietly through her teeth. "I don't suppose 'WDC' is the title of another poem, is it?"

Steven frowned. "What do you mean?"

"I've just entered another coded word, from the next chapter. You haven't transliterated it yet. Looks like we need a different code from here on."

"Oh shit," Steven quietly said. "And where are we going to find that?"

Sara rapidly leafed through Marot's well-worn diary. "I don't know shorthand," she said at last, "but I can read words in capital letters all right. And the next words that Marot wrote that way are HERRENCHIEMSEE and KOENIG. Presumably we won't find out about the titles of those poems until we go to Herrenchiemsee. And as an additional hint, our friend Marot left us that worn-out old word KOENIG for the king."

"Ludwig's castle on the lake, the Chiemsee." Steven laughed despairingly. "My God, that's a whole island! How on earth are we going to find anything there?"

"I don't know," Sara said, staring while lost in thought at the two cones of light cast by the headlights on the road ahead. "But I think this is the time to ask someone for help. Someone who really knows his way around all this Ludwig stuff." She pointed to an exit road that suddenly appeared before them in the darkness. "Turn off there to the right. We're going to see Uncle Lu."

Lancelot held his hand over his right eye socket, from which reddish fluid still ran. His pain and hatred threatened to drive him mad. She had escaped him. A woman! How the hell could that have happened?

It had been pure luck that he'd recognized her in her mask, among all the guests. Erec and Bors had taken a lot of photos of her outside the antiquarian bookseller's shop, but most of them had been shaky or blurred. Basically, it had been his unusually strong hunting instinct at work again. As a former bodyguard, he had developed a sense of what people were like as a whole. He recognized victims by the way they walked and held themselves, or by their nervous movements. Sometime he even thought he could smell fear in their sweat.

As the bookseller had not been with her, it had taken Lancelot some time to recognize the woman. Then he hadn't been able to get close to her among all the guests. But when she finally started along the leafy pathway, he had thought she would be easy game.

She'll pay for this. By God, she'll pay for it.

Half-blinded, he staggered toward the castle, almost knocking into a couple of lovers who fled, screeching, at the sight of him. Finally the giant ducked down behind a hedge and scrutinized the loud, lively activity of the guests from there. There wasn't a sign of the bitch and the bookseller.

Where could they be?

Next moment Lancelot remembered what the woman had said just now: they'd already been searching since *yesterday* and found nothing. So they'd stayed overnight, and where did people stay overnight here?

Lancelot's glance moved slowly to the hotel, and he smiled. If his luck held, the birds hadn't flown yet, and he could give them a nice surprise in their room. He would also call a doctor from the hotel, although he was afraid there would be no saving his eye. But someone would have to pay for that. The giant brushed the dirt off his suit, pressed his white handkerchief to his bloodstained eye socket, and hurried toward the Castle Hotel.

The night porter on duty at reception was tired and unshaven. He had seen too many guests at too many glittering parties already. But when Lancelot leaned over to him, he held his breath.

"What . . . what can I do for you?" he stammered.

"My wife has a room here, with her lover, if you see what I mean . . ." Lancelot's lips distorted into a menacing grin. "The slut's a brunette, wearing a low-cut evening dress and a little red jacket, kind of thing a tart would wear. I'd like to have the key of that room."

"Was that . . . did the other guy do that?" the porter hesitantly asked, pointing to the bloodstained handkerchief held over the right-hand side of Lancelot's face. When the giant nodded, the trembling man handed him the key.

"Room 113," he whispered, secretly picturing what this monster would do to his wife up in the top-floor bedroom. Maybe he'd better call the police?

Without another word, Lancelot ran upstairs. But when he saw the door standing ajar, he knew he had come too late.

Hell and damnation. They're gone!

The room was empty, the beds unmade, two dirty plates and two wineglasses stood on the table; that was all. But on the floor near the door lay something that looked as if it had been forgotten in their headlong flight. Lancelot bent and picked it up.

It was an envelope full of crumpled brochures. They showed, in bright color, Ludwig's three castles: Linderhof, Herrenchiemsee, and Neuschwanstein. The brochures looked well-worn, as if someone had spent a long time poring over them.

Suddenly Lancelot remembered something else that the woman had said.

If anything was hidden, it must be somewhere else . . .

Lancelot smiled. For a brief moment the pain of his eye socket was forgotten. He pocketed the brochures and went downstairs to call a doctor.

That bitch was going to wish she'd never been born.

· 16 ·

I<small>T WAS THE LAST BUILDING IN A HAMLET</small> somewhere in the Bavarian Allgäu area. A low-built, crooked house with a little front garden, where the last sunflowers of the year were blooming, stood right beside the outskirts of the forest. With its weathered fence, its window shutters painted sky blue, and the old stone chimney from which thick black smoke was rising, it reminded Steven of a witch's house. He could practically smell gingerbread. It was early morning; the sun was slowly rising behind the mist clinging to the trees.

"So this is where the leading expert on Ludwig lives?" Steven asked skeptically. "I'd have expected a minicastle, or a late nineteenth-century villa."

"Albert Zöller may be slightly eccentric, but no one knows more about the Fairy-tale King." Sara wearily massaged her temples and suppressed a yawn. "Almost everyone who writes a book about Ludwig the Second makes a pilgrimage to this place sooner or later. Uncle Lu's knowledge is legendary. Leave the car there in front, beside the old oak." She pointed to a stunted tree not far from the house. "Over the last few years, he's retreated from public life more and more. We won't alarm him more than we have to."

"What, by arriving in a car?" Steven raised his eyebrows in surprise.

"Let's say he'd probably rather see us arrive in a horse-drawn cab. But you'll pass nicely as a gentleman of the old school."

The art detective smiled, while Steven looked critically down at himself. He had decided to keep his evening suit from yesterday on; he liked it much better than Sara's ex-boyfriend's casual, loose-fitting garments. Over it he wore a close-fitting black coat that they had also bought yesterday afternoon. In fact the bookseller did look a little like a nineteenth-century gentleman on the verge of middle age.

All I need is a top hat and a walking stick, he thought, *and my grandfather would be proud of me.*

Sara had changed her clothes. Her green woolen dress and hooded jacket were slightly creased, mainly because she and Steven had spent the last few hours sleeping in the car at a roadside picnic area. However, after two cigarettes and a cardboard cup of coffee from a gas station in the Allgäu, the art detective now made a remarkably fresh impression.

"Are you really sure we ought to let this Zöller in on our secrets?" Steven asked as he parked the Mini under the colorful fall leaves of the oak tree. "I mean, I'm still wanted by the police."

"I don't think Uncle Lu would turn us in. And even if he did, we have to take the risk. If we must, we'll just go back on the run." Sara got out and went toward the crooked little house. She pushed the garden gate, which opened on squealing hinges. "If we want to crack the cipher, then we need the help of Albert Zöller. He and my uncle have known each other for decades, and they were always in touch about Ludwig. As far as I know, before he retired, Zöller was an engine driver for German Railways, but the Fairy-tale King has always been his passion. Paul thought that Uncle Lu was way ahead of the experts in his knowledge of the king's last years. He's drawn up a precise account of every day of Ludwig's life."

"Why 'Uncle Lu'?" Steven asked as he followed Sara through the front garden, with its harvested vegetable and herb beds. "His name's Albert, right?"

Sara turned with a twinkle in her eye. "Can't you work that out for yourself?"

She pulled a rusty chain near the entrance, and a bell rang. After a while they heard heavy, dragging footsteps. When the door finally opened, Steven instinctively took a step back. The man standing in front of them in a crumpled shirt and stained pants was nearly six feet tall. He was broadly built, not to say stout, with fleshy cheeks through which little red veins ran. His full head of hair was salt-and-pepper colored and as untidy as if he had just got out of bed. Steven guessed Albert Zöller's age as at least seventy. It was clear to the bookseller at once why Sara called him Uncle Lu.

If the Fairy-tale King had lived a few decades longer, he'd have looked just like Zöller. The thought, unbidden, shot through his mind. *Well, he'd probably have died of gout and heart disease first. This man must have a remarkable constitution.*

"Yes?" the bear in front of them growled. He wore rimless reading glasses that looked ridiculously small on his broad face. Despite the early hour, Sara and Steven had obviously disturbed his studies. "If you're Jehovah's Witnesses, go to hell. I'm the Antichrist."

Sara bobbed an old-fashioned curtsey. "Forgive us for calling on you so early, Herr Zöller. I'm Professor Paul Liebermann's niece, and . . ."

"Liebermann?" The gruff old man's face instantly became friendlier. He looked at Sara with concern. "My God, I read about that gruesome murder in the newspaper. Dear old Paul. I . . . I'm so sorry." His voice had a pleasantly Bavarian note to it, almost like the voice of a kindly fairy-tale uncle.

"Thank you, Herr Zöller. Uncle Paul often talked about you." The art detective took a deep breath before going on. "To be frank, we're here because we want to find out more about his death. We think the murder had something to do with the mysteries surrounding King Ludwig the Second." She pointed to Steven beside her. "My friend here, an antiquarian bookseller from Munich, was the last person to see my uncle alive. Paul left something behind with him. Something mysterious, and we need your help."

"Just a moment." Uncle Lu frowned, which made him look like an angry bison. He scrutinized Steven without moving. What felt like an eternity passed before Zöller finally moved again.

"Aren't you the fellow the police are looking for in connection with Paul's murder?" he finally asked.

"Herr Zöller, I give you my word that Herr Lukas has nothing to do with it," Sara said soothingly. "It's all a big misunderstanding. If you'll let us in, I can explain everything to you."

"Your word of honor, eh?" Uncle Lu shook his broad head thoughtfully, as if he were x-raying the bookseller through his reading glasses. "Very well," he said at last, "but only because you're Paul's niece."

The old man abruptly turned to the house, almost bumping into the door frame. Sara and Steven followed him into a little room that seemed to be both kitchen and living room.

There was an old-fashioned white enamel stove against the back wall. A scratched table with several books open on it stood in one corner. In another, they saw a sofa and a TV set; Steven thought it was probably still a black-and-white one. A door with flowered wallpaper over it led to a backroom.

"I was just going to make myself tea and work on my book," Uncle Lu said. "Would you like some tea yourselves?"

Steven nodded. "Thank you, yes. What kind of book are you writing?"

"It's on Ludwig's connection with Edgar Allan Poe." Zöller shrugged his shoulders and filled three cracked cups with a steaming-hot brown brew. "Not that I expect any publishing house to take an interest in it. Just like my last five books. All the same, plenty of journalists come knocking at my door. Good God, what are you gawking at in that stupid way?"

Steven jumped. He had been staring at the stout old man. His likeness to Ludwig II was indeed striking.

"It's only because . . . er . . ." he began carefully. But Uncle Lu interrupted him with an impatient gesture.

"Yes, yes, I know that I look like him," he growled. "I was often invited to act as his double at meetings of those loyal to the king's memory. But I won't have any more to do with those demented royalists. Too many nut cases, not a serious scholar among them." Zöller slurped his tea with relish. "Well, never mind that. You're here because of Paul. So how can I help you?"

Sara quickly cleared her throat, and then she began telling him their story—about her uncle's murder, the find of the little treasure chest, the mysterious diary, and their search for the crucial keyword. She left out only their pursuit at Linderhof and the Cowled Men. As she told her tale, Uncle Lu sat there as if turned to stone. He seemed to have forgotten his tea entirely. When Sara came to the end of the story at last, he said nothing for some time. Then he spoke up.

"This little chest with the diary," he began quietly. "Could I have a look at it?"

"Of course." Steven unzipped his backpack and took the container out. Reverently, as if he were in a church, Zöller stroked the lacquered wood; then he lifted the lid and took out the photographs, the lock of hair, and the book. He arranged them on the table as if they were magical artifacts.

"Can it be possible?" he whispered. "Did he really write it all down?"

"What do you mean?" Sara asked, looking attentively at the old man. "Have you heard about this book before?"

"There have been . . . theories," Uncle Lu replied hesitantly. "Nothing precise. Shortly after the king's death, Dr. Schleiss von Loewenfeld and Theodor Marot expressed their opinions to a small circle of friends. But the sources are vague. And now this . . ."

He carefully opened the diary and looked surprised to see the secret writing.

"It's the Shelton's shorthand that I told you about," Sara said, and pointed to Steven. "Herr Lukas has managed to decipher it. We've also deciphered part of a Vigenère code. But as for the titles of those poems . . ." She sighed. "To be honest, we're at a loss."

"Ludwig and very likely Theodor Marot, too, were profoundly romantic characters." Uncle Lu leafed thoughtfully through the yellowed pages of the diary. "So it's not surprising if the assistant physician used those poems as a code. More interesting is *what* he wanted to encode. And above all, why Paul was killed for getting involved." He looked deep into Steven's eyes. "I'll believe that you had nothing to do with his murder, Herr Lukas. But if you're lying to me, I'll deal with you in exactly the same way as those deranged men dealt with Paul. Understand?"

"On my word of honor, I really had nothing to do with . . ." Steven began, but Sara interrupted him.

"You haven't told us yet what you know about the book," she said in a loud voice, changing the subject. "Obviously it's far more than we've managed to find out."

"Very well." Breathing heavily, Uncle Lu rose from his chair and adjusted his pants. His stomach hung over his belt like a squashed medicine ball. "It's about time I let you into my holy of holies. And bring that with you, for heaven's sake." He pointed to the little box containing the diary. "It mustn't fall into the wrong hands no matter what."

Without another word, he shuffled toward the door at the back of the room.

"You're . . . er, renovating?"

Disappointed, Steven looked around the room on the other side of the door. He had expected a library, a study, at least a desk covered by documents. But what he saw was a combination of a living room and a temporary toolshed. Newspapers were stacked on a shabby armchair; an old Bakelite telephone stood on an otherwise-empty bookcase along the back wall. To the left was a row of old crates that had once held fruit, with assorted drills, screwdrivers, and a sledge-hammer sticking out of them.

"Forgive the mess, but I have to extend the place again," Uncle Lu said. "And since my wife died—God rest her soul—my housekeeping here has left something to be desired. You get to feel increasingly lonely."

Steven nodded sympathetically, although most of his sympathy was for the dead woman who had put up with this eccentric for so long. He also wondered where Zöller was planning to build an extension in this little house with all its nooks and crannies. At a loss, the bookseller looked at Sara, who merely shrugged.

"What's the point of this?" Steven whispered to her. "The man's a compulsive hoarder. How is he going to help us?"

"Shut up," Sara hissed. "Look over there."

Steven turned back to Uncle Lu, who now stood by the empty bookcase and pushed it aside, breathing heavily. Behind it, an opening came into view, with a flight of stairs leading down beyond it.

"Careful, the stairs are very steep," Zöller said, going ahead. In surprise, Sara and Steven followed him along the narrow downward climb, and finally reached a dark cellar. When Zöller switched on the light, the bookseller gasped.

The room was at least as large as the entire ground floor of the house above them. Shelves of the finest grained cherrywood reached to the ceiling on all sides and were crammed with books, folios, and files. In the middle of the cellar stood an old mahogany table, with a brand-new computer, a laser printer, and a scanner on it. Halogen lamps fixed to steel cables bathed the scene in muted light.

"My cabinet of curiosities," Uncle Lu announced. "It contains everything that has been written about King Ludwig." He pointed to the opposite wall. "And there's another room behind one of the bookcases; I'm extending it at the moment. The torrent of rumors and information about the Fairy-tale King never dries up."

Steven stared, open-mouthed, at the vast archive. He knew several large private collections, but this exceeded anything he could have imagined.

"How . . . how many books do you have here?" he asked reverently.

"Exactly three thousand one hundred fifty-seven," Uncle Lu proudly replied. "Some of them are in Japanese. Some are even in Finnish. As well as countless files, newspaper reports, and much other information that I've scanned onto my hard drive. It's astonishing what an echo a single man can set going all over the world. But here we have the most valuable item."

Zöller went up to a framed oil painting of the king hung between two bookcases. When he took it down, a safe came into view. The old man laboriously entered the combination and finally took out a bundle that he placed reverently on the desk.

Only at a second glance did Steven realize that he was looking at a torn, pale summer coat. On the back there were two black-rimmed holes the size of marbles. The entire garment was flecked with bloodstains.

"The king's coat," Albert Zöller whispered. "The coat he was wearing on the night of the murder."

Sara stuck her finger into one of the frayed black holes. "They really were made by gunshots," she said. She turned to Zöller. "But how do you know that this is really the coat the king was wearing at the time of his death? It could have belonged to anyone."

Uncle Lu shook his head vigorously. "The coat comes from the estate of an old countess who credibly convinced several people in the 1950s that it had belonged to the king. She herself always insisted that Ludwig had been shot and the coat exchanged at the scene of the crime."

"What became of this countess?" Steven asked.

"She died in an unexplained fire in her apartment. Luckily the coat was saved from the flames."

Sara frowned. "Do you really mean she was killed because she knew the truth about the king's death?"

"I don't mean anything." Uncle Lu shrugged. "All the same, I think it's better for as few people as possible to know that this coat is in my hands."

"But what does all this have to do with Marot's diary?" interrupted Steven impatiently.

"Wait a minute," Zöller snapped. "You'll see soon enough."

Once again he went to the little safe, and this time he came back with three notebook-sized portrait sketches mounted on a piece of cardboard. They looked old and were stained. Steven thought he saw the marks left by water when it dried.

"These drawings are by the portrait painter Hermann Kaulbach, who carried out many commissions for Ludwig the Second," Uncle Lu said. With his fat fingers, he pointed to the two outer pictures. "These two are the personal physician, Max Schleiss von Loewenfeld, and the king's equerry, Richard Hornig. There are rumors that they were on Lake Starnberg, with Marot and Kaulbach, on the night of the murder. The sketches were done in the rain, very fast, probably on that ill-omened day, the thirteenth of June 1886. You ought to recognize the man in the central picture for yourselves." Zöller paused while Steven and Sara stared at the portrait of a stout middle-aged gentleman with a beard. His eyes were closed, his mouth open in a silent scream. Dark blood flowed from the left corner of his mouth.

It was the face of the king.

"Some people claim that Kaulbach sketched Ludwig the Second only minutes after his death," Zöller said in a low voice. "Loewenfeld and Marot are said to have been there, and were, so to speak, the first eyewitnesses. The physician's assistant spoke of murder later, and so did Hornig, the equerry. And Loewenfeld was silenced." He heaved a deep sigh. "I haven't been able to prove all this yet. But now here you are, with this diary . . ."

"Can you explain why Uncle Paul had to die for the sake of that little box?" Sara asked. "Obviously someone still cares a lot about this little book, even after more than a century."

Uncle Lu scratched his unshaven, fleshy face and looked up at the ceiling.

"Let me think. A scholar perhaps, wanting to grab the glory for himself? Or maybe the Wittelsbachs. Large parts of the archive of the royal house are still not accessible to the public. The family is very anxious for Ludwig's death to remain a mystery."

"Do you think they would kill for it?" Steven asked skeptically.

Zöller shook his head. "Not really. Although I'm sure the Wittelsbachs would very much like to know what's in the book. But they have barred all access to any form of enlightenment about the matter for decades. If it were finally possible to examine Ludwig's body in St. Michael's Church in Munich, then the cause of his death could surely be established." He sighed deeply. "But you might as well ask them to sell Neuschwanstein to the Japanese. The Wittelsbachs don't play games, especially when it's about Ludwig, a member of their family."

"How about the Cowled Men?" Sara asked." Could they have anything to do with it?"

Uncle Lu laughed so much that his cheeks shook like a fat dog's jowls. "Those crazy bastards? The last time I heard anything of them, they wanted to mint euros with Ludwig on them, because they don't like the Prussian eagle." He leaned over to Sara. "Did you know there's a theory that the Cowled Men are just the invention of a Cologne advertising agency? An interesting idea."

Steven was tempted for a moment to tell Albert Zöller that that crazy bunch had lain in wait for him twice already, but he decided against it. They wanted Uncle Lu to help them. It would be better not to alarm the old man unnecessarily, not that he looked afraid of very much.

Sara changed the subject. "If your story is true, and Loewenfeld and Marot really were eyewitnesses, then it will certainly say so in the book," she began. "And someone or other wants to prevent its coming to light. Only who, and why? And what about those coded words? Obviously there's some far greater secret they don't want aired."

Wearily, she rubbed her eyes. "I suppose there's no other option—we must decipher the rest of the diary. Maybe we'll discover the murderer that way." She pointed to Steven's backpack, which held the diary. "Herr Lukas and I think the next keyword is hidden at Herrenchiemsee."

"Herrenchiemsee?" Zöller asked, astonished.

Steven nodded. "It's the next word written in capitals in Marot's account. Like Linderhof before it. And Marot left us another clue by adding the word KOENIG, king, in capitals. But I rather doubt that we'll find anything at Herrenchiemsee. After all, the island there is much larger than the castle grounds of Linderhof."

Uncle Lu's eyes lit up. "So there's a puzzle to be solved," he whispered. "Am I right in assuming that you want me to help you?"

Sara smiled. "Would you do that?"

"Would I do that?" Once again Zöller burst out laughing, so that his big belly hopped up and down like a being with a life of its own. "You'd have to tie me up and leave me here to make sure I *don't* help you." Suddenly he was serious again. Puffing as he rose from his chair, he went over to the bookshelves and picked out a stack of thick folios. "Better begin right away," he murmured, lost in thought. "There are about a hundred books on Herrenchiemsee here. Do you think we can fit them all in your car?"

Sᴏᴍᴇᴛʜɪɴɢ ɪɴ ᴛʜᴇ ᴄᴀʀ ʙᴇᴇᴘᴇᴅ, but Steven couldn't make out what it was. He twiddled the radio, checked the air conditioning, and tapped the instrument panel, but the beeping went on.

"What the hell is that?" he asked, looking helplessly at Sara, who was now behind the wheel again. "Is your Mini by any chance giving up the ghost?"

"If so it's because we're overloaded." Sara pointed behind her to where Uncle Lu sat on the rear seat like a fat giant in a toy car. Zöller's massive head brushed against the roof, and his knees poked Steven's back through the upholstery. All the same, the old man seemed to be pleased with life, mainly on account of the laundry basket that was slipping back and forth beside him at every bend in the road. It was crammed with books. Now and then Uncle Lu picked up one of these large tomes, leafed through it, and made notes on a greasy little writing pad.

"The Herreninsel in the Chiemsee covers almost five hundred seventy acres, and the lake has a circumference of more than four miles," he growled without looking up. "A small world unto itself. Ludwig even wanted to build a little railroad on it, like the one on the fictional island of Lummerland in Michael Ende's book. You know

Jim Button and Luke the Engine Driver, don't you? Ever heard of that children's book?"

"Herr Zöller, all I can hear right now is beeping," Steven said, his nerves on edge. "And it's driving me crazy."

"Oh, sorry." Uncle Lu put his hand to his right ear and fiddled with something. The beeping stopped. "My hearing aid. Must have misadjusted it."

"Oh." Wearily, Steven closed his eyes and tried to get a bit of rest. They had been on the road for almost three hours, and the car smelled of male sweat, cow dung, and the smoke of Sara's menthol cigarettes. It was making him feel slightly unwell. The drive had taken them along small, winding country roads, through quiet villages, past chapels, and into the Chiemgau district. They had twice had to wait as a farmer drove his herd of cows across the road at a leisurely pace, and once they lost their way so badly that the Mini almost got stuck in a stinking manure heap in a blind alley. Now, at last, the blue waters of the Chiemsee opened out before them, looking near enough to touch and apparently going all the way to the first mountains of the Alps. All around, green hills and meadows lay in the fall sunlight like something out of a glossy brochure from the Upper Bavaria Tourist Board.

"Damn bleak around here," Sara muttered, lighting herself a new cigarette. "I really don't know why so many city dwellers want to move to the country. It stinks of cow shit."

"Ludwig loved these lonely places," came Uncle Lu's deep voice from the back seat. "He disliked Munich. If he'd had his way, he would probably have lived in a remote Alpine valley with a few mountain farmers."

Steven caught himself thinking that he could nurture such dreams himself, although in his case they didn't feature stinking manure heaps, another of which had just appeared by the side of the road.

He rubbed his eyes and stared yet again at the list he had made after decoding the puzzle words in Marot's diary. So far they had deciphered thirteen words with the keyword MARIA. All were clearly the titles, or partial titles, of poems, although some of them meant nothing at all to Steven. Others, however, could be found in any school textbook. He had written down all the poems in order, with the names of their authors if he knew them. But he could still make nothing of them.

"*Erlkönig*" (Johann Wolfgang von Goethe), "The Erl-King"

"*Belsazar*" (Heinrich Heine), "Belshazzar"

"*Thal*"?

"*Zauberin*"?

"*Lorelei*" (Heinrich Heine), "The Lorelei"

"*Winsperg*"?

"*Fluch*"? (perhaps "*Des Sängers Fluch*," Ludwig Uhland?), "The Singer's Curse"

"*Ring*"? (perhaps "*Der Ring des Polykrates*," Friedrich Schiller), "The Ring of Polycrates"

"*Siegerich*"?

"*Taucher*" (Friedrich Schiller), "The Diver"

"*Der Fischer*" (Goethe), "The Angler"

"*Legende*"?

"*Ballade*"?

"I really don't know what Theodor Marot was trying to tell us with these poems," he mused. "The ones I know are all from the German Romantic and Classical periods. And they look back at the Middle Ages or other distant times. But apart from that, I can't see anything in common among them."

"Presumably Ludwig would have liked to live in a poem like those," Sara said. "Or in a booming opera by Richard Wagner. We can only hope we find another clue soon." She pointed to the laptop, which was now in a lady's purse between Steven's feet. "By the way, I transferred all the other puzzle words in the diary to my laptop last night. See for yourself."

IDT, G, NFTQM, WFIFBTQT, GQT, ıDT, WQI, ID,
WFIFBGQTP, WFT, IFGQMT, IFI, IQT, J, JG, JT , W, JTI, JG,
JG, J, JG, JG, JG, IT

"There's one interesting thing," she said thoughtfully. "The words get shorter and shorter. At the end of the diary, most of them consist of just one or two letters."

"Why don't we simply try KOENIG as the key?" Steven suggested, but Sara dismissed the idea.

"I've already tried that. Along with the other usual suspects such as LUDWIG, REX, or ROI. No luck. Nothing comes up. It must be something less obvious."

Steven sighed and looked ahead to where the lake now clearly shone among the hills. At close quarters, it almost looked like an Alpine inland sea.

"Look, we can already see the Herreninsel!" Uncle Lu bellowed in his ear from the back seat. "And the smaller one beyond is the Fraueninsel with its convent of Benedictine nuns. What a picturesque place for a castle."

"And what a terrific tourist magnet." Sara pointed to a ferry, small but crammed with passengers. It plied between the islands and a harbor on the mainland. "Let's hope we don't have to stand around too long. Your books had better stay in the car. I guess you don't want to drag them all over the island."

Albert Zöller gave her a conspiratorial wink. "You just leave that to me. You won't be sorry you brought good old uncle Lu along on this mysterious trip."

A QUARTER OF an hour later, they had parked the Mini down by the harbor.

Little rowboats in which fishermen mended their nets gently rocked on the water, tied up to countless landing stages. On the right there was a jetty bleached by rain, where a paddle steamer whistled as it waited to put out. Somewhere a horn hooted. When Steven looked around, he saw a puffing steam locomotive pulling green cars trundling along behind the boathouses, looking as if it had come straight from the nineteenth century.

"Pinch me, Herr Lukas," Sara said, looking at the locomotive in amazement. "We haven't by any chance just time traveled back into Marot's diary, have we?"

"The paddle steamer dates from 1926, and the steam locomotive made its maiden trip just after Ludwig's death," said Albert Zöller behind them. "So you're right to some extent, Frau Lengfeld. The people here like it when the world changes as little as possible. And so do the tourists." He pointed to the jetty, where Steven only now saw the noisy crowd of tourists waiting for the next steamer trip. They seemed to come from all over the world and were happily snapping photos, from all possible angles, of the locomotive, the steamer, and the fishermen mending their nets.

"Well, I'll see what can be done," Uncle Lu said. Puffing, he heaved the laundry basket full of books out of the car and went, without further comment, toward the rather dilapidated boathouses to their right. Sara and Steven followed a little way behind him.

"Do you know what he's planning to do?" the bookseller asked.

Sara shrugged. "Maybe he's looking for some other way to get to the island. That could only be a good thing for us. See that green Bentley over there?"

Steven turned to look and saw an elegant vehicle, polished until it shone, with darkened windows. It was parked inconspicuously beyond the locomotive with its engine running. "What about it?"

"I may be wrong, but I think it's been following us," Sara whispered. "I've seen it behind us at least twice in the last few hours. And now here it is at the harbor."

"Oh my God. Do you think it's the police?"

The art detective shrugged again. "I don't know how they could have found us. And the police probably don't drive green Bentleys, even when they're out of uniform. Although I bet they'd like to."

Steven glanced back at the car, which could be only vaguely made out through the steam from the locomotive. Now the driver stepped on the gas, and the Bentley disappeared, tires squealing, into a narrow alley leading up to the town.

"We ought not to say anything about this to Albert," Steven said quietly. "Two of us worrying are quite enough."

By now they had reached the boathouses. A wiry man with a wrinkled, weathered face was sitting on a crumbling landing stage, dangling his legs over the planks. He wore green oilskins and was morosely chewing the stem of a pipe; below him, a decrepit boat in urgent need of a fresh coat of paint rocked on the water. As Uncle Lu approached the fisherman, the latter glanced up and uttered an exclamation of surprise. He spat noisily in the water.

"Well, I'll be damned. It's Lu!" he crowed cheerfully. "For a moment I thought the king was back on his island." The fisherman rose and approached Albert Zöller with arms outspread.

"Don't talk nonsense, Alois," Uncle Lu growled. "The king was never as fat as me, even on the dissecting table." He heaved the basketful of books up on the landing stage, then shook hands with Alois. "But thanks for the compliment. Well, how about it? Would you do us a favor and row the three of us over to the Herreninsel?"

Alois put his head on one side and inspected Zöller's companions disapprovingly. "Are they tourists, or are they friends of yours? Because I'm sick and tired of foreigners. There're more of 'em here than whitefish in the Chiemsee."

"They're people on our side, Alois," Zöller told him with a grave expression. "The king needs our help."

The fisherman raised his eyebrows. "The king? Well, of course that's different."

In silence, the little man helped Sara and Steven into his ancient, dilapidated boat. They were followed by the heavy weight of the laundry basket, and the even heavier weight of Uncle Lu, tilting the boat on its side at a dangerous angle.

"Move over to the middle, Lu," Alois said, pushing off from the landing stage with the oars. "Or you'll end up drowned dead like our Ludwig, and that'd be a shame."

Grinning, Zöller made his way to the middle of the seat and then turned to Sara and Steven.

"Many of the simple folk of the Chiemgau area still support the king," he whispered softly. "Alois won't give us away. Most Bavarians stick together when it comes to Ludwig the Second."

"Sorry, but are we talking about the same king as the one who died one hundred twenty-five years ago?" Steven interrupted, smiling. "You talk as if he were still alive."

Zöller put his head on one side and looked at Steven in surprise. "And isn't he?" Then he roared with laughter. "To be honest," he finally said, puffing to get his breath back, "Ludwig the Second is far more than a fat drowned body to many Bavarians. He's their identity and a myth at the same time, and as a myth, of course he lives forever." Uncle Lu pointed to the morose fisherman behind them dipping his oars steadily into the water. "Every myth has its keeper of the Grail, and Alois is one of them. I've always known him as a loyalist. We once met every year at Berg on Lake Starnberg. Alois backs the chloroform theory, but otherwise he's a reasonable man."

"The chloroform theory?" Steven asked, at a loss.

"Its adherents claim that Gudden anesthetized Ludwig with chloroform and then threw him into the water," Sara said. "One of at least a dozen theories about the death of the king."

"Yes, indeed." Zöller smiled and let his right hand dangle in the cool water of the lake. "There's even a theory that only a waxwork dummy was buried at St. Michael's in Munich, and the real king lived on for decades as a wealthy private citizen. As you see, Herr Lukas, by comparison with King Ludwig, all the conspiracy theories about the Kennedy assassination are just cheap soap operas."

By now they were approaching the wooded shore of the island, which was surrounded by a dense belt of reed beds. A small chapel stood on a little promontory, with a boathouse and a landing stage beside it, and the fisherman was rowing that way.

"Want me to collect you later?" Alois asked as he made the boat fast to a post. "They're renovating the Castle Hotel—you won't be able to stay the night there."

"I'll call you when we're ready," Uncle Lu replied. "I'll leave the books in the chapel until then, if that's all right."

Waving to them, the fisherman put out on the lake, while Zöller dragged the heavy laundry basket into the chapel. Then they set off along the path to the middle of the island. Woods and meadows spread out ahead of them, and to their right they saw a fenced paddock.

"Is that the castle?" Steven asked, pointing to a group of white buildings standing on a rise farther up the path.

Uncle Lu shook his head. "No, only the former monastery, probably the oldest in all Bavaria. After secularization, the church was turned into a brewery, and other parts of the building were simply torn down. A real shame." He kicked a stone by the side of the paddock, and some of the horses in it galloped away, neighing. "Then King Ludwig bought the island for 350,000 gulden in 1873, and moved into some rooms in the old monastery of the Augustinian Canons, a vantage point from which he could watch the building work. It was his dream to create a new Versailles here."

"Just like Linderhof," Steven said. "Ludwig must have been obsessed with the Sun King."

"Yes, indeed, and this castle was originally to have been built at Linderhof, but the space there turned out to be too small." Zöller's eyes passed over the green landscape, the crystalline blue of the Chiemsee, and the Alps. "Here, Ludwig began by leveling out the whole site. Woods were cut down, hills flattened. The place had its own housing for the workmen. There were smiths, steam-driven saws, a railroad, too. And all that just for him and his dreams."

"Well, Herrenchiemsee now belongs to the whole world, particularly tourists," Sara said. "Ludwig would turn in his grave if he could see it."

They reached the abbey and looked down on the little harbor, where a ferry had just put in with a new cargo of tourists. A brightly clad, noisy crowd made its way along the narrow path leading past the old monastery and into the woods.

"The castle stands almost exactly in the middle of the island," Uncle Lu said. "Now, around midday, I can see all hell break loose. I'll make you a suggestion: Sara and I will spend the day looking over the rest of the buildings, and this evening we'll take a look at the castle."

Steven frowned. "Won't it be closed by then?"

"Prepare for a surprise." Zöller pointed to Steven's bulging rucksack. "Meanwhile you can get on with transcribing the book. Maybe you'll come upon something that will help us to decipher the next words."

Steven sighed. "I should have known. Very well, we'll meet back at the chapel at six. Have fun searching the place."

He wearily shouldered his backpack and walked aimlessly around the island, in search of a quiet, shady place where he could continue decoding Marot's diary. A path along the shore of the island led him south, until he had finally reached the farthest point of the island. Here, away from the stream of tourists, it was pleasantly quiet, with the tapping of a spotted woodpecker and the wind in the trees the only sounds. Red and yellow leaves lay on the woodland floor like a soft carpet.

Someone had nailed a wooden bench with a sheltering roof around a mighty beech tree, and from there there was a wonderful view over the Chiemsee to the Alps beyond the lake. Steven sat down on it, and he tried to imagine Ludwig sitting there and dreaming his romantic dreams. A figure from the age of chivalry without a retinue, surrounded by scheming ministers and counselors who thought he was deranged. A king who seemed to have come from a past era, born into a modern world that he didn't understand, and didn't want to understand.

His curiosity reawakened, the bookseller took out the diary and set about going on with its transcription. He was used by now to the strange sensation of dizziness that came over him whenever he began reading it. He had become so good at the shorthand that he read the words almost like normal handwriting, except for the strange sequences of letters that were indeed becoming shorter and shorter.

It took him only a few lines before he was immersed once again in the world of a pleasantly faraway century slowly drawing to its close.

· 18 ·

IDT

*T*he next few days at Linderhof passed as if they were part of a dream.

Immediately after my fateful meeting with the king, I drafted a dispatch to Count Dürckheim, telling him the story of my experiences. As I had good reason to fear that most of Ludwig's servants were no longer to be trusted, I paid out of my own pocket for a courier from Ettal, who promised me to deliver the sealed letter to Berg within a day. I knew that the count and also Dr. Schleiss von Loewenfeld were in the king's castle there, waiting for his return. I myself planned to travel to Berg in the next few weeks, with Ludwig's retinue. By then I hoped to have had a chance to speak to him again about the ministers' plans. But my greatest wish was to see Maria as often as possible.

Maria . . .

Since our first meeting under the linden tree, I had been unable to get the girl out of my mind. It was as if her clear chime of laughter and her clever, merry eyes would liberate not only the king, but me as well, from the gloomy atmosphere that loomed like a poisonous cloud over Linderhof these days. So I would lie in wait for her at the servants' entrance. I helped her to carry baskets of fresh eggs to the kitchen, or I carved pipes of willow wood for little Leopold, all just to get her to notice me. Maria laughed a great deal, and her eyes twinkled at me, yet she was always surrounded by a strangely dark aura that I could not interpret. In the middle of playing with me and her son, something empty and at the same time infinitely sad would suddenly come into her eyes.

Over the next few weeks we met more and more often, and once or twice Maria, without Leopold, went walking beside the little river Linder with me, although she always withdrew her hand as soon as I wanted to hold it for any length of time.

"Who does the gentleman think he's looking at?" she once said playfully, raising a finger in pretended admonition. "I'm the king's maidservant, so I answer only to His Excellency." Then she smiled. "What's more, you're not for the likes of me. A doctor who has studied medicine and a woodcarver's daughter—that would never do."

"I'd happily learn the craft of woodcarving if it would bring me closer to you."

Maria chuckled. "Dear heavens, Theodor! Don't talk such nonsense. Anyway, you have two left hands—you'd only cut your own fingers off."

She eluded my grasp and ran ahead, laughing. And lovesick fool that I was, I ran after her, in a starched shirt and a coat that was much too warm, until my brow was beaded with sweat and once again, out of breath, I had to own myself defeated.

It was at this time that jealousy began gnawing at me like an insatiable little animal. Some half a dozen times Maria disappeared, carrying wine, bread, and smoked meats, into the Grotto of Venus, where the king was waiting for her to bring him his dinner. I knew that Ludwig liked to have members of the ordinary folk around him, and it was his wont to ask how they were and give them small gifts. Maria was not the only one; grooms and coachmen also visited him at times—yet I was tormented by the thought that Maria was alone with Ludwig, and I once waited for her at the entrance to the grotto to call her to account.

"Well, and so how is His Illustrious Excellency?" I asked in as casual a tone as possible. "Do the two of you enjoy the wine? Is the marinated haunch of venison to Ludwig's liking?"

Maria looked at me, surprised and injured, but soon she had control of herself again. "The king has toothache, as he often does," she said in a matter-of-fact tone. "I cut up the meat small for him so that he can eat it more easily. That's all."

"You could chew it for him first, to make it even more tender."

Suddenly the angry frown that I had been privileged to admire at our first meeting appeared on her forehead again. "What in the world are you thinking, Theodor?" she snapped. "Who gave you the right to speak to me like that? You know neither me nor the king, yet you pour scorn upon him. Like all the others!"

"Suppose there's a grain of truth in the scorn?" I asked coolly. My anger carried me unthinkingly away. "It's not for nothing that people gossip about him. Believe me, I know from a reliable source that your beloved king is likely to find himself in the madhouse soon. And with all his escapades, with this grotto, with his ancient Germanic play-acting in Hunding's hut, his nocturnal rides, he's digging his own grave little by little." My voice had risen enough to make me fear it could be heard inside the Grotto of Venus. "Don't you see how he is playing into his enemies' hands?" I cried. "And you even feed him as if he were an old dog!"

Maria's face was white as a sheet. "Quiet!" she whispered tonelessly. "What do you know about the king? What do any of you know? Only yesterday they were saying, down in the tavern, that the king sups with his horse in the evening. What nonsense!" She shook her head indignantly. "You all pick up a few stories and make a great bugbear out of them. Just because you don't understand Ludwig doesn't make him a lunatic."

She marched angrily away and left me standing there open-mouthed. Gradually I felt my hatred seep away, leaving me a pitiful picture of misery.

"Maria, I'm sorry!" I called after her, "I didn't mean it that way. Come back!" But she had already disappeared among the trees.

It was a while before she would speak to me again. During that time my jealousy went on seething inside me, and it soon had new food for thought.

I had already seen Maria go over to Oberammergau twice with little Leopold, but now their expeditions became more frequent. And every time she came back with a particularly unhappy expression, so I decided that next time I had the chance, I would follow the two of them in secret. Their way took them along narrow mountain passes below Pürschling and through the valley known as the Graswangtal, ending only after some hours at a tiny house on the outskirts of the village, where a man of about forty with a grim face and a wild black beard opened the door to them. Children were playing around the house, and the man shooed them away with an imperious gesture before finally showing Maria into the room inside. I did not see any other woman from where I was hiding, but there was a clothesline with laundry fluttering on it, and some knitting lay on a garden bench. With an almost touching awkwardness, Leopold gave the man a hug, and the door closed behind the three of them.

I felt mingled grief, relief, and shame. How could I have thought that there was a secret liaison between Maria and the king? It was much simpler and at the same time more tragic than that. Little Leopold was obviously a bastard child, tolerated by his father only when the man's lawful wife was at church or had gone to market. I ventured to doubt whether Maria still loved that grim-looking peasant. The child had probably been an accident, and presumably his father secretly gave her money for the boy. My hopes rose again.

Soon after that, Maria seemed to have forgiven me, and she would talk to me again, although usually about matters of no importance. It was to be some time yet before we were back on such a familiar footing as before our quarrel outside the grotto.

The month of September passed by, with unusually warm and pleasant weather, which in no way reflected the political storms sweeping through Bavaria at that time. On three more occasions, I tried speaking to Ludwig about Dr. Gudden's psychiatric report, and a potential coup by the ministers, but whenever I broached the subject, I came up against a wall of silence on his part. At least the KING seemed to have forgiven the affront that he felt I had offered him on the platform in the linden tree. I read aloud to him at night from Edgar Allan Poe and Homer's *Odyssey*, kept him company at supper, and went with him on an expedition of several days by coach to Schachen, as well as accompanying him on a walking tour up to his lodge of Brunnenkopfhäuser. On this excursion, he told me that the building of his new castle at HERRENCHIEMSEE was progressing well, and he looked forward to showing me the construction work going on there in the near future. I also indulged him in his new passion for photography. The result was some charming pictures of the two of us that I will always carry close to my heart, for despite his moments of absurdity, which have been interpreted in retrospect as derangement, I loved him as I loved Maria, if in a different way.

G, IDT

How great was my joy when I heard that Maria was to accompany the retinue to Berg as a kitchen maid. We set off at last on the evening of 27 September in the direction of the Würmsee, that truly majestic lake south of Munich, known to more and more of the local inhabitants these days as Lake Starnberg. It was a long procession of people and horse-drawn carriages, led by the king's coach. Ludwig sat in silence in a vehicle like something out of a fairy tale, adorned all over with gilded figures and curlicues, and drawn by four white horses. As usual, we traveled by night, and I was reminded of the ballads in which elves and fairies go through the forests by night, casting their magic spells over all who set eyes on them. One thing seemed certain:

the few people who saw us that night would still be telling their grandchildren, years later, that they had met a real fairy-tale king.

Early in the morning, we reached Berg Castle at last, a small residence of the Wittelsbachs where Ludwig had spent perhaps the happiest days of his youth, and which still served as his home in summer. The building itself was rather plain, a small castle with oriels, merlons, and a tower of sinister appearance. As on my earlier visits, I marveled yet again at the rural atmosphere of the place. The corridors and garden were thronged with all manner of domestic servants, as well as chambermaids and kitchen boys. There were mingled smells of homely dishes cooking, horse dung, and the caustic ingredients used in photography. Only the upper two floors, where Ludwig and his mother resided, were furnished with a little more grandeur, although they were not in the least like the rooms at Linderhof.

Maria immediately felt at ease here. She helped the servants carry the king's personal belongings into the house, and then ran with Leopold along an arbored pathway through the garden and down to the lake. I was about to follow her, when I saw Count Dürckheim, in his officer's uniform, standing beside the small fountain in the forecourt of the castle. He was looking very grave, and in silence beckoned me over to him.

"My respects to you," I hastily greeted him. "I hope you received my . . ."

Dürckheim put a finger to his lips and told me to be quiet. "Not here," he said, low-voiced. "We'll go over to the cavaliers' building, where you will meet a carefully selected company of gentlemen. Follow me, but do not attract any attention."

Passing the colored glass globes that servants had put up on stakes all over the garden, we reached the small, secluded building, designed for the king's visitors, by way of an arbored path. In the corridor inside we were received by my mentor Dr. Schleiss von Loewenfeld, who used to spend a great deal of time here. In silence, and leaning on a walking stick, he led us to a modest conference room, and then carefully closed the door.

When I looked around the room, I saw, as well as the royal physician and Count Dürckheim, two other men standing smoking by the fireplace. One was Richard Hornig, Ludwig's equerry and loyal friend for many long years; he served the king as a riding companion and coachman. The other, a pale, thin man in his late thirties, wearing a light summer suit, holding a straw hat, and smoking a cigarette, I recognized only at second glance. He was the Munich painter Hermann von Kaulbach, who had already done several model drawings for the king, and who was also unconditionally loyal to him. When Loewenfeld saw my surprise at this strange meeting, he raised his hands in a conciliatory gesture.

"Never fear, my dear young colleague," he reassured me, leaning on his stick. "We are among friends here." He smiled wearily. "Perhaps the last friends the king still has."

Dr. Loewenfeld, then almost eighty years old, seemed to have aged by years over the last few months. He still sported old-fashioned sidewhiskers, like the late American president Lincoln, murdered twenty years ago. But now his hair was white as snow, and deep lines had formed around his eyes. Loewenfeld had been personal physician to Ludwig's father, Maximilian II, and was a true friend to the Wittelsbach family. Now he had to stand by and watch as the kingdom of Bavaria went to the dogs.

"Well?" Count Dürckheim spoke to me in an urgent voice. "Have you succeeded in convincing the king that he must act?"

I shook my head in silence, whereupon the count nodded understandingly. "As I had expected. But at least we now know what's at stake. An intrigue, supported by the Prussian Secret Service, with the intention of having the king certified insane. That is nothing but high treason." He put his hand to his officer's cap. "I owe you my thanks, Marot. You have done the country an inestimable service."

"A service that, I am afraid, does us no good," replied Dr. Loewenfeld, sighing as he let himself drop into one of the chairs beside the fireplace. "As long as Ludwig lives solely in his dreams, he will be playing into his enemies' hands. Lutz, president of the ministerial council, has already been in touch with Prince Luitpold. Ludwig's uncle has agreed to take over as regent."

"It's in the king's own hands," interrupted Kaulbach the painter, drawing on the thin mouthpiece of his cigarette holder. "If he goes to Munich and shows himself to the people, no one will dare to certify him insane. But as matters stand . . ." He paused, and it was a pause pregnant with meaning. "If he goes on driving through the mountains in his coach by night, and building his fairy-tale castles, he is indeed playing into the ministers' hands. Lutz is having rumors circulated in the newspapers, they are already singing satirical songs in the taverns, and no one does anything to avert it."

Hornig, the royal equerry, nodded bitterly. "The lackeys at court are full of malicious gossip. I've heard that they steal torn documents from the king's wastebaskets, hoping to find incriminating material. Then they pass it on to that bastard Lutz."

"Who can still be trusted?" I asked hesitantly, looking around at the company.

"Apart from the five of us?" Count Dürckheim laughed despairingly. "I wouldn't vouch for anyone else. Count von Holnstein is inciting the last of the loyalists against the king."

"Another bastard!" Richard Hornig spat in the empty fireplace. "And when, thanks to Ludwig, he had a handsome sum from Bismarck."

I could understand Hornig's anger with his immediate superior. The Master of the Royal Stables, Max Count Holnstein, had once been the young king's playmate. But Holnstein was hungry for both power and money, a bull-necked, choleric man who liked to browbeat his subordinates. He had been paid ten percent commission on the millions of the Guelph Fund, money with which Bismarck had bribed the king of Bavaria, after the war in the seventies, to get a Hohenzollern on the throne of the German emperor. Holnstein had been scheming against the king for years.

"How about Dr. Gudden?" I asked. "If he could be convinced that this opinion of his serves only to prepare for a coup, he might be amenable to reason."

"I know Bernhard von Gudden," replied Dr. Loewenfeld, wearily rubbing his temples. "A highly intelligent, ambitious man, and above all a vain one. His expert opinion damning the king will be the pinnacle of his career. He's making himself the talk of all Europe with it. He's not about to give that up."

"I think that Marot is right," Hermann Kaulbach said, turning to the others. "We ought to get in touch with Dr. Gudden. It's always worth making an attempt. Maybe he could be bribed."

"Oh, and what would we bribe him with?" Count Dürckheim snorted angrily and lit himself a second cigar. "The king is no longer solvent. All the same, he goes on building and building. This very night he plans to travel on to Herrenchiemsee, to supervise work on the castle there. This is a never-ending nightmare. Can't you finally grasp that fact?"

"Gentlemen, gentlemen! A little civilized conduct, if you please!" Old Dr. Loewenfeld had risen from his chair. Clutching his walking stick, he looked sharply at all of us. Once again his eyes blazed with the authority for which I had always admired him.

"There is no point in our shouting at one another," he said at last. "That is not the way for us to save our king. I therefore suggest the following: Kaulbach and I will try to get in touch with Dr. von Gudden. Perhaps all is not yet lost. Meanwhile you, Count Dürckheim, and the king's equerry, Hornig, should go on trying to reason with Ludwig and persuade him to appeal to the public."

"You can forget that idea," growled Dürckheim. "His Majesty has just ordered me to travel to England and beg the Duke of Westminster for ten million marks. So I'm obliged to leave Ludwig with the intriguers and lickspittles."

"And you?" Dr. Loewenfeld hopefully asked the equerry.

Richard Hornig hesitated before he answered. "I must disappoint you. The king recently dismissed me from his service. I'm here because I love him, but that love is no longer returned."

"Good God, Hornig!" cried Dürckheim. "In heaven's name, what has happened?"

"Well, he gave me an order that I was absolutely unable to carry out."

"Refusing to obey orders?" The officer frowned. "What kind of order was it, then?"

"I . . . I was to mount a bank robbery in Frankfurt."

A leaden silence fell.

"Someone pinch me, please, to wake me up," said Kaulbach at last. "You were asked to rob a bank for the king of Bavaria?"

The equerry nodded. "Those were His Majesty's orders. If he can't come by money in any other way, he wants to go on building however he can."

"A king as bank robber." Dr. Loewenfeld sighed deeply. "Maybe Ludwig is deranged after all, and the ministers are right."

"He has his whims and fancies, but he is not deranged," I said firmly. "Let *me* try convincing him to go to Munich. He's already indicated that he'll be taking me to Herrenchiemsee with him. Once there, I'll do all I can to bring him to change his mind."

For a moment I felt all eyes in the room turn to me. It was so quiet that you could hear the maidservants laughing in the garden outside.

"Very well." Dr. Loewenfeld tapped the floor with his stick. It sounded like fate knocking at the door. "Then it's decided. Marot goes to Herrenchiemsee with the king; Kaulbach and I will talk to Gudden. And not a word outside this room about today's conversation. Swear by God and the king."

We all raised our hands as we swore the oath. The royal physician looked gravely at us all before, at last, he went on. "One thing must be clear to you all, gentlemen: if Ludwig falls, it means the end of the Bavarian monarchy. And then we'll be ruled by unfeeling bureaucrats. We stand at a turning point in history."

With these words he opened the door, and the five of us went our separate ways. Had I guessed under what terrible circumstances I would see my fellow conspirators again, I would probably have run as far as I could go, screaming. Or emigrated to America at once. As it was, however, I walked down to the lake, feeling queasy, in the hope of meeting Maria there.

I would very much have liked to talk to her about the king and the ministers' terrible plans for him, but I didn't want to put her in such great danger. Anyone who knew about the plot against Ludwig, and our own plans, would be considered a tiresome troublemaker to be eliminated.

And as the oath sealed my lips anyway, I decided to hold my peace.

· 19 ·

Steven had been reading Marot's diary for more than two hours, as if in a trance, when he suddenly heard a sound behind him. He straightened up. Twigs cracked underfoot on the secluded, shady path through the trees. Could some tourists have lost their way and strayed to this remote spot on the island? Or were the Cowled Men after him again? Maybe by now the police had tracked him down? Steven shuddered at the thought of the green Bentley that had followed them to Prien on the Chiemsee.

Who in God's name are all these people taking such a keen interest in the book?

Cautiously, the bookseller put the diary down and scanned his surroundings from his place on the bench behind the mighty tree trunk. He almost expected to meet the magician, or the one-eyed knight, in this dark fairy-tale wood. But it was only Sara who came toward him, waving.

"So here you are," she cried cheerfully. "I see you found an idyllic place to sit and work on the diary."

"Most of all it's a timeless place." Steven closed his notebook. "I'd say this spot looks just the way it did more than a hundred years ago, except that the beech trees have grown a bit."

"Well? Find anything out?" Sara's voice had a serious note in it now. "Any clue to help us work out what Marot could have meant by writing KING in capital letters?"

Steven shook his head. "No clue at all. Right now Marot is still in Berg, meeting the last few men still loyal to the king. It's an exciting political thriller, but there's nothing to give us the next keyword." Briefly, he told her about the pages of the diary that he had just read. Sara listened in silence, then leaned back and let a stray sunbeam fall on her face.

"Nothing to report from our end either," she told him. "We didn't find a single clue, in the monastery or in the other buildings." She laughed softly. "Not a single word on a whole damn island. Might as well be looking for a needle in a haystack. But I did find something else."

She paused for a moment before going on, in a low voice. "You remember the green Bentley over at the harbor? Just now I met three men whose car it could have been. When I was looking around the old monastery with Uncle Lu, they were always just a couple of rooms behind us. I could be wrong, but I think they're snooping around after us. Now, guess what those gentlemen were wearing."

"What?"

"Old-style Bavarian gear, like that charming character who paid you a call in your antiquarian bookshop."

"The Cowled Men!" Steven exclaimed. "That's all I need."

Sara raised a hand, soothing him. "Take it easy. As long as we're with other people, we ought to be safe. And no one followed me here on my way to find you—I'm sure of that."

"Where's Uncle Lu?" Steven asked.

"Stuffing himself in the restaurant and chatting up the waitresses. He can get on your nerves with his know-it-all attitude." Sara made a face. "That's why I walked around on my own, too, for a while, hoping the keyword would simply materialize on the ground in front of me."

"My guess, anyway, is that if we find it at all, it'll be in the castle,"

Steven said. "And by this evening, I hope to have read the next passage."

Sara smiled at him. All of a sudden the bookseller felt his heart rise. He wasn't used to having women smile at him like that these days.

"You're enjoying this, aren't you?" she said in a low voice. "Reading that old book. You'd have liked to live in those days."

Steven shrugged his shoulders. "What, having teeth drawn without anesthetic, getting TB, raking out the stove at five in the morning early in January, that sort of thing? Not to mention the high rate of infant mortality, and the filth and smoke in the cities. I don't know if it's as alluring as all that." His eyes twinkled as he looked at Sara. "But you're right. Sometimes I really do think I'd have felt more at ease in the nineteenth century. A poor poet surrounded by a great many books, in a little cottage. Not a bad lifestyle."

"Quite a romantic one, anyway."

Sara was looking at him in a strange way. She had now moved very close to Steven on the bench, and that made him feel hot and cold at the same time. Yet again, he had to admit to himself that his original dislike of Sara and her brash style had given way to a certain fascination.

For some time neither of them said anything, and there was nothing to be heard but the twittering of the birds in the trees. Steven felt the trunk of the beech tree behind his back, and he thought that Theodor and Maria could have sat in this very place, under the very same beech tree.

"This passion for books," Sara asked, suddenly interested, "does it run in your family?"

Hesitantly, Steven nodded. "My . . . my father was a well-respected lecturer on literature in Boston, specializing in German Romanticism. I was always surrounded by books—my mother probably changed my diapers on a pile of them." He laughed, but it sounded slightly forced. "She was always reading me German fairy tales and poems when I was a child. Then, when her parents died, we went back to Germany, to her parental home. I was six then. We always had a large library, first in the States, then in Cologne."

Sara grinned. "I guess the only book my own mother possessed was a stained copy of *One Hundred Cocktails to Mix at Home*. But she never read aloud to me out of it. That would have been rather boring."

This time Steven's laughter was genuine. "I'm beginning to see why the Internet means so much to you," he said finally. "It must have been a good, knowledgeable friend. Did your father at least read books?"

Sara smiled, but her eyes were curiously vacant. "My father . . . left us quite early. I see him only occasionally. When I do, I always take him a couple of illustrated art books."

"Your father is interested in art?"

"Yes . . . oh yes, he is. Sometimes more interested than is good for him."

Steven felt Sara's attention slip away. In her thoughts, she seemed to be somewhere infinitely distant. Only after a while did she shake herself as if coming out of a cold shower.

"And your own parents?" she asked suddenly. Her voice sounded cheerful again, as if to drive away her own dark mood. "Let me guess. You visit them every week in their little house by Lake Starnberg. You have a cup of tea and read Shakespeare's sonnets aloud to one another. And there's probably a nice fire burning merrily in the hearth."

Steven jumped. It was as if those last words had obliterated all the beauty around him: the shade of the beech trees, the red and yellow leaves on the woodland floor, Sara on the bench beside him. For a moment he closed his eyes and breathed deeply.

The crackling flames, single pages of books brightly illuminated. Thin gray layers of ash falling. The screams from the library as the firefighter carries the yelling, struggling boy away from his hiding place, out to the street swarming with onlookers. The hatred in the eyes of the blond girl, the soot on her braided hair, the charred hem of her dress . . .

"My God, what's the matter?" Sara asked, looking at him in dismay. "You're white as a sheet. Have I said something wrong?"

"It . . . it's nothing," Steven murmured. "Or, rather, yes, it is something." Suddenly he decided to say more; it was far too long since he had talked about it. Too long since he had been inside his memories.

"There . . . there was an accident." His mouth was dry as dust. The past broke over him like a wave. He had suppressed the images for such a long time, but now they were back. Nausea rose in him, and his throat felt constricted. "My parents . . . They died very early," he whispered. "I was still a child."

He got to his feet, unsteadily, and paced a few steps up and down. For a moment he felt as if he were in a ship at sea caught in a heavy swell.

"Oh God, I'm so sorry." Sara jumped up, too, and took him by the shoulders. "What possessed me to ask such a question?"

"You couldn't have known." Steven stopped under the canopy of a beech tree and looked up at the branches overhead. A single red leaf sailed down to him. Finally he tried a slight smile. "What's more, at the age of forty I really ought to have gotten over it—or finally decided to spend some money on a therapist."

"There are some things you never get over, even with therapy." She stroked his cheeks, and he realized that it felt good. "And believe me, we all have our dark places. I mean, look at me. I'm a whole bundle of complexes. The best psychiatrist in the world couldn't get rid of them."

Steven couldn't hold back an involuntary grin. "Well, that would mean letting someone get close to you for once. Are you capable of that?"

"It might be worth a try."

Gently, Sara ran her fingers through his hair. Then her lips were on his, just a fleeting touch, but all the same Steven felt the little hairs on the nape of his neck stand up. Then the moment was over.

"I . . . I'm afraid it's not the right time for this sort of thing," Sara said, taking a step back, almost as if she herself were startled by what she had just done. For the first time, Steven saw something like awkwardness in her eyes.

"Yes . . . you're probably right," he replied after what felt like forever, pushing back a few strands of hair from his face. "I . . . I guess I'm rather nervous at the moment."

Sara laughed. "Not surprising, with the police after you. I'd call those mitigating circumstances." She offered him her hand. "Let's be on first-name terms. After all, we've kind of been brought together by fate."

"Yes, you're right. We really ought to be friends."

"Maybe even a little more." She was smiling slightly. "Sara and Steven. Sounds good. I think we ought to seal the bargain."

"Seal it? What with?"

Sara's eyebrows shot up. "Well, what do you think, you idiot? With a *proper* kiss. That one was just a peck."

She took his head between her hands and kissed him firmly on the mouth.

It was better than a book by Voltaire.

Much better.

THE WHITE YACHT rolled gently on the small, crystalline blue waves of the Chiemsee, while gulls flew above the deck, screeching. There was a strong wind, so that it looked as if the Alps, powdered with snow, stood right on the banks of the lake.

Lancelot was sitting in a deck chair much too small for him, leaning forward, and letting his gaze sweep over the yacht's equipment. Each of the two engines at the stern was 435 h.p., the diesel tank could hold a good four gallons. At almost fifty feet, the yacht was about the length that Lancelot had planned for his own ship, but he would opt for Brazilian rosewood rather than teak for the interior fittings, and he would have a riveted aluminium seat built in for deep-sea fishing. But all things considered, the yacht was roughly what Lancelot imagined when he was planning to enjoy the evening of his days to the full. Apart from the girls in close-clinging bikinis, of course, although they might be a little scared of his new appearance. The black-colored eye patch that Lancelot now wore, together with his black braid and the scar on his right cheek, made him look like a fierce pirate captain—a more menacing Captain Hook.

Well, there is something exciting about fear . . .

Lancelot was so deep in his thoughts that he did not feel the pain until broken glass was lying on the deck around him. The king had thrown a half-full glass of champagne at him, and now the royal's bright little eyes were bent on the vassal. Legs crossed and in a white fur coat, The Royal Majesty sat on the swiveling seat at the controls in the open cabin, looking down disparagingly, as if from a throne, on the giant in the deck chair.

"My best knight," the king hissed. "Loses an eye and lets the book be snapped up under his nose into the bargain. Snapped up by a *woman.*"

"She didn't have the book," Lancelot said, licking warm champagne and a few drops of blood off his lips. "That bookseller had gone off with it. She admitted it herself."

"And you believed her?" The king laughed scornfully. "Women are crafty and cunning. Looking at your face in that state, I'm inclined to think that the woman is the one really pulling the strings. Who is she, anyway?"

"We . . . we don't know that yet."

The king raised an eyebrow. "And this man Lukas? What have you been able to find out about him?"

Lancelot was visibly uncomfortable. In his mind he saw his own luxury yacht foundering somewhere in the Atlantic. "Not much, except that he's a rather eccentric antiquarian bookseller. Professor Liebermann apparently visited him by chance and then decided to hide the book among his wares." Lancelot scratched under the bandage over his eye; the freshly disinfected socket itched horribly. "God knows why the lunatic is running all over with it now. He obviously guesses that the man Marot hid something. But he has no idea where."

Lancelot still felt a slight sense of satisfaction to know that his assumption had been right. The brochures on the floor of the hotel room had pointed him in the direction of the next stop for the bookseller and his unknown girlfriend. There had been two possible destinations; he had posted men at both places. When they had told him at midday today that the couple they wanted had arrived in Prien, he had immediately passed the news on to his boss.

"Looks as if he's found out something already, and now he's curious," said the king thoughtfully. "He's thinking along the same lines as we are. Strange . . ." The king studied freshly manicured fingernails. "He comes from the United States, right?"

Lancelot nodded. "We've had his personal details checked. He has an American passport, although he's been living in Germany since he was six." The giant's gaze was fixed on a place, some way off, where a couple of gulls were fighting over a fish just below the surface of the lake. "Unfortunately, he's left hardly any traces on the Internet. No Facebook account, no e-mail contacts, no homepage. The man's an oddball, if you ask me."

The squawking of the gulls robbed Lancelot of the last of his nerve. Wearily, he wiped blood from his forehead where the king's champagne glass had hit him. He was going to do just this one job, take the money, and then get away from all this lunacy forever. By now, he sometimes thought he was going crazy himself.

"The United States," the king murmured suddenly, eyes curiously empty. "I'm sure it's only a coincidence, but I must be sure. Find out everything you can about the man. His parents, any siblings. I want to know where he went to school, what he likes to eat, what his favorite books are. Everything."

"How are we supposed to do that? The man's a nerd, there are no friends we can pump, no . . ." At the same moment Lancelot knew that this remark had been a mistake. He only just managed to dodge the champagne bottle sailing through the air to smash on the rail of the yacht.

"What do I pay you for?" the king screeched. "To ask stupid questions? You're my best knight, so come up with a good idea, and do it soon."

Lancelot rose, with difficulty, and bowed.

Just this one last job, then I'm off to the Caribbean. But first I am going to wring this crazy bastard's neck with my own hands . . .

"At Your Majesty's orders," he said, and moved in the direction of the stern, walking slowly backward as court ceremonial demanded. "I'll get our people in Munich and New York on it. Meanwhile I'll find the book for you."

"Within twenty-four hours." The king swiveled away from Lancelot and stared abstractedly at the picturesque Alpine range. "I want the book and the man within twenty-four hours. And I want the man alive. If I don't get him, and alive, you can forget about that account in the Caymans."

The one-eyed knight climbed down a ladder at the rail into the little dinghy and started the outboard motor. He was having difficulty controlling his breathing. One minute longer on the yacht and he'd probably have murdered the king—but then, of course, the account in the Caymans would be gone as well. He must get this thing tied up quickly; his employer's lunacy was increasing to an ever greater extent. At first he had thought the king's conduct was mere eccentricity, but by now Lancelot couldn't be sure of anything. He must get out of here, fast. Just this one last job, and then the Caribbean beckoned.

Think of the girls, the champagne, fishing for tuna. Damn big tuna. Their blood will dye the sea red . . .

Lancelot suddenly remembered that he was to deliver that bookseller alive. His glance fell on the small crate at the stern of the dinghy, and he couldn't keep back a grin. A good thing he had kept some of the gear he'd used in Serbia; he had a hunch that he could use it today. At least it would speed things up a good deal; the man wouldn't have the faintest chance of defending himself.

And no one had said a word about letting that woman leave the island alive.

. . .

FOR THE FIRST time in days, Steven didn't feel afraid of anything.

They were lying side by side on a carpet of red and yellow leaves, watching a spotted woodpecker send its messages out into the wood in Morse code. Steven could smell the nicotine seeping through the pores of Sara's skin. Curiously enough, he found it exciting, like a new perfume that he didn't yet recognize.

She had kissed him for a long time, and then placed a finger on his lips to close them, as if any wrong word spoken now would destroy the magic between them. Eventually, they began talking about their favorite songs, about American soap operas unknown to him, and the stupidest weather forecasters they'd seen. They disagreed on whether *Psycho* or *North by Northwest* was the best Hitchcock movie of all time. They talked about everything except the present and their own past lives, and for just under an hour they were far, far away from Marot's diary, the Cowled Men, the magician, and the blinded giant. Only now did Steven realize how long it was since he had exchanged more than a few words with another human being. He had retreated into his books as if into a cocoon.

"What's it like to grow up without books?" he asked Sara, who was cracking beechnuts beside him and munching the kernels with relish.

She laughed. "Is that how I seem to you? A female nerd raised by computers?" She looked at him, shaking her head. "What on earth do you think of me? I'm more interested in the contents of a book than its form, that's all. Why would I need a library when I can download all those volumes to my tablet instead?"

"Maybe because it's pleasant to leaf through books, smell them, sleep with books beside you?" Steven said. "Because books are like nourishment for oddballs like me, and I've always had them around me? Somehow I can't get used to the idea that all that will soon be a thing of the past."

"You're incorrigibly nostalgic," Sara said with a sigh. "But guess what? I like that. You're someone a person could hold on to when time goes racing by too fast." She spat out a couple of beechnut kernels. "Besides, it's not what you think. I did read a lot as a child. I often went to the municipal library in Wedding instead of going to school; I told them I had to study there for my homework." Lost in thought, she cracked another of the dry nuts. "I immersed myself in adventure stories to forget the world outside. Later, my father brought home illustrated books on painting. If you have graffiti and dog turds on your doorstep, a painting by Caravaggio is like a warm, refreshing shower."

"Is your father a painter, then?" Steven asked.

This time Sara's laughter was a touch too shrill. "*A painter?* I think he'd have liked to be an artist. To this day he's addicted to art. My mother is addicted to alcohol and my father to art, and it hasn't necessarily made either of them happy." She abruptly got to her feet and picked up a heap of colorful leaves, dropping them again to rain down on Steven.

"If you were marooned on the proverbial desert island," she asked him, "which three books would you take with you?"

Steven swept the leaves off his forehead. "Only three? That's a difficult question. Let me think." He paused, and then finally went on. "Thomas Mann's *The Magic Mountain*, even though I've read it three times already. Robert Musil's thousand-page epic *The Man Without Qualities*, at least that would last a long time, and then . . ." He stopped, his expression suddenly darkening.

"You'd take Marot's diary, wouldn't you?" Sara whispered. "The book's gotten under your skin."

Steven did not reply for a long time, and then he hesitantly nodded. "There's something about it. It's like black magic, a kind of curse, and I'm afraid I won't be able to shake it off until I've come to the end of the diary. Sometimes I think . . ."

The long drawn-out sound of a ferry's siren brought them back to reality. Startled, Sara looked at the time.

"Hell, four in the afternoon already," she said, brushing the leaves off her dress. "I suggest you get back to that curse of yours. You're

supposed to have the bit about Herrenchiemsee decoded by this evening. Meanwhile Uncle Lu is arranging for us to have a private
guided tour."

"How about you?" asked Steven, who was obviously finding it
hard to leave their enchanted world in the beech wood. "What will
you do?"

"Look around the island for a while." She kissed him gently on the
mouth one last time and then turned to leave. "You don't want me
holding your hand while you work on it, do you? See you at the castle
at six. Look after yourself."

With a final wave, she disappeared among the trees, and Steven
was left alone. He ran his hands through his hair, his mind in a whirl.
He was clearly in love, a tingling spreading through him right down
to his toes. But he had no idea whether Sara felt the same. Steven was
reminded of Maria and Theodor. Marot couldn't be sure either
whether the young maidservant felt anything more than friendship
for him. Why were women always so complicated?

The thought of the assistant physician reminded Steven of the diary that had cast its spell on him. Still in bewilderment, and with a
sense that he was floating on clouds, he sat down on the bench under
the beech tree and returned to reading the memoir of a man long
dead, a man who was turning more and more into a distant ally of his,
a companion linked to him over the years by this book. By now he
had stopped transferring the transliteration of the shorthand to his
notebook. The entries held him spellbound, too much so for him to
have time to make a transcript.

Steven could almost believe he heard Theodor Marot speaking to
him between the pages, the whisper as he turned them like the whispering of the conspirators, and he felt as if the king himself might
step out of the volume and give him a friendly wave.

After only a few lines, the bookseller was back in the nineteenth
century.

NFTQM, WQI, GQT

*W*e traveled to the Chiemsee on the railroad, going by way of Starnberg and Munich. Ludwig and I sat at the very front, in a royal car with furnishings in no way inferior to those of the king's castles. It was as if we were coasting through Bavaria in a golden salon. Snorting like a dragon from the world of the sagas, the locomotive made its way past meadows and fields where a few peasants stood around here and there, waving their hats to us.

Nostalgically, I remembered the brief time before the two great wars, first against Prussia, then against France. At that time, Ludwig still appeared in public, and the people cheered for the tall, good-looking young man who was their king. But in the last few years, Ludwig had turned away from his people. With a curiously storklike gait, which he obviously considered majestic, he occasionally stalked down the lines of elderly dignitaries and young officers, but otherwise he remained alone, surrounded only by his closest companions. It was a self-chosen internal exile that he had left, at the most, only for his friend Richard Wagner, whom he revered and who had died two years earlier.

In silence, eyes closed, he sat hunched in his compartment, and so

I finally decided to go several cars down the train, where I met Maria with several of the servants. The loud merriment here made the silence in the king's private car all the more uncanny.

"If you know the king so well," I said, sitting down beside Maria on the wooden bench, "then tell me what Ludwig thinks he's doing. He acts like a man from another world."

Maria smiled and looked out at the landscape passing by us. "He *is* a man from another world," she replied. "He comes from a time long before ours. At heart he's a boy acting in his own play. With knights, castles, and wicked dwarves. Those are the ministers as he sees them, wicked dwarves." She laughed and pointed to a couple of the footmen in our compartment who were standing at the windows, open-mouthed, while putting their heads outside to feel the wind. "We race through the world, drawn by iron horses. We build machines and factories. But Ludwig stands still and lets all that pass him by. He's like a king from one of those Brothers Grimm fairy tales. Sometimes he reads them to me, and then I'm Snow White and he is the prince turned into a shaggy bear by a bad fairy's spell."

"Prince? Bear?" I shook my head in dismay. "Maria, the king is not a child anymore. He has a country to rule . . ."

"A country that has stopped dreaming," Maria said, interrupting me. "Don't you understand, Theodor? Ludwig dreams for us because we have forgotten how to dream. To him, a king is not just someone who signs documents and moves armies from place to place; he is a dream, an idea."

"An *idea?*" I said skeptically. "Did he tell you so? Does he teach you such things?"

"At least he doesn't treat me like a stupid woodcarver's daughter, as you do."

Maria fell silent and stared out of the window.

Sighing, I decided not to continue this conversation. After a while I returned to the king, who was still sitting with his eyes closed. He looked like a monument to himself.

In the evening we reached Prien on the Chiemsee, and from there we crossed to Herrenchiemsee by water. While Maria and the rest of the domestic staff drove to the castle in a jolting cart, I stayed with Ludwig at the island's little harbor.

I soon noticed that the building work was not far advanced. A little locomotive, whistling and hissing noisily, towed a few trucks laden with stones and timber up to the castle. But even from the bank it was clear that large parts of the building were not yet completed. The side wings looked curiously naked, mere shells, and what would be an avenue in the future was nothing but a dirty transport road. On the western side of the castle, craftsmen were at work hammering and filing the basin of the fountain, and the canal was only half dug. Nonetheless, you could already guess at the design of this castle, in which Ludwig hoped to emulate and honor his great example, the Sun King, as a Bavarian Versailles.

"The sun rises exactly here and sets over there, on the other side of the island." Ludwig, now in high good humor again and leaping about among the workmen like an excited child, indicated a place on an imaginary axis leading from the avenue to the canal. "The castle lies exactly between them," he called to me, laughing. "I can see the chariot of the heavens rising and falling from my bedroom. Isn't that wonderful, Marot? *Mon Dieu!*"

All at once Ludwig's expression changed. Imperiously, he beckoned to an overseer of the building work in a black coat. "Here, you! What's gone wrong with the figures there on the Fountain of Fortuna? The triton is holding his hand *up*. Didn't I give clear instructions for him to hold it down, like the one in Versailles?"

Looking anxious, the man made him a deep bow. "Majesty, forgive us, but there were several different designs, and . . ."

"Different designs?" Ludwig's face flushed red as a lobster. "What's the meaning of this? Only the latest design counts, the one I commissioned myself. What impertinence! By God, this is lèse majesté!" And with his strong arms he suddenly snatched up an easel lying on the ground and began belaboring the overseer with it. "Take that figure away!" he cried like a man possessed. "This instant! Ruemann must cast a new one, the way I damn well told him to."

I hurried over to Ludwig and tried to get the little wooden easel away from him before he beat the poor man to death. "Stop, Your Majesty!" I cried. "It wasn't his mistake. Stop before there's an accident!"

Ludwig suddenly stopped beating the man and looked at me in surprise. For a moment, I thought he was about to thrash me in the same way. But he dropped the easel and turned away from the unfortunate overseer. "You . . . you're right, Marot," he gasped. "I mustn't let myself get so carried away. But there's so much at stake here, an idea towering above all human conceptions. Do you understand? One sometimes must exercise severity."

"An idea?" I hesitantly asked. I remembered what Maria had been trying to explain to me on the train.

"You'll see. This very night you'll see." The king beckoned over a second overseer, who approached only with reluctance. "This evening all the candles in the Hall of Mirrors are to burn," he ordered in a loud voice. "For me and for my dear companion here."

"But that's almost two thousand candles," the man cautiously objected. "I don't know whether we . . ."

"This evening at eight, and I'll suffer no contradiction." Ludwig took my arm and drew me away from the building work. "Come with me, Marot. We will take a simple meal in the monastery. I need a friend now."

WQI, ID

By winding, narrow pathways we approached the old monastery of the Augustinian Canons, which had housed a now-defunct brewery. On the floor formerly occupied by the canons and princes, Ludwig had had a few rooms furnished in Spartan fashion, and from this vantage point he intended to supervise the building for the next two weeks. I myself was given one of the rooms on the second floor, but the king told me to accompany him at once to his meal, which we took in one of the magnificent halls of the old monastery. Reluctantly, I followed him. I had really hoped to eat down in the kitchen with Maria and Leopold.

It was a ghastly dinner. The king did not eat; he gorged. Gravy and crushed green peas spattered his beard and his coat, but it did not occur to Ludwig to clean himself up with a cloth. He tipped great drafts of wine down his throat, and the red liquid ran over his chin and down to his collar. Only on rare occasions did the king dine in a company of any size, and if he did, he would hide himself behind mountains of plates and glasses. He shoveled everything down his throat like some Bacchanalian god of ancient times, as if the food would extinguish an inner fire.

"Help yourself," he said between two mouthfuls. "You'll need your strength for the sight I am going to offer you tonight. You are my chosen one."

"Very good, Your Majesty." I nodded and went on pushing my peas around with a fork. I briefly considered speaking to the king again about the ministerial intrigue but decided against it. This did not seem to be the right time. Ludwig appeared very much in danger of slipping away into his dream world. I would have to wait for one of his more reasonable moments.

"Is something the matter, Marot?" asked the king, and in his surprise he stopped eating. "You know you can say anything to me. I am your king." He smiled, and I saw the festering blackened stumps of teeth between his full lips. "Your king and your friend," he repeated with gravity.

"I know how deeply to appreciate that, Your Majesty," I replied, and felt myself breaking out in a cold sweat. "But I assure you it's nothing. Merely weariness after the long journey."

Inwardly, I shuddered. Ludwig had proclaimed me his close friend several times before, but I knew that his choice of friends never lasted long. Ludwig liked to have handsome men around him. At the same time, the king had never yet made unseemly advances to me, nor could I imagine that he was even capable of such desires, whether for men or for women. He had separated from his fiancée, Princess Sophie of Bavaria, a sister of the Empress Sisi of Austria, after only a few months' engagement. But now he seemed to have taken a fancy to me, and I didn't know what to think of it.

"If you are tired, then I have something that will cheer your heart again." The king rose, breathing heavily, and his chair fell over. "Let us go over to the castle, my dear Marot. It's time we did in any case. Let's hope those lazy dogs have already lit the candles."

We left the monastery down a narrow flight of steps and walked in silence over to Herrenchiemsee Castle, accompanied only by two footmen in costume and powdered wigs. In the west, above the canal, the fiery red globe of the sun was just setting.

WFIFBGGQTQ

It was an amazing sight. In the darkness of the wood, something bright and incredibly large shone like a monstrous lantern. As we left the trees behind us, the castle suddenly emerged. The whole of the second floor was glittering; the windowpanes sparkled with warm light that shone all the way down to the fountains and the flower beds.

"I see all has been prepared," said the king, and an emotional note came into his voice. "Good. Very good. Then follow me, my faithful paladin."

He gave the two footmen a sign, and they bowed low and stayed where they were. The two of us walked on through the entrance hall, which was lined with marble statues, and up a broad staircase to the second floor, where the king had his own apartments. On the way, I saw many unfinished rooms, bare and unplastered, which seemed to exhale a curious chill. The rooms to which we now came struck me as all the more fantastic. The walls were covered with gilded stucco, marble, and paneling in precious woods. Chandeliers sparkled as they hung from the ceiling, and the floor was made of oak, polished until it shone like a mirror, with ornate inlays of Brazilian rosewood. Pictures of the Sun King of France in all his glory hung everywhere. In battle, at court, larger than life in a sweeping royal cloak. Busts and small statues of the French king greeted us from every corner. Louis XIV was everywhere; he seemed to hover over us like the sun itself.

Ludwig strutted ahead of me as if he were alone on a stage, taking long strides, holding his head stiffly upright. He seemed entirely absorbed by the effect of the splendor around him.

"My bedroom," he whispered, pointing to a huge four-poster bed with a blue canopy and silk curtains interwoven with gold thread. In front of it was a gilded stand, on which a glass globe shimmered on the inside with a blue light. The king picked it up as a soothsayer might his crystal ball, and he began caressing it gently. "Right here is the central point of the sun's course, the center of the universe," he said, kissing the globe. "The place from which the king presides over the fate of his people."

"Is that the idea of which you speak?" I asked with a touch of skepticism. "Are you yourself the center of all being?"

The king straightened up to his full height. For a moment his eyes blazed angrily, exactly as they had that afternoon when he had struck the overseer. "God gave us all our stations on this earth," he finally replied, turning away. "Come with me, and you will understand."

Ludwig went ahead, and we crossed a small room on our way to a double door.

"Voilà," whispered the king. "Feel the breath of history upon you!"

He theatrically flung open the two wings of the door, and I saw a mighty hall that surely extended for more than a hundred paces to both right and left. Countless historical scenes in which the Sun King appeared adorned the ceiling. There was a view of the forecourt of the castle from a dozen arched windows. Opposite the windows hung an equal number of mirrors. But most impressive of all were the chandeliers and the gilded candelabra that stood like an army, bearing thousands of candles, on both sides of the hall. The candlelight reflected over and over again in the mirrors, and in this way the whole room shone so brightly that for a moment I had to put my hand in front of my eyes to avoid being dazzled.

"My Hall of Mirrors," said the king, standing in the middle of the room with his arms outspread. "It is larger than the one in Versailles. I can walk here alone by night, giving myself up to my thoughts, like such great kings of past centuries as Louis the Fourteenth." The king looked at me with a dreamy smile. "Did you know that there is a direct link between me and the Sun King? My grandfather was named after Louis the Sixteenth. I feel that I am the heir of the Bourbons, the last to live out the monarchy in accordance with divine principle."

"Is this place the idea that you spoke of?" I asked, indicating the sparkling light of the candelabra all around us. "A light in the darkness? Are you to be the light of Europe?"

Ludwig nodded fervently, and his eyes burned with enthusiasm. "The king is the bright center. All else revolves around him. He is the real picture, not the shadows on the wall. Without the king, the world would be turned upside down, and chaos would follow. Just look around you, Marot." He pointed to the view outside the window. "Wherever the eye falls, there's nothing but war, destruction, estrangement. We are rushing headlong toward a century of cannibalism. Believe me, *I* am not mad; it is the times in which we live." The king sighed deeply. "A God-given responsibility rests on my shoulders. That makes a man lonely, Marot. Very lonely."

Suddenly I realized what I had been feeling for all these last minutes, which made me shiver despite the warmth from the many candles. It was not the chill of fall that wafted through these apartments, but of loneliness itself. We were all alone in the yawning void of this empty castle, with its unfinished rooms, its gold leaf, its imitation marble on the bare stone. There were no laughing maidservants, no whispering footmen, no good smells from the kitchen, no music, no sound of rushing water, nothing. When the lights in the Hall of

Mirrors went out, cold and darkness would invade the castle once more. I could almost smell the king's fear that a sudden gust of wind might blow all the candles out and leave him alone with the night.

"I need a friend," said Ludwig in the silence. "They have all abandoned me. Lutz, the other ministers, my much-loved Wagner, even the faithful Hornig. Be my friend, Marot. I ask it as your king."

"It . . . it would be an honor for me, Your Majesty," I stammered. "But believe me, you are not alone. The people love you. Go to Munich and show them that you return their love."

Ludwig was smiling again, but there was something unspeakably sad in his eyes. "Did the Sun King show himself to his people?" he asked quietly. "Barbarossa? Friedrich, Duke of Swabia? They were all lonely men. I can assure you, a king loses his brilliance if he throws himself at the feet of the common people."

I felt an inner rebellion against such obstinacy. "You have only to show yourself." I implored. "Is that too much to ask? A wave of your hand, and there will be an end to your enemies' scheming."

The king frowned. "I did show myself, Marot. In the past. But since then, there have been two wars that I did not want. The ministers make me their plaything, the smoke of factories hangs over the cities, the people talk of socialism and revolution. This is no longer my world." Ludwig strode through the brightly lit hall now, and his voice echoed back from the walls. "I do not belong in this age, Marot. And if I am to go under, then let it be as the last great ruler. As an example of what monarchy used to mean. As the last true king."

"But Your Majesty," I began in a pleading tone. However, Ludwig waved me away.

"Go now, Marot. Leave me alone." He looked through one of the great windows and out into the garden, and for all his height and portly figure, he suddenly seemed to me like a vulnerable child, like the loneliest human being in the universe, a man on the moon, far from everything that was warm, bright, alive.

I bowed low and hastily went down the stairs. All of a sudden I wanted only to be gone from here, away from those bare rooms, from all the cold splendor, the silence and darkness. I stumbled out and exhaled deeply, as if that would enable me to cough up all the evil in the castle like a poisonous gas.

When I glanced up, the king was still standing there, staring out at the woods.

A bloodless, lifeless waxwork of a king.

IFGQMT, WFT, IFI, IQT

The morning of the next day gave me a warm, bright welcome.

I opened my eyes because the sunbeams were tickling my nose. Last night was only a horrific memory, and I went down in high good humor to the kitchen, where Maria was busy washing dishes. I crept up quietly behind her and put my hands over her eyes, whereupon, laughing, she felt with her own wet hands for my face. Our quarrel of yesterday over Ludwig seemed to be forgotten.

"Stop that, Theodor!" she cried pertly. "Or shall I put soap on your black coat and tell the king?"

"Only if you promise to come out for some fresh air with me," I insisted. "Without Leopold. I promised the boy a new slingshot if he would leave the two of us in peace. In return I promise not to say a word about the king, agreed?"

"Very well," she said with a sigh. "But only for an hour. Then I have to do the laundry."

I let her go, and together we ran out into the green landscape, laughing like children, down the hill on which the monastery stood, and toward the woodland that spread over large parts of the island. I had not yet said anything to Maria about her strange expeditions to Oberammergau, and I decided that it could wait. Perhaps she might tell me about them herself sometime. Until then, I could hope that Leopold was only the fruit of a brief passion that had long ago grown cold, and no other man stood between me and my beloved.

As soon as we were in the shade of the beech trees to the south of the island, I tried again to take Maria in my arms and kiss her mouth. This time she looked at me angrily. Every trace of merriment had disappeared from her eyes.

"If this is what you lured me into the woods for, then let me tell you I'm no loose woman," she snapped. "You can do that with your other girls, not with me."

"There are no other girls," I assured her. "Maria, I really don't understand you. Don't you like me even a little?"

"More than you can know," she said, "but it will never do."

"For heaven's sake, why not? If it's because of Leopold, then believe me . . ."

But she had already turned away and was running farther into the wood. Shaking my head, I hurried after her. Ever since our first meeting, Maria had been a sealed book. I ardently hoped that she loved me, yet she seemed curiously reserved as soon as I showed my love for her. Did she still feel something for the father of her child, even though he had disavowed her years ago?

I finally caught up with her. She was sitting on a mossy stone, beside a little bubbling brook, crying quietly. Her whole body shook.

"He . . . he'll kill me," she whispered. "I can't do it, Theodor, or he'll kill me."

I froze. "Who?" I asked. "Who will kill you? Leopold's father?" At last I decided to break my silence. "Listen, Maria," I hesitantly began. "I know about your secret meetings in Oberammergau. I . . . I followed you one day because I was blind with jealousy. The man there has no more power over you. He disavowed you, and . . ."

"You fool!" she suddenly cried, as if beside herself. "What are you talking about? You don't understand anything. Anything!"

The next moment, a jay called not far away. I started and saw a figure standing behind one of the beech trees, only some twenty paces from us. The figure had moved out slightly from behind the trunk of the tree, presumably to observe us better, and so I could make out a sleeveless black coachman's coat, a top hat, and the ivory-handled walking stick that the man held. Suddenly he turned his face to me, and my heart missed a beat.

It was Carl von Strelitz.

The Prussian agent did not for one moment hesitate. With his free hand, he reached into the inner pocket of his coat and brought out a small black pistol. There was a report, and the bark of the beech tree directly behind me split open as if at the lash of a whip. I seized Maria's arm and drew her behind the rock.

"Do you have anything to do with this man?" I whispered as another shot rang out and dust from the rock rained down on us. "Have you set him on me? Is *he* the man who will kill you?"

Maria shook her head in silence. Fear seemed to hold her in its frozen grasp.

Desperately, I tried to calm my breathing, but my heart beat wildly. "He has a double-barreled Derringer," I said quietly, cautiously peering out from behind the rock. "He fired the same gun at me once before, a few weeks ago. The devil knows how he found me. At least he'll have to reload." I looked deep into Maria's eyes. "Now, we are going to run, do you hear me? Over to the castle, where we'll be safe. Don't turn around. Just run as fast as you can. One, two, *run!*"

On that last word we shot out from behind the rock and ran like hares. The castle was not very far away, and I could only hope that Carl von Strelitz would not overtake us before we reached it. As we ran, all kinds of thoughts whirled through my mind. What was the Prussian agent doing at Herrenchiemsee? Was he still pursuing me? But he must assume that I had long ago told the king about his meeting with Dr. Gudden. So was it simply a wish for revenge that brought him here, or was there some other reason for Strelitz's presence on the island? What had Maria meant when she said, *He'll kill me?*

We ran in haste over small streams and through thick undergrowth, so that my coat was soon dirty and ripped at the hem. Beside me, Maria was gasping for breath, but she bravely ran on toward the castle. It must now be hidden somewhere behind the trees to the northeast. I could only hope that in our wild haste we wouldn't miss seeing it. When, once, I briefly turned around, I saw that von Strelitz still had his walking stick in his hand. Now he pulled the ivory handle, and a long, thin blade appeared. He cut himself a way through the undergrowth with it, steadily gaining ground on us.

Beside me, Maria stumbled and fell full length in the muddy bend of a stream. I heard von Strelitz let out a cry of triumph. I knew at that moment that we wouldn't make it.

"Go on, run to the castle," I cried to Maria, roughly pulling at her dress. "I'll hold him off until you get there."

"But . . ."

"No buts!" I hauled her out of the stream. She swayed, tottered, and finally hurried on.

The Prussian agent was only a few paces behind me now. I could hear branches cracking as he broke through the thickets. I turned to face him. He held the swordstick stretched far out ahead of him; he meant to stick me like a pig. At the last moment I swerved aside and let him run into empty space; the top hat flew off his head.

Without taking my eyes off the agent, I picked up a stout branch lying on the mossy ground and swung it. Von Strelitz jumped back and feinted a move to the left, in order, finally, to thrust from the right. The blade slit open my coat, which was ruined anyway, and struck me right in the chest—where it unexpectedly met with hard resistance. I staggered a step back and looked down at myself in astonishment. I had expected to be mortally wounded. But a lucky dispensation of Providence had preserved me from death for the moment: the thrust of the blade had been deflected by my silver pocket watch!

With fresh heart, I rushed toward my adversary. This time I swung the branch like a scythe and uttered a berserk yell. Von Strelitz swerved, but the branch struck him on the side at chest height and sent him staggering. As he tottered backward, I took aim with the branch again, and this time I struck him on the left temple. Von Strelitz turned up his eyes, dropped the swordstick, and finally collapsed on the ground like a felled tree.

Instead of dealing him the final mortal blow, in my fear I threw the branch far from me, and hurried away. I almost expected von Strelitz to come after me, but suddenly the trees thinned out, and I saw the green, well-tended turf on the western side of the castle before me. On my right were the two fountains and the garden complex, and two gardeners with wheelbarrows stared at me in astonishment as I broke through the bushes like a wild boar being pursued.

Frantically, I looked around for Maria. She must be here somewhere! Or had she run on to the monastery in her panic? At last I found her, lying like the dead beside one of the basins. I stumbled a few more steps, and then I, too, sank to the ground. When I turned once to look back, the trees towered up in silence behind me, like a dark, high wall with evil raging beyond it.

There was no sign of von Strelitz.

"Who . . . who was that?" Maria gasped, as she lay there, still fighting for breath.

My mouth was full of a taste of iron; my rib cage hurt from the thrust of the sword. "An . . . old acquaintance," I finally managed to say. "And you? Are you sure you have never seen the man before?"

"By God, no, never! How could I have known him?" She sat up and looked at me, distraught, her face smeared with dirt and blood running in a fine trickle from an injury to her forehead. "For heaven's sake, Theodor!" she wailed. "What are you keeping from me?"

I shook my head and bent over her to wipe the blood away. "Nothing that has anything to do with you," I said. "Believe me, it is better for you to know nothing about it."

"But how am I to trust you in the future if you don't trust me?"

"I've sworn an oath."

"An . . . an oath?"

I closed her lips and went on cleaning her face and dress, in rough-

and-ready fashion, with water from the basin of the fountain. When I had finished, I turned away and went in silence toward one of the many flower beds.

"What are you doing?" she cried. "Don't leave me here alone."

I began hastily picking a bunch of white lilies. When I had finished, I came back and knelt down in front of her. Reverently and with bowed head, like a paladin before his queen, I offered her the flowers.

"Dearest Maria," I tentatively began. "The . . . the lily has been a symbol of purity and innocence since time immemorial. By the holy Virgin Mary and these flowers, I solemnly swear that none of the terrible recent events can destroy my love for you. I love you, Maria."

With these last words I drew her down to me, the white lilies fell from her hand, and we sank into a sea of flowers in a close embrace. For the first time I kissed her on the mouth. She tasted of mud and blood, of sweat, and of the sweet fragrance of an apple cake that she had baked that morning. I had never in my life tasted anything so wonderful.

At that moment steps crunched over the gravel behind us. I sat up in alarm, fearing to see Carl von Strelitz standing on the path.

But it was not Strelitz; it was the king.

Ludwig did not seem to have slept at all. His face was even more waxen than I remembered it when I had seen him in the night. His eyes glowed with a cold rage that I had never seen in him before.

"How . . . how could you dare do this, Marot?" he said in a hoarse voice, as if someone were constricting his throat with a thin cord. "My friend . . . I trusted you."

"Your Majesty . . ." I hesitantly replied, getting quickly to my feet as I brushed dust and dirt off my coat. "It is nothing that . . ."

"Get out of my sight before I put an end to you!" he shouted. His face swelled red as a turkey cock. He seemed to be inflating himself to twice his usual size, his whole stout body shaking like a mountain about to explode at any moment with the force of a power within it.

"I trusted you!" he roared. Picking up the lilies, he flung them in my face like someone throwing down a gauntlet. "I told you my *idea*, and this is how you repay me? Get out of here, both of you!"

At that moment, I was indeed afraid that the king might kill us both—strangle us with his fleshy paws, or drown us like a couple of kittens in the basin of the fountain. So I turned and ran with Maria toward the nearby castle.

Behind us, I heard Ludwig's bestial roar. But as we moved farther away, I realized that it changed more and more into weeping—a pathetic whining, like the sound of a child whose favorite toy has been taken away.

It was to be many months before I saw the king again.

· 21 ·

SHAKEN, STEVEN LUKAS PUT THE diary down on the bench beside him.

The love story of Theodor and Maria affected him more than he had expected. Maybe his sudden sympathy for them also had something to do with Sara. Like Theodor Marot, Steven didn't know what was happening to him. Angrily, the bookseller brushed that thought aside. When all this was over, and he could finally convince the police of his innocence, there would be time for Sara and him.

But first he must decipher the damn book.

The worst thing was that even after reading those last pages, he couldn't say what the second keyword was. He could only hope that the guided tour of the castle that evening would get him farther.

It was noticeably cooler now in the evening twilight. Steven buttoned up his coat, shouldered the rucksack, and walked back to the castle, where he was to meet Sara and Uncle Lu in half an hour's time.

As he walked along beside the lake under the shade of the beech trees, Steven several times felt as if he were being observed. Something creaked, a twig cracked somewhere, but whenever he turned around, all he saw was the red and yellow of the autumn leaves and the gray trunks of the beech trees forming a labyrinth behind him. He was reminded of the Cowled Men whom Sara thought she had seen on the island. Had they followed him? Steven quickened his step when a large black crow suddenly flew up in front of him and moved away through the air, cawing loudly. The bird sounded as if it were laughing at him.

At last he reached the canal that ran in a straight line from the lake to the castle. It led past hedges, flower beds where the flowers had faded, the empty basin of a fountain, green with algae, and ended at the forecourt of the princely building. There were only a few tourists about at this late hour. The little café in the side wing had closed, and the manager was just bringing in the tables and sun umbrellas. A gardener was wearily loading rakes and spades on a small truck before going off to enjoy his well-earned relaxation after the day's work.

Steven admired the basins of the two great fountains, with the mythological figures raising their arms to the twilight sky, where the air was breathless as if before a storm. He remembered the passage in Marot's diary when Ludwig II had stood exactly here, overcome by one of his famous fits of rage. For a split second Steven felt he had been catapulted back to those days, but he shook himself, and the moment was over.

If I'm not careful, I'll end up as crazy as Ludwig . . .

Steven was looking at his watch, to see if it was time to find Sara and Uncle Lu, when he suddenly heard a click to his left. A man in a voluminous green coat stood behind one of the hedges with a camera in his hands, and he seemed to be taking random pictures of the castle. But then Steven noticed that the lens was trained on him; the soft click sounded like the safety catch of a gun being taken off. Was this character photographing him?

Another man in a similar hunter's coat appeared behind one of the fountains. The stranger slowly raised a pair of field glasses to his face and examined the castle.

Is he looking at the castle or at me? Maybe I'm more paranoid than I thought.

The man in the hunter's coat came toward him, walking with long strides. He took something from under his sleeve; it had a silvery glint in the evening light. The sun was so low over the canal that it dazzled Steven, and he could not see the man properly. But he seemed about to speak to him; he was coming closer and closer; he . . .

"Hey, Steven! Here we are!"

Startled, Steven turned away and looked at the castle. Sara and Albert were standing at the entrance. The art detective waved cheerfully to him.

"Where were you?" she called to him. "We thought the woods must have swallowed you up."

"They almost did," Steven muttered. When he turned again, the man in the hunter's coat had disappeared. So had the man with the camera.

"I have good news and bad news for you," Uncle Lu said when Steven reached the castle. "The bad news is that so far we haven't found a single clue to any possible keyword. The good news is *this*." Grinning, he held up and jingled a bunch of keys. "All Herrenchiemsee, including the glass cases and the alarms, is open to us with these keys. The head of the security firm is a real Ludwig fan. In my time as a double, I once gave him my autograph and put a couple of my books at his disposal. Ever since then, he's thought as highly of me as if I were the king himself. Come along." He strode toward the entrance. "The night watchmen are leaving the emergency lighting on for us, and if it seems a little eerie, I have a couple of flashlights here as well."

"Good to see you again," Sara said quietly as they entered the dimly lit first floor. "I was beginning to miss you."

Steven felt a warm surge of emotion flood through him. "I . . . I missed you, too," he replied hesitantly. "Sorry if I unloaded my family history on you and . . ."

"Forget it." Sara cut him off with a smile. "One of these days I'll tell you about my own picture-perfect childhood." Suddenly her expression turned serious again. "Did you manage to find anything out?" she whispered, looking cautiously around. A few cleaning ladies were still busy with the toilets. Otherwise there was no one in sight. High-ceilinged white corridors stretched out to the right and left.

Steven shook his head with resignation. He briefly wondered whether to tell Sara about his odd encounter outside the castle and then decided not to. Very likely he really was suffering from paranoia. "Nothing that struck me as significant at first sight," he said, "but the story is getting more and more tragic."

For Sara and Uncle Lu, he briefly summed up Marot's arrival at Herrenchiemsee, his encounter with the king in the castle, and the spectacular events the next morning.

"Bound to turn out that way," interjected Uncle Lu, who was walking just ahead of Steven and Sara. "Ludwig falls in love with the handsome Theodor, so he's jealous of Maria. When it came to that sort of thing, the king could be a tricky bastard. According to several sources, he also had an affair with Hornig, his equerry. When the faithful Richard Hornig finally got married, Ludwig threw him straight out."

"But what I can't make out is why that man Strelitz was on the island," Sara said as they walked along the empty first-floor corridors. Their footsteps echoed on the worn, smoothly polished flagstones. "All he was really supposed to do was reassure Lutz and the other ministers that Bismarck was on their side. So what was he doing at Herrenchiemsee? Getting his revenge on Marot? Sounds to me like kind of a flimsy motive."

"We can forget about Strelitz for now," Steven replied. "What we need is the second keyword."

"You're right." Albert Zöller stopped in front of a huge entrance portal at the end of the corridor and took out the key ring. He searched for the biggest key with his greasy fingers and inserted it in the lock. Squealing, the heavy double doors swung open.

"Then we'll see what our friend Theodor made of it at the time," Uncle Lu said. "Let's hope love didn't paralyze his brain."

Two hours later, they stood in the king's magnificent council chamber on the second floor, their heads together over a worn old map spread out on a table covered by a blue velvet cloth.

Night had fallen outside. The few lights left on after the castle closed bathed the gilded stucco hall in a fairy-tale light. When Steven looked out of the windows, which were the height of a man, and stared into the darkness, he thought he saw something intermittently flickering outside. He assumed it was distant lightning portending a coming storm. But it could equally well be the reflection of their own flashlights in the countless windowpanes and mirrors of the castle.

Or someone else's flashlight, Steven thought. *This castle is massive.*

"Let's see," Uncle Lu said, tapping the ground plans of some of the rooms shown on the map. "We've been in the Great Hall of Mirrors, the Hall of Peace, the Hall of War . . ."

"Don't forget that bedroom with the blue globe and the four-poster bed in it," the bookseller said wearily. "As well as the writing room and the Blue Salon."

"We've been in every damn room on the first floor," Sara groused. "Even the ones that were never completed. My feet hurt with all this walking, and still we've found nothing. *Niente. Nada.*"

"There must be something we've overlooked," Steven said. "I'm sure the keyword is here. It's obvious that all the rooms in the castle revolve around Louis the Fourteenth. That's clear from the diary, and there was the word KING as a clue. So we must . . ."

Suddenly he gave a start.

"What is it?" Sara asked. "Did you think of something?"

Steven shook his head. "I heard a sound, footsteps somewhere. Could someone have followed us?"

"Only the night watchman," Zöller calmly replied. "And Franz is a good friend of mine. He knows we're looking around here, but we ought not to put too much of a strain on his patience. So you'd better go on, Herr Lukas."

With some hesitation, Steven nodded. He was still thinking of the two men he had seen on the castle forecourt. Had they really been only ordinary tourists, or were they, too, in the castle now? Were they the Cowled Men whom Sara thought she had seen? Exhausted, Steven rubbed his temples and tried to concentrate on the puzzle.

Very likely Uncle Lu was right, and by now he was simply too jumpy for such adventures.

"Marot mentions all the pictures, statues, and busts of the Sun King," he went on. "The entire castle is a tribute to Louis the Fourteenth, furnishings included. The code word *must* have something to do with him."

"But you've already tried all the words we thought of on your laptop," Zöller said. *"King Ludwig, Sun . . ."*

"Versailles?" Sara suggested. "It may be too long, but let me try it."

She took the laptop out of her bag and typed in the word. There was a soft beep.

"Fuck," she said. "If *NZC* is the title of a poem, then it has to be a pretty modern one, definitely not from the Romantic period." She tried typing in a few more words but soon gave up, swearing to herself.

"Can't you think of anything?" she asked Zöller, her nerves obviously on edge. "After all, you're supposed to be the expert."

Uncle Lu rolled his eyes. "I'm an expert on Ludwig the Second, not on your word games."

"We won't get anywhere like this," Steven said. He stared at the almost life-sized portrait of the Sun King behind the writing desk. It showed Louis XIV in his blue coronation cloak, with a pattern of little golden crosses, wearing a full-bottomed wig and with a cane held solemnly in one hand. He seemed to be looking down on the three of them, trying to solve their puzzle with something close to mockery.

"I'm sure that guy up there is trying to tell us something," Steven murmured. "But for the life of me I can't figure out what. The keyword must be something that's hidden and obvious at the same time, like the name *Maria* carved into the bark of the linden tree."

"What other rooms are there on this floor?" Sara asked, turning to Uncle Lu. "Could be we'll find something in them."

Zöller frowned. "As far as I know, only the robing room and bathroom were even half finished. Oh, and the kitchen with the apparatus working the magic table. Technically very interesting, but not the sort of room where you might expect to find a clue."

"All the same, I think we ought to take a look." Sara was already hurrying to the door, while Uncle Lu, grumbling, rolled up his map. "If only to see what kind of a wardrobe Ludwig had."

They went back to the first floor down a flight of stairs still in a rough state of construction. Now, at night, the echo of their footsteps sounded even more sinister than earlier in the evening when there were still a few other people in the now-empty building. Steven thought he heard soft voices, and gravel crunching outside the windows. He pressed his nose flat against one of the dim panes, but all he could see through it was the tops of linden trees, looking in the dark like the shaggy heads of gigantic rock trolls.

"Oh, come along," Zöller grumbled. "I told you it's only the night watchman. You'll get me shitting my own pants next."

Steven followed the others into a room where the beams of their flashlights revealed a huge metal structure. It looked to Steven like Dr. Frankenstein's dissecting table. Only at second glance did he notice the crank and the weights on either side of it. The platform extended upward to the ceiling.

"We're directly under the dining room here," Uncle Lu explained. "Ludwig used this hydraulic elevator to bring the already-set table up to the dining room above. The famous magic table straight out of the fairy tales. Not bad, eh? But take a look at this." He led Steven and Sara into a bathroom with a marble bath the size of a small hotel swimming pool.

"Ludwig's bathtub. The basin holds more than thirteen thousand gallons of water," Zöller said. "Presumably the king and his men friends . . . er, disported themselves here. But the room was never completed . . . Which means that Marot won't have seen it, and he can't have left a message here. I'm baffled, I'm afraid. End of guided tour."

"Nothing unusual in the robing room either," Sara called from a nearby room. "Apart from the fact that so many mirrors would have a terrible effect on my getting dressed in the morning. Seeing *one* big bum is quite enough. Here I'd see an infinite number of them. Not at all good for the ego . . ." Shrugging, she rejoined them in the bathroom.

Steven passed one hand wearily over his eyes. "I'm still sure we've overlooked something. Let's go through all the rooms again in our heads. The Great Hall of Mirrors, the porcelain room, the Blue Salon . . ."

Another sound stopped him. This time it came from the right, where the stairs led up to the second floor. When Steven turned around, he saw the night watchman, shining his flashlight straight into his face.

"No offense meant," the man intoned, "but I have to go over to the old monastery now. How much longer do you need?"

"Not long, Franz," Zöller replied. "We'll just take a quick look through again, and then we ought to be finished."

"Heavens above, Lu!" the night watchman said. "You got any idea the trouble you could land me in? If admin hears that I'm letting private guests into the place at night, I'll be fired. What are you doing here, anyway?"

"Helping the king, Franz. That's all I can tell you." Albert Zöller raised his hands in a placatory gesture. "Give us another hour and then we'll be off."

"Okay," the watchman said. "But only if you'll appear as Ludwig in the gondola again at our next meeting." He switched off the flashlight and turned away. "I'm going over to the monastery now. When I come back, I'll look in on the museum next door. I'd like you to be out of here by then."

"Just a moment," Steven said, when the night watchman had left. "The museum. We haven't been there yet."

Uncle Lu's brow wrinkled, and he studied the map again. "But what's the point? Yes, it's here in the castle, but it wasn't here when Ludwig was, so Marot can't have left any clue in there. More likely we'd find something in the garden, but we'd have to wait until tomorrow for that."

"But the rooms themselves *were* here at the time," Sara objected. "Steven's right. We ought at least to take a look at the museum."

"Oh, very well, Frau Lengfeld," Uncle Lu growled. "You and Herr Lukas go to the museum, and I'll rattle through the rooms on the second floor again. Let's meet by the cash desk in an hour's time. If we haven't found anything by then, we'll give up for the night. I can't keep Franz waiting any longer, and that's my last word."

Still grousing quietly, the old man moved away and disappeared behind the metal structure of the magic table. The lightning of the coming thunderstorm flashed beyond the windows.

SARA AND STEVEN WAITED UNTIL Uncle Lu's footsteps had died away on the stairs. Now the only sounds were the occasional click of the emergency lighting and their own breathing. In silence, they hurried back along the corridor to the reception desk, from which a narrow passage led to the east wing of the castle. They ducked under a barrier and entered the dark museum.

"Not that I think we'll find much here," Steven said, "but I'd like to go to bed feeling we really have tried everything."

"And it's good for the two of us to be on our own," Sara whispered.

Steven grinned. "Did Marot's tryst with Maria inspire you? If so, we'd better be quick before Zöller . . ."

"Idiot!" Sara snapped. "That's not what I meant. We need to talk about Uncle Lu."

Steven raised his eyebrows in surprise. "Why?"

"Up to now he's played pretty dumb for a genuine Ludwig expert, don't you think? As if he didn't want us to find anything out. And he spent a long time chatting to those guys from security just now. All dyed-in-the-wool Ludwig fans, like that eccentric fisherman who brought us over in his boat. And at midday, he suddenly disappeared for half an hour."

"You mean . . ."

"I mean maybe it was a mistake for me to let someone like Zöller in on the whole story. How do we know he wouldn't like to have the diary for himself? For himself or some organization that he's working for in secret. That green Bentley only began following us *after* we'd visited Zöller."

"The Cowled Men. You really think he's working with them? He himself described them as a bunch of idiots."

"Maybe only to divert suspicion from himself. In any event, we ought to keep our eyes open."

They entered a long corridor, where nothing but vague outlines could be seen in the dim emergency lighting. Outside the windows, distant lightning flashed, and thunder rumbled from the other side of the lake. The king's christening robe, coronation cloak, and death mask hung in glass cases beside the corridor walls. In one niche Steven saw yellowed photographs charting the course of Ludwig's physical decline. He looked thoughtfully from one to another. On the extreme left was a lanky youth with a slightly feminine cast of countenance, a cigarette in his fingers coquettishly stretched out in front of him. On the extreme right was a fat, bloated man in a Bavarian hat, one of the last photographs of Ludwig, taken just before his death. The contrast sent a shudder down the bookseller's spine. What could happen in the life of a person to bring about such a change?

More sparsely lit halls followed, containing furniture, photographs, glass cases, and finally a life-sized marble statue of the king. The statue was in the shadows, so that for a brief moment Steven thought he was looking at a living man. He imagined Ludwig climbing down from his marble pedestal to them, in order to tell them his secret.

The bookseller found the silence around them oppressive; he felt as if he were inside a casket. A black wave of memories lapped against the door of his subconscious mind. Steven saw himself as a boy, standing beside his parents' grave with red-rimmed eyes.

Ashes to ashes, dust to dust . . .

"Is that Neuschwanstein?" he whispered, to take his mind off the memories, looking at the model of a fairy-tale castle set on a plaster rock.

Sara shook her head as she read the plaque affixed to it. "That's Falkenstein Castle," she said. "Another castle that Ludwig intended to build near Pfronten. Unfortunately, his death prevented it, although I suspect his ministers would finally have turned off the money tap before that."

In the dim light, Steven made his way into the next high-ceilinged room, where there were more models. By now he was in control of himself again.

"This is interesting," he called to Sara, who was still standing in front of the plaster model of Falkenstein Castle. "Here's a model of a group of statues intended for the Apollo Fountain down by the canal. Exactly where Theodor gave Maria that bunch of flowers."

Steven looked at the statue of the Greek god on his chariot of the sun. "The sun as a symbol again. I really could have sworn that was the keyword."

His eyes fell on a decorative vase beside the model. An inscription told him that it, too, came from Herrenchiemsee. Again the sun stood in its glory over the portrait of Louis XIV, which was surrounded by fine porcelain flowers. Farther down was the crest of the Sun King: three golden lilies on a blue field.

Suddenly Steven stopped dead. In his excitement, he almost forgot to breathe.

Three golden lilies . . .

Heart thudding, he remembered the last entry in the diary, the exact passage where Theodor confessed his love to the shy Maria.

The lily has been a symbol of purity and innocence since time immemorial . . .

The royal physician's assistant had not chosen flowers at random for Maria, but very special flowers. They had been *lilies*, white lilies. Could that be mere coincidence?

And Steven also recollected where he had already seen the same flowers—in the council chamber, more precisely on the picture of the

Sun King. His cloak had been plastered all over with lilies. He simply hadn't recognized them as flowers.

I'm sure that guy up there is trying to tell us something. Something that's hidden and obvious at the same time . . .

"Sara!" he cried as his heart beat faster and faster. "I . . . I think I know what the keyword is."

"*What?*" Sara hurried over to him. "You found it? Here?"

Laughing, Steven shook his head. "It was around us the whole time. Do you remember what flowers Marot picked for Maria? They were lilies. The lily is the crest of the Bourbon rulers, the sign of the Sun King." He pointed to the flowers on the decorative vase. "See for yourself. Three golden lilies on a blue field!"

"My God," Sara groaned. "It really was all over the place on the second floor. I even saw it on the benches in the Great Hall of Mirrors."

"And on the painting in the council chamber," Steven added excitedly. "The Sun King's coronation cloak. It was covered with golden lilies. Marot was practically rubbing our noses in it. He built lilies into his story on purpose. Those remarks about innocence and purity should have tipped me off. And what's more, lilies flower in midsummer, not in October."

"Three big wet kisses if you're right." Frantically, Sara dug her laptop out of the bag, put it on one of the glass cases, and typed the word *Lilies* into the decoding program. A few seconds later disappointment clouded her face.

"Damn!" she swore quietly, turning the screen so that Steven could take a look at it. "Just another jumble of letters."

Steven stared at the Input and Output fields.

XVI . . .

Input	IDT
Key	LILIES
Output	XVI

The bookseller stopped. "Just a moment," he said finally. "That's not a tangle of letters—it's a Roman numeral. Sixteen. Suppose XVI stands for Louis the Sixteenth? After all, he was the Sun King's grandson, and another Bourbon."

"You mean . . ." Sara typed the next coded words in the puzzle into her computer, and a row of figures appeared on the screen.

V, XVI, CXIII, LXXXXIII, XV, LXXXXVIII

LIX, VII, XXVIII, LXI, XXX, XII

"You're right," she said. "Roman numerals, thirteen of them in all."

"I wonder whether they're for some royal dynasty?" said Steven, baffled. "German or French rulers?"

"No idea." At top speed, Sara entered a few more words from Marot's diary into the laptop. "All I know is that this can't be the whole solution to the puzzle. The last third of the diary contains coded letters that can't be deciphered, with LILIES as the keyword." She smiled. "I assume you know the next word in Marot's account written in capitals?"

Steven groaned. "NEUSCHWANSTEIN . . . the third part of the puzzle. Of course, Ludwig built three castles, so there are three places in the puzzle. We might have guessed. And the last keyword?" He went to get the little treasure chest out of his rucksack, but Sara waved him away.

"Don't bother. I already looked. It's WAGNER." Smiling, Sara closed the laptop. "At least we know we're getting somewhere. So now let's . . ."

There was a rustling sound behind them. Steven turned around, expecting to see Uncle Lu.

"Herr Zöller, I thought we were meeting . . ." he began. But the words died away on his lips.

Three men were standing in front of a large painting of the Fairytale King as if they had just walked out of the picture. They wore Bavarian suits and green hunter's coats, and two of them wore green Alpine hats. It must have begun to rain outside, because large drops fell from the brims of their hats, forming puddles on the floor. The man in the middle had sparse gray hair and wore an old-fashioned pair of pince-nez. He looked like a schoolteacher in an old movie. At that moment, bright lightning flashed outside the museum windows, followed by a crash of thunder.

"Good evening, Herr Lukas," the stranger said in a grating voice. "I did say we'd be meeting you again."

· 23 ·

INSTINCTIVELY, STEVEN LUKAS TOOK a step back. The stranger before him was none other than the elderly gentleman who had turned up at his antiquarian bookshop five days ago, the man who, dressed as a magician, had waved the hood of a cowl at him at the party in Linderhof. And presumably also the man he had seen outside by the fountain earlier that evening. So he had not been imagining those voices and footsteps in the castle.

"You . . . you're the boss of the Cowled Men . . ." Steven stammered. The man nodded while at the same time he watched Sara frantically search her purse.

"If your charming companion is thinking of producing a gun from her makeup case, then you should strongly recommend she do no such thing," he said. A small black pistol gleamed in his hand. "This is a Walther PPK, a deadly large-caliber toy that I normally use only on wounded wild boar." The little eyes behind the pince-nez twinkled craftily at Sara and Steven. "My great passion, you see, is hunting, which includes hunting for rare antiquities. Particularly when they have some connection with Ludwig the Second." With his gun, he indicated Sara's purse. "Put that down on the floor, please. Believe me, this is all a misunderstanding."

Cautiously, Sara put down her purse. "A misunderstanding?" she snapped. "You want the book and we have it. So don't bullshit me, Herr . . ."

She paused, and the man gave her a smug smile. "You may call me Huber, a good Bavarian name. I am what you might call the steersman of our little association. The gentlemen to my right and left are my two valued lieutenants, Herr Meier and Herr Schmidt." The two men in hunter's coats bowed. "As for the book," Herr Huber continued, "you are right, we do want it. But not to take it away from you. On the contrary, we want to help you decode it."

"Help us?" Steven stared at the leader of the Cowled Men.

"You heard me." Herr Huber put the pistol in the side pocket of his Bavarian coat and then raised his hands in a placatory gesture. His face looked gray as rock in the emergency lighting.

"We are a very old order," he said in a soft Bavarian singsong. "When Emperor Frederick Barbarossa drowned in the river Saleph while on the Third Crusade, his knights wrapped themselves in black cloaks and covered their heads with black hoods. Ever since then, we have paid honor to great emperors and kings. Ludwig was the last of them who stood for those old ideals. We will not rest until his murder has finally been explained and atoned for." With slow, almost majestic strides, the man who called himself Herr Huber paced through the room and sat down on an armchair with a gilded frame. In his voluminous coat, he reminded Steven of a stern storybook king on his throne. The two lieutenants placed themselves behind their leader. Judging by their physical size, they could well be the two Cowled Men who had chased Steven over the Theresienwiese in Munich.

"Then why are you following us if, as you say, we all want the same thing?" he asked the leader. "Why put on this show?"

Herr Huber shook his head. "You don't understand. *We* were not following you—that was always the others."

Steven frowned. "The others?"

"The people who killed the professor, and who are going to kill the pair of you if you don't watch out for yourselves." Herr Huber leaned back on his throne. "Let me illuminate the situation for you," he said. "It was about three weeks ago that Professor Liebermann first got in touch with us. He spoke of Theodor Marot's diary, a book that has always been rumored to exist and that is said to prove that our king was murdered. And now it did indeed seem to have turned up at an Internet auction, where Paul Liebermann acquired it for a ridiculously small sum. The professor came to us for help with its transliteration."

"Came to *you* for help?" Sara's mouth twisted in a mocking smile. "Why would my uncle have done that?"

"Your . . . uncle?" For a moment the leader of the Cowled Men seemed genuinely bewildered, but quickly recovered. "We wondered what part you are playing in this game," he said. "But to return to your question: among our ranks we have several of the leading experts on Ludwig. Where finding lost files from that time is concerned, we can do it faster than anyone. Professor Liebermann knew that, and so he contacted us. He even came to Munich on purpose to see us. But then he broke contact."

"Why?" Steven asked, torn between fear and curiosity. He was still staring as if spellbound at the self-styled steersman in his wide-skirted coat. The Cowled Man looked like someone out of a different era, like a sepia picture in an otherwise brightly colored catalog. In addition, he radiated natural authority—but did that mean he could be trusted? Suppose this was a trap? Suppose all these men wanted was to get their hands on Marot's diary?

"We suspect that someone else got wind of the book and put the professor under pressure," Herr Huber said. "Maybe Liebermann thought we had something to do with this unknown person. At any rate, he did not get in touch with us again, and we began shadowing him to find out why. And during one of these shadowing operations of ours, it finally happened."

"What finally happened?" Sara asked impatiently. "This is like pulling teeth."

"Liebermann left his hotel carrying a package and went straight to Herr Lukas's antiquarian bookshop. When he came out, a black Chrysler was waiting, and two men dragged him into the car. The book seemed to have disappeared." The steersman rose from his throne and went over to the white marble statue of Ludwig in the other corner of the room. He gently ran one finger over the king's stone cloak. "At first we were baffled. But on the evening of the same day, I visited Herr Lukas myself. We had to make sure that he had nothing to do with the professor's abduction."

"And chasing me, wearing cowls, across the Theresienwiese?" the bookseller asked. "What was the point of that? You scared me half to death."

Herr Huber smiled. "That was exactly the point. We wanted to show you that we are not to be trifled with. We were going to increase the pressure on you gradually. If you had really known anything about the abduction, you'd soon have cracked."

"Thanks a lot," Steven muttered. "Next time why not wear grim reaper masks and swing a scythe?"

"The fight down in the cellar storeroom of the bookshop wasn't part of this planned terror scenario, then?" Sara asked.

The steersman shook his head and pointed to the silent lieutenant standing on his left. "That was Herr Schmidt. He went to take another look around your stockroom. And suddenly he came upon that other man . . ." He sighed deeply. "You know the rest. Herr Schmidt owes his life to the two of you. We Cowled Men, therefore, are in your debt." The man who called himself Schmidt again bowed silently.

"Oh, and that's why you tried to scare me to death again in Linderhof?" replied Steven. "My heart all but stopped when I recognized you dressed as a magician."

"What was I to do?" The leader of the Cowled Men turned away from the marble statue. "We knew that some unknown power was after both of you. Fortunately, one of our informants at the ticket office recognized you. I had to make contact with you at Linderhof while remaining incognito, or I would have put myself in danger." He briefly smiled. "After hunting, my other great passion is for doing magic tricks. None of the security staff noticed that no magician had been hired to perform at the party. And as for the trick with the hood . . ." Herr Huber bowed like a cheap variety artiste. "I'm sorry, but I couldn't help myself. We Cowled Men have always been inclined toward the theatrical, a quality that, as it happens, we share with the king."

"You weren't exactly inconspicuous here on the island either," Sara said. "I saw all three of you in the monastery. And there was no missing that green Bentley in which you followed us from Albert Zöller's house."

The elderly gentleman looked at her in surprise. "Green Bentley? We don't drive any green Bentley." He set off with his silent lieutenants into the next dimly lit room. "Your friend Albert Zöller isn't the only one who knows members of staff here. Two of the security guards are our people, and so are several of the gardeners and the man down at the harbor ticket office. He informed us of your arrival. Unfortunately, we lost track of you for a while, Herr Lukas, and picked up your trail again only outside the castle. Now, follow me this way, please. I want to show you something interesting."

Sara and Steven entered a smaller room where a wooden boat stood on the left, among some artificial reeds. An oil painting behind it showed a kind of jungle garden stretching into the distance.

"This boat comes from Ludwig the Second's conservatory, which once stood on the roof of the Residence Palace in Munich," explained Herr Huber, pointing to a few old photographs on the opposite wall. "Sad to say, the roofed winter garden was demolished soon after the king's death. It was enormous, almost two hundred thirty feet long, and as tall as a church. There were palms in it, orange and banana trees, a grotto with stalactites, waterfalls, a hut thatched with reeds, and a small lake." The steersman's voice almost cracked with emotion. "Imagine such a refuge for our politicians today on the roof of the Reichstag in Berlin. They could walk at their leisure up there, debate, indulge in their dreams. Who knows, perhaps many of their decisions would be quite different."

"Maybe hookah pipes and hashish ought to be distributed to the parliament?" Sara suggested. "The federal president invites you to a course in drumming and fire dancing."

The leader of the Cowled Men briefly closed his eyes. "It hurts me to hear such sentiments from the mouth of Professor Liebermann's niece," he said. "Your uncle was a great romantic."

"But not a romantic lunatic, that's the difference."

"Be that as it may," Herr Huber said. "All I want to say to you both is this: Ludwig the Second was a genius, a shining light who has been dragged through the dirt for far too long. We cannot allow his reputation to be further sullied by the memoirs of some low-born lackey. So I am afraid I must insist on being allowed to see that diary before it becomes public property."

"But what makes you think that Theodor Marot meant the king ill?" Steven asked. "I've read large parts of the diary. Marot was true to Ludwig to the end."

"Obviously *too* true." The steersman took off his pince-nez and began nervously cleaning the lenses. "There are rumors that Marot was, well . . . homosexual, and made advances to the king. Not that Ludwig would have fallen for such a thing. God forbid. However, certain protestations of love on Marot's part could nonetheless cast a poor light on the king . . ."

"That's ridiculous!" Steven exclaimed. He felt rising anger. "Theodor Marot wasn't gay—Ludwig was. And you know it. You're trying to falsify history. Can't you just accept that your precious king was gay? Is it such a big deal?"

"I can only repeat myself," Herr Huber said as his two assistants moved menacingly toward Sara and Steven. "The king's honor must be defended by every means at our disposal. I will therefore ask you to hand me the book at once." Suddenly the black pistol was back in his hand. "Don't make me use force. The king was a pacifist, and I am really a pacifist, too. Up to a point."

Now the two lieutenants were standing beside Sara and Steven. As one of them positioned himself threateningly in front of the art detective, the other reached swiftly for Steven's rucksack.

"Hey, you can't just . . ." Steven began, but the Cowled Man had already wrenched the rucksack from his grasp and threw it to his boss. Herr Huber worked frantically at the zipper, finally pulling it open. He triumphantly lifted the little wooden treasure chest.

"At last," he whispered, his voice husky. "My dream becomes reality. After more than a hundred years, soon we will find out who . . ."

There was a faint pop, and the steersman's voice died away midsentence. Astonished, he looked at a small red circle on the chest of his coat. A thin stream of blood flowed from it.

Herr Huber moaned and collapsed between his two lieutenants, his trembling hands still clutching the treasure chest.

A moment later the light went out, and the inside of the museum was suddenly dark as a grave.

Thick mist began rising from the floor.

· 24 ·

LANCELOT WAS ANGRY. Very angry.

He had served in Iraq and in several African states, the names of which he had long ago forgotten. But this Bavarian job was becoming more and more complicated, with incalculable risks and an insane boss. He had already paid for it with one eye, and he had no intention of losing any other parts of his body, let alone his reason or his life.

Think of the Caribbean, think of the girls.

Directly after getting in touch with the Munich and New York control centers about that damn antiquarian bookseller, he had gone back on the trail. But at first it was as if the earth had opened and swallowed up both that little bitch and Steven Lukas after they reached Herrenchiemsee. When Lancelot had finally seen a light in the castle that evening, he had slipped in and, to his delight, had found the couple on the second floor. A fat old guy was with them, but he wouldn't present any problems.

Then, unfortunately, an armed night watchman joined the three of them, and Lancelot decided to put off attacking. Instead, he followed the woman and the bookseller into the museum, where he could eavesdrop on their conversation from the next room. Now he knew that the woman's name was Sara, and he also knew the second keyword—an advantage that he could turn into hard cash from The

Deranged Majesty. In addition, he had found the power distributor box for the museum in the ticket office. A couple of switches thrown, the smoke bombs he had brought with him from the dinghy set off, and the museum would turn into a haunted house.

With Lancelot as the chief attraction.

Hey there, Sara. Afraid of the Dark Man, are you?

Everything was going as planned until those three men arrived, at least one of them armed. When they were about to make off with the book, Lancelot finally lost his cool and fired a shot. Now one of the men was wallowing in a pool of blood, the other two were yelling blue murder, and the bookseller and his slut were about to disappear, taking the book with them.

In other words, it was time to act.

Lancelot fired his Glock 17 with its fitted silencer into the distributor box twice. At once the museum was plunged into total darkness. Then the giant threw the smoke bombs into the middle of the room, where they exploded with a faint hiss. Swirling mist spread like an overdose of incense.

Lancelot changed the magazine of his semiautomatic pistol, pulled down the gas mask he had brought with him, and plunged into the smoke.

Coughing, Sara staggered through the room, which was rapidly filling with dense smoke. Soon everything was invisible: the boat, the painting, the two surviving Cowled Men. Their uncertain footsteps were the only sign of their presence. But soon they moved off and finally died away entirely. Apparently the two men had succeeded in getting out of the museum.

Suddenly that faint pop came again, once, twice, three times. It sounded as if glass cases were smashing somewhere; then there was quiet, with only a slight hissing from where the mists were thickest.

"Steven!" Sara called into the smoke, trying to breathe in as little of it as possible. "Steven, where are you ? Where . . ."

She stopped midsentence when it struck her that it wasn't particularly clever to shout in a room where a murderer might be hiding. Silently, she groped her way through the room, until she suddenly stumbled over something large. She fell to the floor and found herself looking straight into the rock-gray face of the steersman of the Cowled Men. His mouth gaped in surprise, as if he still couldn't understand that he was really dead.

As Sara struggled up, her right hand met the little box containing the diary. She snatched it up and crawled on through the smoke-filled room on all fours. She heard suppressed coughing somewhere, and soon after that saw someone curled up in a corner, barely moving. Cautiously coming closer, she saw that it was Steven. He had drawn up his knees in the fetal position and was staring apathetically into the smoke. A slight tremor ran through his body.

"Steven, what is it?" Sara whispered. "What's the matter?"

"The . . . the fire," the bookseller answered. His eyes were vacant. "It's like that time in the library. My parents . . . they're somewhere in there."

Sara shook him. "You're dreaming! We're in the museum at Herrenchiemsee. Your parents died years ago."

"I . . . I heard screaming. They're burning alive. It's my fault; it's all my fault!"

"You didn't hear your parents—it was the Cowled Men," Sara hissed desperately. "Someone shot their boss. And it's not a fire in here—it's some kind of smoke bomb. There's someone in this room, and if we don't hurry, he's going to shoot us the way he shot that Herr Huber."

"Must . . . must hide," Steven whimpered. "I've ruined everything. The library's on fire. Mom and Dad won't find me in the teahouse . . ."

"Damn it, what teahouse? What are you talking about? Steven, you leave no choice." With all her might, she gave the trembling bookseller a slap in the face that brought him halfway back to consciousness. He shook himself and, dazed, felt his cheek.

"That hurt."

"It was meant to. Now, we have to get out of here."

Sara hauled the still-lethargic Steven up by his arms until he could stand on his own. Then, together, they stumbled and groped their way through the room, hoping to find a way out through the smoke.

"I think we ought to look for that boat," Sara gasped, the smoke constricting her throat more and more. "There was a door into the next room with the marble statue there. Then if we go right and straight ahead, we ought to . . ."

She stopped dead when she heard soft footsteps only a few yards away. There was a steady hissing sound, as if from a pair of bellows being blown.

"Oh God, there's someone here!" Sara froze where she was and clung to Steven. They waited in silence until the footsteps and the hissing sound died away. The bookseller signed to her to stay quiet, then drew her into the back right-hand corner of the smoke-filled room. His expression was tense but concentrated. Sara heaved a sigh of relief; Steven seemed to have overcome his strange trauma.

Suddenly there was a scraping sound, this time from the other side of the room. Sara still held the little treasure chest, clutching it to her breast like a talisman. Her heart thudded; she expected to hear the "pop" of the silencer at any moment, followed by unbearable pain. The smoke around them was still so thick that she couldn't see more than a pace in front of her. With difficulty, she fought down her urge to cough. Any sound now, however slight, might give them away.

She was about to steal along beside the wall with Steven, hoping to find one of the two passages at some point, when a figure emerged from the vapor ahead of them.

The figure looked like a giant out of a fairy tale, and this giant was in a very, very bad mood.

The strange figure was more than six feet tall. He wore jeans, a black leather coat, and a close-fitting pullover. In one hand he held a long, slim pistol with a silencer; in the other a flashlight the length of his forearm. The worst thing, however, was his head. His face was covered by a black gas mask, which gave him the look of a monstrous fly.

"Hello, Sara," Lancelot said. His voice came through the gas mask in a curiously muted hiss. "Not very nice to Papa, were you? But now you have all the time in the world to make up for it."

STEVEN FOUGHT WITH all his might against his rising faintness. Once again, parts of his childhood took shape before his eyes.

When he saw the giant striding toward him through the smoke, he thought at first he was seeing the firefighter in the gas mask who had carried him away from the ivy-covered teahouse on that dreadful evening. His parents' screams had died away, and Steven had opened the pagoda door a little way to glance out at the fire, now lighting up the whole street like a hundred searchlights. The party guests were still standing around the large garden in dinner jackets and evening dresses, staring at the burning villa. Many of them were shedding tears; others held handkerchiefs over their mouths to protect themselves from flying ash.

All my fault . . . Mom and Dad will be very cross . . .

Steven had finally been given away by his whimpering. The gigantic firefighter had found him in the teahouse, picked him up like a kitten, and carried him through the smoke and outside.

But when he saw the black pistol in the giant's hand, Steven knew that he was facing not good but the depths of evil. This must be the man who had lain in wait for Sara at Linderhof; now the bookseller could understand why she had called him the worst nightmare of her life.

And you are my nightmare, too, although you don't know why . . .

Beside him, Sara screamed, while the tall stranger calmly trained his gun on the bookseller.

"Good evening, Herr Lukas," he growled. The smoke was beginning to clear, and the man pushed his gas mask up. He had a scar on his face and wore a black-colored eye patch. "I have a score to settle with your girlfriend," he went on in a deep, sonorous voice. "I suggest you go to sleep for a while now, and then the two of us will be taking a little journey." He smiled and ran the muzzle of his pistol over his lips, which were moist with sweat. "Sara will be staying here, I'm afraid. She has been a very, very naughty girl. Goodnight now, Herr Lukas."

Without any warning, the giant swung the pistol and struck Steven a blow over the temple. The bookseller staggered, everything went black before his eyes, and he collapsed.

Surprisingly, he did not entirely lose consciousness; the blow had not been quite hard enough for that. From the floor, Steven saw the dead leader of the Cowled Men lying in front of him, covered in blood. He watched, despairingly, as the giant marched through the drifting smoke toward Sara. There was a fire in her eyes that Steven had never seen there before.

"One more step, you great castrated ox," she hissed, "and I'll scratch your other eye out."

"I hardly think so," the giant said. "This time I'm better prepared." He pointed with the pistol to the body of the steersman of the Cowled Men. "I suppose you don't want to end up like that. So put that damn box down on the floor very slowly, understand?"

Sara nodded and bent to put the treasure chest with the book in it down. At first Steven was surprised to see the art detective comply so quickly, but then he saw how Sara's eyes were feverishly moving over the floor.

She's looking for her purse. The thought flashed through his head. *She's looking for her purse with the pistol in it.*

Cautiously, the bookseller turned his head the other way. There, only six feet from him, lay Sara's green purse. Steven swiftly worked out the length of time he would need to draw the pistol and shoot. Two seconds to jump up, with his head still ringing from the giant's blow, and grab the purse. Then at least three more to open it, take out the gun, and pull the trigger.

Five seconds. Too long, damn it!

Unless someone distracted the giant . . .

At that moment his eyes and Sara's met. The detective seemed to have guessed at his thoughts, because as soon as she was standing upright again, she spoke to the giant with the pistol.

"I don't know what you plan to do with the box, but help yourself. You're welcome to it," she said in a firm voice. "Good luck finding the book, though."

The giant looked at her grimly. "And what do you mean by that?"

"I mean the book isn't in that box, you idiot. The bookseller hid it somewhere. Unfortunately, you've knocked him unconscious, and I have no idea where it is. You'd better think something up quick if you don't want to piss off your boss."

"If you're trying to fool me . . ." The giant bent over the container and picked it up. Curious, he opened the little box.

At that moment Steven jumped up and ran to the purse. The seconds stretched endlessly. He grabbed the green purse, unzipped it, and brought out the pistol. Shaking, he aimed it at the giant, who had frozen where he stood, and pulled the trigger.

Nothing happened.

"Ah, you always have to take the safety off a gun first," the giant said, smiling and pointing to a small lever on the butt of his own pistol. "*My* gun's safety is already off, by the way." At his leisure, he aimed the pistol at Steven's legs. "The boss did say to take you alive," he growled. "Never specified in what condition, though. Watch out, this is going to be very, very painful."

Steven closed his eyes and waited for the shot.

It didn't come.

When he opened his eyes again, he saw that the giant was staring at the door on his left in confusion. In the now-clearing smoke, a broad-shouldered figure stood in a voluminous royal cloak, one hand raised in admonition or greeting, his black-haired head angrily thrust forward.

It was Ludwig II.

Steven's mouth hung open in astonishment. No doubt about it, the man in the vapors was the Fairy-tale King. Incredulous, Steven closed his eyes and then opened them again. But the king was still there.

Am I losing my mind? Is there something in that smoke that sets off hallucinations?

The giant seemed baffled at first, too. He seemed unable to assess the situation. Slowly, he lowered his gun.

"But, Your Majesty . . ." he stammered. "You're here? I thought . . ."

"Stay your hand, unworthy man," said a deep, resonant voice, "before my anger strikes you like a flash of lightning from a clear blue sky!"

When Steven heard the voice, he started in surprise. Only now did it occur to him that, even for Ludwig II, the figure was decidedly fat. The smoke was still drifting quite densely over the floor, but the bookseller could see beige front-pleated pants under the royal mantle, and a pair of casual shoes splashed with mud.

Furthermore, this Ludwig wore glasses.

Steven looked at Sara, who had also been staring at the figure in the mist. At the same moment, she seemed to realize, as he did, who the king really was. It took the giant a moment longer.

That was his mistake.

Steven flicked off the safety, aimed into the smoke, and pulled the trigger. After the "pop" of the silencer on the giant's gun, the sound of the shot that followed was deafening. In spite of the small size of the weapon, the recoil was so violent that the bookseller almost dropped the pistol. For a moment Steven thought he had missed, but then the giant dropped his own pistol and staggered several paces back until the smoke finally swallowed him up. To be on the safe side, Steven fired a few more shots, and then he ran over to Sara.

"Is everything okay?" he cried, reaching for the little treasure chest.

She nodded. Together, they went over to the doorway where the fat king still stood.

"I stole the coronation cloak from one of the broken glass cases," Albert Zöller panted. "His Majesty will never forgive me, but I had to distract that lunatic's attention somehow, before he shot you both. Who was he, anyway? Just as I was going over to join you in the museum, the lights went out, there was a crashing and a clanking, and two men came toward me, screaming."

"We'll tell you all about it later," Steven said, ushering the group at a run to the museum exit. At last they reached the castle entrance, where the door was wide open. Outside, rain poured down in torrents, the night was starless, and only occasional flashes of bright lightning passed over the sky. Not until they had reached the fountains did the three fugitives stop to catch their breath.

"Where . . . where do we go now?" Sara asked, turning and looking around her. In spite of the cool fall air, sweat ran down her face, joining the rain to form small streams. "Over to the monastery? At least there'll be a few people there."

"I don't think that's a great idea." Zöller frowned. "The security staff will probably have us up against the wall for lèse majesté. I did switch the alarm system off, but when they see all this, they'll put two and two together. There are some fanatical Ludwig fans among the night watchmen. I doubt that they'd settle for just banning us from Herrenchiemsee for life." Uncle Lu searched his pants pocket and brought out a scratched cell phone. "I tell you what we'll do. I'll call Alois at the Prien fisheries and tell him to pick us up down at the chapel. And then I'll give myself until morning to work out how we can extricate ourselves from this mess."

"One way or another we'd better hurry," Sara said suddenly. "Looks like there's no way to kill that knight."

Steven glanced back at the castle, where a figure in a leather coat was staggering through the exit. The man was clutching his right leg, but otherwise he seemed to be uninjured. Pistol in hand, he looked searchingly into the rain-lashed night.

"He's alive and kicking, Steven, damn it!" Sara cursed. "Where the hell did you learn to shoot? At the Oktoberfest carnival?"

"I wish I had. To tell you the truth, I'd never held a gun in my life before."

"Get out of here . . . He's seen us." Puffing and panting, Albert Zöller ran over to the small tool-filled truck that the gardeners had parked there. The giant seemed to have spotted them. He limped toward them, his gun raised.

"What's the plan?" Sara called to Uncle Lu, who was now sitting, legs apart, in the driver's seat of the truck. "Are you planning to hot-wire the truck? We don't have time for that."

"Didn't I tell you the head of the security staff gave me all the keys to Herrenchiemsee?" Zöller produced the large, rusty bunch of keys from his pocket. "As far as I remember, there's a single key for all the minitrucks on this island," he muttered. "The only question is, which is it . . ." Slowly, he tried to put one of the many keys into the ignition. "No, not this one."

"Damn it, hurry!" Sara screamed. She and Steven had clambered up on the bed of the truck. "That lunatic will be in firing range any second."

Sure enough, Steven heard a hiss, and soon after that, stone dust sprayed up from the rim of the basin of the fountain.

"Let's try this one," Uncle Lu muttered. "This could be it. Oh no, not this one either."

Another bullet struck one of the statues in the Fountain of Fortuna. In spite of his injury, the giant was astonishingly fast. He had now covered almost half the distance between them, and Steven could see his face distorted by hatred. He was dragging one leg, and seemed to be in great pain. Now the man stood still again and aimed at the truck. Steven instinctively knew that he wasn't going to miss this time.

There was a rattle, and the rusty truck leaped forward. With a tinny sound, three more bullets riddled the load surface.

"There we go!" Zöller cried in relief. "As usual, the last key. Now, where's first gear on this?"

At last the little truck began to move, rattling. It reached a speed of 18 m.p.h., and soon they had left the castle forecourt behind. The figure of the giant grew smaller and smaller. Steven thought he heard one more faint hiss pass above him, and then the woods swallowed them up.

"He'll follow the tire tracks," Sara said, staring into the darkness behind them. Small twigs whipped her face, but she didn't seem to notice them. "He's not going to give up so easily. Not him."

"I don't think he'll be able to get far with that wound," said Steven, shrugging his shoulders. "The way he's limping, I did at least hit his lower leg."

Sara grinned. "Not bad for five shots fired at point-blank range. Wyatt Earp would have been proud of you."

"I'd settle for you being proud of me," Steven said, drawing her close. The little treasure chest, wet from the rain, lay safely on his lap. In spite of Sara's body heat, he was shivering slightly, and not because of the wind and storm. The dark dreams had disappeared, but Steven knew they could come back at any time.

In front of them Uncle Lu, in the king's voluminous cloak, was squawking into his cell phone. Alois, the fisherman, didn't seem to be especially amused by his old friend's nocturnal call, but Zöller had some persuasive arguments. Finally the old man put his cell phone away and grinned at his two passengers.

"I've promised Alois the king's cloak," he said, turning to them in the back of the truck. "And I'll probably have to back his chloroform theory at the next meeting. Ah well, it isn't really such a crazy theory."

"No crazier than a diary, a dead Cowled Man, and a contract killer in a castle museum," Sara replied.

A few minutes later they finally reached the little harbor near the chapel. Alois, the fisherman, was waiting for them, with his outboard engine chugging. The stormy wind whistled over the Chiemsee, and the boat was bobbing up and down on the waves like a wet paper ship, but that didn't seem to bother Alois. The promise of the cloak had improved his temper considerably.

"Lord almighty!" the old fisherman said. "I took you for the king himself. What the devil were you doing over there, Lu?"

"I'll tell you back at your hut over a beer," Zöller said. "Now, let's go, damn it. Otherwise we'll both be lying dead in the water like Ludwig and Gudden."

LANCELOT STOOD ON the bank, watching the bobbing boat as it grew smaller and smaller across the heavy swell of the lake. The wound on his left leg hurt like hell, but the giant was sure it was only a graze. A fresh dressing, some disinfectant, and the hunt could go on. That was the good news.

The bad news was that they had escaped him again.

Cursing, Lancelot kicked a rotting wooden post into the water. The king would go berserk. As so often, there would be threats to flay Lancelot alive, or to have him deported to Papua New Guinea.

Lancelot breathed in the fresh air of the lake deeply.

At least he had one card to play. He knew the second keyword— and he knew where the trio was going next.

Neuschwanstein.

All was not yet lost. Lancelot would get back on the trail. But this time he would take Tristan and Gawain with him, maybe Galahad and Mordred as well. He'd take a whole damn army if need be.

Next time they wouldn't get away.

Once again he stared at the boat slowly moving away over the Chiemsee, which lay before him, an infinitely black, surging surface, its waves crowned by white foam. Then he limped back into the woods.

When his cell phone rang a little later, it took Lancelot some time to fish it out of his blood-soaked pants pocket. It was the king. In a hasty whisper, Lancelot explained what had happened in the castle. Then he said no more for quite a long time as he listened in silence.

The Royal Majesty was not angry. The Royal Majesty had a plan.

· 25 ·

THE BED IN THE OLD BOATHOUSE creaked and squealed if Steven moved so much as a centimeter. It was so narrow that he was in constant danger of either falling out or forcing Sara over the side of the bed. It also stank of old fish.

He stared at the rotting ceiling and tried to find some peace and calm, in spite of the rain pattering down and the events of the last few hours. Alois, the fisherman, had given them the key to his old boathouse down in Prien harbor. After they had hidden the Mini in a nearby garage and told Uncle Lu about their experiences in the museum, the old man had disappeared with Alois into a bar somewhere to give him a slightly doctored account of the last few hours. Meanwhile, Sara and Steven had crept into the crooked boathouse, hoping that the killer wouldn't find them there. But whenever the shutter over the window rattled, Steven imagined he saw the one-eyed giant suddenly appearing in the hut.

Far worse, however, were the memories that overwhelmed him like flashes of lightning.

Steven kept seeing his parents' burning villa before him, heard the crackling of the flames and his mother's shrill scream from the library. When he closed his eyes, there was a furious girl with long blond braids, trying to scratch his eyes out. But whenever the picture was about to become clearer, it dissipated. There was nothing beyond it but endless black.

Damn you, dreams. Why have you come back?

"Can't you get to sleep either?" Steven asked, after he had been tossing and turning for what felt like an eternity.

The art detective sat bolt upright in bed. "Thanks for asking," she snapped. "Even ignoring the lice in this place, a deranged giant in a gas mask tried to murder me tonight. And when I close my eyes, I see the leader of the Cowled Men wallowing in his own blood. So, no, I can't get to sleep either."

Steven switched on the rusty lamp beside the bed and turned to Sara. Her hair was tousled and still damp after their flight from the island. It had small leaves in it. He looked at her in silence for quite a long time.

"We still don't know who that colossus is," he said at last, lost in thought as he stroked Sara's hair. "No friend of the Cowled Men, anyway, that much is clear now. I wonder if he was following us from Uncle Lu's house in that green Bentley?"

A particularly violent gust of wind rattled the shutter, and the rain slapped against the wood like a wet cloth. Sara gave a nervous start. She reached for her crumpled pack of cigarettes beside the bed and lit herself a partly smoked one. "No idea. Maybe, or maybe it was some third party we don't even know about. Or friends of Albert Zöller keeping us under observation."

"Do you still think he has something to do with your uncle's murder?" Steven shook his head. "Forget it—he saved our lives just now, putting on that Ludwig act. We ought to be grateful."

"All the same." Sara drew deeply on her cigarette. "There's something wrong. Uncle Paul knew Zöller. So why didn't he turn to him for advice if Uncle Lu knows so much about the king? Instead, my uncle went straight to the Cowled Men."

"But then something must have happened," Steven replied. "That guy who called himself the steersman of the Cowled Men did say that his contact with Paul Liebermann was suddenly broken. And the professor came to my shop instead because he needed material to help him decipher the shorthand."

"Oh hell." In annoyance, Sara ground out her cigarette on one of the bedposts and threw the cigarette butt on the floor. "I'm sure my uncle would know what those poems and roman numerals mean. It's like the farther we go, the more we're groping around in the dark."

"And the greater the danger that we'll pay for this adventure with our lives," Steven said. "Whoever's behind it all, I never should have gotten involved."

"Damn it, Steven, don't you see?" Sara looked him straight in the eye. "Solving the puzzle is our only chance. Or do you want to tell the police about what happened in the museum?"

Steven ran his hands through his hair. Once again a wave of memories was rolling toward him. "I just don't know how much longer I can stand this. I feel as if something is reaching out to me, something . . ." He hesitated briefly before going on. "Something even worse than that nightmare in the museum. A dark place, a black hole deep inside me. And it has something to do with that damn diary. Sometimes I think I'm turning as crazy as Ludwig himself."

Another gust of wind shook the thin wooden walls of the boathouse. The wind whistled through the shutters, and to Steven it sounded like the wailing of a small child.

A child crying out for his parents, he thought. *Crying out for his parents, who died long ago.*

Sara leaned over him and covered his face with little kisses. "Whatever it is, Steven, you can tell me," she whispered. "Okay, so I'm no psychiatrist, but I can listen just as well as Dr. Freud." She tried to smile and then turned serious again. "Does it have something to do with the way you fell apart back there? With the weird stuff you were stammering? Something about a fire and a library. And a teahouse. What do you mean, a teahouse, Steven?"

The bookseller shook his head. "It . . . it's so long ago. I was only six at the time. I can . . . I can hardly remember."

"Try."

He took a deep breath. "My childhood memories don't really be-gin until we were living in Germany," he began hesitantly. "We were living in a big house in Cologne—it had belonged to my maternal grandparents before us. My father was crazy about the library, which dated from the early 1870s. And so was I . . ." Steven closed his eyes. "To this day I can see it: the tall oak bookshelves, the rolling ladder that allowed you to soar along the rows of books like an eagle, the yellowing oil paintings on the walls, the shimmer of dust outside the window . . ." He looked at Sara again and sighed. "I was new to Germany. I didn't have any friends to play with, and that library, in the empty house with all its high-ceilinged corridors and rooms, be-came my playroom, my secret realm. I taught myself to read in the library, using an illustrated edition of the fables of La Fontaine and a stained old edition of the fairy tales of the Brothers Grimm. Even then I liked to hide away behind heavy tomes. They offer me protec-tion, as maybe you can imagine. But back then . . . back then they brought death."

Sara looked at him, wide-eyed. "What happened?"

"A few months after we moved into the villa, my father threw a housewarming party, a ball," Steven went on. "There were a few dis-tant branches of the family in Germany, and friends and colleagues—the kind of guests you invite to a party like that. It was to be a glamor-ous occasion. The men all wore tuxedos or tails, the women wore evening gowns, a small chamber orchestra played Haydn, Mozart, and Schubert in the salon. I . . . I remember being bored. So I went up to the library on the second floor to be alone. I couldn't reach the light switch, so I lit a candle. No, not a candle—it was a Chinese lantern. And there was this safe behind an old oil painting of Bismarck . . ." He paused and tried to recollect. "That night the safe happened to be open. My father must have forgotten to close it . . ."

"You looked inside?" Sara interrupted him.

Steven nodded. "There was something in there, but I . . . I simply don't remember what it was. From that point on, there's this black void in my head. But if I concentrate, I always see a girl with blond braids trying to scratch my eyes out. Her white dress is burning; I hear crackling and hissing; there's acrid smoke everywhere . . ."

"My God," Sara said breathlessly. "You accidentally set the library on fire. That's why you went into shock in the museum. The smoke aroused your memory."

Steven pulled the thin woolen blanket tightly around himself and nodded. "The next thing I remember is running through my grandparents' garden, which was decorated with Chinese lanterns. I ran and ran to this little teahouse at the end of the garden. I . . . I was thinking that Mom and Dad would never forgive me, so I crept away and hid there."

It was some time before he mustered the will to continue. The fall wind, howling and whistling, rattled the shutters over the windows as if to prevent Steven from telling any more of his story.

"When they realized that the house was on fire, my parents fled into the garden with their guests," he said, his voice flat and emotionless. "But when they didn't find me out there, they went back into the house in spite of the flames. They kept calling my name—I could hear them from the teahouse. But I was too frightened to answer. Dad could get very cross if I damaged any of his books, and now the whole library was blazing, the whole house. I crawled under the table and put my hands over my ears. My parents' screams are the last thing I remember . . . their screams from the burning library . . ."

"They died in the fire?" Sara asked quietly. "Both of them?"

Steven nodded. "Because I didn't answer them. They must have gone looking for me until they were trapped by the fire, and finally the smoke smothered them. When the firefighters arrived, one of them heard me crying in the teahouse and finally found me under the table. Then I was adopted by a family who had been friends of my parents."

He smiled wearily. "I could have done worse. My adoptive father was Hans Lukas, a highly regarded professor of English literature at

Munich University, and my adoptive mother, Elfriede, was the soul of kindness. They both died only two years ago, one not long after the other. My birth parents had left me a handsome inheritance, which I squandered on old books. All the same . . ." Steven briefly wiped his eyes. "All I still remember of my real mother is that she knew wonderful fairy tales and songs from her native Cologne. I suppose my love of Germany is based on those memories. Maybe I'm still looking for those fairy tales in my books." He laughed despairingly and struck his forehead. "Now I really do sound like a patient on a therapist's couch. I hope you've been busily writing all this down."

"Idiot." Sara gently swatted him on the nose. "Don't joke. I'm glad you told me. Maybe I understand you a little better now."

Steven smiled. "I'd like that. You know, I don't think we go so badly together. Who knows, when this adventure is over, maybe there could be something more permanent between us." He was staring at her thoughtfully. "And maybe it's time you told me your own secrets, Miss Mystery. I have a feeling I'm not the only one here with a dark hole in my past."

Sara laughed quietly. "Another time. One patient on the couch per session, okay? Tomorrow we're going to go to Neuschwanstein and finish this thing."

She passed her finger over his lips, then kissed him lightly in the hollow of his throat. "Until then, the two of us will have to find some way to pass the time."

Directly after that, Steven stopped caring about the way the bed creaked and squealed.

WHILE SARA SLEPT soundly beside him a couple of hours later, Steven lay with his heart thudding and his eyes open, staring at the ceiling. The events of the last few days, feeling Sara so close, his memories of the fire at the villa in Cologne more than thirty years ago, all combined to keep him awake.

What really happened back then? Why are the images coming back?

By now the rain had stopped. Steven turned restlessly in the bed, finally gave up, and reached for the diary lying on the floor beside him. The book was like a drug that he couldn't do without, like a magic powder out of a fairy tale. He had a feeling that he wouldn't be able to rest until he had read it to the end.

· 26 ·

JTI, JG

I must now write an account of the king's death, and I swear to
God that every word is true. Even if the ministers, the newspapers, the whole world claims otherwise, I know what happened. I
and a handful of others who, however, hold their peace out of fear or
because they are already dead. We were threatened, some of us were
bribed, or made compliant in other ways. But I cannot keep silent any
longer, and so I am now going to tell the true story.

After that terrible incident at Herrenchiemsee, I lost sight of the
king for a long time. He did not want me near him now, so I confined
my meetings with him to the few times that I accompanied Dr.
Loewenfeld on a visit. Otherwise I listlessly went about my work at
the Surgical Hospital in Munich, and pored over scientific books in
my small attic room in the Maxvorstadt district, while only one name
rang through my head.

Maria.

My love for her grew and grew in the months that followed, and
so I traveled as often as possible to Linderhof, where she went about
her work in a small farmhouse not far from the castle, and continued

to keep the king company. Ludwig had forgiven Maria more quickly than me, and so she was usually somewhere near him. I did not venture to appear before both of them together yet, but whenever His Majesty set off to spend a few days at NEUSCHWANSTEIN and Hohenschwangau, Maria stayed behind at Linderhof on her own, and then my hour came.

I gave her small but precious gifts and sweetmeats. I rode with her through the Ammergau woods. Once we were caught in a thunderstorm and had to spend the night in a barn, but it was a chaste night, for I sensed that Maria still resisted confessing her love to me. I was sure that this reluctance was connected in some way with her son, Leopold, and that she was still devoted to the child's father, even if he had abandoned them both. But if I broached the subject to her, she remained obstinately silent, and so I finally gave up, hoping that in time even that deep wound would heal.

On a cold winter's evening, when the king was once again roaming the forests in his fairy-tale sleigh, I found her under the linden tree where we had first met. Its branches groaned under the weight of the snow they bore. Maria's face showed that she had been weeping, and tears still ran down her cheeks.

"What's the matter?" I asked in concern, stroking her hair, where a few snowflakes glittered. "Is it young Leopold? Has the boy been up to mischief again?"

She shook her head and blew her nose noisily. "I'm anxious about the king," she said softly. "Day by day he's getting . . . stranger. It's as if he is moving more and more into another world. At first I thought it was just that he's different from us ordinary mortals, but recently . . ." She broke off, and looked at me sadly. "Tell me, Theodor: outside the Grotto of Venus in the fall, you said that his enemies wanted to put him in a madhouse. Is that true? Do the king's ministers want to have him certified insane? And what will become of him then?"

"I . . . I can't tell you any details," I murmured. "I mustn't, for your own safety. But there's still hope." I caught her hands. "If Ludwig would only go to Munich, if he would give up some of his whims and fancies. Can't you speak to him? He still seems to listen to you, at least."

Wearily, Maria shook her head. "Ludwig lives in a country of his own, like Emperor Barbarossa under tons of rock deep below the Kyffhäuser hills. Not even I can reach him now."

THE LONG WINTER passed, and at last spring came. Rumors that the king had lost his wits swelled louder and louder. Lutz and the other ministers had done all they could to ruin His Majesty's reputation. Articles about Ludwig's state of mind and his vast burden of debt were published in newspapers at home and abroad; his earlier obsession with Richard WAGNER was discussed again. Ribald songs about deranged "Herr Huber" were sung in the taverns of Munich, and the police did not intervene.

However, the king did nothing to quell these rumors, looking like the very image of a lunatic. On my few official visits, I saw that he was declining ever more swiftly. His teeth were falling out by the dozen, his neglected mouth stank, he ate huge quantities of food, and loudly abused the lackeys and ministerial officials who persisted in refusing him money for his castles. After his former equerry Richard Hornig had declined to rob banks for him, he sent couriers and dispatches to places as far afield as Constantinople, Tehran, and Brazil; he toyed with the idea of emigrating to a Pacific island and continuing his building there; he ordered officials to set up a secret army in preparation for a coup d'état; he shouted, raged, and scolded like a small child whose toy has been taken away—but whatever he did, he was not granted another pfennig.

Our small circle of conspirators watched this conduct with horror, but we were powerless. The attempts of Kaulbach and Loewenfeld to win Dr. Gudden over to our side had been fruitless. Instead, we learned through our contacts that the lackeys at court were still assiduously fishing compromising notes of the king's out of wastebaskets and even the toilet. In addition, Prince Luitpold had publicly declared himself ready to assume the regency. It was five minutes to midnight, and the clock was inexorably ticking on.

Finally the bombshell exploded.

Late in the afternoon of 9 June 1886, I received a letter from Dr. Loewenfeld in which he earnestly asked me to travel to Lake Starnberg at once. Richard Hornig had a villa there in Allmannshausen, where we few who were still the king's friends met on occasion to discuss what could be done. It was clear from Loewenfeld's letter that this was a matter of the utmost importance; the doctor spoke of life and death.

When I arrived in Allmannshausen around eight that evening, in torrents of rain, the other conspirators were already sitting around a card table in the smoking room, looking grave. Through the haze of cigar smoke, I saw Dr. Loewenfeld, on whose face the last few months had engraved deep lines of anxiety, as well as Hermann Kaulbach, the painter, and Richard Hornig, the equerry. Only Count Dürckheim was missing.

"Where's the count?" I asked, bewildered. "Has he been held up?"

Loewenfeld shook his head sadly. "Sycophantic courtiers have suspended him from his post and sent him to his estate in Steingaden," he said. "Because they know that he is the king's most faithful friend. We tried to send him warning, but obviously someone intercepted our messenger."

I let myself drop into one of the upholstered armchairs by the fireplace. "My God, what's happened?" I said. "Is Dr. Gudden really going to certify the king insane?"

"He'll do it today," replied Kaulbach, flicking the ash off his cigarette into the glowing logs. "At the latest tomorrow. All is lost."

"Today?" I leaped up. "But . . . but why haven't we heard anything about it before?"

"The operation was planned well in advance," growled Richard Hornig, who was slumped in his chair like a clod of earth. "The Black Cabinet took care that no one would get wind of it too soon."

I nodded, and thought, with a shudder, of the department of the

266 • OLIVER PÖTZSCH

police authority in Munich that must have helped to hatch the plot on orders from the ministers. Count Dürckheim had often told me about those police officers who operated in secret. This so-called Black Cabinet had been intercepting all letters to Ludwig for months, including a communication from Bavarian bankers who wanted to offer him credit. Only selected newspaper articles were laid before the king, and apart from Count Dürckheim, he was surrounded exclusively by officials and lackeys in league with the ministers, who had been instructed by Johann Lutz, president of the ministerial council, to lull Ludwig into a sense of false security.

"Damn it all, we should have known!" Dr. Loewenfeld banged on the floor with his walking stick. "Ever since Ludwig planned to turn to parliament for the money back in April, they've all been in turmoil. Just think, the opposition would have granted the king millions, gaining ministerial posts in return. Lutz *had* to react, or it would have cost him his head. If only we had made a move earlier."

We were all silent, and for a while there was nothing to be heard but the ticking of the tall grandfather clock in the corner.

"What are the ministers planning to do?" I finally asked, breaking the silence. It seemed as if the others had already resigned themselves to Ludwig's fate.

"A delegation of officials, led by that scoundrel Count von Holnstein, set off for Neuschwanstein this afternoon, along with Dr. Gudden and several asylum attendants," replied Loewenfeld, his face pale. "They intend to present Ludwig with Gudden's medical report and then depose him. And tomorrow Prince Luitpold will take over as regent in Munich."

I bit my lip. The situation did indeed seem hopeless. Yet I still pursued the point. "Does Bismarck know of this? Maybe, if the Prussian chancellor were to stand firm against them . . ."

"Good God, you know better than any of us that Bismarck will approve of this operation," Richard Hornig interrupted me. His eyes blazed with anger. "Clearly his agent Carl von Strelitz had more meetings with Lutz. All this was rigged in advance."

Carl von Strelitz.

When Hornig mentioned the Prussian agent's name, I closed my eyes for a moment. I was still sometimes plagued by nightmares in which Strelitz attacked me with his swordstick and ran me through the chest. In my dreams, bright blood spurted from the wound like the jet of a fountain, and I always woke up screaming. So far I had been unable to find out why Bismarck's agent had been on the island at the end of September, let alone why, just before his appearance, Maria had uttered those remarkable words.

He'll kill me.

I was soon to find out.

"We must warn the king!" I cried now to the company around the table. "Let us telegraph to Füssen at once."

"Do you suppose we didn't think of that?" barked Kaulbach, the painter. He had lit himself another cigarette and was nervously drawing on his long, ivory cigarette holder. "We have to assume that the Black Cabinet has also taken over the telegraph office in Füssen, and if those dogs intercept any message of ours, all is lost."

Loewenfeld nodded his agreement. "If I were Lutz, I'd keep the castle under observation, station some of my own men in the telegraph office, and make sure the king thinks himself safe. The minister may be a traitor, but he's no fool."

I said nothing for a moment, while the smoke from the men's cigars and cigarettes hovered like a dark cloud above our heads.

"Then we must find some other way to warn the king," I finally said. "Hornig, do you have any horses here?"

The equerry raised his right eyebrow. "You're thinking of sending a mounted messenger? It's a good fifty miles to Füssen. In the weather out there, he'd need at least four hours to cover the distance. And the delegation, with Gudden, will be arriving there in . . ." He took out his gold pocket watch. "In exactly two hours' time. So you can forget that idea. In any event, it's useless. The king is too obstinate to listen to any of us. He's dismissed me from his service, he's fallen out with Kaulbach over the sketches for the picture of the ruins of Falkenstein

Castle, the doctor here is too old, and Dürckheim has been suspended and sent away. So which of us could go?"

"I could," I said firmly.

"You?" Hermann Kaulbach looked at me skeptically. "As far as I'm aware, the king banished you from his circle of friends forever after that wretched business at Herrenchiemsee. When I last saw him, he spoke of having you horsewhipped and transported to the Antilles."

"I must try, nonetheless," I replied. "I am sure that Ludwig still has some fondness for me. And when he hears the news I bring, he will forgive me."

"Or chop your head off," growled Richard Hornig. "Anything is possible with him." He sighed and then rose to his feet. "Be that as it may, I can see that we have no other option. Come with me, and I'll see if I can find a horse in my stable that won't throw you at the first crossroads it comes to."

WE DECIDED ON two fast young black horses. I was to ride them alternately, and in that way I could cover the whole distance to Neuschwanstein at full gallop.

In the past, I had accompanied Ludwig on many a nocturnal ride, and I considered myself a reasonably good horseman, yet the next few hours were hell on earth. Torrential rain was falling, the roads were softened and muddy, and I could hardly see my own hand before my eyes. Raindrops whipped into my face like hailstones, and after a few minutes my clothes were already clinging to my body. Beyond Hohenpeissenberg, the rain finally slackened, but it was still difficult for me to see the right way to go in the darkness.

Shortly after midnight, a few lights showed ahead of me at last, telling me that I had reached Füssen. A little later, I approached Hohenschwangau Castle, where Ludwig had spent much of his childhood. On a height opposite it, Neuschwanstein Castle stood, faintly illuminated. Large parts of that imposing building were still surrounded by scaffolding.

I reined in my horse and looked around me. What now? So far I had thought only of reaching Neuschwanstein. Now that the castle lay ahead at last, I hesitated. Suppose Gudden, Holnstein, and the others were already up there with the king? Suppose soldiers were already stationed on guard around the castle? All at once this whole venture seemed pointless. I was freezing, as if shaken by a fever. Hunger gnawed at me, and I felt more exhausted than ever before in my life.

At that moment I saw a large man walk unsteadily through the entrance to Hohenschwangau Castle and down to the valley. For a brief moment I thought I was looking at the king, but then I recognized the massive figure as that of Count Holnstein, once a close friend of the king. He seemed to have been drinking heavily. He swayed as he approached the stable, where a coachman was just leading two horses out by their reins. I quickly slipped behind a nearby shed with my two mounts and watched what happened next from there.

"Hail, my man!" bellowed Holnstein, twirling his mustache. "What are you doing here?"

"I . . . I'm to get the carriage ready for the king," stammered the coachman. "His nightly drive . . ."

"Unharness those horses at once," the count snapped at him. "We have a different carriage ready for the king."

The coachman looked at Holnstein's gigantic figure, baffled. "But the king gave me orders to—"

"The king is giving no more orders!" barked Holnstein. "His Royal Highness Prince Luitpold has assumed the regency. So you can go to the devil!"

The wiry little man's mouth dropped open. At first he seemed about to say something; then he bowed and took the horses back into the stable. Holnstein looked grimly after him, and then, treading heavily, went back into the castle, where I could now see, in outline, a large company seated around a table on the other side of several lighted windows. My heart was racing; I hadn't arrived too late! Obviously the distinguished gentlemen were amusing themselves over supper before going to tell the king the bad news.

Leaving one of my horses behind the shed, I galloped the other up the steep hill to Neuschwanstein. Fortunately, there were no soldiers to be seen. After I had knocked hard on the castle gate several times, the sleepy castellan opened it to me. I knew the man from my earlier visits. After a brief exchange of words, I was let in, and I stormed into the lower courtyard and from there up the steps to the palace to take the king the news.

I found him high up in the Singers' Hall.

Ludwig was an even more pitiful sight than I remembered from our last meeting. He was so fat that I feared the buttons of his coat might come off at any moment. His face was pale and bloated, and there were food stains on his shirtsleeves and vest. As I came in, he was holding a small book in his greasy fingers, silently declaiming some lines of verse. His lip movements were reminiscent of a pale carp's. Although I had made a lot of noise as I raced into the hall, he did not seem to notice me.

"Your Majesty!" I cried. "You are in great danger!"

At last he turned his mighty head my way, but he obviously did not recognize me.

"Kainz?" he asked. "Did I summon you to give a performance?"

I grimaced. The king obviously took me for one of his actors. Had Ludwig lost his wits after all? Had his critics been right? In the magnificent Singers' Hall, with its high ceiling, its mural paintings from *Parsifal*, and its gilded chandeliers, his desolate figure looked like that of a beggar in a fairy-tale castle. He was standing on the small stage at the end of the vaulted room, in front of a roughly painted backdrop showing a wood with trees, bushes, and deer. Suddenly his expression changed, and his eyes narrowed to small slits.

"Marot!" he exclaimed when at last he recognized me. "I thought I had made myself clear. I do not want you anywhere near me now. Your conduct was *dégoutant*."

Although the king went on roundly abusing me for some time, I was immensely relieved. At least Ludwig seemed to know who I was and had not entirely fallen prey to delusions.

When the worst of his rage was spent, I hurried to the stage and bowed like a knight to his ruler. And in that castle, I really did feel like a character from the world of the sagas, like Parsifal or Tristan, reporting to his king before going away in search of the Holy Grail.

"Your Majesty," I began quietly. "I know that I have failed you. Nonetheless I come to you in this dark hour because I must warn you. Count Holnstein, Dr. von Gudden, and several officials and madhouse attendants are on the way here to have you certified insane and depose you. You must flee at once!"

Ludwig looked at me in astonishment. "Nonsense. If any danger threatened, Hoppe my barber would long ago have . . ."

"Forget your lackeys," I interrupted him. "Most of them are already working for the ministers. Your Master of the Stables, Holnstein, has been inciting them."

"I can believe it of him, corrupt as he is." The king put his head on one side and scrutinized me curiously. All at once he seemed to me as reasonable as in his younger years.

"Marot, it is to your credit that you have come to warn me. A king can forgive. Stand up." He called to his faithful servant, Weber, who had been waiting behind the door. "Lock the castle gates and let no one in," he commanded in a firm voice. "Fetch the local gendarmes from Füssen and the firefighting forces from the countryside around. We'll see if those fine gentlemen can lay hands on me without so much as a by your leave."

My heart leaped for joy. This was the king as I had known him in the old days! The king for whom I was ready to die. His eyes, no longer vacant, fixed on me with an alert and friendly expression. He went down the few steps from the stage and clapped me on the shoulder so hard that I almost fell over.

"It's good to have you back with me again, Theodor," he said, smiling. "Now, find something dry to wear before I lose the best of my knights to a chill. That, truly, would be ridiculous."

JT, W

The next few hours passed in tense expectation. The castle was barred, and several of the country gendarmes from Füssen had taken up their position outside the main entrance. In spite of the rain and the early-morning hour, a number of people had already gathered, having learned of the shameful intentions of the Munich officials.

From one of the tower windows, I watched several peasants standing together, arguing wildly. Many of them had brought scythes and flails with them, and torches lit up the dark scene. In spite of the menace in the air, I could not help smiling. Once again, it was clear that Ludwig was still venerated like a saint in these rural areas. The men and women out there would let themselves be torn to pieces rather than have anyone hurt a hair on their king's head.

At last, in the first light of dawn, the traitors approached.

It was a strange picture that presented itself to me in my vantage point by the window. Count von Holnstein; Count Crailsheim, foreign minister of Bavaria; and several other officials came driving up in carriages splashed by dirt and mud. When they climbed out, I saw in the rising mist that the noble gentlemen wore gold-embroidered gala uniforms, with old-fashioned tricorne hats on their heads. Dr. von Gudden, another doctor, and the four madhouse attendants wore plain black, which made them look like hungry ravens. When they realized that the local gendarmes and the peasants had them encircled, they looked anxiously around. Only Count Holnstein preserved his composure.

"We are here to arrest the king and take him to Linderhof!" he called to the crowd, in the tones of one accustomed to command. "For his own protection. It has been proved that Ludwig is insane.

From this day on, Prince Luitpold is regent in his place. So make way there and let us into the castle!"

However, the people gathered together outside the main entrance, and angry murmuring was to be heard, as threatening as the sound of an angry animal.

"What you are doing here is a crying shame. A sin and a shame," said an elderly lady of distinguished appearance wearing a monstrous hat. She seemed to be one of the local landed aristocracy. "Letting these ministers harness you to their own purposes," she scolded, pointing to the hesitant officials. "Your children will be ashamed in times to come when they hear of this high treason." She swung her umbrella menacingly, while her little poodle began to yap furiously. People in the crowd cheered for the king.

Count Holnstein looked around for help, sensing that the situation was getting out of control. He nervously mopped the sweat and the rain from his brow, seized one of the hesitating madhouse attendants, and with him went up to the local gendarmes, who had formed a human chain outside the castle gate.

"In the name of Prince Luitpold, rightful regent of Bavaria, will you finally open this gate!" he roared. "Otherwise I'll have you all—"

At that moment the butt of a rifle hit the madhouse attendant in front. A small bottle fell from his hand to the ground and broke with the soft sound of splintering glass. There was a second of horror, and then wild shouting rose in the air again.

"That smells like chloroform! The dogs want to send us all to sleep! Seize them!"

It was only with difficulty that Count Holnstein, Dr. Gudden, and the others got back to their carriages. The peasants seemed to be on the point of throwing several of the most prominent men in the land into the Pöllat Gorge. By this time even the firefighters had made haste to the king's aid. The doors of the horse-drawn carriages slammed, the coachmen cracked their whips, and to the accompaniment of angry abuse, the officials fled back to Hohenschwangau.

When they had disappeared around the next bend in the road, loud cries of jubilation rang out. The enemy had been routed.

When I returned to the castle courtyard, I saw that the servant Weber, one of the last to be loyal to the king, was talking to a few of the local gendarmes. He seemed to be greatly agitated.

"What is it?" I asked at once. "Surely these officers are not about to arrest the king?"

"On the contrary." Alfons Weber grinned at me. "His Majesty has just given orders to have that whole gang who were here just now arrested. We'll pick them up down in Hohenschwangau." He clapped his hands with glee, like a child. "At last there's a fresh wind blowing here!" shouted Weber right across the courtyard. "You wait and see, Marot. The king will go to Munich and dispatch all those ministers to the devil. And everything will be all right again."

I nodded, although I was not yet ready to believe in this peace. However, not two hours later the first to be arrested did indeed stumble into the castle precincts. They were Count Holnstein; Count Crailsheim, the foreign minister of Bavaria; and Count Toerring, whom the ministers had designated the king's future companion. They still sported their gala uniforms, but now those garments looked like costumes for clowns. The men's tricorne hats hung askew over their faces, their gait heavy and dragging. True, they were not fettered, and the gendarmes walked a little way behind them, but the crowd lining the road made any idea of flight impossible. They were running a gauntlet that I wouldn't have wished on my worst enemies.

"I'll put your eyes out if you don't go faster!" one Allgäu farmer shouted to Count Crailsheim. A young peasant woman pointed to the staggering prisoners, who were deathly pale, and called to her little boy loud enough for everyone to hear, "When you're grown-up, you can tell your own children how you once saw the traitors."

I expected the first stones to fly through the air at any moment, the first flails to smash the heads of the officials like clods of earth, but nothing of the sort happened. And so Holnstein, Gudden, and the other traitors toiled up to Neuschwanstein, where they were locked up together in a sparsely furnished room in the tower building.

I stood in the courtyard, a smile on my lips, and looked up to where the sun was just rising behind the castle walls. The king, it seemed, had been saved.

Only a few hours later, I was to be bitterly disappointed.

A STRONG AROMA TICKLED STEVEN'S NOSE. He awoke with a start and saw a young woman before him, holding out a mug of steaming coffee. It took him a moment to recognize her as Sara. He had been dreaming again of the girl with the blond braids. They had been struggling, with something lying on the floor between them. When he tried to pick it up, the aroma of coffee had brought him back to reality.

"You grind your teeth horribly in your sleep," Sara said, smiling. "Did you know that? I hope it wasn't to do with what you were reading last night."

Wearily, Steven sat up in bed and gratefully sipped the hot brew as he tried to shake off his dream. "If I was grinding my teeth, it was more likely because of our experiences last night," he said. Yawning, he told her what he had read before sleep had overcome him at last, long after the first dawn chorus of birds began to twitter.

Sara listened thoughtfully as she took small sips of her own coffee. "As far as I remember, that corresponds almost exactly to what's already known about Ludwig's last days," she said when he had finished. "Maybe Zöller knows more."

"You trust him again?"

She laughed softly. "Far from it. I saw him down by the lake just now, along with some unshaven character in a Windbreaker and dark sunglasses. They were having a lively discussion about something, but unfortunately I wasn't able to catch any of it. But, wait until you hear this." She paused for dramatic effect. "A quarter of an hour later, I managed to get a quick look at Zöller's cell phone; he'd left his jacket over a chair down by the kiosk. I went through the latest numbers he called, and guess who Uncle Lu called no less that five times recently?"

In spite of the coffee, Steven's mouth felt dry. "Don't keep me in suspense like this," he said. "Who was it?"

"A detective agency."

For a moment the bookseller looked at Sara, bewildered. "A detective agency?" he finally asked. "Why in the world would Zöller be getting in touch with a detective agency?"

Sara shrugged. "No idea. I called the number and then checked the name of the company on the Internet. It's a small place in Garmisch, run on a shoestring. Nothing special, it mainly investigates insurance fraud and missing persons. But why would Zöller be calling a detective agency five times? And he made a few calls to the States, but before I could try out any of those numbers, he came back."

"A detective agency in Garmisch and a few calls to the States . . ." Steven skeptically shook his head. "I don't know. It could all be a coincidence. Maybe he's desperately searching for a distant relation and was phoning his sister in the States about it. I'm beginning to think you're as paranoid as I am."

"Could be you're right." Sara got off the bed. "Could be I'm working myself up about nothing. Either way, it's about time we were off to Neuschwanstein. It's after ten already."

"After ten?" Steven stood up and found that every bone in his body ached. He felt as if he hadn't slept for more than half an hour. "What day is it?"

"Saturday. Why?"

Steven sighed wearily, buttoning up his shirt. "Exactly the day for an expedition to Neuschwanstein. We probably won't even be able to see the castle for all the tourists. But so what? Tomorrow will be no better."

Outside the weather had cleared, the sun shone brightly down from the sky, and only a few puddles of rain on the asphalt still bore witness to last night's storm. The old Prien steam locomotive was approaching from the village, whistling and hooting, to bring a new set of tourists down to the pier, and it promised to be a beautiful fall day, a final farewell to summer.

Zöller was already waiting in the back seat of the Mini Cooper. He had bought himself a bag of buttery Bavarian pretzels from a stall and was now munching his way through them. He nodded to Sara and Steven, and offered them his bag of greasy delicacies.

"No, thank you, I feel a bit queasy already," Steven said, getting into the front passenger seat. Sara got behind the wheel, and the car, squealing, turned the corner.

"I spoke to a few of my people at Herrenchiemsee," Zöller said, as he desperately tried to stretch the seatbelt over his belly. "No one has heard anything about those two Cowled Men who ran for it, and I guess no one will. The police are sure to want to ask them some tricky questions. Those officers like to poke about in the dark." He grinned and picked a few crumbs of pretzel out of his teeth. "My friends among the night watchmen have promised to keep us out of it for now. Especially because otherwise it would come to light that they gave me the key." Zöller tapped Steven's shoulder from behind. "Find out anything new from the diary?"

The bookseller told him, briefly, what he had read the previous night. But Zöller could not make anything out of the latest diary entry he had deciphered either.

"All common knowledge already," he grunted. "The arrival in Hohenschwangau of the commission to take the king away, the midnight supper, the arrests . . . All of this was known apart from the conspiracy about Marot and Dürckheim—I'll admit that I never heard about that before."

"How about the descriptions of the castle?" Steven asked, pursuing his point as they drove along narrow country roads toward the western Alps. "Marot meets the king in the Singers' Hall. Maybe the final keyword is something to do with those Parsifal murals in the Hall. Or anyway one of Wagner's operas. *Wagner* is the second word written in capital letters, after *Neuschwanstein*."

"You can find those sorts of saga characters in every corner of the castle," Uncle Lu said, wiping his greasy fingers on his pants. "Parsifal, Tannhäuser, Lohengrin, Sigurd and Gudrun, Tristan and Isolde . . . The whole of Neuschwanstein is nothing but a setting for Wagner operas. Ludwig wanted to build a memorial to his favorite composer, the man he idolized. Along with all the entire legendary world of the Middle Ages. He'd been fascinated by it since childhood."

Steven frowned. "But I can't help noticing that Marot deliberately refers to that world of legend in the Singers' Hall." He took out the diary and leafed through it. "Here. He says he feels like Parsifal or Tristan setting out in search of the Holy Grail."

"Just a moment," Zöller said. "Tristan doesn't go in search of the Grail—that's Parsifal."

"Yes, but I'm inclined to think that the search for the Grail as a whole stands for our attempt to find the solution to the puzzle. We have to find the keyword, and it's concealed somewhere in the Wagnerian legends."

"Oh, wonderful," Sara groaned. "I can just about remember who killed Siegfried, but if the keyword has to do with any other characters, I'm afraid I have to pass."

Uncle Lu grinned. "Good thing you have me, then." He rummaged in the crate of books on the back seat beside him. "There must be a reference book on the old hero sagas in here somewhere. We'll soon find out what friend Theodor was really trying to say."

Steven thought of Sara's research into Zöller's cell phone. Could kindly Uncle Lu really be plotting against them? But then why had he helped them up to this point? Thinking hard, Steven leaned back in his seat and tried to doze, but the constant bends in the road kept bringing him back from dreams teeming with heroes, magicians, and kings.

They drove westward on small country roads running along the foothills of the Alps. At the sight of the freshly mown flower meadows, the moors, the colorful foliage of the woods in fall, and the old farmhouses standing in the sunlight to the right and left of the road, Steven once again thought he understood why Bavaria liked to think itself a special place. Here at the southernmost tip of Germany, time did indeed seem to stand still. Here you still felt you were in a less complicated time, while the modern world was top-heavy with longing, clichés, and false notions.

And Ludwig the Second is the idol adored by the people here . . .

After a good two hours on the road, they had finally reached the small town of Füssen and approached Neuschwanstein and the older castle of Hohenschwangau that stood opposite it. The two castles clung to the walls of a narrow valley bounded on the south by a small mountain lake. While Hohenschwangau—the castle where Ludwig had spent his childhood—was rather modest in appearance, Neuschwanstein was the quintessential fairy-tale castle. Steven knew, of course, that no medieval castle had ever looked like that, but the building, on its rocky plinth and with its turrets, battlements, and pointed roofs, all as white as confectioner's sugar, was the archetypal building of the Middle Ages as many wished it to be.

How many, in fact, became clear to Steven only when they made for one of the large parking lots in the valley. The narrow road between the two castles was lined with hotels, restaurants, souvenir shops, and overpriced snack bars. Along it surged a noisy crowd of Americans, Japanese, nouveaux riches Russians, and people of a dozen other nationalities on their way to the ticket office.

When they stopped in one of the last vacant and wildly expensive parking spots, Sara noisily drew in her breath. Steven stared through the windshield and could not help a nervous start. A police car with its engine running stood right by the kiosk at the entrance.

"Oh well," said the bookseller, resigned. "They've found us. Now what?"

"What do you think?" Sara replied, defiantly. "We wait. So there's a police car. No big deal. Maybe the nice officers want to visit Neuschwanstein. Or maybe they're simply hungry. There, see for yourself." She pointed to a kiosk not far away where a stout police officer stood with a curry sausage. Leisurely, the officer strolled back to the car where his colleague was waiting, looking bored and drumming out a rhythm of some kind on the instrument panel.

Relieved, Sara smiled. "What did I tell you? Nothing to worry about."

Suddenly the stout policeman stared their way and stopped dead in the middle of the road. Steven felt as if he scrutinized them forever before he finally strode quickly toward them.

"Bloody hell," he said. "He's recognized us. We've got to get out of here."

"Right now that really would be the stupidest thing we could do," said Zöller, speaking up from the back seat. "This is the time to keep calm. Just act bored. And Frau Lengfeld, you start the engine very slowly."

Sara turned the key in the ignition, while Steven tried desperately to look like any other American tourist. They rolled gently past the stout officer, who went on walking straight ahead. In the rearview mirror, Steven saw him throw his paper napkin into a trash bin and call something to his colleague in the car. Shortly after, Sara's Mini turned into a nearby parking lot, and the police officers did not reappear.

"Three cheers for German bureaucracy and the sanctity of the lunch break," Sara said. "Half an hour later, and you can bet they would have checked up on us. Now, quick, let's get lost in the crowd." She grinned. "At least *that* shouldn't be too difficult here."

Steven squeezed out of the Mini and looked at the teeming mass of school classes, tourists, and shouting kids holding hands with their parents and obviously getting on their nerves. Horse-drawn carriages without a single vacant seat rattled along the road, and farther back a bus crammed as full as possible was trying to drive up to the castle.

"How we're going to find a keyword to solve the puzzle in all this hustle and bustle is a mystery to me," Sara said a few minutes later as they and Zöller were buying their tickets to the castle. "Sure you don't know a night watchman here, too—someone who'd let us into the castle when it's closed for the night?"

Sadly, the old man shook his head. "I'm afraid not. Security at Neuschwanstein was taken over by a new outfit recently. And even if I did, I don't think that after what happened at Herrenchiemsee, any of my contacts would let us in."

Before they entered, Steven went to one of the souvenir shops and bought himself a crooked Bavarian walking stick, a T-shirt with a castle motif printed on it, and a cheap Bavarian hat. He took his entrance ticket without a word and strode ahead in his new garb. "Not one word," he said on seeing Zöller's grin. "The sight of that fat cop just now was too much for me. At least no one will recognize me so easily in this ridiculous getup. Now, bus, period carriage, or on foot? Any preferences?"

The bookseller was about to change to the other side of the street when a white Maserati raced past him so close that he had to jump back.

"Bloody bastard!" he shouted at its driver. "This is Neuschwanstein, not the autobahn!"

The car suddenly stopped and reversed.

Wonderful, thought Steven. Not only are you wanted by the police, and there's a lunatic trying to shoot you, but now you get some provincial in a Maserati trying to kill you in a fit of road rage.

The tinted driver's window lowered, and so did Steven's jaw.

"Hello, Mr. Landsdale. Is that folksy Bavarian costume for back home in Milwaukee?"

Luise Manstein gave him a friendly smile. She had pushed her sunglasses up into her short gray hair, and she wore a close-fitting pantsuit like the one she had worn on their meeting outside the Grotto of Venus at Linderhof.

"What . . . what are you doing here?" Steven stammered.

"I could ask you the same question, Mr. Landsdale." The president of Manstein Systems neatly raised her right eyebrow. "You left my birthday party rather suddenly. Was your plane taking off in the middle of the night, I wonder?"

"No, no." Steven forced a smile. At the last minute it occurred to him to fake an American accent. He was frantically wondering what newspaper he had said he worked for. At least Luise Manstein didn't seem to know about the gruesome events at Linderhof.

"Oh, I had a call from the editorial offices in Milwaukee," he explained. "The boss wants another background story, on Neuschwanstein this time. So I had to get an early night. I hope you had a good time even without me."

Luise Manstein's glance turned to Sara and Zöller, who had approached the Maserati, suspecting nothing. "And your two companions?" she inquired.

"Er, this is only Al . . . Adolf, my German photographer," Steven said hastily. "And the girl there is Peggy, my assistant."

Steven looked desperately at Sara and Zöller, making small signals with his hand. Zöller was about to say something, but Sara was quick to get in first.

"The tickets, Mr. Landsdale," she squawked with a broad Texan drawl. "We gotta be up at the castle at one P.M." Zöller let out a small cry of pain when Sara's heel kicked him in the shinbone.

"You're not going up to the castle right *now*, are you?" Luise asked in surprise. "I wouldn't recommend it. It's a madhouse up there—you might as well write about Disneyland."

Steven shrugged. He was beginning to feel more assured in his role as a provincial American reporter. "I know, but I have to have the story ready by tomorrow at the latest. And I wasn't able to book a press tour at such short notice. Anyway, I'm more interested in . . . er . . . the historical facts."

"Ah, I see. The *historical facts*." The industrialist looked at him for some time with a narrow smile. Steven felt the sweat under his Bavarian hat beginning to run down the back of his neck.

"I'll tell you something, Mr. Landsdale. I like you," Luise said. "I have a weakness for the States and their way of making facts into fairy tales. We ought to have a longer talk about that sometime . . ." Her eyes twinkled as she looked at him, pausing for rather longer than was necessary. "So I'll make you a proposition: what would you say to a nighttime tour of the castle?"

"A . . . nighttime tour?" The bookseller blinked at her in surprise. "But how . . ."

She smiled more broadly. "You don't think I'm here at Neuschwanstein for pleasure, do you? Some time ago, Manstein Systems undertook a big contract for this place. The castle needs a general technological overhaul. An interactive museum, improvements to the logistics and transport system, new software to deal with bookings . . . but above all a modern security system with a new alarm complex." She pointed to one of the horse-drawn carriages trotting past with a set of Japanese tourists on board. "Technologically, this place is still in the last century, although it accommodates a world cultural heritage worth billions. It's lucky that no terrorist gang has thought of blowing the castle sky-high." Shaking her head, she looked up at the proud building towering above them, radiant white like something out of a Disney movie. "The contract is mainly advantageous for my firm's reputation. There really isn't much money in it."

"And you'd really get us into the building when it's empty this evening?" Steven asked in surprise.

"Us?"

Steven pointed to Sara and Zöller. "I'd need my assistant and photographer with me, of course."

"If you like." Luise Manstein sounded several degrees cooler now. "I have to go in again myself. The new CCTV cameras were installed only yesterday, and there are still a few minor glitches in the alarm system. I'm one of those annoying bosses who likes to check up on everything herself." Her eyes twinkled again. "And I must admit I'd be really interested to see Neuschwanstein by night, particularly the king's bedroom." The tinted window on the driver's side of the car went slowly up again. "Think it over, Mr. Landsdale. I'll be up there at the gatehouse at nine this evening. Maybe we could get a martini after. So long!"

The car's engine roared, and the Maserati disappeared past the nearest souvenir shop.

"Peggy and Adolf!" Sara blurted. "I suppose you couldn't think up anything sillier? Sounds like Stan and Ollie, or Tom and Jerry. And what do you mean, I'm your *assistant?* You should be so lucky."

"I couldn't think up anything else on the spur of the moment," Steven replied. "Anyway, she bought it, and now we have a way to get into the castle when it's empty, so stop complaining."

"Oh, I'm to stop complaining, am I?" Sara said crossly. "The old cow has the hots for you, and you're going along with her game."

"Only because it's a way to get us into the castle, damn it!"

"Would one of you be kind enough to tell me what's going on?" Zöller asked. "Why am I suddenly a photographer called Adolf?"

Steven mopped his brow. "It's a long story," he said with a sigh. "I'd better tell you while Sara books us a hotel. It looks like we'll be here at least until tomorrow."

AFTER SOME SEARCHING, they found an overpriced, old-fashioned place to stay in the town center of Schwangau, not far from Neuschwanstein. When Steven saw the shabby hotel furnishings down in the lobby, dating from the 1960s, he was reminded of what Luise Manstein had said. The place really was still stuck in the last century. If terrorists bombed it, there wouldn't be much loss, apart from the two castles.

This time they booked a double room and a single room, so that Sara and Steven had a little time to themselves during the next few hours. However, their friendly conversation soon died away, and they lay in silence on the bed, staring at the wood-paneled ceiling.

"One way or another all this will soon be over," Steven said.

Sara turned to look at him. "How do you mean?"

"Well, either we crack the puzzle of the third keyword tonight and find out what Theodor Marot was trying to say, or . . ."

"Or?"

"Or I go to the police with that damn diary. I've reached the point where I don't care whether I'm wanted for two murders or even three. I just want it to be over."

Sara sat up. "You can't say a thing like that!" she exclaimed. "Not so close to finding the answer. Do you want it all to be for nothing? And what's more . . ." She took Marot's diary off the bedside table and held it in front of Steven's nose. "Didn't you yourself say the book held a magical fascination for you? That something about it seems to have to do with your past? If you give up now, Steven Lukas, you'll never learn the whole truth about yourself."

"Do I want to?" he asked. "The whole truth? I've managed okay without it so far." He looked thoughtfully at Sara. "Besides, people who live in glass houses shouldn't throw stones. Who are you, Sara Lengfeld? Everything I know about you would fit on a postcard. So don't *you* talk to me about secrecy."

For a moment Sara seemed about to say something, but then she dropped a kiss on his forehead and got off the bed. "All in good time. Right now I'm too busy making sure that wrinkled old industrialist doesn't seduce my Parsifal. She's crazy for you." Her eyes sparkled. "Now let's go for something to eat. I have a feeling we'll both need to keep our strength up."

On the hotel terrace, they met Uncle Lu. The wiener schnitzels were so tough that they could hardly chew them, and the beer tasted like dishwater. After that they had to kill time somehow until their date at the castle.

As if by mutual consent, neither Sara nor Steven said any more about the diary. There was tense expectation in the air. While the art detective surfed the Internet in the hotel lobby, and Uncle Lu rummaged in his crate for books about Neuschwanstein and the medieval legends, Steven went up to his room. He picked up the account written by Theodor Marot and made himself as comfortable as he could on the creaking hotel bed. There were only a few chapters left to read. Steven felt that he would soon discover the real background to the death of Ludwig II.

And maybe, also, the truth about himself.

· 28 ·

JTI, JG

*T*ime in the castle ran on inexorably slowly, like the sand in an hourglass.

In retrospect, those hours seem to me the real turning-point in the life of Ludwig. How different the history of this country would have been if he had only acted with decision! But like Hamlet, he hesitated, and when the king finally made up his mind to flee, it was already too late.

Directly after the arrest of the doctors and officials in the tower building, Ludwig telegraphed his loyal adjutant, Count Dürckheim, who was still in Steingaden after his suspension from his duties. It turned out that the Füssen telegraph office was not, as we had expected, in the hands of the enemy. Furthermore, the traitors had even neglected to tell the local gendarmes in advance about the change of regime. Yet instead of firmly giving the signal to attack, the king continued to vacillate between boundless hatred and weary apathy. Like a caged panther, he paced up and down the throne room, uttering fearsome curses.

"Put out the traitors' eyes; whip them until the blood comes!" he shouted, as spittle flew from his lips. But the next moment, lowering his voice, he was asking the servant Mayr for the key to the tower so that he could throw himself from it.

"Your Majesty, the key . . . the key has been mislaid," stammered Mayr, bowing low several times. Like many of the servants, he had long ago gone over to the enemy, although as yet Ludwig had no idea of this. "I . . . I'll send people to look for it at once."

Ludwig merely nodded in silence and went on pacing. It was as if he were waiting for his downfall.

The disaster began with Sonntag, chief district officer of Füssen. Shoulders hunched, kneading his green felt hat in his fingers, he turned up at the castle toward noon. The portly official was visibly embarrassed, but nonetheless he walked with a rapid tread over to the chamber in the tower building where the prisoners were being held.

"Set these gentlemen free," Sonntag ordered the local gendarmes guarding them. He flourished a document that was wet with rain. "Prince Luitpold's proclamation has just been telegraphed to Füssen. The gentlemen in there are correct: King Ludwig the Second has indeed been deposed."

The chief district officer handed the document to the surprised gendarmes and firefighters, and then unlocked the prison door with his own hands. Holnstein came out, his eyes flashing.

"And high time, too," growled the count. "This has gone on long enough. Now let's put an end to this farce."

"I would advise you to leave the castle one by one, and secretly," whispered Sonntag. "The king does not know that you have been freed, and I can't guarantee the conduct of the populace."

Holnstein nodded in silence, but his glare let the local gendarmes standing around know that he would have liked to put them all up against the wall. When the count saw me in the second row, his mouth twisted into a scornful grin.

"Don't think I'm unaware who's behind all this, Marot," he said sharply. "You'd better find yourself a position as a horse-doctor. That is, if the prince regent leaves your fine friend the equerry a few horses after what's happened."

I bowed and looked as if I had no idea what he meant. "I'm sorry, Your Excellency, but I really don't know what you are talking about."

"The devil with you, Marot." Count Holnstein was so close to my face now that I could see his mustache bristling. "Did you think your little conspiracy was a secret from us? We didn't eliminate your group only because you're none of you anything but squealing rats." He laughed contemptuously. "What difference did it make whether you warned the king or not? The man's deranged—surely you can see that by now. He won't accept help from anyone. So now good day to you; we'll be seeing each other again soon."

The count turned away, and I raised my hat to him with a smile, hoping that he did not see my fear.

One by one, the prisoners left the castle. Dr. Gudden kept looking nervously up to where the throne room stood, as if the king might yet scratch his eyes out at the last minute. A hunting carriage was waiting outside the portal to take the gentlemen back to Munich, by way of Peissenberg.

The first act of the tragedy was over.

I had been watching the liberation of the officials in horror from the courtyard side of the gatehouse, when a rider suddenly galloped through the entrance on a whinnying horse. It was Count Dürckheim! On seeing me, he waved me over, and I told him briefly what had happened in the last few hours.

"It may not be too late," said the count, tearing his sweat-drenched army cap off his head. He had ridden all the way from Steingaden to Füssen at a full gallop. "Take me to the king at once."

We found Ludwig in his study, bent over a sheet of paper on his desk. As we entered the room, he was just imprinting his seal on a large envelope with his signet ring. A second and considerably smaller letter lay beside it, looking more like a folded message. Ludwig pushed both documents aside and looked at us with happy surprise.

"Count Dürckheim! How good to see you here," he cried, rising from his chair. "I hadn't expected you so soon."

"I rode like the devil, Your Majesty," replied Dürckheim, bowing. "At this moment, we are in haste. You must come to Munich at once."

The king looked at him in surprise. "To Munich? But why?"

For a moment it seemed that the count's face fell, but then he pulled himself together. "Because it is your last chance to escape deposition," he said in a calm, objective tone. "If you show yourself to the people, the ministers will never dare to have you declared insane. We will write a proclamation of our own, arraign Prince Luitpold for high treason, and . . ."

"Oh, Dürckheim. Munich!" the king interrupted. "Look at me. I am tired and sick. City air does not agree with me."

"Then . . . then at least take refuge in the Tyrol," I begged him fervently. "The empress of Austria is your cousin. She will help you. In a few hours' time, Count Holnstein will have sent a battalion of Munich police officers here to surround the whole castle."

"My dear Marot, what would I do in Austria?" Shaking his head, Ludwig returned to his desk. "Look down from the mountains at my castles, which wouldn't be mine anymore? Write a counter-proclamation on my behalf if you think it really necessary, but don't trouble me any further with it. I have other plans." He put the larger letter into Count Dürckheim's hand. "My dear count, I have only two requests to make of you. This sealed document must be taken to Linderhof as fast as possible. It may well be the most important missive I have ever written in my life, so take good care of it. *This* message," he added, picking up the smaller, folded sheet of paper that had been lying on the table, "tells you to whom you are to hand the document. Do not read it until you have reached Linderhof. *Compris?*"

Count Dürckheim nodded. "I understand, Your Majesty. And your second request?"

"Get me some cyanide."

Neither Dürckheim nor I said anything for some time; the king's words had taken our breath away.

"My king, you mustn't do a thing like that!" the count finally exclaimed. "Bavaria needs you. What is to follow you?"

"Other times," said Ludwig quietly. "Times in which I do not want to live."

Count Dürckheim clicked his heels. "Majesty, forgive me, but that is the first order you have ever given me that I cannot obey."

The king smiled mildly at him. He seemed to be in a distant world once again. It was as if, in his mind, he had withdrawn into one of the mural paintings of the *Tannhäuser* saga that surrounded us on all sides in the study, an ideal medieval world in which knights, minstrels, and real kings still existed. "Very well, Dürckheim, very well," he said at last. "Leave me alone now."

The last thing I saw as I turned away was Ludwig throwing letters one by one into the fire burning on the hearth, where they briefly flared up blue and green, and finally fell to ashes.

JG, J

The next blow of fate came hurrying toward us in the form of a battalion of police officers from Munich. They arrived at the castle at eight o'clock that evening and promptly took control of it.

By now all letters to or from the king had been intercepted. From this point on, he was entirely cut off from the outside world, and his orders held sway only as far as the castle gate. However, that did not seem to trouble him much. He had spent all afternoon burning old letters in the study, and then he wandered lethargically around the great halls of his castle. Sometimes he stared through the window for minutes on end, so that I began to fear he might jump out. But since asking for cyanide, he had expressed no more thoughts of suicide. Ludwig seemed to be resigned to his fate. A leaden weight lay over the castle; it was like being in the castle of the Sleeping Beauty, in expectation not of a prince but of the arrival of the traitors. The first of the servants had already left.

The thirty Munich police, commanded by four officers, sent the last of the loyal local police home and barred the castle gate. They cut off the telephone, that newfangled invention with which Ludwig might have telegraphed messages to Füssen. They turned off the warm-air heating system, and forbade the king to go for walks. From this point on Ludwig II was a prisoner.

At midnight I lay down to rest in one of the second-floor servants' rooms, but I could not sleep properly. I tossed and turned restlessly; in my dreams I saw Maria, who was running away from me as I pursued her. But whenever I had almost caught up, and tried to reach for her, she was several steps ahead again. Suddenly she stopped, turning to me, and her face was the face of a rotting corpse. Her mouth opened, maggots crawled out of it, and I heard her hoarse voice in my mind.

He'll kill me . . .

Suddenly I was awoken by someone shaking me hard. When I opened my eyes, I saw Count Dürckheim standing over me. He wore his uniform, his coat, and his officer's cap, as if he were about to leave. Outside, it was nearly dawn.

"We must talk," he whispered. When I opened my mouth, he put a finger to his lips. "Not here—the walls have ears. The police from Munich are all over the castle. Follow me."

Drowsily, I pulled myself upright and accompanied him to the stairway, which we climbed in silence. On the fourth floor, the count led me through the various rooms until finally we were outside the door of the king's bedchamber.

"But . . ." I began as Dürckheim pressed down the door handle.

"Never fear," he told me. "The king is not here. He is pacing up and down in the Singers' Hall like one of the undead. At the moment the bedchamber is the safest place. The servants know that the king never spends the night here, only the day. So no one will think of spying on us."

His Majesty's adjutant pushed me into the cold room and closed the door behind us. With the gray light of morning falling through the window, the outline of the huge bed with its magnificently carved canopy could just be seen. All around us were imposing murals telling the tragic story of Tristan and Isolde, from the fatal love potion to their union in death. The two ceramic figures above and at the side of the tiled stove also showed the lovers. I could not help thinking of Maria and myself; in one of the paintings the loving couple embraced as closely as the two of us had done a few months earlier at Herrenchiemsee.

Count Dürckheim, exhausted, sat down in one of the armchairs and looked at me with red-rimmed eyes. He did not seem to have had a wink of sleep.

"The counter-proclamation is written and printed," he said, rubbing his temples. "We have had thirty thousand copies distributed, but, to be honest, I don't think it is going to work. Presumably the police will confiscate most of the pamphlets before they get into circulation."

"Then what are we to do?" I asked.

"We?" The count smiled wearily. "You overestimate my powers. I've already received orders from the War Ministry, three times, to return to Munich at once, on pain of arraignment for high treason. Now that Luitpold has taken over as regent, I serve another master." He sighed at length. "The way it looks, Marot, you will soon be the last of our little group of conspirators able to stand by the king."

"My God, Dürckheim, don't leave Ludwig now, when he needs you most," I exclaimed. In desperation, I sat down on the blue damask coverlet and ran my hands through my hair. For a moment I entirely forgot that I was sitting on the king's bed.

The count raised a hand to soothe me. "Don't be alarmed. I am going to leave, but before I reach Munich, I'll make sure a message gets to the equerry Hornig and a few friends to tell them to do all they can to prepare for the king's flight."

I frowned. "For that, we'd need to know first where Gudden and Holnstein mean to take His Majesty."

"Ah, here at least, there's a glimmer of hope." For the first time a slight smile passed over Dürckheim's face. "I still have a few reliable sources of information, and they report interesting news. Dr. Gudden plans to detain Ludwig at Linderhof Castle. They intend to make the place a kind of prison. So we must act fast." He stood up, smoothing down his uniform jacket. "I have several capable people in the Linderhof area, and they will organize an escape. From the castle, it is not far to the Tyrol. All is not yet lost, Marot."

Suddenly he put his hand to his breast pocket. "Damn it, I almost forgot. The letter." He took out the large envelope and the small folded note. "I gave the king my word to hand it over in Linderhof. But now I must go straight to Munich if I don't want to end up in front of a court martial."

I thought for a moment and then put out my hand. "Give it to me. I'll take the letter to Linderhof with me and give it to the recipient there."

Dürckheim looked at me doubtfully. "I gave my word," he said. But then a sigh escaped him. "What does it matter? If I can't trust you anymore, whom can I trust? But remember that the letter is to be given only to the person named in the note. And you are not to open the note until you are at Linderhof."

I nodded, then took the letter and the note, stowing both safely away in my vest pocket just below my heart.

"I must go." The count gave me his hand in farewell, and the first pale rays of the morning sun fell on his face. "For God and the king."

"For God and the king."

Without another word, Count Dürckheim turned away and hurried down the stairs of the palace to the first floor. A little later I heard a horse neighing, and I looked through the window, where nocturnal drifts of mist were dispersing. Leaning low on his horse, like a miscreant, the count galloped out of the castle gate.

The morning twilight quickly swallowed him up.

· 29 ·

A KNOCK AT THE DOOR BROUGHT Steven out of his reading. It was Albert Zöller, standing in the doorway of the small hotel room that the bookseller shared with Sara.

"Adolf the photographer reporting for duty," he announced, saluting like a soldier. Around his neck hung an unwieldy camera that he had scrounged up a few hours ago in a photographic equipment store in Schwangau. "Always wanted one of these," he said, grinning as he waved the old-fashioned camera in front of Steven's face. "I thought it looks more professional than those newfangled digital cameras." He looked at his watch. "Eight thirty already. We'd better go up to the castle quickly, if we don't want to miss our date."

Steven started in surprise. "So late already?" He packed the diary away in his rucksack and put on his shoes. Then he and Zöller went down the well-worn hotel stairway.

"Anything new?" Uncle Lu asked, pointing to the rucksack with the book in it.

Steven shook his head slightly. "Only that just before his death Ludwig wanted to send what was obviously an important letter to Linderhof. According to Marot, he considered it possibly the most important document he had ever written."

Zöller paused for a moment on the stairs. "How remarkable," he murmured. "There's nothing in the scholarly literature about any such letter. Does Marot say what was in it?"

"I'm afraid not," Steven replied. "But maybe the letter will come up in his diary again."

"Maybe. If it does, you absolutely must tell me about it. It matters, do you understand? It matters a great deal."

Steven scrutinized the old man, who was now thoughtfully running his hand over his mouth. It seemed to him that Zöller was keeping something from him. Obviously Sara had been right in her assumptions about those phone calls. But why in the world had Uncle Lu been in touch with a private detective agency? And what was so important about the king's last letter?

Suddenly Zöller's expression changed. He grinned and patted a shopping bag full to bursting that he had brought out from behind his back. "Well, never mind that now," he said happily. "I have twenty pounds of books that could help us in here. Critical literature, illustrated books, a collection of ballads . . . I even have the librettos of *Tannhäuser* and *Lohengrin* with me."

"So long as you don't start singing from them." It was the voice of Sara, who was standing at the bottom of the stairs. She clapped her hands impatiently. "Hurry up, you two. Or we'll be too late for Steven's tryst."

It was already dark outside. A drizzling rain had begun to fall, blowing into their faces as they went up the broad road to the castle. Steven had refrained from wearing his disguise of the traditional hat and Bavarian T-shirt. It was too dark for anyone to be able to recognize him, anyway. The road stretching before them was empty of people. A black ribbon through the woods, it lost itself in the darkness after only a few yards. Only the steaming heaps of horse dung, the crumpled tickets, and the ice-cream wrappers by the roadside still bore witness to the hectic activity of the daytime. It occurred to Steven that Theodor Marot had hurried to the side of his mentally disturbed king through this very wood 125 years ago. Many of the trees around them might date from that time.

"You know, Neuschwanstein should be glad to have a famous firm like Manstein Systems seeing to its modernization," Sara said as they hurried ahead through the wood. "When you think that more than a million visitors from all over the world come here every year, the place could do with a more distinguished touch."

"If I understood Frau Manstein correctly, the firm is more concerned with the security aspect," Steven said. Feeling cold, he buttoned up his jacket. "Since she mentioned potential terrorists, I've had a distinctly queasy feeling. I think Manstein was in charge of all the security for Oktoberfest in Munich. And how about this place? A terrorist could easily attack it if he wanted to."

"Don't go inviting trouble," Zöller said, gasping for air. "And I'd be glad if we could go a little slower, or you'll lose your Ludwig expert without needing any terrorist attack."

When they came to the next bend in the road, all three stood spellbound for a long moment.

The castle towered ahead of them, radiant with almost unearthly glory in the beams of countless floodlights. At night, Neuschwanstein looked even more like a Grail castle than in the day. Its battlements and towers were almost dazzlingly white, standing out against the black wood around them. Somewhere an owl called, and a large bird of prey flew by in front of the bright crescent moon, disappearing on the other side of the castle. Steven could not suppress a smile. Ludwig II and Richard Wagner would both have appreciated this spectacle.

He looked away and was about to go up the drive to the gatehouse, when two more lights came on below the Knights' house, as it was known. They were the headlights of a car.

"Looks like *la baronne* is waiting for you," Sara said, and went over to the Maserati, walking as if she were stumbling clumsily on the wet cobblestones. "Right, so I'm silly Peggy from Texas."

The lights were switched off, and Luise Manstein got out of the car. After glancing with disapproval at Sara and Uncle Lu, she greeted Steven with a brief nod. "Good evening, Mr. Landsdale. I see you brought your charming companion. Pity, I would have liked to be alone with you. But as you wish." She looked at her silver watch. "You're late. I was about to go in without you."

"I'm sorry, but it took Peggy a little time to do her face." Steven smiled. "You know what young assistants are like these days. They think of nothing but their makeup."

The industrialist cast a mocking glance at Sara, who went pale and bit her lip. Luise pointed to a small iron door at the foot of the castle. "Well, one can't always choose one's own staff. Come along, then. I don't have all night."

Steven looked up at the white walls of the castle towering into the air once more. All of a sudden Neuschwanstein looked genuinely menacing, like a castle in a ghost story with gates that might close behind them forever. He shook off the thought and followed Luise Manstein to the iron door.

To the right of the entrance, a small keypad was set into the wall. The head of Manstein Systems tapped in a numerical code, put her thumb on a panel, and stared into a convex lens at eye level. After a few seconds the safety door opened with a quiet hum. Together, they entered a long corridor with a vaulted ceiling stretching ahead farther than they could see. The light at the entrance illuminated only the first few yards, but whenever they came to a new section of the tunnel, a red emergency light flicked on. As they went along, Steven felt that they were walking at least twice the length of the castle.

At last, by means of a stairway, they reached a souvenir shop on the first floor of the castle. The tall room was crammed to the ceiling with kitschy cups, plates, and jigsaw puzzles in boxes, every item bearing the famous portrait of the king. Ludwig beer mugs, Ludwig wooden platters, Ludwig dolls, Ludwig coloring books, and even

Ludwig pencil sharpeners in the shape of a white plastic swan covered tables and racks set out all over the room. There were several posters behind the cash desk, showing Ludwig II in the prime of his youth. None of the pictures were of the fat, toothless tyrant who had died at the age of forty in Lake Starnberg.

If the king could see all these knickknacks, he'd probably be turning in his grave, thought Steven. *In fact he'd be positively spinning in it.*

Luise noticed his glance and looked at him sardonically. "Did you know that Ludwig wanted to blow up his castles rather than have them desecrated by the unworthy?" she asked. "Maybe that would have been a better solution. As it is, the world is full of this tasteless junk. But what's to be done?" She pointed to a plastic dinner service with the design of a golden castle. "What do you think Neuschwanstein makes annually out of this tatty stuff and tickets to see the castle? More than six million euros. The king has repaid his debts a hundred times over."

"Great, I'll put all that in my . . . er, story," Steven said, taking out a notepad. "It would be terrific if we could take a little look at the royal apartments."

"Ah, the Americans and their proverbial superficiality." Luise smiled ironically. "Forgive me. I didn't mean to give you a long lecture on cultural history. I'm going to the security control room now, and meanwhile you can walk around the palace as you like. We'll say two hours, all right?" She pointed to a door at the back of the souvenir shop. "Keep going straight ahead, but please don't touch anything, or you'll get a firsthand experience of the new alarm system, and the police will turn up with a hundred officers."

She turned away and disappeared through an iron door on the right, which was secured by another numerical code. For a while Steven and the others stood in the room in silence, and only when the footsteps beyond the door had died away did Sara clear her throat loudly.

"'You know what young assistants are like these days,'" she said, mimicking Steven. "'They think of nothing but their makeup.' Ha, ha, very funny, Mr. Landsdale."

"Only joking, nothing to get jealous about." Steven winked at Sara and then walked ahead. "Now, let's get this over with. We only have two hours, and if we haven't solved the puzzle in that time, I'm going to throw the damn book into the Pöllat Gorge and turn myself in to the police."

· 30 ·

THE KING'S APARTMENTS WERE ON the third and fourth floors of the palace, on the west side of the castle.

As soon as they were up there, Zöller tipped out his books on the mosaic floor of the throne room and declared the high vault of the hall, with its massive chandelier, their headquarters. The place was gigantic, reminiscent of Byzantine architecture, with a cupola bedecked with stars. It occupied the full height of those two floors, and it had a gallery running around the room halfway up.

They set out from there to investigate the separate rooms, but a first, superficial inspection produced not a single useful clue. In addition, they dared not touch the furniture and mural paintings, for fear of setting off the alarm. Small cameras in the ceiling showed that security featured prominently in Neuschwanstein these days. Zöller took pictures of some of the furniture with his new camera, but he was looking more and more distracted. Steven even thought he detected a trace of panic in Zöller's expression. However, he had no idea why that might be.

At a loss, Steven stood in the middle of the enormous hall and looked up, as if he might find the keyword there. Beneath the vault of the cupola, there were pictures of pre-Christian rulers, and in the apse the bookseller saw Jesus Christ, the twelve apostles, and six more kings. The murals in the room celebrated the heroic deeds of saints, and Steven was struck, in particular, by the figure of St. George stabbing the dragon in the eye. While the battle between knight and monster went on in the foreground, the background of the painting showed a castle on a mountain looking very much like Neuschwanstein itself.

"Where's the throne?" Steven asked, and his voice echoed in the high spaces of the room. "After all, this is the throne room." He pointed to the empty apse, and a broad flight of steps leading up to it.

"Ludwig died before the throne was finished," Zöller said. "But there are drawings. It would have been huge, made of gold and ivory, intended to outdo the thrones of both Charlemagne and Louis the Fourteenth. Everything here was to be just like the music of Wagner: grandiose and a little too loud." He chuckled and pointed up. "Most of this stuff is only smoke and mirrors, anyway. The cupola is an iron structure, the columns are stucco, and glass drops hang from the chandelier. The entire castle is a theatrical setting."

Groaning, Uncle Lu levered himself down to the floor and began leafing through a thick volume.

"Let's just sum up," he announced. "Supposing the keyword really does have something to do with Richard Wagner, then we're looking at five thematic areas here. Each of the state rooms in the palace is based on an old legend. In the salon, the murals tell the story of the legend of Lohengrin; in the study, it's Tannhäuser; in the bedroom, Tristan and Isolde; and finally, in the Lower Hall, Sigurd and Gudrun."

"I've already fed all those names separately into the laptop," Sara complained. "*Nada*. But that would have been too easy."

Steven turned to Zöller. "Which do you think is the most likely room?"

"*Lohengrin* was Ludwig's favorite Wagner opera," Uncle Lu said thoughtfully. "It impressed him in his youth. And it's perfectly possible that Marot concealed a clue in the Lohengrin pictures in the salon."

"Who exactly was Lohengrin, anyway?" Sara asked. "All I really know about him is that he crosses the lake singing, in a boat drawn by a swan."

Uncle Lu cleared his throat. "The character goes back to the Parsifal legend. Parsifal is the Grail king, that's to say the keeper of the Holy Grail, and Lohengrin is his son. As the Knight of the Swan, Lohengrin travels to the Duchess of Brabant to protect her. But she must never ask him his name . . ."

"Which, of course, she does anyway," Sara interrupted. "Naturally. Now I remember the story. And *Tannhäuser*?"

"Deals, among other things, with the medieval singers' contest at the Wartburg castle. The Singers' Hall on the fourth floor is modeled on the hall in the Wartburg." Zöller opened a thick, well-thumbed book. "The story of Sigurd and Gudrun, in turn, goes back to the legendary Germanic world of the Edda." He looked at Steven and Sara, his eyes twinkling. "You two probably know the romance better as the Nibelung legend featuring handsome Siegfried and his prim and proper Kriemhilde. The legend is easily the best-known story in Wagner's operas. All most people really know about Tristan and Isolde is that they were a couple of lovers."

"Hey, wait a moment." Steven suddenly pricked up his ears and leafed fast through the diary, his voice growing more and more urgent. "Theodor Marot described the paintings and figures of the two lovers in Ludwig's bedroom at some length. And Marot and Maria, after all, were another couple of lovers. The other two keywords were MARIA and LILIES. They're both kind of connected with love. Couldn't 'Tristan and Isolde' be the legend we're after?"

"And suppose it is?" Sara was sitting beside Zöller on the mosaic floor, tapping the keyboard of her laptop listlessly. "I've fed the names *Tristan* and *Isolde* in about a dozen times. All I get out of that is garbage."

"Then let's go back to the bedroom," Steven said, already making for the exit. "Maybe we'll find a clue that we've overlooked so far. There simply *must* be something, I'm sure of it. We've been too blind to spot it so far, that's all."

IN THE FLICKERING emergency lighting, they hurried along the dark corridors and chambers of the castle. As a teenager, Steven had once gone on a guided tour of Neuschwanstein, but at night the building looked little like the fairy-tale tourist attraction of his childhood. In the darkness, the castle was gloomy, cold, and almost unreal, like a theatrical backdrop in which painted characters suddenly came to life. Knights with faces distorted by pain, pale aristocratic maidens, kings, and warriors stared out of the murals at Steven and seemed to follow every step he took. The heavy wooden doors creaked and squealed, and several times he thought he heard footsteps directly overhead, as if the king were still wandering restlessly through the Singers' Hall. Sara, too, kept looking up at the ceiling, intrigued.

"All the cameras are making me paranoid," she said softly, pointing to another lens mounted in a corner. "You really do feel you're under observation the whole time."

"Any idea how many people go around this place every day?" Zöller said, standing in contemplation of the furniture. Once again, Steven felt that something was troubling him. "It's sometimes up to ten thousand a day in the summer. Ten thousand idiots who think they can paw everything here. Without security cameras, you might as well shut up shop."

Zöller went ahead as they finally, by way of the anteroom and the dining room, reached the king's bedchamber. The magnificent neo-Gothic furnishings were as impressive as the stage set for a Wagnerian opera. In the left-hand corner stood the broad bed with its carved wooden canopy. Next to it was an equally ornate washstand with a silver swan providing water. Two doorways led to the private chapel next door and a small, artificial grotto with a conservatory. The bedroom walls were covered by mural paintings from the legend of Tristan and Isolde, and here again the small cameras made sure that improper behavior by any visitors was immediately detected.

Lost in thought, Steven looked at the bedside table. Its wood looked curiously thin and cheap. Once again, the bookseller thought of what Zöller had said just now.

Most of this stuff is only smoke and mirrors . . .

"So let's see what we have here," Uncle Lu said, leafing through a booklet about legends of the Middle Ages. He then scrutinized the paintings and furniture. "The washstand has running water, and there is a flushing toilet," he lectured. "Ludwig always made use of the latest technology. Nonetheless, the fittings and furnishings were so grotesquely like something out of a fairy tale that only a few weeks after Ludwig's death, Prince Regent Luitpold threw it open to the public as evidence of the king's insanity. This bed, for instance . . ."

Suddenly Zöller stopped short. He adjusted his reading glasses and inspected the lavish carvings on the canopy.

"What is it?" Sara asked. "Have you found something?"

"No," the old man murmured, shaking his head as if waking from a nightmare. "I must be mistaken. Anything else would be . . ."

He chuckled as if he had just heard a bad joke. Then he shrugged and pointed to a mural on the left, showing a pair of lovers in the shade of a broad treetop. "The lady in the white dress there is Isolde," he said. "So the man embracing her so soulfully must be Tristan. Aha, and over there he is handing her the fatal love potion."

"Maybe it would be helpful if you could give us a brief summary of the plot," Sara said. "I'm apparently the only person here who doesn't know her way around the world of the old Germanic legends."

Uncle Lu grinned. "You don't know the most famous love story in Germany? Very well, here's the short version." He cleared his throat. "King Rivalon is burning with love for the beautiful Blanchefleur, but their relationship must be kept secret. Just when she becomes pregnant, Rivalon is killed by the wicked King Morgan. Blanchefleur dies of love and grief, and her child grows up without ever knowing his real parents. That child is Tristan."

"So what about Isolde?" Sara asked.

"Don't be so impatient." Uncle Lu raised his hands in a placatory gesture. "Much later, Tristan is to pay court to the Irish princess Isolde on behalf of King Mark of Cornwall. On the crossing to Britain, the two of them accidentally drink the love potion that was really meant for Mark and Isolde. And then fate takes its course."

Zöller pointed to a mural showing Isolde mourning at the bedside of a mortally sick Tristan. "Tristan loves a woman who is betrothed to another man. A theme popular to this day in romantic novels and soap operas. The handsome young man does marry another girl, who as it happens is also called Isolde, but even his marriage cannot extinguish his love for the true Isolde. In the end they both die after a few complications so unbelievable that no TV producer would allow them to pass. End of story."

Sara applauded slowly. "Thanks for the lesson, Herr Zöller, even if I still have no idea what the keyword is. My head is positively ringing with all those names instead." Sighing, she enumerated them. "King Rivalon, Blanchefleur, Morgan, Mark, another Isolde . . ."

"And I've left out most of the names, too." Uncle Lu grinned. "Otherwise it would be a performance to fill a whole evening."

Suddenly, something clicked inside Steven's head. It was as if a piece of a jigsaw puzzle that he had spent a long time looking for had finally moved into the right place.

Was it possible?

"Just a moment! What was the name of Tristan's mother again?"

Zöller looked at him in surprise. "Blanchefleur. Why do you ask?"

"Blanchefleur . . ." The bookseller frowned, and his eyes lingered on the woman in the white dress in the mural. "Maybe it's just a co-incidence, but if my French isn't letting me down, then Blanchefleur means . . ."

"White flower," Sara muttered. "White like the lilies that Marot picked for Maria. Do you really think *Blanchefleur* is our keyword? There are an awful lot of letters in it."

Steven nodded eagerly. His voice almost cracked. "Why not?" He held up three fingers. "The first keyword was *Maria*, the second was *lilies*. And number three, *Blanchefleur*, is both a woman *and* a white flower. So the word stands both for a lily and for Maria. It's the sum of the two first keywords." In his excitement, he pointed to the mural. "And Blanchefleur and this King Rivalon also had to keep their love secret, just like Tristan and Isolde and just like . . ."

"Theodor and Maria!" Sara struck her forehead. "I think you've got it." She took out her laptop and typed the name . . . "Bingo. Although . . ." A shadow clouded her face.

"What's the matter?" Steven asked. "Is something wrong?"

"Damn it, all we get is roman numerals again." Sara pointed to the monitor and a row of capital letters shimmering on it.

I, IV, II, V, III, IV, IV, I, IV, IV, IV, IV, II

"First the titles of those poems, and then nothing but two sets of figures," she said crossly. "I'm beginning to think that friend Theodor is playing an elaborate joke on us."

"Suppose it's not the keyword?" Zöller suggested. "Maybe the name is a false trail?"

"Nonsense!" With one finger, Steven tapped the mural showing the lady in white and Tristan. "*Blanchefleur* is the third keyword, I'm sure it is. If only I knew . . ."

Suddenly he stopped in alarm and looked up at the ceiling, where one of the CCTV cameras was mounted above the mural.

"Listen, I may be wrong," he murmured, "but wasn't that camera just pointing in a different direction?"

All three stood there as if turned to stone and stared up at the ceiling, like small children caught stealing cookies.

Finally Sara broke the silence. "Hell, Steven, you're right," she whispered. "The thing must have moved. But how . . ."

There was a faint humming sound, and the lens moved several

degrees to one side. All at once Steven had a feeling that the camera was looking straight at him, like the eye of some unearthly being staring down at him with interest.

Sara nervously pulled at his sleeve and pointed to a second camera behind them. It, too, turned in their direction, also humming softly. Only now did the bookseller notice a detail that had escaped him entirely in his excitement.

A small black microphone was fitted over the lens of each camera, and a little red light blinked wildly whenever they made the slightest sound.

"Oh shit," Sara said.

Still humming, the two cameras now moved their lenses down, as if to greet old friends.

LANCELOT LOUNGED ON the comfortable, black leather sofa in the middle of the control room, playing with the regulators on the control panel. Above him flickered more than two dozen monitors, each showing one of the rooms in the castle. Most of them were empty; in one of them there was panic.

They had obviously noticed what he was doing, but that didn't matter. He knew what he wanted to know. The king would be grateful to him. Well, maybe not grateful exactly, but at least Lancelot had fulfilled the major part of his contract and could hope for a good fat fee. He knew the third keyword; he had brought together everything that was worth knowing about this man Steven Lukas and his woman. Now all he needed was the diary, and then his mission would be complete.

Caribbean, here I come.

He had to admit that the king's plan had worked perfectly. They had fallen into the trap like so many mice, and now they were gaping stupidly at the camera lens like mice staring at a snake. With a tingling sense of anticipation, Lancelot zoomed in on the face of the little slut who had put his eye out. Her expression was partly baffled, partly terrified. He could see every bead of sweat on her brow. Now he moved the camera a little lower, so that he could admire her heaving breasts.

Nice cleavage. A pity I can't get the camera to look up her skirt.

Suddenly the young woman's expression changed. Her bewilderment and fear vanished, and her eyes flashed angrily. With determination, she approached the camera.

Sara showed him her middle finger, took a piece of chewing gum out of her mouth, and stuck it over the lens. The monitor went black.

What the hell . . .

A moment later, the other screen showing the bedroom went blank as well. Snarling, Lancelot stood up from the leather sofa and took the safety catch off his well-oiled Glock 17. He had been having fun long enough.

Now it was time to tidy up.

SARA STUCK THE last remnant of her chewing gum on the second microphone and turned furiously to her two companions.

"I don't know what's going on here," she whispered. "But someone seems to be watching us. And probably listening to everything as well."

"One of the security guards, maybe?" Zöller suggested. "Or the head of Manstein Systems herself? It could be that Frau Manstein is just checking the system and having a little joke at our expense. She did say she was going to the control room."

"In that case she's not going to be very happy that you've stuck gum all over her expensive cameras and microphones," Steven said. "Although that's exactly what Peggy from Texas would do, with her adolescent sense of humor."

"Very funny." Sara rolled her eyes nervously. "Come on, admit that you're terrified. And still no one has said that . . ." Suddenly she stopped dead.

"What is it?" Steven asked.

"The picture," she said slowly, pointing to the mural showing the woman in white. "In your excitement just now, you touched that picture."

"So?"

"Frau Manstein said she'd switched the alarm system on. But no alarm went off, even though you tapped the painting several times. So someone switched the system off again." She looked cautiously out at the corridor leading to the artificial grotto. "Someone who doesn't want to be disturbed in his work."

"Sara, please don't turn paranoid," Steven replied skeptically. "This unknown Someone would have had to get into the castle to switch off the system. You saw for yourself how complicated that is. Numerical code, fingerprint, facial recognition—who'd be able to get past all that?"

"I don't know," Sara said, looking around the room. "But someone has to clean this place. There are tour guides, watchmen . . ." She suddenly fell silent and bent down. Steven blinked and tried to get a clearer view.

Beside the tiled stove with the two figures of Tristan and Isolde, there was a small electronic distributor box at knee level, as black as the cameras. An adhesive label on it showed the logo of a company and some writing. Sara cried out in surprise.

Now Steven knelt down as well to get a better look at the label.

"*Camelot Security,*" he read aloud.

But it was not the words that drained the color from his face; it was the logo underneath them.

It showed a golden swan with outspread wings. Below it, there was another inscription in tiny, old-fashioned script, forming part of the logo.

Tmeicos Ettal.

It took Steven some time to remember where he had seen that logo and the inscription before. The realization struck him like a blow in the pit of the stomach. It was the same as on the amulet worn by the dead Bernd Reiser, the man in the cellar of his antiquarian bookshop in Munich. Steven felt his heart beating faster as everything suddenly fitted together. Was this possible?

Camelot Security . . . It's a case of combining the old and the new.

The bookseller groaned under his breath. He didn't want to believe it, but the longer he thought, the clearer it all became. It made no sense, but nonetheless it was logical. Even before he could follow his train of thought all the way to its terrible end, a sound startled him.

"Time to go," Lancelot said, suddenly appearing in the bedroom doorway. His good eye sparkled mockingly as he sketched a small bow.

"Allow me to escort you," he growled in his deep, bass voice. "The Royal Highness awaits to grant you an audience."

· 31 ·

THE KING RECEIVED THEM IN the throne room, sitting ramrod straight on a plain wooden chair without arms or a back, a mere stool, placed exactly on the raised part of the apse where Ludwig's throne had once been destined to stand.

To the left and right of this improvised throne the paladins Gawain and Mordred stood guard, holding their automatic Uzis in front of them, like lances adorned with pennants. To hold audience, the king wore the royal cloak of white ermine from which the professor's blood had been removed by chemical cleaning. A thin aristocratic hand tightly gripped the same Derringer the king had used to spray Paul Liebermann's brain matter over the forest floor. In honor of the day, the king wore a little mascara and some discreet lipstick. The makeup harmonized perfectly with the king's short gray hair, and equally gray pantsuit.

"Welcome to my castle, Herr Lukas," Luise Manstein said. "I must confess that you have given me considerably more problems than I assumed you would. Strong blood flows in your veins."

Steven stood in the middle of the throne room as if frozen, staring at the industrialist, who was scrutinizing him sardonically from the marble stage of the apse. Sara and Albert Zöller were also incapable of any movement.

"But . . . but you're . . ." Steven stammered.

"A woman. I know." Luise nodded. "You made the mistake of taking me for a man once before, do you remember?" A smile, narrow as a knife blade, appeared on her face. Steven thought of their first meeting at the Grotto of Venus. What had the industrialist said on that occasion?

Women in leading positions always have to contend with that prejudice . . .

"I . . . I don't understand." Steven stood there, his shoulders drooping, his mouth open, and could make no sense of the scene before him. The woman who was head of a leading German IT company sat there, wearing a royal cloak and holding an old-fashioned pistol.

"Do you seriously believe that *you* are Ludwig the Second?" Steven asked.

He had certainly heard that there were lunatics who thought they were Ludwig reincarnated, but the idea of a successful woman like this, head of a large company, falling victim to that delusion left him speechless. He cursed quietly. When he saw the logo of Camelot Security and saw the connection between Bernd Reiser, who had died in his bookshop, and Manstein Systems, he ought to have guessed that the head of the firm was involved in all this somehow. But by then, of course, it was too late anyway.

"You disappoint me again, Herr Lukas," Luise said. "Of course I am *not* Ludwig. The king has been dead for more than a hundred years. All I want is the book." She gave him a thin smile and pointed to his rucksack. "Or let's say what is hidden in the book."

By now Steven had recovered from his initial surprise. Unbridled fury rose in him. "*You* set that lunatic on us, then? *You* handed us over to him at Linderhof and Herrenchiemsee?" With revulsion, he indicated Lancelot, who still stood behind Sara with his gun at the ready. "But why? With all your money, you could simply have bought the damn diary."

Luise Manstein leaned forward on her wooden stool. "Do you think I didn't try? When I found out that the professor had discovered the diary in someone's effects, I wanted it at once. I offered him any price he cared to ask. But he remained obstinate. And then, when I was going to . . . well, question him, it was too late. He had already passed it on to you." She frowned. "Unfortunately, Herr Lukas, you preferred to go underground. Even the police couldn't find you."

"Then *you* tipped off the cops and left Uncle Paul's clothes in the bookshop," Sara said, as Lancelot dug his Glock into her back. "I always wondered who had told the police about the connection between Steven and my uncle."

Luise caressed the butt of her Derringer and played dreamily with the trigger. "Just a little trick. Of course, my attorneys would have ferreted out Herr Lukas twenty-four hours later and brought him to me, along with the book. But you had to stage a dramatic escape." She sighed and cast a theatrical glance up at the cupola. "It was pure chance that I met you at Linderhof, Herr Lukas. A dispensation of Providence, if you like. But unfortunately you gave me a false name at the time, and I did not know what that ominous character, the antiquarian bookseller Steven Lukas, really looked like. Your picture does not appear on Facebook, or any other website. Most old-fashioned."

"I knew there was a good reason for me to steer clear of the damn Internet," Steven murmured.

"Well, well, you are a little antiquated, with all your books." Luise smiled. "Be that as it may, only the description given by one of my paladins made it clear to me that the blundering provincial journalist Greg Landsdale was really Steven Lukas, a wanted man. So I simply waited for you at Neuschwanstein and finally lured you here." Luise's right eyebrow rose. "Although I would have been very glad to meet you on your own. Just the two of us. But never mind, this way we'll sort everything out."

Unbidden, memories flared up in Steven again, like little flashes of lightning striking before his eyes. And here was that sense of nausea again.

The Chinese lantern lying crushed on the ground, the burning pages, the struggle, the flight down the long corridors, out through the window, down into the garden by climbing down the ivy . . .

What was all this? What was going on in his head? He forced down the impulse to retch and tried to concentrate on the woman sitting in front of him in the royal cloak.

"What do you want the book for?" he asked. The two gorillas to the right and left of Luise Manstein hadn't moved an inch, yet it seemed to Steven that they were just waiting for a pretext to fire their Uzis at him. "To prove that King Ludwig was murdered? Professor Liebermann would have done just that."

"I suspect it's about something very different," Zöller said, speaking up for the first time. His voice sounded curiously calm, almost apathetic. "Something beyond the power of your imagination, Herr Lukas. This woman is . . ."

"*Silence, you scoundrel!*" Luise leaped off her wooden throne and pointed the little Derringer straight at Zöller. Her hands were trembling, her eyes cold and piercing. "Why I need that book is no business of anyone here. All that matters is for me to have it in my hands at last. For the damn riddle to be solved after more than a century."

Zöller took a step back and held his tongue, but Sara intervened.

"I suspect that Uncle Lu was about to say, 'This woman is a total nut case.'" She turned to the bookseller. "Come on, Steven! Look at her! She thinks she's a new Ludwig, and these thugs are her paladins. You can't *get* crazier than that. And this giant monkey here," she added, turning furiously to Lancelot, who was just behind and towering above her, "is just her favorite toy knight."

"You have made Lancelot very angry, Frau Lengfeld." The head of Manstein Systems sat down on the stool again, but now her voice was cold as steel. "Very angry. You are part of his fee, did you know that?"

Lancelot grinned, then winked at Sara with his one sound eye.

"I'll make you an offer, Frau Manstein," Steven said. He opened his rucksack and went over to the gallery, holding the little cherrywood chest. "I'll give you the book. The book and the little treasure chest. And in return, you let us go. The police would never believe us anyway, and you'll save yourself a great deal of trouble."

"She'll never let us go." Zöller shook his head. He seemed like an old man again. "We know the secret of the book, or at least almost. And what's more, we could always tell the police about this lady's large-scale art theft."

"Art theft?" Sara asked, baffled. "What are you talking about?"

A slight tic on the industrialist's face showed Steven that Zöller had found out something important. The two guards to the left and right of the throne exchanged nervous glances.

"You can deceive millions of tourists, maybe the castle administration as well, and a few self-styled experts, Frau Manstein," Zöller growled. "But you don't deceive me. I've taken a very close look at the bed, the washstand, and the rest of the furnishings of the castle, and I've taken photographs. It's only a matter of tiny details, but I've seen too many pictures of the original fittings and furnishings to miss seeing the difference."

"Nonsense," hissed the industrialist. "The copies are perfect."

"The *copies?*" Bewildered, Steven looked from Uncle Lu to Luise Manstein. "What copies?"

"Herr Lukas, do you really think that Manstein Systems accepted the commission in Neuschwanstein just for the prestige of it or out of pure love for humanity?" Zöller laughed quietly. "A leading German IT company renovates a dusty castle? Sees to unimportant details like personally hiring the security staff? That struck me as odd all along. When I had a chance to take a look at the furniture in the royal bedchamber today, I couldn't believe it at first. I thought I must be mistaken. But now I know that we are witnesses to one of the greatest art thefts of the century. For that very reason alone, Madame here isn't about to let us go."

"Are you saying that all the furniture and works of art in the castle are only . . . *duplicates?*" Steven remembered how thin and cheap the wood of the king's bedside table had looked to him just now. Could it be possible? All at once he felt as if the ground had been pulled from under his feet.

Most of this stuff is just smoke and mirrors . . .

"I don't know exactly how many pieces of furniture," Zöller said. "The bed, the chairs, and the washstand in the bedchamber, in any case. Presumably on the nights when Manstein Systems' people were installing the security system, they gradually dismantled everything here, bringing in the duplicates at the same time. The furniture in the study and the dining room also struck me as a little different. And here . . ."

He looked curiously up at the ceiling, where the great chandelier hung, with nearly a hundred candles.

"We did a good job," Luise boasted. "The chandelier weighs approximately a ton. A fragile, unique work made of Bohemian glass. I think it looks magnificent in its new location."

Spellbound, Steven looked around him in all directions. The chandelier, the candleholders that were as tall as a man, the magnificent tables and chairs in the neighboring rooms . . . Had they all been stolen? Did nothing but *duplicates* still stand in Neuschwanstein?

"Where in God's name did you take all those things?" he asked, horrified. "To a storeroom? Are you going to sell them? Surely you have enough money already."

Luise laughed out loud; it was an almost girlish giggle. "I see you still don't understand me, Herr Lukas," she said, smiling. "Ludwig never wanted ordinary mortals walking around his castles, desecrating the pictures and furniture here by staring at them. I have had the exhibits taken to a sacred place where I alone can look at them."

"Ah," Sara said. "Your living room, I presume. Because you are no ordinary mortal, are you? Other people get reborn as a butterfly, Napoleon, or a potted plant, but you, of course, are the reincarnation of Ludwig the Second."

"*How dare you insult me,*" Luise cried, jumping up from her temporary throne. She aimed the Derringer straight at Sara now, while her voice rang through the hall. "You'll find out soon enough who it is you're dealing with. Lancelot, teach this insolent bitch a lesson."

With a swift movement, the giant pressed against the hollows of Sara's knees from behind, so that she bent over, with a cry of surprise, and dropped to the ground. Then he swung his leg back and kicked her in the stomach with all his might. Sara folded like a pocketknife; a gurgling sound emerging from her throat, and she brought up gall and saliva.

"You . . . you bloody bastard!" she gasped, writhing in pain.

Steven watched this scene as if he were in a trance. Then he dropped Marot's little treasure chest and ran, fists up, toward Lancelot, who stood two heads taller than he did. The giant swerved aside at the last moment and delivered a right hook to the bookseller's chin. Fighting for breath, Steven fell to the floor. For a moment everything around him was black, and then, unsteadily, he got to his knees. He was holding his lip, and blood dripped to the mosaic flooring. Suddenly he felt incredibly weary.

"Damn it, what the hell are we doing here?" he cursed quietly. He leaned down to Sara and caressed her trembling body. A shudder ran through her; she seemed to be weeping silently. "Why did your uncle have to come to *my* bookshop?" Steven asked. "So many booksellers in Munich, but no, he had to pick me."

Steven felt a hand on his shoulder. When he looked up, he saw the anxious face of Uncle Lu. For the first time he noticed the deep lines on the old man's face and the infinite sadness in his eyes.

"Herr Lukas, it's time you learned something very important about yourself," Zöller began in a quiet voice. "It wasn't by chance that Paul went to you. He knew you and your parents. And he knew that . . ."

The gunshot rocked the throne room as if lightning had struck the cupola. Albert Zöller staggered several steps back, clutching his stomach. For a moment Steven thought it was only the noise of the shot that had alarmed the old man, but then Zöller put out his hand and stared incredulously at his fingers.

They were red with blood. Thick liquid dripped from them onto the brightly colored mosaic floor.

Now Steven could also see the red stain on Zöller's shirt, almost exactly where his navel had to be. The stain spread and spread, and soon his pants and shirt were wet with blood. Uncle Lu groaned quietly, then tipped forward and lay motionless.

Luise lowered her Derringer, from which a small puff of smoke rose to the cupola, and breathed out deeply.

"You . . . you've killed him." By now Sara had scrambled to her feet. She was still bent over in pain and clutching her stomach, but at least she could speak again, more or less. "Damn you! What did that old man ever do to you?"

"He poked his nose into things that are none of his business." Luise stood up and handed the little pistol to one of her paladins. "And he's not dead. See for yourself." She pointed to Zöller's body. A slight tremor passed through it; his rib cage rose and fell faintly. "I suppose the bullet didn't hit a major organ. Maybe he can still be saved, but he doesn't have much time left."

"Then call a doctor!" Steven cried. "At once!"

The industrialist smiled. "I'll call a doctor. I'll even have a specialist flown in from Munich if it's necessary. But not until you tell me the answer to the puzzle. So where did Marot hide it?"

"Hide *what?*" Steven turned Zöller's heavy body over on its back. He looked at Luise, bewildered. "Why would Marot have hidden anything?"

"*Don't lie to me!*" the industrialist screeched. Once again she seemed to have slipped into the world of her delusions. "The puzzle leads somewhere. Out with it, before I shoot another one of you."

"What are you raving on about?" Sara asked defiantly. "We don't know of any place. All we have are the titles of a few poems and a whole lot of numbers, nothing more." Meanwhile she had hurried over to Zöller and unbuttoned his shirt. Cautiously, she felt his weak pulse. "You ought to have waited a little longer before firing that shot.

Without Uncle Lu, we'll never find out what the solution to the puzzle is. Steven hasn't even finished reading the book yet."

Briefly, Luise Manstein closed her eyes. Steven thought she was going to give her henchmen the order to mow them both down with their Uzis, but she regained her self-control.

"Very well," she whispered, "very well. Then I'll tell you what we'll do. You three stay here in the throne room with the diary. I'll give you three hours." She held three fingers up in the air as if swearing an oath. "Three hours, no more. If you can tell me where the secret is hidden then, I'll call a doctor for this stubborn old man. You have my royal word of honor on that. If not . . ." She turned to go, and her henchmen followed her in silence. "If not, there'll be another couple of mysterious deaths in the Ludwig case."

Royal cloak billowing, The King's Majesty stalked out of the throne room toward the study, with the two paladins. Only Lancelot lingered behind for a moment in the doorway, fixing Sara with his one good eye.

"You and I are going to have fun soon, baby," he whispered. "And if you two cute kids think you can call for help with your cell phones or the laptop, forget it. Up here there's no cell service, no wireless network, nothing. Tried it myself. Neuschwanstein is deep in the Middle Ages."

The two wings of the door slammed shut.

IN THE SILENCE that followed, all they could hear was Albert Zöller's tortured breathing. He kept his eyes closed, his eyelids flickering nervously now and then. Sara tore strips of fabric off her jacket and began improvising a bandage for the old man.

"This man needs help!" she shouted at the top of her voice, hoping that someone outside could hear her. "My God, is there no one here who'll help us?" But the silence around them only felt more oppressive.

"What kind of situation have we gotten ourselves into?" Steven cursed, running his hands through his graying hair. "I should have burned that damn diary back in my bookshop."

"Then that madwoman would probably have burned you as well," replied Sara. "Stop whining, and think how we can get out of here. It's the only way Uncle Lu may have a chance." The art detective seemed to be back in control of herself to some extent. Once more she felt Zöller's pulse and mopped the sweat from his brow. Her improvised bandage was already wet with blood.

"I don't think Uncle Lu can last much longer. Not three hours, anyway," Sara whispered. "That lunatic. She really does think she's Ludwig reborn. I'd guess she's built herself a little palace somewhere, where she lives out her royal dreams surrounded by the original Neuschwanstein furniture. How crazy is that?"

"But then why the book?" Steven asked. "What does Marot's diary have to do with it? And what place did she mean—this place we're supposed to find for her?"

Sara shrugged. "The woman's downright deranged. Who knows what goes on inside her head?"

Suddenly she got up and stood, legs apart, in the middle of the room, her face turned to one of the cameras under the ceiling. "Hey, you, Queen of Hearts!" she shouted. "Can you hear me? Ludwig would never have done a thing like this. Maybe he was a little eccentric, but you are totally deranged. Do you hear, *to-tally de-ranged!*"

When there was no reaction, Sara looked all around her, searching frantically, and finally hurried over to a small door on the left of the apse. She opened it, and Steven felt a cold draft of air.

"I'm sure there's a great view from up here in the daytime," he heard Sara saying from outside. "But the only way down is a sixty-five-foot drop. *Fuck!*"

She closed the door and turned back to Zöller, who was breathing heavily. Gently, she laid his head on what was left of her jacket. "I suppose there's nothing to do but to go along with that deranged old bat's proposition," she said. "Not that I think Luise will let us go then, but maybe we can at least save Uncle Lu."

"Whom, incidentally, you suspected for no good reason," Steven interjected with annoyance.

"As if that matters now." Sara rolled her eyes. "I guess we'll never find out what he was doing with that private detective agency, and those phone calls to the States. Or at least, not if Uncle Lu doesn't get to see a doctor very soon."

Steven frowned. "What did he mean when he said it was no coincidence that your uncle came to see me?" he asked. "He said Paul Liebermann had known my parents. How could that be?"

"Who knows," Sara said. "Luise shot Zöller the moment she heard him. Obviously she didn't want you to know any more."

"More about what? Uncle Lu said it was time I learned something very important about myself. What the hell was it?" Steven sighed and rummaged listlessly around in Zöller's books, which were scattered all over the mosaic floor. There were smeared bloodstains on some of them. "We've solved the third puzzle, we've made it to Neuschwanstein, and we still don't know any more than we did at the start."

He stared at the picture of St. George fighting a green dragon in front of a small castle on a rock. That was just how Steven felt: he was fighting, struggling, thrashing about, and still he didn't move from the spot.

"I'm beginning to feel fairly sure that all this is to do with my childhood memories," Steven said quietly. "I don't know how and why, but there's some kind of connection between me and the diary. The sensation of dizziness that I get when I read it, the memories of earlier times . . . it's as if something were knocking at the door to my consciousness with all its might. The diary takes me back to my childhood. And Zöller knows what the connection is." His voice rose, echoing in the high cupola. "Hell, why didn't he say something sooner? How does he know what I'm not supposed to know?"

"Crazy Luise was talking about a hiding place just now," Sara said. "Presumably the ballad puzzle takes us there. But what can the something be? A treasure? Obviously it's something that's extremely important to her."

Steven cleared his throat. "Up to this point we've always thought that finding out about the true background to Ludwig's death was all that mattered. But maybe it's something else. Something to do with my own past." He picked up the diary, which bore a large drop of blood. "Only one thing to do," he said, wiping the drop away with his last white handkerchief. "I have to finish reading the damn book. Luckily there are only a few pages left."

"If Uncle Lu's going to have any chance, you'll have to read fast," Sara told him, mopping the sweat off Zöller's forehead. "I don't think he has much time left."

"Then you'd better listen to the end of Marot's story. Maybe you'll spot something that I'd miss."

Steven sat down on the steps up to the gallery, opened the book, and read the penultimate entry in the diary out loud.

· 32 ·

JG, JG, JG

*T*hey came at midnight to take the king away.

By now most of the servants had already left the castle. Only four had stayed with Ludwig, and an almost unreal silence reigned. Even before this, Neuschwanstein—with its scaffolding and half-fin-ished rooms, its bare corridors floored only with loose boards, and its fairy-tale furnishings—had seemed to me like a ghost castle. Now I actually thought I felt a touch of evil seeping through its walls.

I had lain down to get a little rest in one of the servants' bedrooms and had fallen into a restless state of half sleep, from which I was awoken by the sudden sound of several loud voices. When I hurried up the steep spiral staircase, I saw Ludwig's massive form standing in the bedroom doorway. Two attendants were positioned, one on his right, the other on his left, holding the king with their strong arms. Ludwig himself looked pale and bloated; he had clearly been drink-ing. His voice sounded soft and apathetic, as if he were already re-signed to the inevitable.

"What . . . what do you want?" he stammered. "What does this mean? Let go of me!"

Dr. von Gudden, with his assistant, Dr. Müller, beside him, stepped out of the group of madhouse attendants and addressed the king.

"Your Majesty, what I have undertaken to do is the saddest task in my life. Your Majesty has been certified by four doctors who are specialists in insanity, and on the basis of their opinions, Prince Luitpold has assumed the regency."

"But how can you call me insane?" asked Ludwig in a muted voice. "You did not come to see me and examine me first."

"Your Majesty, that was not necessary. The material in the files is extensive and positively overwhelming."

Ludwig suddenly looked at the doctor with a steady gaze. As so often, his mood seemed to change from one second to the next, and now he seemed extremely reasonable.

"How can you, as a serious neurologist, have so little conscience as to make out such a certificate?" he asked in an objective tone. "A certificate that decided the fate of a human being whom you have not seen for years? How can such a thing happen?"

"The . . . the certificate has been made out on the basis of evidence from your servants," replied the doctor, looking nervously at his assistant. "As I said, it is more than sufficient."

From my vantage point on the staircase, I sensed that Dr. von Gudden was becoming less and less certain of himself. He took off his pince-nez and began polishing the lenses with ceremony. Obviously he had expected to confront a babbling lunatic, not a man with his mind clear. Meanwhile, Ludwig was growing heated.

"A medical certificate based on statements from paid individuals?" inquired the king indignantly. "And by way of showing their gratitude, they have betrayed me."

Gudden was not going to broach this subject. "Your Majesty," he said huskily, "I have orders to accompany you to Berg Castle this very night. The carriage will be brought at four in the morning."

I gave a start of surprise. So the king was going not to Linderhof but to Berg! Obviously the plan had been changed at short notice. Ideas raced through my head. Dürckheim was planning an escape from Linderhof, but that plan was now invalid. What was I to do? Time was running out for us, for the longer Ludwig was in the power of the conspirators, the more unlikely did his liberation become. Berg Castle was probably being converted into a prison at this moment, and the people's indignation at this coup d'état would die down with every passing day. We had to act immediately.

I was still standing, as if transfixed, in a niche on the spiral staircase. So far neither Gudden nor the king had noticed me. Only after a while did I make my decision. I crept quietly down the staircase and was about to step out into the castle courtyard, when I saw some of the gendarmes at the gate patrolling back and forth. Obviously they had strict instructions to let no one else out. The black-roofed carriages that were to accompany Ludwig to Berg already waited in the courtyard.

Cursing under my breath, I went back inside the castle to look for another way out. I must, *must* warn my fellow conspirators! At this moment I thought of the throne room on the upper floor. The balcony on its western side was indeed at least fifteen feet from the ground, but it was unlikely that the gendarmes would be guarding that side.

After a moment's hesitation, I hurried back to the servants' rooms, where I purloined several sheets from the beds and went upstairs with them. I could still hear the voices of Gudden and the king from the direction of the royal bedchamber. Taking no more notice of them, I went to the throne room and quietly closed the two great wings of the door behind me. Alone in that high, vaulted room, with its starry cupola and mighty chandelier, I felt almost as if I were in some Far Eastern funerary monument.

Reaching the balcony at last, I hastily began knotting the sheets together. From time to time I looked at the depths below, where the castle walls came to an abrupt end in the undergrowth. Farther to the south, I could see the Pöllat Gorge in the moonlight, spanned by the slender Marie Bridge that Ludwig had had built for his mother, who liked walking long distances. Although it was June, up here on the balcony an icy wind blew, and dark rain clouds were coming down from the mountains.

After a good fifteen minutes I had knotted the sheets into a long rope, and I now tied it fast to one of the columns. I tugged at it to try it out, then took a deep breath and swung myself out silently above the void. Cautiously I clambered down, using several stone gargoyles below the balcony as handholds, until after what seemed like an eternity, I felt solid ground beneath my feet.

I crossed to the Pöllat Gorge along a narrow path. It led past the little Pöllat River, winding its way beside waterfalls, scattered rocks, and finally into a wooded valley not far away.

At last I had reached Hohenschwangau, where one of my horses was still stabled. The coachman, Osterholzer, had taken good care of him, and he whinnied happily when he recognized me. I opened the stable door, led him out into the night, and rode away into the darkness.

Just as I left the sleepy little town behind me, the rain set in.

IT RAINED WITHOUT stopping, a thin, wet, all-enveloping drizzle that accompanied me for the next few hours, making my clothing as heavy as lead. I had only this one horse, so I had to ride more slowly in order to spare him. As we approached Lake Starnberg, which could hardly be made out through the wet mist of the rain, my faithful steed's trot became unsteady, and I realized that he had lost a shoe. He swerved to the left and to the right, then shook his head reluctantly, and I had to dig my heels into his sides to make him go on.

At last, in the gray light of dawn, I reached the royal equerry Richard Hornig's estate in Allmannshausen. When my horse recognized his old stable, he broke into a final gallop and stopped at the stable door so abruptly that, exhausted as I was, I fell forward and off his back. With the last of my strength I scrambled up and ran to the manor house, where lights were already on despite the early hour. I knocked frantically at the door, until finally Hornig, unshaven and in a bad temper, opened it. When he saw me, his annoyance gave way to an expression of astonishment.

"My God, Theodor! What are you doing here?" he asked. "Count Dürckheim has sent us a dispatch saying that the king will be brought to Linderhof. We thought that you were with Ludwig . . ."

"The king isn't going to Linderhof," I interrupted. "He's being sent to Berg Castle. They'll already be on their way here. We must set about planning his escape from Berg."

"Berg, here on Lake Starnberg?" Hornig looked at me, taken aback. "Well, that changes things, of course. But it isn't necessarily the worst of news. I have many friends around here." Only now did he notice my pitiful appearance, and he clapped me sympathetically on the shoulder. "But what am I talking about? Come along in and warm yourself up."

As I entered the room where a fire blazed, I saw that we were far from being alone. As well as Hornig and his brother, here in the large, smoky room were Dr. Schleiss von Loewenfeld, Kaulbach the painter, and a dozen other persons, some of whom were very clearly simple, earthy fellows. However, I also saw Count Rambaldi from Allmannshausen and Baron Eugen von Beck-Peccoz from Eurasburg. All things considered, they were a motley crew of daring men who now stared at me suspiciously as their conversations died away.

"Never fear, gentlemen," said Hornig reassuringly to the company at large. "This is Theodor Marot, a good friend of the king. He brings important news." Turning to me, he helped me out of my wet over-coat. "Tell them, Theodor."

Briefly and hastily, I gave an account of what had gone on at Neuschwanstein during the last two days. When I had finished, an awkward silence fell in the room. The air in the place was stale and sultry, and combined with all the smoke from the men's pipes and cigars, it made me feel dizzy.

"My dear Marot," said Dr. Loewenfeld, breaking the silence at last, "we must all be grateful to you. As you see, the last of the king's loyal subjects have assembled here to stand by him. Until now, however, we have assumed that any escape must be from Linderhof. Your news changes everything, but it is far from being bad news."

"Indeed, quite the opposite," interrupted Hornig, lighting his pipe with a pine splinter from the hearth. "I know the land around Lake Starnberg like the back of my hand, and I have contacts. As for these men . . ." He pointed at the determined expressions of the company. "They will do everything to set their king free."

"Assuming that he will let them," growled Kaulbach the painter. "If I understand you correctly, Theodor, he is not so keen on the idea. Obviously His Majesty prefers cyanide."

"At the end, I thought him very determined again," I replied, warming my back at the crackling fire on the hearth. "I think that when Ludwig sees his escape will be crowned by triumph, he will not refuse. But as long as he sees a fate like that of his brother, Otto, ahead of him, death will seem the only way out."

Dr. Schleiss von Loewenfeld struck the wooden floor with his walking-stick. "Then we must act quickly! As soon as the king is free, he must go to the Tyrol and regain his kingdom from there. We will make out a medical certificate of his sanity revealing Gudden's as a shady, tendentious pamphlet. Then we can arraign Holnstein, Lutz, and the other ministers for high treason." He shook his head angrily. "A medical certificate made out by a man who hasn't once spoken to the patient. Any district medical specialist in insanity will debunk that. It's nothing but a badly planned coup d'état."

A murmur of agreement rose. Several of the common folk present sent up three cheers for the king and raised their glasses.

"When do you think the king will arrive at Berg?" Richard Hornig finally asked.

I shrugged. "Gudden said the carriages would be ready to leave at four in the morning. So they can't be taking much longer."

"In that case we must hurry." Hornig took out a notepad and scribbled a couple of words on it. "The villains will probably stop for a rest in Seeshaupt, if only to change horses at the posting station. So we'll try to get a message to Ludwig there. I suggest that for safety's sake we form several rescue commandos who—if Ludwig decides on flight—will wait for the king at different locations on Lake Starnberg."

"Ought we not to let his cousin Sisi know?" I asked. "After all, she goes to stay at Rose Island in the lake, and she is a friend of his."

Kaulbach the painter shook his head vigorously. "I consider that too dangerous. The empress of Austria is a member of the Wittelsbach family. Who knows, maybe Prince Luitpold has already been in touch with her." He buttoned up his white linen jacket and rapidly smoothed it down. "The fewer people who know about this operation, the better."

"Very well, then that's decided." Dr. Schleiss von Loewenfeld rose ponderously from his armchair. "Who's going to tell the king when he arrives in Seeshaupt?"

"I'll do that," I offered. "He trusts me."

Kaulbach frowned. "But Gudden and Holnstein will recognize you."

"Leave that to me." I put my wet hat on again and slipped into my overcoat, which was now steaming with the damp. "It won't be the first time I have made myself out to be someone else. And if it goes on raining like this, even my own mother wouldn't know me in these garments."

THE PARTY BRINGING the king arrived in the village of Seeshaupt shortly after eleven in the morning.

Rain still poured down in torrents; it was as if heaven itself wept for King Ludwig's fate. After sleeping for far too short a time and eating a frugal breakfast at the Hornig brothers' house, I set off on a fresh horse for the posting station at the southern end of the lake. In addition to my overcoat and hat, I wore a patch over one eye, and I had brought a stick with me, so that I looked like a disreputable drunken veteran of the French campaign of the year 1870. I killed several hours in the tavern at the posting station, drank a couple of glasses of beer, and practiced my new role by limping through the saloon bar of the place several times, swearing like a trooper at the top of my voice.

When I finally heard the whinnying of many horses, I and several other guests hurried outside, where we witnessed a dismal spectacle. The commission that had taken the king was on its way with four covered black carriages. The drivers looked darkly down from their high boxes at the whispering crowd. A couple of the madhouse attendants stretched their legs. Dr. von Gudden himself was nowhere to be seen; he was presumably waiting with his assistant in one of the carriages, where they were both sheltered from the rain.

From my place in the curious crowd, I tried to make out which of the vehicles carried the king, and at last I saw his pale, bloated face in the window of the front carriage. Several spectators also seemed to have recognized Ludwig, and restrained huzzahs were heard, but there was an overall atmosphere of anxiety. The people realized that their king was a prisoner. A woman, obviously the landlady of the tavern, stepped forward, bowing several times, and handed the king a glass of water, which he gratefully drained.

As the people, gaping but with a certain caution, approached the royal carriage, I plucked up my courage and limped toward the window from which the king was greeting the crowd, waving wearily.

"Your Majesty," I whispered, after I had looked around for the attendants one last time. "It's me, Theodor."

The king looked at me in surprise. Only when I took off the eye patch did recognition cross his face.

"Marot," he murmured. "Have you come to say goodbye to me? Those in this gang are going to lock me up in Berg. They'll treat me like a lunatic, like my brother, Otto." He smiled faintly. "But I will fly away like a swan. I'll fly where none can follow."

"My king, all will be well." I kept my voice low, almost inaudible. All the same, I was afraid that the attendants or coachmen could overhear me. "Hornig and the others were already preparing for your escape. Boats are ready and waiting."

"Truly?" Ludwig briefly closed his eyes and took a deep breath. "Then perhaps all is not lost."

I looked anxiously around. One of the madhouse attendants had his eye on me. He whispered something to his colleagues and pointed my way.

"I must go now," I said. "We'll get a message to you in Berg when the moment for flight has come. Until then . . ."

"Wait one more second," the king interrupted. "I have a gift for you."

He reached under the seat in the carriage, and I could see that strong leather straps had been fitted to it, and the door handles had been unscrewed on the inside. Ludwig gave me a small book.

"This contains poems and ballads," he said in a tone of nostalgia. "Goethe, Schiller, Heine . . . They inhabit a world that is far more mine than this prison that we call reality."

"My . . . my king," I said, hiding the book under my overcoat. "I thank you. But now I really must . . ."

"Many of those poems are very close to my heart," he went on, lost in thought. "Sometimes only lines, or single words. But they mean a great deal to me. Goodbye."

He gave me his hand in farewell. I was about to turn away, but he held my hand so firmly that I could not tear it from him.

"And one more thing, Theodor," he said. "I have forgiven you about Maria. Something grew between me and that girl that is stronger than hatred and jealousy. Promise me that you will look after her when I am no more. Look after her and the boy."

A shudder ran through me, and I found it hard to hold back tears.

"I . . . I promise you that," I said quietly.

"Then go with God."

I suddenly felt a hand on my shoulder. It swung me around, and I was looking into the angry face of one of the madhouse attendants. He had been among the men who came with the first group charged to take the king, and who had been imprisoned on Ludwig's orders.

"Hey, what do you think you're doing?" he growled. "This is no king of yours now. He's a lunatic in need of treatment." He laughed unpleasantly. "Better be glad he didn't gouge out your eyes. He's been known to do that to your betters, you know."

I gave the madhouse attendant a foolish grin and prayed to God that he wouldn't recognize me.

"I was only bawling him out for not supporting us old soldiers in the old days against France," I said. "I thought him crazy even then. A man who doesn't place himself at the head of his army doesn't belong on the throne," I told him. "You don't get a chance to speak your mind to a king every day of the week." I pointed derisively behind me at the carriage, taking care to sway back and forth.

"Well and good, then, well and good," grumbled the attendant. "And now clear out before you throw up on my coat."

He gave me a shove, and in relief I tottered away. Once I was at a safe distance, I turned back once more, but Ludwig's face had already disappeared into the interior of the carriage. Only the attendant was still looking at me, shaking his head. When I put my hand under my overcoat, I felt the king's book directly over my heart.

My promise was to bind me until death and beyond.

· 33 ·

THE SOUND OF ZÖLLER'S HOARSE coughing made Steven pause for a moment. He had been reading aloud to Sara in a whisper; now he looked anxiously at the old man. But Uncle Lu seemed to be in a semiconscious state, muttering in his sleep with his eyes closed. Sara mopped the sweat from his brow yet again and then turned to the bookseller.

"Damn it, none of this gets us any closer to solving the puzzle," she said. "We're running out of time. Isn't there another word written in capital letters farther on? Some kind of clue to what those stupid roman numerals could mean? Luise was talking about a place. Is there anything about a special place?"

Steven leafed hastily through the diary, then shook his head. "I'm afraid not. No special place, no clue to the numerals, and none to the titles of the poems in the first part of the memoirs—" He stopped short.

"What is it?" Sara asked.

Steven turned a page back and let his finger run along the text. "The poems," he said quietly. "Marot says that Ludwig gave him a book of ballads in Seeshaupt. It could be just coincidence, or it could be ..."

"A clue. You may be right." Sara was on the alert now. "Read that bit again."

Leafing back, Steven read out the passage once again: *"Many of those poems are very close to my heart. Sometimes only lines, or single words. But they mean a great deal to me."*

"Do you think . . . ?"

"I think that sounds very much like a clue," Steven said. "After all, a third of our puzzle words refer to the titles of poems. But then what would the roman numerals mean?"

Roman numerals . . .

For a brief moment there was an eerie silence in the throne room, and then Sara burst out laughing. She opened her laptop and brought up the file with the deciphered code.

"How could we be so stupid?" she cried. "The king mentions *lines* and *words*! We never tried getting the roman numerals to stand for lines of poems and single words."

Steven frowned. "Wait a moment—there are thirteen titles of poems, the thirteen numbers worked out with the second keyword . . ."

"And the same number of numbers worked out with the third keyword," Sara interrupted him excitedly. "The poem, the line, the word. Just like Marot wrote. What was the first title again?"

Steven rapidly leafed through the diary. "'Erl-King,' it was the 'Erl-King.' The first roman numeral is XVI, which would be line sixteen. That would mean . . ." He closed his eyes for a minute so as to concentrate on remembering the poem. ". . . *Be calm, my dear, keep calm, my child, In the dry leaves rustles the wind so wild.* Those are lines fifteen and sixteen, so the first word would be *in.*"

"The second poem is Heine's 'Belshazzar,'" Sara said. "That's no problem, I still remember learning that one in school. How did it go again? *The midnight hour was coming on, In peace and quiet lay Babylon . . .*" She glanced at her screen. "Line five, as far as I remember, is *Up there in the royal hall,* so the fourth word is *the.* Put the words together and we have *In the.*" She snapped her fingers. "I think we're getting somewhere." She glanced with satisfaction at the screen, where the first two poem titles and the relevant roman numerals had formed into a table.

Ballad	Line	Word	Solution
Erl-King	XVI	I	In
Belshazzar	V	IV	the

"Gold star, Frau Lengfeld, well done," Steven said. "Although the third word is *Thal* for valley, and I haven't the faintest idea what poem that refers to. I have nothing for *Zauberin*, *Winsperg* and *Siegerich* either."

"Maybe the words are each just part of a line of poetry. Think about it. You're the bookseller here."

Resigned, Steven shook his head. "Forget it. Like you say, I'm a bookseller. I don't spend my life reciting poetry. Damn!" He threw the book down on the cold mosaic floor. Suddenly it all seemed to him pointless. He was tired, very, very tired. He would have liked to lean against Sara and go to sleep.

"Why didn't we think of all this before?" he cursed quietly. "They'd probably have had a book of German poetry in the library."

Sara's own nerves seemed stretched to the breaking point. She was tearing her hair, her face was pale, her mascara smudged. All the same, at that moment she looked to Steven almost impossibly beautiful.

As beautiful as Maria, he thought. *Except that she and Marot weren't at the mercy of a raving lunatic who thinks she's the reincarnation of Ludwig and shoots people in cold blood.*

He glanced in concern at Albert Zöller. The old man still lay on the floor close to them, breathing heavily, and the makeshift bandage was already drenched with blood.

"The library," she mused. "You've given me an idea. Just before we left the hotel, Uncle Lu said there was a book of poetry among the stuff he brought, do you remember?" She frantically rummaged among the pile of well-worn books. "It must be here somewhere. We can only hope that . . . voilà!" Triumphantly, she held up a shabby little book with a blue binding. "*German Ballads*! Published in 1923. Not the latest thing, but poems don't deteriorate as time goes on. And unlike us, Uncle Lu thought of bringing a poetry book along. It may save his life now." She opened it to the table of contents. "Now we just have to find the right titles."

Steven picked up the diary from the floor in front of him. He had a feeling that their time was running out, that they were scurrying around like hamsters on a wheel yet getting nowhere. "I hope you're right," he said. "I suggest you put your mind to the ballads while I go on reading. We don't want to miss another important clue at the very end."

And if I'm going to die anyway, I'd at least like to know how Ludwig lost his life, and what it all has to do with my own past, he thought gloomily. *Because we're never going to get out of here. Luise Manstein will spare our lives for as long as we're useful to her, not a minute longer.*

He leafed back through the diary again and began to read. There were only a few pages left.

· 34 ·

JG, IT

We divided up between three boats going back and forth on Lake Starnberg by day and night.

So as not to attract unnecessary attention, we usually changed places on the boats, and there were also times when the three of them gently rode the swells side by side, like fishermen in search of fat freshwater whitefish. We wore dark coats by way of camouflage, and they were soon dripping wet. The rain, which only occasionally fell more gently, made it hard to see the banks of the lake, and we used field glasses as an aid. But they, too, could not penetrate the gray haze in the castle park.

Now we had to play a waiting game.

We knew from those we trusted in the castle that the king was a prisoner. His keepers had unscrewed the door handles and bored peepholes in the thin doors so that they could watch every step that Ludwig took. Although all seemed quiet, we knew that the subversives were expecting resistance. After dark, those inside Berg Castle were forbidden to leave, and gendarmes patrolled the park day and night.

By means of small notes stuck to the underside of plates and serving dishes, we had let the king know about plans for his escape. Ludwig was to persuade Gudden to take a walk beside the lake. At the sound of a whistle, he was to shake off Gudden and wade a few yards into the deep water, where we could finally pick him up in a boat. Not a bad plan, except that there was no sign of the king all that Saturday. And at first we waited in vain on Whitsunday as well.

"Gudden is scared stiff of going out," growled Hornig, while the rain dripped off his hat and into the boat. Together with Kaulbach, Loewenfeld, and me, the equerry was in the smallest of the three boats. It was nearly midday already, and still nothing had happened, except that the showers had given way, for the time being, to a slight drizzle. A stormy wind whipped up the surface of the lake into small waves.

"Our informants have told us that the psychologist is rather nervous," Hornig went on. "Dr. von Gudden has obviously had a long conversation with His Majesty and realizes that Ludwig isn't as crazy as he thought. Now he sees his hopes dashed."

"As long as they keep Ludwig locked up in Berg, no one will ever know that he is *not* crazy," interjected Kaulbach the painter. "The ministers will probably build a wall around the castle and make it the most expensive prison in Bavaria."

"Or else they'll kill him."

It was Dr. Schleiss von Loewenfeld who had spoken. All at once there was complete silence in the boat. Not a sound was heard but the steady pattering of the rain.

"Kill . . . kill him?" I asked. "Kill the king?"

"Think about it, gentlemen." The old physician looked sadly around at us. "The whole affair is nothing but a failed coup d'état. The king has been certified insane, and now they realize that he is not. If we don't get him out, Ludwig will probably demand a second opinion from the castle. He will turn to Bismarck and stake his claim to have his throne back. And Lutz and the other ministers . . ."

"Will be arraigned for high treason. Damn it all, you're right."

Hornig spat into the murky water. "Yes, I can believe that this villain-ous gang would murder their own king and make it look like suicide by a man with the balance of his mind disturbed."

"If we don't rescue him first. There—see for yourself." Hermann Kaulbach pointed to the bank, where several figures were emerging from the trees. I held my breath.

Gudden and the king were there, but with guards.

We had expected that the psychiatrist wouldn't move from Ludwig's side. But Dr. Bernhard von Gudden was already more than sixty, and a small, frail figure. It would have been easy for the king, at just under six feet tall, to overpower him and get away. That was not the case, however, with the powerful attendant and the armed gen-darme, who were both keeping to the background but could be seen well enough behind the bushes in the park.

"Confound it all!" said Richard Hornig under his breath. "As long as that madhouse attendant and the venal police officer stay so close to the king, we can't make the attempt. They might well level fire-arms at His Majesty."

"But who knows whether such an opportunity for flight will come again?" I objected. I was suffering from a slight shivering fit, but I tried not to let it show. Nonetheless, my voice sounded tired and shaky. "This could be the last walk Ludwig will take for a very long time."

"We must risk that." Dr. Loewenfeld put away the field glasses that he had just been using to watch the bank. "That police officer is looking our way. Presumably he's suspicious. We ought to send the other two boats away, in any event. Three small craft together are too conspicuous."

"You're right." Richard Hornig gave the other two boats a sign to turn away. "This boat will have to be enough. And now let's pray that His Majesty appears in the park again in more favorable circum-stances. We should also take a few security precautions."

In a few words, he told us his plan.

. . .

AT EXACTLY QUARTER to seven in the evening, we had our second chance.

This time our boat was waiting very close to the bank, behind a small promontory densely overgrown by reeds and willow, so that from the bank it was out of sight. Meanwhile, I had hidden in the undergrowth of the park to keep an eye on the situation and give the boat a signal when the police officers and attendants were far enough from the king. Only then would we risk the attempt at flight.

The rain had almost stopped now, and dark gray clouds covered the sky, casting a gloomy twilight over the park. I was crouching behind a bush near the path and felt the damp slowly creeping up my back. I kept taking out my pocket watch, but the hands were moving at a snail's pace. I felt as if I had been sitting behind this bush for days. My limbs hurt, and a slight fever made me shiver all over.

At last, when I hardly believed it would ever happen, I heard footsteps crunching on the gravel path from the castle. After a short time, I saw Ludwig and Dr. von Gudden walking down the path. They both carried furled umbrellas; Gudden wore a top hat and a black coat, as if he were going to a funeral, while the king had on a pale summer coat, unbuttoned at the front, and a fashionable bowler. I waited a little longer while the king and his doctor came closer to me. There were no guards in sight.

Was it possible? I had expected to see the attendants following at a suitable distance. But now it looked very much as if they had been left behind in the castle on purpose, along with the gendarmes.

I watched in suspense as the mismatched couple came closer and closer to my bush. Sixty feet, thirty feet . . . To my horror, they stopped right in front of me. What was I to do? This was the moment when I ought to be giving the agreed signal. But by doing that, I would have given away my hiding place. If I did that, Dr. von Gudden would certainly recognize me and report me to the authorities.

While I was hesitating, the king began to speak. To the day of my death I shall never forget the minutes that followed; every second of them is branded on my memory forever.

"You know that you have made a mistake," began the king quietly but firmly. "Out of pure vanity, you have let the ministers make use of you for their own purposes, and now your good reputation is endangered. Retract your diagnosis, Dr. von Gudden, and I promise that you will live on as a man of high position and authority."

"Your Majesty, I really do not know what you are talking about," replied the doctor. His voice sounded strangely hoarse, almost panic-stricken. At close quarters, I could also see that his face was ashen gray. Something seemed to be terrifying him. "I have already told you several times that no closer observation was necessary," he managed to get out. "The evidence is convincing. In addition, it is very common for the mentally sick to appear normal at first after their committal to an asylum. That doesn't necessarily mean anything. My medical opinion is incontestable."

"Who's behind this?" Ludwig's tone of voice was more aggressive now, and he stepped up to the little man, towering over him. "Is it Lutz, or Count Holnstein? Prince Luitpold himself? Tell me! It must be clear to you that all of those here are trying to kill me. I have seen it in your face, Gudden. Just now, at supper. I saw the light of naked fear in your eyes."

"Your Majesty, I swear . . ."

Ludwig had now taken the frail little doctor by his collar, and he began shaking him. Gudden went as red in the face as a turkey cock.

"Don't swear, Gudden!" growled the king. "You lie as soon as you open your mouth. You realize that you can't lock me up here forever. I will telegraph Bismarck; I still have influential friends. I am not a slobbering idiot like my brother, Otto; I am the king. And when I get out of here, then . . ."

At that moment a shot rang out in the gray twilight, and directly after it another. Neither made a loud sound; the reports were muted like a paper bag exploding. All the same, my blood froze in my veins.

I saw Ludwig open his eyes wide in surprise. For a moment he stayed on his feet, supporting himself on Gudden; then he slumped like a sack of coal and fell to the ground. The doctor let out small, shrill sounds of fear that almost reminded me of a child crying. He stepped aside in horror and stared at the king's body. There were two black holes on the back of his white coat, and bright blood was trickling out of them.

"I seem to have arrived just in the nick of time."

Instinctively, I started at the sound of that grating voice. It had come from a bush not far from my own hiding place. Now a lean figure rose from behind the bush and stepped onto the lakeside path. In his right hand, the new arrival held a gun of unusual appearance, with a club-shaped stock. At the sight of the assassin, I had to bite my tongue to keep myself from crying his name out loud.

It was Carl von Strelitz.

"Maybe the king was crazier than we assumed after all," said the Prussian agent, putting his gun aside. "What a violent-tempered giant." With practiced movements, he turned Ludwig's heavy body over and felt for any pulse in his carotid artery. Then he nodded, satisfied.

"Mission accomplished. He's dead." Smiling, von Strelitz stood up and turned to the psychiatrist. "Do you know what I should have done?" he said, his voice expressionless. "I should simply have sat in that bush waiting. Probably the king would have throttled you and then waded out into the water in despair. A nice, clean job. On the other hand"—he looked out at the lake—"the water is only waist-high here. Drowning himself probably wouldn't have worked. Well, this way was safer, at least."

"My God, you shot him!" croaked Gudden. "I almost died of fright. I thought that, using chloroform . . ."

"You thought I'd just anesthetize the king and then throw him into the lake?" Von Strelitz made a dismissive gesture. "No, no. My mission was clear. To eliminate the king without running any risks whatsoever. And that's what I've done."

"But the bullet wounds," whispered Gudden. "And the noise. They'll come after us."

"Not if you do exactly as we've agreed." Von Strelitz took out his pocket watch and glanced at it. "It's now exactly seven o'clock. The attendants and gendarmes have instructions to keep away from the scene for at least half an hour, and only then raise the alarm. Furthermore, I used a Girandoni air rifle." He looked appreciatively at the gun at his feet. "An excellent invention. No powder smoke, no cartridge cases to give away what happened, no muzzle flash, and the sound of the report is well within bounds. So we have all the time we need. Now, kindly help me."

Carl von Strelitz began unbuttoning the dead king's coat and stripping it and his vest off him. He carefully made a neat pile of the bloodstained garments, having first taken Ludwig's pocket watch out of the vest pocket. "Pity about this handsome watch," he murmured. "Well, at least posterity will know His Majesty's exact time of death."

Then he brought fresh clothes out from behind a bush and fastened the watch to another vest.

"This way, we can convince the first eyewitnesses of His Majesty's suicide by drowning," explained von Strelitz, reaching for a clean linen shirt. "However, before the autopsy, Holnstein and Lutz ought to spend a few little sums of money on the doctors in Munich. I've heard that they are all pledged on oath to bear us out." He shook his head dismissively. "If you ask me, we can forget that. In cases of doubt, only money and threats will work. You don't get yourself a fine country estate by swearing solemn oaths."

"But . . . but it's a dark winter coat that you have there," stammered Gudden, pointing to the new garment in the agent's hands. "You can see, the king was wearing a light-colored . . ."

"Damn it, I was told he'd wear a dark coat," whispered the Prussian agent angrily, as he went on cleaning the blood off Ludwig's body and dressing it in the clean shirt and vest. "If your ministers are too stupid even to plan an assassination properly, it's not my fault." The sweat stood out on von Strelitz's brow. It looked as though, even after death, the king was defending himself against this degrading process. From my hiding place, I watched as Ludwig's head lolled back and forth like a puppet's. I was in such a state of shock that I was incapable of movement. The king was dead, murdered before my eyes! Contrary to my own better knowledge, I hoped that all this was only a dreadful nightmare from which I would wake at any moment.

"All this is nothing but a farce," said von Strelitz, still annoyed, as he threw the new coat and an undergarment a long way out into the water. "When Lutz told me to gather material that would incriminate the king, I assumed that you had at least a *little* substantial evidence on your side. But there was nothing except the complaints of a few servants whose feelings had been injured." He laughed contemptuously. "And to cap it all, that little informer crosses my path again at Herrenchiemsee and almost gets past my camouflage. *Quelle merde!*"

I started behind my bush. At last I realized why von Strelitz had been on the island in the Chiemsee. He had been collecting evidence of Ludwig's insanity, and I had gotten in his way. But what had Maria meant when she murmured, *He'll kill me*, just before von Strelitz appeared in the wood? Was there something else that I didn't know?

"You . . . you really have no cause for complaint." By now Gudden had recovered his old academic arrogance. Nonetheless, he stalked back and forth on the bank, looking nervously around him, as von Strelitz dragged the king's body over to the lake. "How much did Holnstein pay you for this mission?" snapped the doctor. "How much were you paid to change sides and work for the Bavarian government? Thirty thousand reichsmarks? Fifty thousand?" He stamped his foot angrily. "If you had done your work properly, if you had collected evidence, or forged it for all I care, we wouldn't have had to resort to such means as these. You were probably paid a good bonus for committing the murder, isn't that so?"

"He was a king, after all; don't forget that," grunted von Strelitz, pushing Ludwig's corpse into the waist-high water. "Killing a king has always been well paid. It's been the same ever since the time of Judas. Now, for heaven's sake, help me." He beckoned impatiently to Gudden. "Don't be so squeamish; you're welcome to get wet. After all, you're to tell everyone, later, that you tried to save Ludwig when he decided to drown himself in the lake."

Dr. von Gudden sighed and gingerly made his way into the water, which was far too cold for June. After taking a few steps, he had reached the agent. The body of Ludwig, face-down, bobbed in the water beside them like a buoy.

Paralyzed by shock, I crouched behind the bush. I ought to have gone running along the lakeside path, calling for help. By this time, however, I was no longer sure exactly who was involved in the plot. I decided to leave my hiding place and steal back to the promontory beyond which the boat was still waiting. But I had hardly stepped out on the path, which was bordered by tall reeds at this point, before I heard the doctor's voice again. Looking past the reeds, I could easily see the two figures now standing in the lake, some sixteen feet from the bank.

"And I'm not sure that we'll be believed when we say it was suicide," whined Dr. Gudden. "There will always be doubts. The king has been too reasonable for a potential suicide these last two days. He even said we were trying to kill him."

"You're right," replied Carl von Strelitz calmly. "There will indeed always be doubts. Unless the king had done something shortly before his death to make him look deranged in the eyes of one and all."

The psychiatrist looked at von Strelitz, baffled. In his wet coat, which was swirling around him in the knee-deep water like mourning ribbons, he resembled an overgrown, agitated coot. "I . . . I'm afraid I don't entirely understand you."

Carl von Strelitz carelessly pushed the floating corpse aside and waded toward Gudden. "You really don't? I thought you were cleverer than that, Doctor. *Au revoir.*"

With these words, the agent put his strong fingers around Gudden's throat and tightened them. The small, frail doctor had not the slightest chance. He grunted and panted for breath, tugging at his attacker's arms, but von Strelitz simply kicked his legs out from under him and held him down below the surface of the water like a puppy. At first Gudden struck out wildly; then he began thrashing his limbs about so that the water foamed up around him in white jets. Those movements changed to twitching, and finally his body went limp.

Von Strelitz held Gudden under the surface for a little longer and then gave the corpse a slight push. Like a piece of driftwood, it floated toward the middle of the lake.

At that very moment my friends' boat appeared on the choppy water. They had obviously suspected that something was happening. I could see Hornig and Kaulbach, both rowing against the wind as hard as they could. Dr. Schleiss von Loewenfeld sat in the bow, his hair blowing around his head. When he saw the Prussian agent, and the two corpses in the water, he cried out in horror.

"My God, the king!" he cried. "Hornig, look!"

Without hesitation, Loewenfeld leaped into the waist-high water and waded toward Ludwig. Meanwhile, Richard Hornig had thrown down his oar to dive straight into the water, and now he plowed his way through the lake like an ocean-going steamer. He soon reached Carl von Strelitz, who was waiting for him with his fists raised.

The two men were soon engaged in a life-or-death struggle, each vying in turn to push the other under the water. Hornig punched von Strelitz with a right hook to his chin, so that he staggered back and fell on top of Gudden's corpse. Von Strelitz struggled up again and flung himself on the royal equerry with a piercing cry. Richard Hornig was a fit, muscular man, but he was no match for the sheer malice of the Prussian agent. Von Strelitz spread the fingers of his right hand like a tiger's claws, digging them into his adversary's face, and at the same time thrusting his knee forward to strike Hornig between the loins. The equerry doubled up with pain, and Carl von Strelitz struck the back of his head with all his might. Hornig sank into the waters of the lake with a gurgling cry.

"Kaulbach, do something!"

It was Dr. Schleiss von Loewenfeld who had called out to the painter. With almost superhuman strength, Loewenfeld was tugging at the king's body, trying to drag it to land. Meanwhile, Hermann von Kaulbach was still sitting in the boat, his hands clutching the rail, rigid with horror and incapable of any movement. No one yet seemed to have noticed me behind the tall reeds.

While von Strelitz held the royal equerry down underwater, I looked desperately around. For a moment I was tempted to call for help at the top of my voice, but then my eye fell on the air rifle lying only a few paces away from me. I ran to it, snatched it up, and took aim.

In my time as a student in Strasbourg, I had been considered a good marksman, and I had also twice acted as a man's second in a duel. But this weapon was new to me, and I had no idea whether I could fire it with precision. The steel was cold against my cheek. I loaded another ball from the magazine and aligned the sights on my target. Von Strelitz was only fifteen paces away and did not appear to have seen me. He was still holding Richard Hornig down under the surface of the lake, where white foaming bubbles were rising. Now Dr. Loewenfeld caught sight of me.

"Marot, heaven sends you!" he cried. "For God's sake, pull the trigger!"

Startled by Loewenfeld's voice, Carl von Strelitz briefly let go of his victim and turned his head to me. His face was a mask of hatred and alarm. A mocking smile played around his lips. He slowly raised his hands, and a coughing, retching Hornig emerged from the lake before him again.

"Don't do anything stupid," von Strelitz called to me. "I have in-fluential friends—very influential. You can still decide to back the winning side." He pointed behind him, to where Dr. Loewenfeld stood up to his waist in the water beside Ludwig's corpse. "The king is dead, and believe me, that's the best thing that could happen to your country. A deranged dreamer, that's what he was. Is a man like that fit to lead Bavaria into the twentieth century?" He laughed and stroked his wet black hair down over his head. "Trust me when I say we'll meet with challenges to which no dreamer is equal. Bavaria needs a strong king, not a starry-eyed idealist. In a few years, no one will care a whit about Ludwig. So be reasonable, and . . ."

"Go to hell, von Strelitz."

I pulled the trigger and once again heard the muted, pleasingly quiet report of the air rifle. Carl von Strelitz staggered two steps back, but he stayed on his feet. He stared at me, his eyes full of hatred, one last time; then his gaze moved down in surprise to where blood was staining his white shirt red.

"You damn . . . fool," he groaned. Then, at last, the agent fell backward and hit the water with a splash, his arms flung wide. Streaks of blood spread out around him like long, red threads.

I stood on the bank as if in a trance. The gun slipped from my hands and fell on the gravel path that ran along the bank. Only Richard Hornig's coughing brought me back to the present. He had scrambled out of the water by now, but he was still fighting for breath. "God in heaven, Marot! You . . . you saved my life," he groaned. He was pale as a drowned corpse, but otherwise he seemed to be in good shape. Now he took hold of the body of von Strelitz, scrutinized it disparagingly, and then threw it back into the lake like a piece of rotten wood. "That bastard nearly drowned me. Who in the name of three devils was he?"

"The man who murdered the king," I said quietly. "We came too late."

There was a moment of absolute silence, in which only the cawing of a single crow could be heard. A cloud of red had formed around Ludwig's corpse and was slowly dispersing in the murky water. His thick black hair floated like seaweed in the gentle swell of the lake.

We stood on the bank as if numb, staring at our dead king, at Dr. Gudden, and the Prussian agent, all three of them drifting, facedown, in the water of the lake. Tears glistened in Hornig's eyes, mingling with the raindrops, and none of us said a word. It was as if the world as we had always known it had stopped turning.

Not until we heard cries in the distance and saw the flickering of torches through the trees did we run into the night, without another word.

ONLY AN HOUR later the five of us sat, brooding, in the smoking room of Baron Beck-Peccoz, who had waited for the king in vain at the gate of his castle park with his carriage. When he heard of Ludwig's death, he seemed paralyzed by shock at first. Finally, he drove us in the carriage to his estate of Eurasburg, which was very close to Berg Castle. We were now staring, our eyes glazed, at the glowing logs on the hearth, while the stormy rain lashed the windows.

"If there were any traces left to show how the king really died, then they'll have been removed by now," said Richard Hornig. "They'll take the body of the Prussian agent away and make the whole thing look like the suicide of a deranged king. No one will ever know the truth."

The rest of us nodded in silence. It was as if, after so much hectic activity, apathy had overwhelmed us, leaving us unable to speak of what had happened. The king was dead, and nothing could bring him back.

Suddenly Kaulbach the painter rose to his feet. With shaking fingers, he ground out his cigarette in the ashtray and looked at us one by one. "It was a mistake for us to run like hares," he said angrily. "We must go to the Starnberg police. At once! This crime can't go unpunished."

"Go to the police? Don't be childish, Kaulbach." Dr. Schleiss von Loewenfeld shook his head wearily before going on. "Don't you understand? This thing has been engineered from the very top. Are you really planning to oppose the future prince regent, all the ministers, and the majority of the Bavarian nobility? Only with the king alive and at our side did we stand any chance of reversing the coup d'état. It's too late now."

For some time no one said anything. In the midst of the silence, Hermann Kaulbach suddenly took his wet hat from the fireside and turned to the door.

"What are you going to do, for God's sake?" asked Dr. Loewenfeld in surprise.

"I am at least going to pay the king my last respects," he said firmly. "And if you gentlemen have a spark of good feeling in you, you'll do the same."

Kaulbach disappeared into the rain outside, and after a little while the rest of us followed him. Only the baron still sat by the fire in a melancholy mood, watching the fire slowly burn down. His face was hard and gray as rock.

IT WAS JUST after midnight when we finally returned to Berg. Bright lights blazed everywhere in the castle and the park; people were running around in agitation, many of them weeping or embracing; gendarmes hurried through the wood like restless spirits. The bodies of Ludwig and Dr. Gudden had been found only about an hour before. They had drifted north from the original scene of the crime. We suspected that the dead Carl von Strelitz had already been taken away by police officers who knew his intentions.

In the general turmoil, it was easy for us to gain access to the castle. After all, Dr. Loewenfeld had been the king's personal physician, although he had seen less and less of him in recent years. It was Dr. Loewenfeld, too, who made it possible for us to pay our condolences to the body of the dead king.

Contrary to our expectations, His Excellency had not yet been taken to Berg Castle but was lying in the boathouse with Dr. Gudden. They had been covered up to the throat with cloths, but in the general atmosphere of haste, no one had thought of washing Ludwig's face. His mouth was open as if in a silent scream, and a thin line of dried blood stuck to his cheek.

"Do you see all that blood on the floor?" Dr. Loewenfeld whispered to me. "I'd assume that came from your Prussian agent before he was spirited away from here in secret. Either from him or from Ludwig himself. In any event, they'll have to clean this boathouse thoroughly to get rid of all the traces."

The four of us took off our hats and stood in silence before our king, whom we had wanted to save, and who was now taken from us forever. I felt the sense of something ending. The fairy tales disappeared with Ludwig, as did the last spirit of an epoch that had once teemed with fabulous creatures, strong warriors, elves and dwarves. They would be succeeded by pragmatists, by bureaucrats.

All at once I heard a faint rustling, and I saw Hermann Kaulbach bring out a sketchpad, damp from the rain, from under his coat. With quick movements, he captured the image of the dead king on paper. He also did little portrait sketches of Richard Hornig and Dr. Schleiss von Loewenfeld.

"Even if they fake everything else, there will be a record of this moment," said Kaulbach quietly. He looked at the door of the boathouse, which was only half closed. The gendarme on duty had just gone out for a cigarette.

"Let us promise not to forget all this. We owe His Majesty that."

We nodded gravely and murmured our promise.

Only a moment later, a thought flashed through my mind. Kaulbach's words had reminded me of something. I, too, owed a duty to Ludwig.

The king's letter!

Hadn't Ludwig himself called it the most important missive he had ever written? I had promised to deliver it to some person unknown at Linderhof. And in all the turmoil, I had forgotten about it.

I felt for my left-hand vest pocket, finding the letter, and the note bearing the name of its recipient. Who might that recipient be? Who could be important enough to receive the last letter of Ludwig's life?

I had been told not to discover the recipient until I reached Linderhof. But time was short. And maybe it was too late anyway, now that the king was dead. So I took out the little note, unfolded it, and read the name.

At that moment, I understood.

H EY, WE WERE RIGHT! WE really were right!"

Sara's voice brought Steven out of his thoughts. He was so absorbed in reading the book that her words came through to him muted.

"What . . . what do you mean?"

Sara pointed to the monitor of her laptop. "The lines of poetry and the roman numerals. They really do spell out a sentence. See for yourself."

Ballad	Line	Word	Solution
Erl-King	XVI	I	In
Belshazzar	V	IV	the
Women of Winsperg	XVI	IV	king's
Count of Thal	CXIII	II	fourth
Enchantress in the Forest	LXXXXIII	V	castle
Ring of Polycrates	XV	I	a
Song of Siegerich	LXXXXVIII	IV	scion
The Singer's Curse	LIX	V	shows
Lorelei	VII	I	the
The Angler	XXVII	IV	dearest

The Diver	LXI	IV	of
Legend	XXX	IV	his
Ballad	XII	II	treasures

Steven looked at her and at the screen, on which a greenish table was shimmering.

In the king's fourth castle a scion shows the dearest of his treasures.

The bookseller frowned. "What in the world . . ." he began.

"*Fluch* really did stand for Ludwig Uhland's poem '*Des Sängers Fluch*,' 'The Singer's Curse,' just as you suspected," Sara said. "'*Legende*' and '*Ballade*' are two not very well-known poems by Goethe. The most difficult ones to track down were *Thal* and *Winsperg*. But thank goodness, there are also a few ballads now rightly forgotten in that little old book." Sara triumphantly held up Zöller's volume of poetry. "*Thal* is *Der Graf von Thal*, The Count von Thal, by Annette von Droste-Hülshoff, and *Winsperg* refers to a rather boring poem by Adalbert von Chamisso called '*Die Weiber von Winsperg*,' 'The Women of Winsperg.' Taken together with the roman numerals for lines and words, we get this sentence . . ." She emphasized every single word. "*In the king's fourth castle a scion shows the dearest of his treasures.* We've finally solved the puzzle. That's the place that crazy Luise was blathering on about."

Sara gave a V for victory sign, grinning broadly. "Now we just have to go to the king's fourth castle and . . ."

Steven raised his eyebrows. "Fourth castle? As far as I know, Ludwig built only three castles. Linderhof, Herrenchiemsee, and this one, Neuschwanstein."

Sara bit her lip. "Damn it, you're right," she said quietly. "There's something wrong." She frowned. "How about Ludwig's hunting lodge on the Schachen, in the Wetterstein mountains? Or Berg, maybe? It's a castle, after all, even if Ludwig didn't build it himself. Could that be it?"

"I don't know. It strikes me as illogical. All that trouble, just to lead us to Berg. We might as well start at the Residence Palace in Munich itself." Steven sighed. "Whatever we do, we have to do it fast." He glanced at Albert Zöller, who was still lying on the cold mosaic floor. His large paunch rose and fell like a pair of bellows, sweat poured over his face, which was white as a sheet, and he was breathing heavily. "Uncle Lu isn't going to last much longer."

"Do the last pages of the diary maybe give any information about this fourth castle?" Sara asked, nervously crumpling up her cigarette pack.

"Not so far." Steven opened the diary again. There was only one last entry to read. "But at least I think I now know what's driving our dear friend Luise, and what that treasure really is."

"You know . . . ?" Sara stared at him, wide-eyed. "Come on, then, what is it? Gold? A crown? The truth about Ludwig's death?"

Steven shook his head. "That's just what we're supposed to think. Yes, Marot tells us how the king lost his life. But that's not Ludwig's greatest secret, not by a long shot."

"Then what is?"

"Solving the puzzle has already given us the first clue," replied Steven. He ran his fingers over Marot's closely written lines. "But suppose you give me another five minutes to read this, out loud if you like. Then we'll know the whole truth."

· 36 ·

I reached Linderhof castle late that morning. The meadows were wet with rain and dew, and the morning heat of the summer's day made the moisture rise as mist. The whole park was embedded in white clouds. It was like a dream world through which I trudged, weary and feverish, in search of my beloved.

I found Maria by the linden tree where we had first met. She was playing with her son, Leopold. The boy, laughing, was running away from his mother, who had tied a white scarf around her eyes and was groping about in a circle like a dancing bear. Quietly, I stole up behind her and placed a hand on her shoulder.

"Ludwig, is that you?" she whispered. "Have you come back from Neuschwanstein at last? We've missed you."

I took her blindfold off and turned her firmly to face me. Her eyes looked at me in confusion as she blinked in the sudden bright light.

"You? But . . . ?"

"Ludwig is dead," I said quietly. "His pursuers killed him." I gave her the sealed letter. "He asked me to give you this. Maria, why didn't you tell me that . . ."

My voice died away as her eyes told me that I had been right. Seeing the pain in her face hurt me almost more than the loss of my beloved king.

She took the envelope in silence, incapable of any movement. In a few brief words, I finally told her what had happened. Then we stood beside the linden tree for a long time without a word, until I saw that tears were falling on the letter.

Maria was weeping.

"I knew this would happen someday," she whispered. "His enemies were too powerful. I think that at heart it was what he wanted. He simply did not fit into this day and age."

"Mother, what's the matter? Why are you crying?"

Leopold was standing beside us. He stroked Maria's apron with his slender hand. Only now did his likeness to his father strike me. The black curls, the grave expression, the tall stature. He would be a handsome man, as handsome as his father had once been. Would he also inherit his father's deep grief, his world-weariness, and all his little eccentricities?

"It's nothing, Leopold," said Maria, forcing herself to smile. "Go and play, and I'll be with you in a moment."

The boy went away, with a slightly sulky look, and Maria's glance was serious again. "How long have you known?"

"About you and Ludwig? Not until I saw who was to be given this letter." I heaved a deep sigh. "For months I thought that Leopold's father was a married man from Oberammergau. I followed you there, Maria. Forgive me, I was sick with jealousy. I . . . I'm so sorry." Ashamed, I put my face in my hands. "I was watching you from the house on the outskirts of the village of Oberammergau, I saw the embroidery things on the bench . . . I was sure that Leopold was a child born out of wedlock to you and that . . . that farmer."

"You idiot." Her face wore a melancholy smile. "That farmer is a woodcarver and, as it happens, my elder brother. Now and then I go to see him, taking Leopold so that my child will have at least a little family life. And after that I always feel most strongly how much I miss having a strong man at my side, a father for Leopold . . ." Once again, tears came to her eyes. "But the king needed me so much. I couldn't leave him alone. I . . . after all, I was one of the few who understood him . . ." Her voice failed her, and we were silent for a moment.

After some time, I went on, hesitantly. "The way Ludwig treated you. That jealous scene in Herrenchiemsee . . . I should have guessed it far sooner. I thought he was jealous of you, but he was jealous of *me*. Because he loved *you*. And how about you?" I felt my throat constrict. "Did you love him, too?"

"Oh, Theodor. There are so many kinds of love. Love for a child, for parents, for a brother, a lover . . ." I breathed a sigh of relief; it did me good to see her smile, as she went on. "The king could never really show his love. And it was only a single night at his hunting lodge on the Schachen, and he was as shy as a schoolboy. Even then, he was a child at heart, often a dreamy child. And sometimes very angry."

"'He'll kill me.' That's what you said on the island at Herrenchiemsee." I was almost inclined to laugh. "I thought for so long that you meant Carl von Strelitz, but it was Ludwig you meant."

"He could be insanely jealous. Of men as well as women. When he was disappointed in someone, it was as if something in him broke."

"I found that out for myself." With some hesitation, I pointed to the letter in her hand. "Don't you want to open it?"

"I think I know what's in it." She folded the letter and tucked it into her bodice. "It will be a . . . what is it called . . . ?" She searched for the right word. "A . . . a statutory declaration. Ludwig always promised me that someday he would acknowledge Leopold as his son. But whenever I brought it up, he withdrew. A bastard in the house of the Wittelbachs, a liaison with a simple maidservant. It would have been only one more reason for them to have him declared insane." Her face clouded over. "Well, the letter will do Leopold no good now in any case. On the contrary, if those wretches in Munich learn about him, they'll probably have him assassinated. As Ludwig's only son, he would have a claim to the throne, wouldn't he?"

"Not if the statutory declaration was made by a madman. Ludwig's adversaries would presumably base their arguments on that."

Thoughtfully, I nodded. "But you're right; that gang can be credited with any vile act. We must keep the secret. If necessary even beyond our own deaths. Who knows . . ." I smiled mysteriously. "Who knows, maybe someday the truth will come to light. And people will recognize that Ludwig was not insane and did not commit suicide. Then, to be sure, his son could lay claim to the throne."

"Or his son's son, or even his son's great-grandson." Maria sighed. "I don't think the murder of Ludwig will ever be properly explained. Too many powerful men have spun that web of lies."

"We'll see." I put my arm around her shoulders, the clouds parted for a moment, and the sun shed a thin ray of light on us. "Until then, in any case, we must conceal that letter," I said firmly. "And if we die before the secret of Ludwig's death can be aired, we must make sure that only those who do not want to harm his reputation know of the hiding place."

"But how will you do that?" she asked. "How can you make sure that the statutory declaration doesn't fall into the wrong hands?"

I hesitated, but then a plan suddenly began to form in my mind. It was such a fantastic plan, like something out of a fairy tale, that I'm sure Ludwig would have liked it. I held Maria's hands firmly, and at that moment I felt a bond between the three of us—Maria, me, and the king.

"Didn't you say yourself that there were very few people who really knew Ludwig?" I began. "Who knew about his most secret wishes, the many themes and symbols of the world he dreamed of? About his fairy-tale castles and plans for the future?" My voice was firmer now, and I raised my hand as if to take an oath. "I promise you, Maria, I will think of a puzzle that can be solved only by those who really understand the king. None of the ministers, none of the bureaucrats who thought Ludwig was insane. And this puzzle will lead to the place where I shall hide the statutory declaration."

Maria looked at me, baffled. "What kind of puzzle?"

I smiled and drew her gently down into the tall grass under the linden tree.

"It will be our story, Maria. Ours and Ludwig's." Tentatively, I dropped a light kiss on her cheek, and I felt her trembling. "And now tell me all you know about the king. His deepest secrets and wishes. The whole truth. I will devise a puzzle worthy of a fairy-tale king. Even if it is more than a hundred years before it is solved."

We sank into the grass and saw clouds moving in the sky overhead in the shape of fabulous creatures.

"Is that the end of the diary?" Sara asked, nestling close to Steven for warmth. She fished the last cigarette out of her pack and lit it. A small cloud of smoke rose to the cupola in the roof.

Steven leafed through it and shook his head. "No, there's one page left. It was written almost a full year later."

"Then read it aloud," Sara said, drawing deeply on her cigarette. "I want to know how the story ends."

In a faltering voice, Steven read.

AFTERWORD, WRITTEN ON *the morning of 28 July 1887*
This is our story.

The puzzle has been written, and I have hidden the statutory declaration. Maria does not know where. I am going to keep it a secret from her, for fear of endangering yet another human being. May those who understand and love the king as Maria and I did find the place someday.

It all happened just as we feared. A year after the murder, the new ruler's men are out and about everywhere, intent upon silencing every possible witness to their plot. One of Ludwig's servants is alleged to have committed suicide; others have died in unexplained ways, or were incarcerated in asylums, or are said to have disappeared. Those gentlemen have also muzzled my mentor, Dr. Schleiss von Loewenfeld, threatening him. Hornig and Kaulbach are keeping quiet, whether out of fear or because they have been bribed, I cannot say.

They will not find me.

I am sitting outside our little house in a remote valley of the Werdenfelser Alps, watching Maria and Leopold playing. I resigned from my position as assistant to the royal physician directly after Ludwig's death, even before the prince regent could send me packing. The simple country folk here can do with a qualified doctor; until now they have always had to make do with rustic barber-surgeons. I splint broken bones and treat coughs with camomile, echinacea, and coltsfoot; I put my stethoscope to old women's chests and listen to their tirades about unfaithful, good-for-nothing husbands; I mix medicines in scratched stoneware pots and mortars, yet I can imagine no better profession.

For Maria is with me, Maria and Leopold. We are a family, and even if I am not the boy's father, I feel that all the same there is an invisible bond between the three of us that no one can break now.

Only occasionally does one of the local farmers ask about Leopold, and why he does not look at all like me. Then I tell the truth, saying that his father is dead. The men say no more and nod. There is not much talking in these remote, deep Alpine valleys, and that is just as well.

Here come Maria and Leopold running over the mown fields of stubble toward me, the boy with his arms outspread as if to take off in flight. The sun is climbing above the mountains, and its light wanders from tree to tree, from house to house. Maria's laughter rings out in the air like the clear sound of bells.

At this moment I feel like a king.

Signed,
Dr. Theodor Marot, in the year of our Lord 1887.

PS: I will keep this diary for posterity, together with a lock of Leopold's hair and a few carefully chosen photographs. After Maria and I die, it will pass into the possession of Leopold, the only son of Ludwig II, then to the hands of his children, and so on, until at last the time is ripe for the truth.

· 37 ·

AFTER THAT LAST SENTENCE, THERE was silence for some time in the throne room, broken only by Albert Zöller's rattling breaths.

"Ludwig had a *son?*" Sara asked at last, incredulously, grinding out her cigarette. "Is that the secret that was kept for so long?"

Steven nodded. "As far as I know, there have always been rumors about an heir. Zöller mentioned something like that once. To all appearances Ludwig was gay, yes, but certain women fascinated him. He's even thought to have had a relationship with the sculptor Elisabeth Ney." He tapped the sentence giving the solution to the puzzle in Sara's laptop. "Remember. *In the king's fourth castle a scion shows the dearest of his treasures.* That scion was obviously Ludwig's son, Leopold, and the statutory declaration bears it out."

"Just a moment," Sara objected. "So you think the treasure in that fourth castle is nothing but the statutory declaration made by Ludwig at the time?" She shook her head. "All that suffering, all those deaths, for a single scrap of paper? But why . . ."

Their conversation was interrupted by a yapping cough. When they turned around, they saw that Zöller had hauled himself, with difficulty, into a sitting position, and was leaning against the wall.

"My God, Uncle Lu!" Sara cried. "You mustn't try to stand up. We hope there'll be a doctor here soon . . ."

"Forget the doctor, children," Zöller moaned. "You don't seriously think that Manstein woman will get treatment for me, do you? It's probably far too late for that anyway."

"But Herr Zöller," Steven reassured him, "you're not in such serious condition that . . ."

"Nonsense." Zöller gestured impatiently. "I can tell for myself what kind of condition I'm in. So don't pretend to me. It's much more important for you to understand at long last, Steven."

"Understand?" Steven blinked incredulously at the old man. "I'm afraid I don't see what you mean."

"Don't you realize why the Manstein woman shot me just now?" Zöller winced in pain. "Because I was on the point of telling you the *truth*."

"What truth?"

"The truth about that damn diary! The reason why Frau Manstein is after it like a Fury, why she's climbing over corpses to get her hands on it. Why Paul made sure he left the diary with *you*." The old man took another deep breath, while Steven and Sara stared at him in suspense.

"Go on," Steven whispered. "I want to know."

"Two months ago my old friend Paul Liebermann came to see me," Zöller began, breathing heavily. "He said he had bought the estate of an old junk dealer at auction over the Internet. A pile of worthless books, but among them a curious little box containing the diary of a certain Theodor Marot, along with several old photographs and a strand of dark hair. Paul knew that this man, Marot, had been the assistant to the royal physician Max Schleiss von Loewenfeld. There has always been speculation that the diary would contain the truth about Ludwig's death."

"Herr Zöller, we know all this already," Sara said gently. "You really must spare yourself now."

"Kindly let me finish what I was saying." For a moment the old annoyance flashed into Zöller's eyes, but then he had to cough again. It was a while before he could go on.

"Luise Manstein got wind of that auction when the book had already been sold to Paul," he said. "She wanted it for herself and showed my friend a family tree demonstrating that . . ." He took a deep breath and coughed up blood. "Demonstrating that her family is descended from a certain Leopold from Oberammergau, whose mother Maria had been a maidservant of Ludwig the Second's."

Silence reigned for quite a while, and finally Sara whistled softly through her teeth.

"So loopy Luise is really a descendant of Ludwig the Second?" She looked disbelievingly at Zöller. "Is that true? That's why she wants the diary?"

"I'd already suspected it was something like that," Steven said wearily. "And it was probably for the same reason that Frau Manstein made off with Ludwig's furniture from Neuschwanstein. She thinks she's his legitimate descendant. All she needs as proof is that statutory declaration."

Zöller nodded and held his stomach. He seemed to be in great pain. "Luise Manstein showed Paul a letter authenticated by a notary, in which . . . in which Theodor left the diary to Maria after his death. Marot fell at the front in France in 1916, as an army doctor of distinction. From then on, the book officially belonged to the former Oberammergau maidservant and her descendants."

"But Professor Liebermann didn't give Luise Manstein the book?" Steven asked.

"My God, no!" Zöller laughed, a rattling laugh. When he wiped his mouth a moment later, bright blood showed on the back of his hand again. "Paul was quick to realize that the woman isn't exactly all there. She became more and more insistent. She set her thugs on him. All the same, the diary really did belong to her family. Then Paul remembered the family tree that Luise Manstein had shown him. He asked to see it again and secretly made a copy." Zöller paused for a moment to get his breath back again.

"With its help he . . . he succeeded in tracing a second branch of the family," he finally went on. "You see, my friend Paul was hoping that there was another descendant, someone to whom he could entrust that valuable book with a clear conscience. And guess what, he did find such a descendant. He, too, like all members of the family, initially bore his great-great-grandmother Maria's surname, which was also the surname of her son, Leopold." Groaning, Uncle Lu took a deep breath and looked Steven intently in the eyes. "Herr Lukas— the maidservant's name was Maria . . . *Berlinger.*"

Steven felt dizzy and had to lean against the wall of the throne room for support. He saw his parents in front of him, the dusty little street lined with Fords, Buicks, and Chevys with the paint chipping off; the decrepit elevator that took them up to their tiny apartment in Boston; the nameplate on the door with the handsomely curved letters that, at the time, he couldn't yet decipher.

GEORGE W. AND KAREN BERLINGER

"Berlinger?" he whispered. "But that's . . ."

Zöller elaborately searched his jacket and finally brought out a folded document with spots of blood on it. "I have the complete family tree here with me, Herr Lukas. Kindly take a quick look at it."

Zöller pushed the document over to him. Steven put the diary to one side and reached for it as if it were radioactive. Slowly, he unfolded the sheet of paper. It showed a family tree of the kind he had often seen in old books, except that he knew the names listed on this one. Taken together, they added up to a kind of formula, with the answer, as in an arithmetical calculation, at the bottom right.

It was his own name.

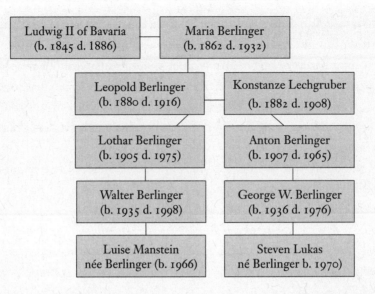

The brightly colored Chinese lanterns shining in my grandparents' gar-
den, the crackling flames in the library, the book with its pages fluttering on
the floorboards in the wind . . . the girl with the blond braids who wants to
scratch my eyes out, her burning dress . . .

"Do you understand, Steven?" Zöller asked. "Ludwig's son,
Leopold, had two sons, one of whom emigrated to the United States.
That son, Anton Berlinger, is *your* grandfather. You are a direct descendant of Ludwig the Second, just as Luise is. She is your cousin."
He coughed again, and blood spilled from the corners of his mouth
as he went on. "Paul wanted to get in touch to find out more about
you, Steven. When events began moving thick and fast, he hid the
diary in your bookshop."

Zöller sighed and let out a loud, halting breath. "I have done some
research in the States and even engaged a private detective, because
I couldn't believe what Paul said. And then, suddenly, there you were
standing at my door asking *me* for help . . ." Uncle Lu laughed quietly.
"At first I wanted to make sure that I wasn't being taken in by a fraud
and a murderer. But it's all true."

All at once, Steven felt as if he were behind a wall of opaque glass.

He vaguely saw Sara opening her mouth, obviously saying something to him, but he couldn't hear her. Slowly, he slipped to the floor, clutching the family tree like a child holding his teddy bear as if it were the last thing that could still save him from the all-destroying fire . . . from the stifling, billowing, nightmarish clouds of smoke that slowly withdrew, and showed him, at last, all that he had suppressed for so long.

The book took him back to his childhood. Suddenly he could remember everything . . .

. . . A SEA of legs before him, women's legs under long ball gowns, men's legs in black front-pleated evening pants, hands patting Steven on the head, someone pushing a plate of wobbly green dessert over to him. They all speak the same kind of clipped English as his mother, very different from his father's soft English. It sounds like wood breaking in the forest, the same as in the scary fairy tales that Mama is always telling him.

Steven feels bored; he is only just six, and there are no playmates here. Just a lot of uninteresting grownups and a girl who is about ten years old and bigger than he is. She has long blond braids and is wearing a white dress. She gives him a bad-tempered look and hides behind her father . . . Steven has forgotten her name. Daddy says she's his cousin and they should play together. The girl's eyes flash like burning coals, and she frightens him. He runs out into the corridor, away from the girl, down the broad spiral staircase . . .

The music of piano and strings can be heard on the second floor. Steven hears the laughter of the guests, sometimes shrill, sometimes menacing, the clatter of cutlery, the clink of glasses, but it gets quieter and more muted the closer he comes to the library at the end of the corridor, which is the room where he plays, his dusty citadel. Many of the books here are more expensive than a car, his father once told him. "One of them is even irreplaceable. You will inherit it one day, but don't ask questions now. Let Daddy read in peace . . ."

Steven pushes the heavy double doors, and they open with a squeal; eve-

rything is dark in here, the switch for the light is much too high up for him . . . but Steven has brought one of the brightly colored Chinese lanterns from the garden with a candle inside it to light the way.

The bookshelves tower up in front of him; he can smell the dust between the pages of the books; he wants to go on reading those animal stories by the man with the funny name. Or the story of the wolf and the seven little goats . . .

"You'll know him by his rough voice and his black paws, the mother goat tells her kids . . ."

Suddenly Steven catches sight of a picture above his father's armchair. It shows an old man with stern, piercing eyes and a huge mustache. He has often seen it up there, but this time it is standing out from the wall a little way, like a small door standing ajar.

Steven cautiously moves the picture aside, and behind it he sees a second door, made of iron. That door is open as well, and there's a pretty little treasure chest inside it, containing an old book, with a white swan on the cover. It looks like a book of magic spells. Steven decides that he really must ask his parents if they will give him the little treasure chest so that he can keep his plastic knights in it.

He opens the book, and something about it is strange. There are letters in it that he has never seen before. They look like magical signs—maybe it really is a book of magic spells. Steven holds the shining lantern closer to the curly letters; he wants to know what they say; he guesses that it must be something very, very important. This is the book that his father was always talking about . . .

All of a sudden Steven feels a draft of air behind him. He turns around and sees that girl from downstairs standing there in her white dress, with her long blond braids. She points her fingers at the little treasure chest on the floor, and the book with the white swan on the cover in his hands. "Give that here!" she shouts. "It belongs to Grandfather! Give it to me, you bastard, you beast, you thief!"

She falls on Steven and tries to grab the book, but he takes it away from her. They fall to the floor, and she scratches his face. Steven shrieks; her fin-

gernails are boring into his eyelids; she is thrusting them into his eyes like needles; green and yellow flashes go through his head . . . "You bastard, you dirty thief! Give it here! Give it here!"

All at once she cries out in pain and rolls to one side. Steven sees little flames licking at the hem of her dress. The Chinese lantern with the candle flickering inside it lies crushed on the floor beside her. The girl screams and rolls back and forth; the books around her catch fire. The girl sets more and more of the books in the shelves and on the desk alight. Now she looks like an angel falling from heaven, like an angel in a purgatorial fire made of books . . .

Gray smoke rises, enveloping the bookshelves. Steven reaches for the book of magic, puts it in the little wooden chest, and runs out into the corridor, toward a window. With the little chest in his hand, he slides down along the ivy and into the garden. He must get away from there, away from the crackling, smoking books, away from the girl with her burning dress.

At last, on the outskirts of the garden, the dilapidated teahouse emerges in front of him. Steven pushes the crooked door open, crawls in on all fours like a baby, and gets under the table. Mom and Dad will be very cross with him for playing with fire. The library is their greatest treasure, they always say; they will scold him. Steven crawls farther in, behind the dusty, folded garden chairs, and the moldy-smelling tablecloths stacked up in piles in the teahouse, but he holds the little treasure chest tight. He is a stone, a silent stone in the earth, and no one can see him.

All at once he hears many voices coming from the garden, a firefighters' siren wailing in a crescendo. Steven also hears his parents' voices: "Steven! Steven!" But he doesn't dare to call back.

Suddenly they are shouting so loudly that Steven has to cover his ears. No, they are not shouting; they are screaming. Steven shouts back. He shouts, "Stop it!" After all, he is a stone, a mute stone in the earth. But Steven is not mute anymore; he shouts until at last silence reigns. The door opens, and there stands a tall firefighter in his helmet and armor like a real knight. He carries Steven out to his car with the flashing blue light on top. Someone takes the little treasure chest away from him and gives it to one of the police officers. The little chest sways up and down in his hands like a jack-o'-lantern, becomes a tiny dot, and suddenly disappears behind two parked cars.

The little chest . . . the little chest . . . my little chest!

A LOUD REPORT brought Steven back to the present. He saw Zöller suddenly fall aside, blood spurting from his body, a great deal of blood. With horror, Steven saw that something had blown the whole left-hand side of Zöller's face away. The old man was dead before he even hit the floor.

Luise Manstein stood behind the balustrade, with her smoking Derringer in her hands. She leaned against a man-sized opening that had been hidden behind one of the pictures of heroes in the upper part of the great hall.

"Hello, Steven," she hissed from the balcony, pointing to Zöller's body. "Did the old man talk in the end?" She looked at her silver wristwatch. "I came to tell you that your time has run out. But what does that matter? You know the truth now."

The industrialist spread her arms out. In the royal mantle, she looked like a tall, white angel.

Just as she looked back then in her white dress, Steven thought. *Except that she doesn't have those blond braids now.*

Luise gave an almost childish smile, then swept her arm in a circular gesture around the throne room, with the body of Albert Zöller lying in his own blood in the middle of it.

"Welcome, my dear cousin. Make yourself at home here in our great-great-grandfather's castle."

· 38 ·

As Luise looked down on them, the double doors opened, and Lancelot came into the throne room with three of the other bodyguards. Each held a submachine gun.

"You're the girl from all those years ago," Steven said. "The girl with her dress on fire. The girl with the blond braids who tried to scratch my eyes out in the library."

"Correct. And it's a great pity that I didn't succeed. That would have spared us all a lot of trouble." Luise pointed to Sara's laptop on the throne room floor. "But now it will all be set right. Looks like you've solved the whole puzzle."

Lancelot had reached the middle of the throne room. He cast a glance at the laptop and frowned.

"It says something about a fourth castle, Your Excellency," he growled. "And a scion showing the king's dearest treasures there. Can you make anything of such nonsense?"

Luise was taken aback for a moment; then she began to giggle. Briefly, Steven wondered if she was about to tip over into full-blown insanity.

Or maybe I am.

"Can I make anything of it?" she asked at last. "That's a good one, very good. Theodor Marot had a real sense of humor."

"Whatever's so funny, I hope it chokes you. You and your entire bunch of deranged gorillas." Sara's voice was shaking, and tears of rage glittered in the corners of her eyes. "You're none of you anything but a gang of crazy murderers." She pointed to Zöller's body. "That old man was no danger to you, and yet . . ."

Lancelot waved that away. "Stop making such a fuss. He wouldn't have lived much longer anyway. It was just putting him out of his misery." He grinned. "Better start worrying about your own future instead, girlie."

"Stop blathering, paladin, and pick up that diary," Luise hissed.

Lancelot strode toward Steven, bent slightly, and picked up the little wooden treasure chest from the floor. The bookseller still felt numb. Before him lay Uncle Lu, shot in cold blood, just after he had told Steven his true origin. Yet he did not have the strength to look down at the body of the murdered man.

I am a descendant of Ludwig the Second, Steven told himself. *How much of Ludwig is there in me? My yearning for past times, my dreams, the way I like to immerse myself in books—is all that a mild form of insanity? Ludwig's brother, Otto, was raving mad, and so is Luise. What about me? Do I, too, carry the germ?*

Suddenly he remembered what Sara had said about him back at Linderhof.

Sometimes I think you're living in the wrong century, Herr Lukas . . .

"I admit it's hard to grasp, Steven," Luise said gently. Still wearing the royal white cloak, which dragged over the floor behind her, she had come down a flight of steps and entered the throne room.

"I myself have known who I am since my earliest childhood. My grandfather was always telling me about it, the way other children get told the story of Baby Jesus. It never meant much to Papa, but I spent most of my time with my dear grandpa. He and I were . . . very like each other." Luise looked at Steven with a spark in her eye. "My grandfather and yours were brothers, Steven. Brothers and at the same time mortal enemies. May I?" She picked up the bloodstained family tree from the mosaic floor and examined it, wrinkling her brow.

"Leopold, son of Ludwig the Second," she murmured, running her finger down the line of her and Steven's forebears. "To the day of his early death on the battlefields of Verdun, Leopold never knew anything about his real father. Marot thought it too dangerous. The prince regent's agents never rested." Luise shook her head, lost in thought; she now seemed to be in an entirely different world.

"When the good Theodor died a short time later, working as an army doctor on the Somme, only Maria still knew the secret of the diary. On her deathbed, she left it to her two grandsons. Lothar and Anton, the legitimate heirs of Ludwig, were to bring the truth to light after so many years."

"If you've inherited anything from Ludwig yourself, dear cousin, it can only be insanity," Steven said. "Insanity and, I hope, an early death."

"Quiet!" she snapped. "You still don't understand anything. You and your whole despicable branch of the family. My grandfather Lothar was telling people about his true origins back in the 1930s, but the folk of Oberammergau thought he was crazy, just fantasizing." She shook her head indignantly. "Your grandfather Anton didn't want to know anything about it. He disowned his family. They quarreled, and then . . ."

Her voice rose again; her eyes seemed to be spraying fiery sparks. "And then your damn grandfather went to the States and simply took the diary with him, like a cheap souvenir, that . . . that thief, that *bastard!*" She tore the copied family tree into small pieces and threw them in the air, where they sailed down to the floor like a rain of white paper sprinkled with red. "He stole the diary. Grandfather Lothar told me all about it. He described the book and the treasure chest to me in such detail that I saw them in my dreams. He even sent detectives to the States, but they failed to find his damn brother and the book." She watched the scraps of paper sucking up Zöller's blood from the floor.

"Unfortunately, my grandfather left us far too early." She sighed. "Only a few months before you and your wretched family came back to Germany. He'd been looking for his brother's descendants all that time, and now there, they suddenly were in Cologne, smiling at a housewarming party and trying to shake my hand." She laughed, and it sounded like the squeal of a ten-year-old. "I kept my eye on you at that party, Steven. After all, you were one of the family of that brood who cheated us of our greatest treasure. When you went up to the library, I followed you. And then I saw you with that book, the one Grandfather was always talking about. *My* book." Her eyes narrowed to slits. "You got away from me then, Steven. I thought the book had been burned. And you may as well have disappeared from the face of the earth."

"Because I had taken the surname of Lukas," Steven said. "My adoptive parents' surname." Images from the past went through his head again, like drifting mist, and he instinctively shivered. "The book reminded me of that time again. That was why I couldn't stop reading it. It really is a book of magic, a book of magic with a curse on it. The curse of my descent."

"Well, ultimately that . . . book of magic has come back to me," Luise said, closing her eyes as if in prayer. "And now it's time to go on a little journey. I was going to show you the castle, wasn't I?" Smiling, the industrialist pointed to the door. "I know a place where you can see the building in all its glory."

· 39 ·

ALONG WITH LANCELOT, THE THREE armed bodyguards, and
Luise Manstein, they left the throne room and climbed down the
broad spiral staircase to the first floor.

Steven and Sara staggered rather than walked. The experiences of
the night made the paintings, arched doorways, vaults, and theatrical
backdrops around them freeze into a single nightmare. As they felt
the muzzles of the semiautomatics in their backs, they stumbled along
the branching system of corridors until they finally came out into the
open air.

A cold fall wind blew around Steven. They were on the northern
side of the castle, not far from the gateway through which they had
entered Neuschwanstein what felt like an eternity ago. Steven had
lost all sense of time. He assumed it must be just before sunrise; he
thought he saw the first faint hint of the light of dawn in the sky.

"Where . . . where are you taking us?" he gasped, still breathless
after going down all those steps and corridors. The men had driven
them like cattle going to the slaughter.

"You'll soon see, dear cousin." Luise pointed the Derringer to the
left, where a small path ran along beside the castle walls. "There's no
better viewing place in all Neuschwanstein."

She switched on a long flashlight to show them the way through the dark wood. Luise's henchmen also carried flashlights, and thin beams of light flitted over the well-trodden path that finally brought them to a wider road. After a few minutes, they left this road and stumbled over a small, tree-grown rise in the ground. They heard the rushing of a mountain stream in the distance.

At last Luise stopped, pointing her flashlight straight ahead, and Steven saw a narrow bridge leading through the night ahead of them. In the darkness, it looked like the entrance to hell.

"The Marie Bridge over the Pöllat Gorge," she said with awe. "See for yourself; the view is astounding." She gave Steven a push, and with Sara he staggered toward the bridge, while two of their guards got into position in front of them and two behind them. Now the sound of water was very close.

The panorama was indeed incomparable.

Below them lay the Pöllat Gorge. A giant waterfall roared down into a rocky basin, flowing on and down to the valley as a rushing mountain stream. Mighty rocks stood to the right and left. Toward the east, Neuschwanstein rose like a white fairy castle among the trees in their fall colors. At exactly this moment, the first faint red glow of the morning sun showed behind the castle.

"Well, did I promise you too much?" Luise leaned dreamily against the chest-high metal railing, looking at the sunrise. She made a wide gesture over the misty mountain world of the Alps. "A beautiful place to die, don't you think, Frau Lengfeld? We are entirely alone; the first hikers won't be around for a few hours. And then an unfortunate tourist woman will be found at the bottom of the Pöllat Gorge, a victim of her own stupidity." Shaking her head, she looked at Sara's high-heeled shoes. "You really shouldn't walk in the mountains in pumps like those. Didn't you read the warning notices?"

Sara tried to fling herself on Luise, but Lancelot held her back by the shoulder with his huge paws.

"You crazy viper!" Sara yelled. "You won't get away with this.

Questions will be asked. I left a message behind at home. If anything should happen to me, then . . ."

"Oh, Frau Lengfeld, do stop," Luise interrupted. "Don't you think you've told enough lies? That naïve idiot beside you may have swallowed all your stories, but you won't get anywhere with me."

"Lies? What . . . what do you mean?" Steven asked.

"What do I mean?" Luise raised her right eyebrow. "Well, dear cousin, we have gathered information not only about you but also, of course, about your charming companion here. And do you know what's so funny about it?" She paused for a moment and then winked at Steven. "Professor Liebermann has no niece."

Steven's jaw dropped, and his legs threatened to give way. What kind of game was she playing?

"Sara . . ." He looked at the art detective, who was standing by the bars of the bridge and was unusually silent, with her lips narrowed. "Is that true?"

"Steven, let me explain . . ."

"*I want to know whether it's true!*" When Sara nodded, he had to hold on to the handrail of the bridge to keep from crumpling.

"And it gets even better, Steven," Luise said. "Has Sara ever told you about her dear papa? No? Then I will." She paused for dramatic effect before she went on, relishing the situation. "Peter Lengfeld is an art thief, the terror of museums, with an unfortunate tendency to steal objets d'art. He has about a dozen break-ins to his name. At the moment, he's serving his third term in prison, waiting to get therapy. We've made inquiries, Steven. While you were at Linderhof, Sara Lengfeld visited her father at Stadelheim Prison in Munich. Ask her what she was doing there. Well?"

Sara was silent. She closed her eyes and breathed deeply and heavily. But Luise Manstein wouldn't let the subject drop.

"This woman is a liar, Steven," she repeated. "A liar and a criminal. I've seen her file on the police computer. Sara Lengfeld has a criminal record for breaking and entering. She has helped her father more than once in his thefts from museums. And she is *not* the niece of Professor Paul Liebermann."

Steven felt hot tears running down his face. This was all too much for him. Which of them should he believe?

"My God, Sara, I trusted you," he whispered. "I told you all about myself. I loved you . . . Say it isn't true. Say you weren't lying to me from the start!"

"Steven, it's not the way you think!" Sara was pleading now. "Okay, it's true about my father, but that's a long time ago. I've changed. And this isn't about him at all. Don't you see how she's trying to play us off against each other? Let me explain . . ."

"You lied to me, Sara *Lengfeld.* Or whatever your real name is. Who can I still trust? Tell me, who?"

"Steven, believe me . . ."

Steven abruptly turned away from her and stared down into the gorge. Suddenly he thought of all the little ways in which Sara had involved him more and more deeply in this business. The plan to solve the puzzle had been hers. Again and again she had advised him against going to the police. She had urged him to go on. And her strange coolness at the sight of the dead man in his bookshop made sense now. Was this woman nothing but a stone-cold criminal? Had she needed him just because he could read Marot's shorthand?

Had she . . . used him all along?

For a moment he was tempted to climb over the handrail and let himself drop—drop to the bottom of the gorge, where darkness and endless oblivion awaited him. But then it occurred to him that others were about to make him do that anyway.

"Unfortunately, Frau Lengfeld hasn't yet told us who she is actually working for," Luise said. "Whether for her father or for someone else. But maybe a look at the depths below will make her a little more forthcoming. Well, Frau Lengfeld, what about it?"

"You're going to kill me anyway," Sara replied, "so why should I tell you anything?"

Luise shook her head disapprovingly. "You're forgetting that some ways of dying are quick; some take much longer. Lancelot will think himself lucky to try either way on you. So talk."

Sara's lips were a narrow line, and she kept her arms folded.

"Very well." Luise gave a theatrical sigh. "Then it will take a long time. A very long time."

She tapped Steven on the shoulder. "Come along, dearest cousin. Family duties call. You have solved the puzzle, and now I know where we must search. A perfect division of labor, don't you agree?" Luise turned away, and the three bodyguards pushed the trembling bookseller along ahead of them, until they had left the bridge behind again, with only Sara and Lancelot still on it.

At that moment he heard the throb of rotor blades coming from the east. A helicopter came up from the valley and prepared to land in the castle courtyard. The industrialist took a deep breath.

"Let's forget that little snake," she said, leading Steven away. She held the treasure chest with the diary in a firm grip. "Lancelot will take care of her. Our taxi is waiting in the upper courtyard. It will take us to the fourth castle and the end of our quest."

Meanwhile Lancelot, his gun raised, advanced on Sara. He lifted his eye patch so that she could see the dark socket behind it.

"Hey, baby," he called, vying with the noise of the helicopter. "Today you're gonna learn to fly."

40

Luise, her three paladins, and the exhausted, staggering Steven hurried toward the castle, while the helicopter, making an infernal racket, came down in the upper courtyard of the castle. Ducking, the five of them approached the roaring monster as it rocked, like an intoxicated dragon, a few hand's-breadths above the ground.

Luise pointed her Derringer to its interior. "In you get, Steven!" she shouted. She gave one of the armed men a few instructions, and then she, the other two, and Steven climbed into the helicopter. The door closed, and they took off.

"Mordred and a few of the other knights will see to the throne room and Zöller's body," she said, staring out of the window, through which the castle below them got smaller and smaller. "When the first tourists arrive at ten, no one will be able to tell what happened here last night. Tristan and Galahad, on the other hand . . ." She pointed to the two bodyguards who sat to the right and left of Steven in their black leather jackets, staring straight ahead. "Tristan and Galahad will accompany us on this quest. Besides Lancelot, they are my best paladins, and they have instructions to shoot you at once if there is any danger of your trying to escape. So don't think that you can try anything clever."

"Where are we going?" Steven asked as he looked ahead through the cockpit window, where the Alps were emerging from the mist. Steep peaks rose among the clouds, which were slowly dispersing in the morning light. Steven still felt numb; in the last hour his life had turned into a nightmare from which he didn't seem to be awakening. The damn book had cast its spell on him, and in the end it had thrown him into hell.

"Where are we going?"

Luise laughed. "To the fourth castle, of course. You yourself were kind enough to find out the hiding place for me. Don't you remember the solution to the puzzle?" She chanted Marot's words like a strange kind of melody.

"*In the king's fourth castle a scion shows the dearest of his treasures.* The irony behind that is truly too delicious."

"But Ludwig built only three castles," Steven wearily objected. "There was never any talk of a fourth."

The industrialist smiled broadly. "You're right, Cousin. Only three castles were built. However, a fourth was *planned*. Your expert friend Albert Zöller could have told you that, I'm sure. Ah, there it is."

She wiped condensation off the pane beside her, and through a small hole Steven looked down on a wooded mountain, one of the foothills of the Alps. Its precipitous peak, maybe some three hundred or more feet high, was treeless, and on its rocks he saw a dilapidated ruin that must once, ages ago, have been a castle.

Suddenly a memory surfaced in Steven's head. He thought of the model castle in the museum at Herrenchiemsee. The hill on which it stood had looked very like the mountain below him. At the time, Sara had even read the information about the planned project. What had the place been called . . .

"Falkenstein Castle! An ideal hiding place. I should have known." Luise's voice brought him back to reality. "Ludwig's dream of a castle fit for a true king. And incidentally, at the highest altitude of any castle in Germany." She looked reverently down at the ruin. A modern complex of buildings lay at its foot.

"The castle that stood here in the Middle Ages was a powerful signal from Count Meinhard of the Tyrol, who wanted to incorporate the land around Füssen with his domains," the industrialist went on. "As an inhabited fortress, however, its situation was too high and inhospitable, and so it fell into ruin. Ludwig wanted to build his tomb here, but he died before the building work really began. Marot couldn't have chosen a better place."

"And that new building down there?" Steven asked, pointing out of the window. "That can't be part of the castle."

Luise smiled broadly. "An elegant little luxury hotel that I acquired some time ago, and to which I have added some . . . well, extensions. If I'd known that Ludwig's statutory declaration was only a few yards away . . ." Laughing, she shook her head.

The helicopter was now losing height, and it came down on the parking lot outside the hotel. In spite of the noise, the hotel windows were dark, and there was no one in sight.

"Fortunately, I have been using the off-season to do some renovations," Luise said as the rotor blades slowed. "The hotel is closed. So we're all alone up here."

She took the little treasure chest off one of the back seats, put it in a nylon bag that she had brought with her, and opened the door. Icy cold mountain air blew into the interior of the helicopter.

"Come on, Steven," Luise said. "Time to claim our inheritance."

41

LANCELOT STOOD IN THE MIDDLE of the Marie Bridge with his semiautomatic Glock 17 in one hand and an Uzi in the other. He grinned at Sara as the footsteps of Steven, Luise, and the other men slowly died away in the wood.

"Just the two of us, girlie," he said at last. "Looks like it's time for the showdown."

The giant hummed a tune, and it took Sara some time to work out that it was supposed to be Simon and Garfunkel's "Bridge over Troubled Water." Lancelot put his two guns down on the ground in front of him and came toward Sara, still humming, his huge hands raised. He looked like the crazed priest of some ancient, forgotten deity.

Keep your head clear, she thought. *This guy is a sadist pumped full of testosterone, a fit fighting machine, a murderous mercenary, but apart from that, he's a perfectly normal human being. And human beings make mistakes.*

"'When darkness comes,'" sang Lancelot in his deep growling bass, "'and pain is all around . . .'" He smiled broadly. "I don't need a gun for what comes next. I'll be doing it by hand. And tomorrow morning I'm booking the flight that will take me to my yacht in the Caribbean. Too bad you won't be able to come, too."

Sara stood in the middle of the bridge, which vibrated slightly under Lancelot's footsteps. The giant was only a few feet away. She looked frantically around, trying to calculate her chances of flight. They were very few. The situation was, to put it mildly, hopeless.

If I turn around and run for the forest on the other side of the gorge, he'll pick up his Uzi and shoot me. If I stay where I am, he'll throw me off the bridge. If I fight, he'll throttle me. Which would hurt less?

Day had dawned now, and the first rays of sun were bathing the bridge in an almost unreal light. The chest-high handrails to the left and right were made of metal, and the planks of the bridge were solid, stable timber with narrow cracks between them. Through one slightly wider crack, Sara could see that the bridge rested on an arched iron structure anchored in the rock on both sides of the gorge. Suddenly she stopped short.

Could *that* offer a chance?

Looks like I don't have any choice . . .

Quick as lightning, Sara kicked off her impractical shoes, then feinted a movement to the right, and the next moment climbed over the handrail on her left. Lancelot was so surprised that he let valuable time pass before finally moving after her with a roar. When he reached the middle of the bridge, Sara had already climbed down to one of the iron girders. The giant leaned over the handrail and stared at her, his one sound eye full of hatred.

"That won't get you anywhere, you bitch!" he shouted. "I'll pick you off like a bird with a broken wing!"

Running back to the two weapons, which were still lying on the planks of the end of the bridge nearer the castle, he thrust the Glock into his belt and reached for the Uzi semiautomatic. Meanwhile, Sara made her way hand over hand farther down her girder, and from there she climbed down onto a horizontal strut directly under the bridge. She held two posts firmly, one in each hand, and now ventured a brief glance down.

The sight made her suddenly feel nauseated. For a brief moment, the strength went out of her fingers. She just barely managed to cling to the iron.

Some three hundred feet below her, the waterfall poured through a small basin and into the valley. The walls of rock dropping to the bottom were breathtakingly steep. A slight wind blew through her hair and tugged at her clothes.

Now the bridge itself began to swing. It took Sara a moment to realize that the swinging was not the work of the wind but of Lancelot, who was running along the planks with all his weight. She couldn't see him, but she could hear him all the more clearly for that.

"Where are you? Where?" he shouted into the wind. "Have you flown away, little birdie? Damn it, where are you hiding?"

Sara breathed a sigh of relief. Obviously Lancelot couldn't see her from where he was behind the guardrails. She heard his heavy boots stamp over the planks, back and forth, faster and faster as he looked for his victim.

"Bloody woman."

Suddenly the Uzi semiautomatic barked. In alarm, Sara looked up and saw with horror that several bullets had come through the planks. One shot hissed by close to her ear.

"Where are you, Sara?"

Lancelot's voice was almost cracking. Once again, several planks splintered. Sara pressed her lips together to keep from screaming, and thus giving her hiding place away. What now? It was only a matter of time before one of the bullets hit her. Below her, on the north side of the bridge, she saw an iron basket structure about six feet wide, presumably fitted for building workers. Maybe she could take refuge there? But how on earth was she to travel the hundred feet or so to the structure below the bridge? Sara knew that if she looked down again, everything would probably go black before her eyes. Moreover, any movement would give away her whereabouts. There had to be some other way to do it.

Sara's brain was working at top speed as bullets pinged off the metal structure around her. At last she formed something like a plan in her head, clouded as it was by adrenaline. She had once done some judo as a child. She didn't remember much about it, but one rule stuck in her memory.

Your opponent's weight is your own strength . . .

Sara nodded grimly. More than two hundred pounds could mean a lot of strength.

She took off the belt of her dress, a thin polyacrylic cord that had been nipping at her waist. Experimentally, she tugged at her improvised rope. It seemed as if it would take some weight. The question was, how much?

Holding her breath, she pushed herself in the direction of the guardrail until she was back on the vertical girder by which she had climbed down. Finally, she crawled up, centimeter by centimeter, as if on a climbing pole, until she was directly below the sides of the bridge.

Lancelot peppered the planks with bullets, the floor of the bridge shattering into hundreds of wooden splinters. The noise was so infernal that Sara was afraid she would go deaf. The shots must have been heard down in the valley, but it would certainly be too late for her by the time anyone placed them. She had to act now.

And she did.

In a brief pause between two volleys of shots, she gave a quiet little whimper. It was a very slight sound, but loud enough for her to be sure that Lancelot would hear it.

"What the devil . . ."

She heard his footsteps marching over the bridge, coming toward her faster and faster. Nine feet, six feet, one foot. . . Now he must be directly above her. Sara let out one last whimper, and then Lancelot's arm, holding the Uzi, appeared over her head. He was bending over the side of the bridge. The semiautomatic, his finger on the trigger, his hairy arm . . . At last she saw Lancelot's face as he leaned over the guardrail, which came only up to his stomach. He squinted his one sound eye, aiming at her face.

"Game over, baby," he growled. "Now you'll find out what . . ."

At that moment, Sara seized the wrist of the giant just above her with her right hand. Closing her eyes, she took her other hand off the girder . . .

And let herself drop.

In a fraction of a second, Lancelot's expression changed to panic. He waved his free arm about; he staggered; then his heavy body toppled over the guardrail like a block of stone. A shot went off, and Sara felt a burning sensation on her right temple. For a brief moment their eyes met, and then Sara let go of Lancelot's hand. Screaming, he fell to the depths below with outstretched arms, while the Uzi and the Glock fell after him like a couple of plastic toys.

The scream stopped abruptly as the giant's head smashed into a rocky wall. His body turned over in the air a few times, and then he fell into the rushing water in the stone basin. Like a rotten piece of wood, he bobbed up and down, until the falling water washed him down in the direction of the valley.

Sara hung from the cord belt of her dress, swaying gently back and forth at a height of almost three hundred feet.

"Yacht in the Caribbean, eh?" she shouted down into the gorge as tears ran down her face. "Have a good trip down the river, asshole! And you'd better not try to haunt me. Then I'll . . ."

An ugly tearing sound stopped her. One by one, the threads of her cord belt were giving way. She spun helplessly in the wind. She moved her legs, then rocked back and forth, trying to reach the safety of the iron girder diagonally above her. More threads gave way. She desperately reached out her right arm; she wriggled and twitched, until she finally managed to catch hold of the iron with her hand and pull herself up.

Sara clung to the thick pole like a child clinging to its mother. The cord of the belt was almost entirely gone but for one thin thread. Almost lifelessly, she slid down the iron pole, pressing her legs to the cold metal and closing her eyes.

She felt an overpowering sense of faintness rise in her, and the gorge rushed toward her like a fist ready to strike.

· 42 ·

___

While the sun rose in the sky, a glowing red globe to the east, Luise, Steven, and his two guards went up a well-worn flight of stone steps to the peak of the Falkenstein. The entire Alpine mountain chain stretched out before their eyes like a never-ending ribbon of rock running all the way to the horizon. The abyss dropped steeply away beside Steven's feet; only a step farther and he would fall more than one hundred sixty feet to the depths.

"See that little white mark over there?" Luise handed him a pair of field glasses. When Steven looked through them, he could indeed make out Neuschwanstein between the trees.

"You can see Falkenstein from the window of the throne room on a clear day," the industrialist told him. "Ludwig immortalized the castle on a picture there of St. George."

Steven remembered the model in the museum at Herrenchiemsee, the fairy-tale plaster castle with its battlements and bay windows. But the ruin up here on the peak was not in the least like a legendary king's castle. He stared blankly at a ruinous wall, about sixteen feet high and made of crumbling blocks of stone. In many places empty windows and embrasures could still be seen. More recently, a stairway with a rail had been fitted inside so that visitors could enjoy the magnificent view from a platform. Otherwise, the castle looked more like the remains of a tower battered by wind and weather for many hundreds of years. Steven studied a rusty notice giving information that had been put up beside the ruin.

"*In 1889 lightning struck here, and since then the whole of the eastern gable wall has been missing,*" he read aloud. "I assume that over the last century tourists have left no stone unturned here. So how are we supposed to find a single document? It probably fell to pieces long ago, and . . ."

"*It exists and it is here!*"

Luise's shrill cry cut through the otherwise-peaceful morning silence, and even her two paladins turned around, startled.

"And if necessary, we ourselves will leave no stone unturned. Not a single stone. I have time. My family hasn't waited more than a hundred years to lose patience now, at the last moment. If need be, we'll stay here until we have dug up the entire peak."

The glances exchanged by the two guards told Steven that they were far from enthusiastic at this prospect. Nonetheless, they obediently picked up their shovels and picks and began digging.

Meanwhile, the bookseller was staring across at the little white dot to the east that was Neuschwanstein. Steven's thoughts were with Sara. What had Lancelot done to her? She had obviously been lying to Steven; yet he still loved her. Had she merely been using him to get her hands on the diary? Had it all been just an act? Sara had made him feel able to break away from his lonely, dusty world of books at last; she had made him feel young again. But the way it looked now, she was nothing but a fraud.

And probably dead already.

With tears in his eyes, Steven sat down beside a contorted old tree not far from the entrance to the castle and looked down into the yawning gulf. The damn diary had taken him back to his childhood and finally brought him here. Once again, he felt a desire to jump.

Then perhaps I'll meet Sara again.

Tristan and Galahad picked about at the niches in the walls first and then began breaking several large blocks of stone out of the walls.

Meanwhile, Luise prowled up and down the small courtyard of the castle like a panther in a cage.

"It must be here somewhere!" she cried. "Search, dig, keep those shovels working! Maybe Marot left a sign of some sort behind, something scratched on the rock, *something*."

"Have you seen the gigantic heap of stones on the north side of the castle?" Steven asked, pointing behind him with a weary smile. "I suppose you've heard of Sisyphus, Luise?"

"Very funny, dear cousin." Luise Manstein tossed him a shovel encrusted with mud. "I suggest you start in on that heap of stones right away. Galahad will go with you, so don't get any stupid ideas."

THEY DUG FOR more than an hour, and in spite of the chilly fall wind, Steven soon had sweat running down his forehead. The mountain of rubble stretched the entire length of the castle ruins, a waste of limestone bedrock in pieces large and small, and to make matters more difficult, they were sometimes wedged together. Galahad kept looking at him darkly.

"Once we've found that bloody letter, it'll be your turn," he said. "I'll stone you with my own hands. Every rock I have to turn over I'll throw at your head."

"This could take quite a while yet," Steven replied, straightening up with a groan. His back ached from the unaccustomed manual labor. "If we're out of luck, my beloved cousin will have us tear the entire castle apart."

Steven went over to the contorted tree, where there were several bottles of water ready for them. As he drank deeply, he glanced down at the hotel. The helicopter still waited on its pad. A light drizzle of rain had set in, but all the same the pilot had already had to get rid of two early-morning hikers with Nordic walking sticks. Steven was briefly tempted to call to them for help. But probably that would have cost not just his own life, but also the lives of the innocent elderly couple.

Breathing heavily from the hard work, he sat down on a rock beside the tree and watched Luise and Tristan digging holes at random in the castle courtyard while the industrialist shouted and cursed at the top of her lungs. She had now switched to speaking of herself in the royal plural. Indeed, she seemed to be getting more deranged every minute. She reminded Steven more and more of the defiant ten-year-old who shouted, ranted, and wanted to scratch his eyes out. It seemed as if Luise simply did not realize how pointless all her efforts were.

"The letter will occupy a special position in Our castle," she gasped, and struck the rocks so hard with the pick that splinters of stone sprayed up. "Right beside Our bed, or maybe in the throne room next to the picture of St. George. We will have a chapel built, a vault for the worthy descendants of Ludwig."

"And where is this pretty castle of yours?" Steven called to her. "It's strange that I've never heard of it. Must be quite large if all the furniture from Neuschwanstein fits into it."

"That's none of your business," Luise said. Her gray suit was torn and dirty from all her grim digging; her hair stood out around her face in confusion. She looked like a furious little gnome wielding a pick.

Like Alberich in search of the Rhine gold, Steven thought. *But I am neither Wotan nor Siegfried.*

Thoughtfully, he ran one finger through the soil mingled with roots under the contorted tree. Rotting fall leaves clung to his hand. He rubbed them off and let them drop to the ground. They were withered, brown linden leaves, the typical heart shape.

Suddenly he stopped.

Linden leaves . . .

Could it be possible? Steven looked all the way up the tree. It appeared to be old, almost two hundred years, he estimated. The linden must have been standing here when Marot came to Falkenstein in search of a hiding place.

But considerably smaller at the time . . .

Once again, the answer to the puzzle went through Steven's head.

In the king's fourth castle a scion shows the dearest of his treasures . . .

Steven felt the blood throbbing in his temples, and all of a sudden his throat seemed as dry as a piece of sandpaper. They had assumed all along that *scion* meant Leopold, Ludwig's son. But what if *scion* meant something different? What if it referred to its horticultural meaning of a little tree, a young shoot that, someday, would grow into a strong trunk?

A mighty linden tree.

Steven dug his hands far into the heap of withered leaves and then the soil beneath them, and his heart began to beat faster. His fingers slipped as if of their own accord over the roots and up to the trunk, until they met with some tiny indentations that must have been carved in it by someone long ago. They were letters, distorted and almost covered by the bark as it grew with every year's passing, but Steven recognized them without looking.

Maria.

Steven instinctively smiled. The beginning and the end; it all came full circle here in Falkenstein. The journey was over, and the letter . . .

He felt Luise looking at his back as if her gaze were the tip of an arrow. When he slowly turned around, he saw her standing at the entrance to the castle. She was leaning on her pick and giggling wildly.

"I knew you'd lead me to the hiding place, dearest cousin," she said, pointing to the linden tree. "I really ought to have figured it out myself." She shook her head, laughing. "A scion that shows us Ludwig's son. Friend Theodor really was a poet." Her face transformed into a frozen grotesque. Her lips narrow and bloodless, she turned to her two companions.

"Tristan and Galahad, we need ropes and an ax. And hurry up! We are going to dig my cousin a grave worthy of him."

Luise Manstein took the pick, and with an ardent cry she drove the implement deep into the bark of the tree.

• • •

THEY FOUND THE container about six feet down. It was rusty iron, and so dirty that at first the men thought it was a clod of earth. The beautiful linden tree, felled, lay on the ground, its roots torn apart and shredded as if a bomb had hit it. Luise danced around the wreck of the tree, holding her face up to the drizzling rain.

"Here it is!" she shouted, her voice almost breaking. "Destiny is fulfilled! I have the proof!"

She had the heavily breathing paladins give her the container, and she carefully scratched the layer of mud away. Underneath it was a lid riveted in place and a rusty padlock.

"Quick, a knife!"

Galahad handed her a knife, and, with a well-aimed thrust, Luise Manstein broke the now-brittle padlock open. She reverently put the little container on the ground, knelt down, and lifted the lid.

Inside lay a sealed envelope, damp and sprinkled with spots of mold, but otherwise intact.

Luise took it out and stroked the seal, which showed a swan with its head raised. The knife passed under the seal, which crumbled into small red fragments. With her fingertips, she took the letter out of the envelope and carefully unfolded it. She seemed to be trembling all over.

"I've waited so many years for this moment," she whispered. "Ever since I was a child. And now my dream has come true at last."

Luise fished a pair of reading glasses out of her breast pocket, put them on, and silently moved her lips, as if incanting a magic spell.

"*Thursday, the tenth of June 1886,*" she began quietly. "*I, King Ludwig the Second of Bavaria, do hereby declare, being in full possession of my intellectual powers, and in the best of health, that . . .*"

At that moment the sirens wailed.

· 43 ·

LUISE LOOKED UP IN IRRITATION. Tristan, Galahad, and Steven also turned around, startled. The bookseller could hardly believe his ears. He was hearing good old police sirens, similar to the fanfare in old Westerns as the cavalry rode to the aid of the beleaguered fort.

But how can this be possible? Steven thought. *It must be a dream, a beautiful dream, no more.*

However, the sirens were distinctly too loud for a dream. Three green and white Audis and a bus, blue lights flashing, raced up the narrow, winding mountain road to the hotel. A second bus followed. When the pilot down in the parking lot saw this large contingent coming, he ran to the helicopter and started the engine. Soon after that, the rotor blades began to turn faster and faster, until finally the helicopter rose from the ground and disappeared among the clouds.

Only seconds later, the police cars had reached the hotel parking lot. Gray-clad men poured out of the two buses, wearing balaclavas and equipped with MP5 submachine guns and Kevlar bulletproof vests. They took up their positions behind the cars. Some of the officers swarmed out into the woods below the peak. There were clicks of safeties being taken off, and then there was an almost eerie silence.

"This is the police!" a croaking voice suddenly announced through a megaphone. "We know you're up there, Frau Manstein! Give your-self up. Any resistance is useless!"

Luise froze, her face distorted in a grimace of horror, insanity, and bewilderment. For a moment Steven thought she would put the letter down on the ground and surrender. But then she drew out her small pistol from under her suit and put it to Steven's head.

"Not a step closer!" she shouted. "Or I'll blow his brains all over the castle!"

With a strangely calm demeanor, she tucked the envelope into her neckline and gave her two paladins a sign.

"Open fire," she ordered, and then ran with Steven into the shelter of the castle courtyard. "Distract them until the chopper comes back."

Tristan and Galahad looked at each other uncertainly. Then they threw down their shovels, drew their semiautomatics, and got into position behind the embrasures of the ruined building. Soon after that, the clatter of the Uzis rang out, interrupted by occasional shots from the police officers. Looking through a moss-covered window opening, Steven saw at least four masked men, wearing bulletproof vests and armed with sniper rifles, sprinting from tree to tree and constantly looking for cover. Just before reaching the peak, they finally crouched down behind some rocks and waited.

"I don't know who tipped them off," Luise snarled, "but don't think it changes your situation in any way." Her voice was close to Steven's ear now; he could smell her expensive perfume. "The helicopter was really just supposed to take the new antenna over to the tower at Neuschwanstein. But now I'll have to get myself rescued from here in genuinely majestic style." She held her cell phone to her ear and waited impatiently for someone to answer.

But however long she waited, no one did.

"Damn it!" Luise shouted at last, throwing her BlackBerry down on the stony ground of the courtyard, where the display smashed into tiny splinters. "That filthy bastard of a pilot has run for it. When I get my hands on him, I'll . . ."

"Whip him until the blood comes and put his eyes out?" Steven suggested, trying to ignore the cold muzzle of the Derringer against his temple. "Have him sent to a penal colony in Papua New Guinea? Oh, come on, Luise. Don't make things worse than they already are. Even if you were to get away from here—you heard it for yourself: the police know who you are."

"You think I should surrender?" Luise laughed as her paladins launched into a new orgy of noise with their Uzis. Splinters of stone sprayed off the rocks where the police marksmen had taken cover. "Never! I have plenty of money in my overseas accounts. More than Ludwig could ever have dreamed of. I'll move to a small, unknown island and realize his dream there. Away from this sick civilization that gives romantics like us no scope. I will . . ."

A scream was heard, and Steven saw Tristan stagger back with a bleeding wound gaping in his left arm. One of the snipers behind the rocks had aimed through the embrasure and hit him.

"The battle of the Burgundians in King Etzel's hall," said Luise. "You remember the Nibelung saga? *Hundreds now lie slain, by my hand alone* . . . The heroes fall one by one, and the floor of the hall is wet with blood."

"You are totally out of your mind!" Steven yelled. "Give up! It's not too late!"

"Would Ludwig have given up? What do you think?" But Luise seemed unsure of herself. She gnawed her lower lip, and the mascara ran over her mud-stained face, making her look like a vampire drained of blood.

Then she seized Steven's arm.

"No. I don't think Ludwig would have given up. On the contrary."

She pulled him away behind the castle and toward the abyss. Only now did the bookseller see, to his horror, that sparkling new iron rungs led down the precipitous wall, now wet with rain.

"Follow me, Cousin," Luise commanded, with a grave and majestic expression. "It is time for you to set foot in our great-great-grandfather's halls."

· 44 ·

THEY CLIMBED DOWN THE ROCKY WALL one after the other, while the bullets went on rattling overhead.

Steven looked down, his heart thudding, as he made his way from rung to rung, using those above him as handholds. It must have been a good hundred thirty feet down to the grassy ground below, over-grown with small bushes. Flight was out of the question; Luise was right above him. She had slung the nylon bag with the little treasure chest inside it over her shoulder, and she kept stopping and threaten-ing Steven with her pistol to make him hurry.

At last he felt ground beneath his feet, and soon after that Luise was beside him. A narrow path wound its way along the precipitous rock wall to the hotel. There was nothing to be seen now of the chaos raging in the castle above. Only now and then did the sound of shots come down to them.

"Right, keep going," Luise ordered, pushing her cousin forward. "Who knows how long my faithful paladins up there will hold out."

Steven staggered along the muddy path that ended, just below the hotel building, at a square, wooden annex. A narrow flight of steps led into a small room made of pale spruce planks with an aromatic scent of resin. Several old etchings showing Falkenstein Castle at an earlier date hung on the wall; there was a model of the castle in a glass display case, and notices provided information about the details of its history.

"The Falkenstein Museum," Luise explained as she searched the pockets of her suit. "The previous owner of the hotel had it built for his guests, but I have found another use for it."

She took out a small key and inserted it into a keyhole fitted to the side of the display case. There was a quiet hum, and then the case moved aside to reveal a flight of stairs leading down. They climbed down the stairs until they reached an elevator with doors that slid soundlessly aside.

"Welcome to Hades."

Luise sketched a slight bow before ushering Steven into the elevator. "This is really only my escape hatch. I would have liked to show you my hotel suite. But the way things seem, I fear we have no time for that now."

She tapped a combination of several numbers into a keypad, the doors closed, and the elevator, humming, went down.

When the doors opened again, Steven was in the Middle Ages.

A long corridor lined with wood veneer stretched before him, and like the rooms in Neuschwanstein, it was adorned with life-sized murals from the world of the Germanic legends. Chandeliers with white candles in them hung from the ceiling, giving a faint light, and from somewhere came the soft notes of one of Wagner's overtures. Only when he looked again did he see that small halogen bulbs and not candles were burning, and the music came from tiny loudspeakers mounted everywhere in the corridor. On closer inspection, he found that the corridor itself had a rather temporary appearance: some of the planks under the thick rugs were missing, and the ceiling had not yet been fully plastered.

Like Ludwig's own building style, Steven thought. *A half-finished castle cobbled together from several different periods.*

"I have rebuilt large parts of Neuschwanstein," Luise announced as they walked down the long corridor. "In one or two years I would have finished the work. Only the murals are new. I think they are even more successful than the originals, don't you agree?"

"Just as gloomy, anyway."

The corridor suddenly veered left, and they were now walking farther and farther into the mountain, through dimly lit rooms. Luise seemed to have hollowed out the whole Falkenstein like a Swiss cheese. The rooms were carved directly into the rock, and some were shaped like caverns. Instead of windows, there were landscape paintings, one providing a view of a medieval idyll. Behind dusty glass, Steven saw castles on steep peaks, towers, and deep green forests.

In due course, he really did recognize all the furnishings of Neuschwanstein in the countless, labyrinthine series of rooms. They passed the plainly furnished servants' rooms with their rustic wooden bedsteads, then the magnificent dining room in which, as in the original, there was a table with a marble and gilded bronze centerpiece. They walked through the dressing room, the bedchamber, and the salon with its columns and Byzantine arches; even Ludwig's bed with its valuable carvings stood here, just as Steven remembered it. Beyond a passage he saw the sparkling red and blue lights of a grotto reflected on the surface of an underground lake.

She really has had all this stuff brought here to realize her own dream of a fairy-tale castle. How long was it in the planning?

"What you see here is the labor of many years," Luise said proudly, as if she had read his thoughts. "When my husband died, I was able to devote myself entirely to my hobby. A not-inconsiderable part of the resources of the Manstein firm has gone into this project." She turned in a circle, the Derringer in her hand and her head raised to look at the ceiling. "Our great-great-grandfather would have done just the same. Then he would have been spared seeing half the world trample his heritage underfoot. Ludwig wanted to keep his castles to himself. *I* am the one who has made that dream come true."

"Luise, Ludwig is dead," Steven said wearily. "If anything survives, it is only his *idea* in people's minds. He's one of the best-known figures in German history. Do you think he would have been if his castles were hidden somewhere underground?"

Luise sighed and directed Steven on along the corridor with her gun. "You don't understand, Steven. How could you? Yours is the branch of the family that has not bred true to its stock and must be cut off. I'm sorry to put it so bluntly."

By now they had reached the end of the corridor. Ahead of Steven, a mighty hall almost fifty feet high opened up—a perfect copy of the Neuschwanstein throne room.

Or in fact the original itself.

He looked at the colorful mosaic images of animals on the floor, the paintings on the walls, the blue columns and the massive chandelier hanging from the ceiling by chains. Luise's footsteps echoed behind Steven as he walked into the middle of the room. Once again the industrialist looked all around her, and there was mingled grief and resignation in her face. Then, with great care, she put the nylon bag containing the treasure chest down on the mosaic floor and took Ludwig's statutory declaration out from her neckline.

"I have looked for it for so long," she murmured, kissing the letter, and then she tossed it carelessly away, so that it sailed to the floor like a tired moth. "All over."

There was silence for a moment. Then Luise's expression changed as a crazed smile played around her lips. She fished a small black device the size of a cell phone out of her pants pocket and began pressing keys. It made a beeping, buzzing noise like a badly set alarm clock.

"Of course I knew I must be prepared for such an attack," she went on. "You must always be prepared for anything, don't you agree? As Ludwig was. It is said that he would have liked to blow his castles sky-high rather than leave them in the hands of those unworthy of them. And that is exactly what I am going to do now."

Steven missed a breath. "You're going to do *what?*"

Luise looked at her cousin with vacant eyes. "I have had a number of explosives built into my pretty little castle, and I can set them off whenever I like by remote control. You have to know when the end has come. Three, two, one . . ."

"Luise, no!" Steven tried to wrench the little device out of her hand, but it was too late. She had already pressed the last key, and she threw the little black box high in the air and away from her, From somewhere on the other side of the walls came a regular beep repeated at intervals of a second.

"We have five minutes," Luise said dreamily. "The last five minutes in my palace. Come along, Cousin. Let us pray together. This is the end of our family. The end of the line."

Steven stood rigidly beside her. Only seconds later did he seem to awake from a nightmare. "If you think I'm going to die with you, you're much mistaken. You . . . you psycho!"

He turned to the exit, but Luise's cutting voice stopped him in his tracks.

"You're staying here."

Steven spun around and looked down the steel barrel of the Derringer.

"What a disgrace," Luise growled. "If you haven't lived like one, then at least *die* like the descendant of a king."

"Never. You can go to hell on your own."

Without thinking, Steven flung himself at Luise, his arms spread wide. He heard a report, a bullet hissed past close to his cheek, and then he was on her. He pressed her body to the floor with his full weight and tried to seize Luise's hand holding the Derringer.

It's like back then, he thought. *All those years ago in the burning library. And our fight is only now coming to an end.*

But although she was slightly built, the industrialist was surprisingly strong. She rammed her knee into his groin, and Steven fell on his side, groaning. Then she aimed her gun straight at his face.

"Die, you filthy bastard. You thief. You're a traitor to the family. Now . . ."

Steven seized hold of the Derringer and turned it aside. Luise tried to kick him again, but this time he was ready. He brought up his knee and used the short moment of uncertainty to bite Luise's wrist as hard as he could. She screamed and dropped the gun. The next moment Steven was holding the pistol. Still lying on his back, he aimed it at his cousin.

Luise Manstein stood over him, her makeup smeared, her short gray hair standing out on all sides around her head. She looked like a defiant ten-year-old throwing a tantrum. She raised her painted fingernails like claws, and naked madness gleamed in her eyes.

"How . . . how dare you bite My Majesty?" she screeched. "You useless little lackey, you filthy bastard . . ."

Steven pulled the trigger.

Luise stood there for a moment as if turned to stone, and only then did she realize that the bullet had missed her. She broke into deranged laughter.

"You're a coward and a failure, Steven," she said. "You may have Ludwig's blood in you, but your branch of the family will wither, and no one will ever speak your name again. You . . ."

Luise fell silent as an extraordinary creaking and squealing sound was heard from somewhere.

The explosives! thought Steven. *They're going off!*

But then he looked up and saw that the chandelier had moved much closer. One of its chains had broken.

I hit the chandelier!

Steven rolled to one side and, out of the corner of his eye, saw his cousin staring upward in horror. One more creak, and then the chandelier with all its weight came down on Luise like a shooting star.

The chandelier made the mosaic floor vibrate as it smashed down on the floor. Stone dust rose; pieces of iron and splinters of glass flew through the air. Briefly, Steven saw a hand with a ring on it still twitching under the heap of rubble, and then he turned away and ran along the corridor to the elevator. The beeping around him was getting louder and louder.

Out of here! The explosion could come any moment!

At last Steven reached the elevator at the end of the corridor. He frantically pressed the button, and only then saw the keypad right beside the door.

Damn it, the code!

Steven desperately tried to remember what numbers Luise had tapped in on their way down, but it was no good. He simply had no idea. He closed his eyes and wondered what combination Luise *might* have used. It had been eight numbers; he did remember that. Luise's own birthday? Steven remembered the date of the birthday party at Linderhof three days ago, and he tried the sequence 20102010, but the doors stayed closed. Maybe Ludwig's birthday? When was that? It had been in the diary, right at the start—Marot, Dürckheim, and the others had celebrated Ludwig's birthday up on the Schachen. Steven concentrated, and then he tried those eight numbers.

25081845.

Nothing happened. There was only the regular beeping, crescendo now.

Steven cursed and hit the keypad. What else was there? If not the king's birthday, then perhaps . . .

What had Luise said as they entered the elevator?

Welcome to Hades . . .

Steven knew this was his only chance. He thought of Marot's diary and tapped in the date of the Fairy-tale King's death.

13061886

Without a sound, the doors slid open.

Steven let out a cry of joy, ran into the elevator, and pressed the button for Up. Rumbling, the elevator began to move, and spat him out only seconds later in the little museum, where the glass display case still stood beside the opening. Breathlessly, he ran down the steps and out into the open air. He stumbled, rolled down a slope, and turned over several times before he finally came to a halt in a thorny juniper bush. The thorns dug into his skin, but this was no time for crying out.

At that moment, well over three hundred feet above him, the hotel blew up.

The blast was so strong that the shock wave blew into his face, hot and dry like a desert wind. A fireball rose above the site of the hotel, and blazing pieces of wood, splinters of stone, and ashes flew up as far as the tallest treetops. Smaller explosions shook the ground three more times, to be succeeded by an almost unearthly silence. Only the crackling of the fire could still be heard, and sirens wailing on the road in the valley.

Steven stared at the fire, just as he had stared at his parents' burning house when he was seven. He had a feeling that something inside him had clicked back into its right place.

It's all over.

Only later did he hear a great many people shouting. He breathed in smoke and saw the monotonous blinking of a blue light reflected in a puddle. Crawling out of the juniper bush, Steven staggered up the steep slope until he had reached the hotel forecourt. Firefighters in gas masks ran around with hosepipes; farther away the gray-clad men of the Special Unit Force carried the two injured bodyguards, Tristan and Galahad, to a police car. Steven was about to go up to the officer and identify himself, when he saw, among the rocks farther away, a small, delicate form.

Sara had thrown a woolen blanket around her shoulders as protection from the rain and the wind. Her mascara was smeared; she had a bandage around her forehead; her green dress was hanging off her, dirty and torn.

And she was smoking.

· 45 ·

"My god, Sara. You're alive!"

Steven hurried across the forecourt, which teemed with firefighters and paramedics, and took Sara in his arms. The smell of her glowing menthol cigarette suddenly seemed like an exotically fragrant perfume. He held Sara so tightly that he could feel the beating of her heart.

"Squeeze me a little harder and you'll finish me off," she groaned, throwing her cigarette away. "That crazy knight on steroids had nothing on you."

"I . . . I'm sorry." He let her go and looked intently into her eyes. "It's just that . . . I never expected to see you in this world again."

"I didn't expect to see you either."

Steven laughed out loud with relief. "I must say I've missed you. Even if I still don't know why I'm going around with you."

"Luise Manstein was right," Sara said. "My father is a career art thief, serving time in prison at the moment, and as a teenager, I really did stand guard for him a couple of times when he was breaking in somewhere. But that had nothing to do with us."

"Why didn't you tell me about it before?"

Sara smiled wearily. "Maybe because you had quite enough childhood history for both of us? As for the bit about my alleged uncle . . ."

"Perhaps I can help you there," said a deep voice with a pleasant Bavarian note to it. "I believe we owe you an explanation, Herr Lukas."

Turning around, Steven saw a tall, elderly man standing among the firefighters. He wore a brown hunter's coat and a large felt hat that hid much of his face. However, he took the hat off to Sara and Steven, and offered the bookseller his hand. He had a full beard and a mustache with twirled ends, an aura commanding respect, and two watchful eyes with which he scrutinized Steven in a friendly manner. Somehow he looked familiar.

"Who are you?" Steven asked while his hand was almost squashed in the other man's large paw. "A senior police officer?"

The man smiled. "By no means. Although Frau Lengfeld's phone call to us did bring the police on the scene particularly promptly. We have a certain . . . well, amount of influence."

"He's my client," Sara said. "After my little fracas with Lancelot on the bridge, I phoned him at once. I ought to have done it much sooner."

Once again Steven had an odd sense of having seen the man somewhere once before. On TV, perhaps, or in the magazines that were always lying around at the barber's. Yes, that was it; there had been an article in one of them about a certain brewery that didn't have permission to sell its product at this year's Oktoberfest, although it brewed the beer favored by the Wittelsbachs.

Wittelsbachs?

Steven was speechless for a moment. He cautiously cleared his throat.

"You are . . ."

The man made a dismissive gesture. "No names. I'm not really here at all. If the press gets wind of it, there'll be exactly the trouble we wanted to avoid." His eyes twinkled at Steven. "Or do you want to have the police after you for murder again?"

"They aren't after me anymore?"

The man without a name glanced at the burning hotel. "Well, let's say I managed to convince the investigators of the case that they were following a false trail. The gentlemen here have enough to do, keeping a deranged industrialist who thinks herself one of our family a secret from the press. Obviously the board of Manstein Systems knew about Luise Manstein's unusual hobby, if not about its extreme degree." He watched with interest as the firefighters tried to stifle the conflagration with foam and fire extinguishers. Flames still licked up from the ruins of the hotel.

"But first, maybe you will tell us just what happened here," the man went on.

Steven nodded and hastily told his story about the search in the ruins of Falkenstein, the finding of the statutory declaration, and his flight from the hotel cellars.

"Luise Manstein dismantled the entire contents of Neuschwanstein and brought them here," he ended, looking regretfully at the man before him. "Sorry as I am to say so, all the original pieces have been burned to ashes. There are only duplicates in the castle. I suppose you'll have to tell visitors that they're forgeries, and . . ."

The man before him was smiling so mildly that the bookseller broke off, intrigued.

"That's an interesting theory of yours," the bearded man said, scratching his chin. "However, I am sure that our experts will come to a different conclusion. We know that Frau Manstein had *copies* of items in Neuschwanstein made. Very good copies, in fact, but no more."

"But that's not true. You can't—" Steven began. However, a glance from Sara silenced him.

"As I said, I have asked the chief of police to discontinue any investigation of you," the man went on, in a pointedly casual manner. "However, I can always call him and ask him to resume if you would rather."

Steven gave a start. "That won't be necessary."

"Wonderful." The man nodded, satisfied. "Then I think it's for the best if Frau Manstein died tragically in a gas explosion in her hotel.

If only for the interests of our country." Smiling, the man turned to Steven again. "I am sure the chief of police will see it the same way. He and I will discuss the matter this evening over a good bottle of wine."

For some time there was nothing to be heard but the crackling of the fire and the shouted orders of the firefighters. Finally, Sara cleared her throat.

"It was the Wittelsbachs who hired me to find out more about the diary, Steven," she said quietly. "I admit I was lying when I told you I was Professor Paul Liebermann's niece. But no more lies now. My name *is* Sara Lengfeld, I *am* an art detective, and I love you."

"And incidentally, one of the best art detectives who has ever worked for us," the nameless man said. "Frau Lengfeld has often been extremely ingenious in tracking down valuable items from our widely dispersed family possessions. We value her experience and her . . . well, rather unusual methods. She was to get hold of the diary for us in her capacity as a go-between."

"Unfortunately, Professor Liebermann was stubborn," Sara went on. Shivering, she pulled the blanket around her shoulders. "Even when the Wittelsbachs offered him half a million euros for it, the idiot refused. And the next I heard, he had been abducted and murdered." She smiled wearily at Steven. "You were my only link with him and the book. So I pretended to be his niece. You know the rest."

"You used me," Steven said reproachfully. "All your warnings about the police and dangerous strangers were only to get me to decode the book for you."

"Please understand, Steven," Sara said. "It was my job to find out what was behind all those puzzles. But that could be done only with your help. I couldn't decode the book on my own. And I did think, at least at first, that we were safe."

"We have been in constant contact with Frau Lengfeld," said the elderly man. "In Munich, in Linderhof . . . although after what happened at Herrenchiemsee, we were on the point of calling the whole thing off. However, at a meeting in Prien, Frau Lengfeld convinced us that we should continue." He sighed deeply. "If we'd guessed what dangers awaited you both at Herrenchiemsee and later at Neuschwanstein, we'd have brought the police in at once."

"The green Bentley down at the harbor in Prien," Steven groaned. "It wasn't the Cowled Men, or Luise's bodyguards; it was you."

"I didn't know that myself at first." Sara smiled. "We didn't meet until the next morning, when you were still asleep. I'll admit that for a long time I still suspected Zöller." She pointed to the ruins of Falkenstein Castle and the scene of the fire below it, which was now only smoking. "I wanted to know who was behind it. Do you understand, Steven? We might have laid hands on Lancelot and the other men, but we wouldn't have had any evidence at all that Luise Manstein was responsible for everything here. So I kept my mouth shut, and I asked the Wittelsbachs to give me a free hand."

"But why all this?" Steven asked, staring angrily at the bearded man. "Granted, Luise Manstein was out of her mind. But why were *you* willing to pay so much money for an old book? Half a million!" He hesitated. "You wanted to destroy it, right? You wanted to make sure that no stain on Ludwig's reputation would ever be in the public domain." Steven had worked himself up into a fury. "You haven't let anyone see the files since Ludwig's death. The archive isn't open to the public. The coffin in St. Michael's Church in Munich isn't allowed to be opened for forensic investigation. You don't want anyone to find out that the king may have been homosexual, that the prince regent, Luitpold, may have known of his murder, that the Wittelsbach family itself has Ludwig on its conscience. Isn't that so?"

The man smiled. "Oh my goodness, Herr Lukas, all these wild conspiracy theories. The Wittelsbachs at the center of a diabolical intrigue. Could we make it any more melodramatic if we tried?" He chuckled. "Do you really think that it would bother anyone these days if my forebears, more than a hundred years ago, were involved in a murder plot? And a homosexual can get to be foreign minister now." He waved the subject away. "No one is interested, not anymore."

"But if that's so," Steven pointed out, "why don't you open up the archive and the grave? Why did you try to steal the diary?"

"Steal it? We didn't want to steal it." The man lit himself a cigarillo and began puffing on it with relish. "We only wanted to know what was in it. If real evidence of the murder of Ludwig had emerged, in all probability we would have bought the book from you. Could you have resisted half a million euros, Herr Lukas?" He threw his match on the wet asphalt. "But that's an idle question now. Or do you still have the book?"

Steven felt a momentary pang. He could have done a lot with half a million euros.

A cruise around the world with Sara, for instance, a few really rare books, a new antiquarian bookshop . . .

"It . . . I'm afraid it was burned down in the hotel," he hesitantly admitted. "Along with the little treasure chest that contained it, the photographs, and the lock of hair." He sighed. "And of course the statutory declaration. The whole search was for nothing."

"A pity," the nameless man said. "We'd have been really interested in that declaration. A fascinating document for our archive, maybe even more so than Marot's diary."

"Why would that sheet of paper suddenly be worth so much to you?" Steven persisted. "Didn't you yourself say that no one today cares how Ludwig died? Or are you afraid I might demand my inheritance?"

The man in the hunter's coat drew deeply on his cigarillo and laughed out loud. "God forbid! Whether we Wittelsbachs were or were not involved in a murder really has no legal consequences now. And, of course, no kind of claim to an inheritance could be derived from that statutory declaration. All the same, it's a case of keeping the *secret*."

"The secret?" asked Steven, baffled. "What secret?"

Sara sighed and nestled close to him. "Oh, Steven, don't you understand yet? Ludwig is Germany's best-known advertisement. It's not just the Wittelsbachs. He's worth millions to the tourist industry, the hotels, the whole country. And why? Because he's the mysterious Fairy-tale King, because there's a *secret* attached to his life and his death. If there's no secret any more, then Ludwig becomes just any old dead-and-gone monarch."

Steven's jaw dropped. "You mean the Wittelsbachs would have paid half a million euros to make sure that Ludwig's death remained a mystery?"

The man nodded. "The Wittelsbachs, and presumably the state of Bavaria, too. The Ludwig trademark has to be protected, if only for economic reasons."

"But that's absurd."

"Is it?" The nameless man looked curiously at Steven. "People pay millions for souvenirs, books, guided tours of the castles, and for the very reason that Ludwig was mysterious, and died even more mysteriously." He ground out his cigarillo with the heel of his shoe. "That's what people are like, Herr Lukas. They need secrets, and we ensure that those secrets are kept. Even secrets concerning Neuschwanstein Castle." He turned to the parking lot. "Now, come along, I'll take you to Munich with me. Unless you'd rather be taken home in a police car."

As Steven stumbled after him, he saw a gleaming green Bentley on the rainy tarmac in front of the still-smoking hotel. A chauffeur touched his cap and, with a smile, held the door open for him and Sara.

For a moment the bookseller wondered what it would be like to be a recognized heir to the Wittelsbachs. With a handsome castle on Lake Starnberg, a butler, and a family tree as long as the way to the moon. But then Sara moved close to him, and he smelled a mixture of smoke, sweat, and rain.

It was time to go home.

EPILOGUE

THEY DROVE PAST FIELDS AND hilly meadows, and the Alpine mountain chain behind them grew smaller and smaller. By comparison with Sara's compact little Mini Cooper—which the police had not released to her yet—the Bentley was a spacious saloon car. The leather upholstery of the interior smelled like a racing horse's polished saddle, and the light of the sun trying to break through the clouds was reflected back from the fittings. The representative of the Wittelsbachs and his chauffeur occupied the front seats, while Sara nestled close to Steven on the rear seat and looked through the window, lost in thought.

Steven closed his eyes and, after all that had happened over the last few days, tried for the first time to calm himself again. Before they could get into the Bentley, the police had taken their personal details. The local police captain had not seemed particularly happy to let them leave, and Steven would have to go to the Munich police station to make a statement tomorrow. Too many questions were still open, and at least three cases of murder were unexplained. But the man with the twirled ends to his mustache had made it clear to the police, in his firm voice, that he was not about to take no for an answer. Steven suspected that the police captain knew about the convivial evening over a bottle of wine planned by that high-up Wittelsbach and the police chief.

"How do you feel as a great-great-grandson of Ludwig the Second?" Sara suddenly asked. She was stretched out on the soft leather, enjoying the view of the Alps' Bavarian foothills.

"Not so different from before," Steven said. "Except that now at least I have a good reason to be eccentric. I guess you'll have to put up with my oddities."

Sara couldn't help laughing. It was good to see her in a happier mood. In the last half hour she had told him about her struggle with Lancelot, hesitantly at first, her voice then becoming firmer and firmer. Just before she fainted as she slid down the pole of the bridge structure, the local police had arrived, saving her from falling to her death at the last second. Now she seemed almost cheerful. It had obviously done her good to talk about that horror. She had taken off the bandage on her head; that last shot from Lancelot's Uzi had only grazed her temple, and the wound had stopped bleeding.

"At least this is a car worthy of His Majesty's last descendant," Sara went on. She stroked the smooth leather. "All we need is some Wagnerian music and a swan on the hood of the car."

"A horse-drawn coach would probably have been more suitable." Steven leaned over her and dropped a kiss on her cheek. "Or maybe your bright yellow Mini, but it would have been rather cramped for three."

A shadow passed over Sara's face, and Steven realized that he had made a mistake.

"I can't help thinking of Uncle Lu," she said. "Not that he was my uncle any more than Paul Liebermann was, but all the same, I grew very fond of him. To think that he's not around now is . . ." She hesitated and looked into the distance.

"At least he doesn't leave a wife or children," Steven said. "Those last few days with us were probably the best he'd had in a long time. I wonder who will inherit his huge archive?"

"The Bavarian State Library," the man with the twirled ends to his mustache said, speaking up for the first time from the front seat. "Zöller was well-known to the Wittelsbachs; he once told me himself that he planned to have his archive thrown open to the public after his death."

"Then at least it won't end up in your top-secret archive," Steven replied acidly. He thought of Kaulbach's portrait, and the king's shirt with bullet holes in it down in Zöller's cellar. "And then other people will be able to form a picture of the real life and death of Ludwig."

"His real life and death?" The man laughed. "Do you know what Voltaire once said? 'History is the lie commonly agreed upon.'"

"But the truth . . ." Steven objected.

"We'll never know what really happened. There are always several versions of the truth; we all fix on the one we need."

The rest of the journey passed in silence. After a little less than an hour, they had reached Munich, and finally the Westend district of the city. When they turned into Gollierstrasse, where the antiquarian bookshop stood, Steven instinctively held his breath. He felt as if he were coming home from months of traveling around the world, although only a few days had passed since his headlong flight. The police had fixed a seal to the shop door and temporarily patched up the broken display window with foil, but otherwise it looked the same as when he went away. Steven broke the seal, with apprehensive expectation, and unlocked the door. At his first glance into the sales area, a pang went through him.

What in the world . . .

He had entirely forgotten Luise's bodyguards saying that they had searched the shop a second time. The books that he had tidied up after the first break-in were scattered all over the floor again. Broken beer bottles lay everywhere, and the place stank of alcohol and stale cigarette smoke. Obviously other hooligans had been amusing themselves here. Graffiti was sprayed on the back wall of the shop, and there was a stench of urine and vomit in one corner. Steven raised the shredded cover of a book and ran his hand sadly over the worn leather.

It'll never be the same as before, he thought.

"Looks as though you'll have to clean this place up thoroughly," said the man with the twirled mustache, who was standing in the doorway looking at the scene with disgust. "Better get someone to come and take all this garbage away."

He gave Steven a business card. "If you have any problems with the police, you can call me at any time. And also, of course, if you come upon another such valuable find sometime. For instance, the diary of Lidl, the king's personal fisherman, which is also lost." He winked. "Not that I think you'll have much success. In that case we have been extremely . . . creative."

He made a brief farewell bow and walked back to the Bentley. Soon after that, Steven heard the pleasant hum of its engine as the car moved slowly away.

"Steven?" Sara's voice brought Steven back to the dismal reality. He turned a gloomy face to her.

"Yes?"

"About the destruction of the original stuff from Neuschwan-stein . . ." she began. "You mustn't see it in such narrow terms. Don't you remember what Uncle Lu said? The furnishings were never anything but cheap glass, iron, and plaster. It was a historical forgery, and now, well, it's a forgery of the forgery." She smiled. "Why spoil the idea of a fairy-tale castle that the people love so much?" She knelt down and began to pick up one of the overturned bookshelves. "If we hurry up, you can reopen in a few weeks."

"Sara, forget it." Steven dropped the wrecked cover of the book that he had been holding so tightly on the floor. "It'll never be the same as before. And I don't have the money for expensive renovations. I'll be lucky if I can pay my next month's rent. I guess I'll have to give up the bookselling business."

"You're right," Sara said, without interrupting her clearing up. "It will never be the same as before. It will be better. The place needs a new coat of paint anyway. And you could build in a trendy seating corner, and have a coffee lounge where customers can drink their *latte macchiato* while they dip into your wares." She rolled her eyes. "Hey, Steven, this is the Westend district of Munich. If you have to sell books, then at least you might get with the times."

Steven looked at her, bewildered. "Didn't you understand? I simply don't have any money, and what's more . . ."

"Oops, what's this, then?" With feigned surprise, Sara picked up a book from the floor. "Has it been lying here the whole time, or did it just drop out of my purse?"

She held the thin little booklet out to him. When Steven recognized it, he was speechless for quite a long time. As if in a trance, he stared at the title.

Memoirs of Theodor Marot, Assistant to Dr. Max Schleiss von Loewenfeld.

"But . . ." he began hesitantly. "How? I mean . . .?"

"You mean the book was burned in the Falkenstein hotel?" Sara's eyes twinkled at him. "That's not entirely so. The little treasure chest was burned, along with the photographs and the lock of hair. But the diary . . ." She held it up triumphantly. "It was lying on the floor of the throne room at Neuschwanstein with all the other books. I simply pocketed it when no one was looking. Luise was carrying its empty container around with her."

"You're . . . you are . . ." Steven was at a loss for words.

"Brilliant? Ingenious? Drop-dead gorgeous? How would you put it?" Sara grinned. "You're forgetting that I'm the daughter of a thief. I'll make you a suggestion. First thing tomorrow, we send that arrogant dope of a Wittelsbach a copy of the opening of the diary. And then we'll see whether he isn't ready to pay half a million euros for it." She grinned. "Maybe even a bit more. After all, I'm an art detective, I can commission experts to take a very close look at the furnishings of Neuschwanstein. They'll wish they never worked with me."

Laughing, Steven shook his head. "How did I ever get by without you?" He took the book from her hand and kissed her long and hard on the mouth. Sara closed her eyes in enjoyment and suddenly pulled him over to behind one of the overturned bookshelves.

"Sara, you can't . . ."

"Who says you have to be Ludwig the Second's last descendant?" she asked, beginning to unbutton his dirty shirt. "The line hasn't died out yet, not by a long shot."

Marot's diary fell fluttering to the floor, but Steven was past noticing it.

AFTERWORD

When I began my research for this novel, one expert on Ludwig warned me that anyone who starts studying the Fairy-tale King will end up deranged himself.

After reading a few dozen nonfiction books on Ludwig II, visiting his castles, and attending university lectures on schizophrenic disorders and megalomania, and above all after endless phone conversations with mysterious Cowled Men, owners of diaries, and other conspiracy theorists, I now know what he meant: the subject of Ludwig II of Bavaria is a morass, both bewildering and fascinating, because new pieces of the jigsaw puzzle and new inconsistencies keep surfacing. In other words, the case of Ludwig's death is the perfect crime.

Many of the incidents described in this novel correspond to historical fact, absurd as they may sound. I have invented or embroidered upon other elements. There is no historical evidence for the character of Theodor Marot, but his superior, Dr. Max Schleiss von Loewenfeld, certainly existed. He was indeed personal physician to the king, and, according to art historian Professor Siegfried Wichmann of Berlin, wrote a diary in which he described the murder of Ludwig II. Wichmann acquired this book, with the rest of Loewenfeld's literary estate, at an auction and placed it in an archive overseas "for reasons of security." Like Marot's diary in my book, it is bound in blue velvet and ornamented with ivory carvings. Whether it is written in a secret cipher I do not know, but anything is possible in connection with Ludwig's death.

The paintings of artist Hermann Kaulbach are also said to have shown bloodstains from the king's lungs. Professor Wichmann, at the time chief curator of the Bavarian State Collection of Paintings, had them photographed privately in the 1960s; since then, they have gone missing, along with Ludwig's coat and his shirt, both of which allegedly show bullet holes.

Furthermore, there is solid authentication for most of the anecdotes about the Fairy-tale King and other characters in this novel: the equerry Richard Hornig, Counts Dürckheim and Holnstein, and the painter Hermann Kaulbach. And yes, the secret society of the Cowled Men does exist (and of course its present head, unlike his fictional counterpart in my novel, is in the best of health). Bavaria would be much the poorer if it had no such eccentric fraternities.

In addition, there is documentary evidence for the course of the last few days in the life of the Fairy-tale King, some of it even in the form of transcribed conversations. I mention that only because it was in those very passages that my wife several times criticized my exuberant imagination. I was always pleased when I could tell her that my account matched exactly with the contemporary reports. However, we shall probably never know exactly what happened on that last walk taken by Ludwig beside the Starnberger See.

The Wittelsbach family archive is indeed closed to the public. Anyone wishing to know about the king's death will often find that his request falls on deaf ears. The royal family has also forbidden any investigation of Ludwig's casket for reasons of piety. But of course it is unthinkable that the Wittelsbachs could be involved in any conspiracy such as the one in this novel. Any similarity to living persons is therefore out of the question.

To give readers some idea of what is true and what is speculation, I have provided a small glossary for conspiracy theorists. Enjoy the puzzle, working it out, and conspiring.

At this point I would like to express special thanks to the two experts on Ludwig, Erich Adami and Alfons Schweigert, whose book on the last days in the life of King Ludwig II is the best general survey of the Fairy-tale King's death. Erich Adami also put several important books at my disposal, as well as a CD that, so far as I am aware, is the most extensive summary of the facts about Ludwig II ever to have been assembled.

Heartfelt thanks, also, to Dominik for all the information about historical and modern weapons, to my cousin Julian for IT and computer information, to the lady whose name I don't know who was my guide at Linderhof Castle and showed me the king's linden tree, to the kind lady in the kiosk at Neuschwanstein for her meatloaf rolls, to my father and Florian, my brother, for medical information, and of course, once again, to my first readers and proofreaders: my wife, Katrin; Marian; Gerd; and Uta. I am sorry if, this time, I have made a nuisance of myself right to the end of the book. I hope the work has turned out to be worthwhile.

Oliver Pötzsch, November 2010

A Little Glossary
for Conspiracy Theorists

Air rifle: An air gun used by the Prussian secret police, among others. Thought to have been a possible murder weapon. There is a Girandoni brand air rifle in the Munich Museum of Hunting and Fishing.

Attempted assassinations: Supporters of the theory that Ludwig was murdered generally base their thinking on a single would-be assassin who is said to have fired an air rifle (see above). Another theory suggests that a rustic gendarme hit the king by accident, inflicting a mortal wound, when he fired at the two men fighting in the water.

Bank raids: Ludwig really did intend to organize raids on banks in Stuttgart, Frankfurt, Berlin, and Paris in order to finance his castles. Fortunately, these plans were never put into practice.

Berg Castle: This might be described as Ludwig's holiday villa. He died there on 13 June 1886. Originally the king was to be interred in Linderhof Castle, but fears of protest by the local population meant that a last-minute decision was made to keep him at Berg, which was closer to Munich.

Bismarck, Otto von (1815–1898): Chancellor of the German Empire and regarded as the archenemy of Bavaria. Some conspiracy theorists see Otto von Bismarck as the invisible hand behind an assassination because Ludwig, tired of the business of government, had allegedly threatened to cede Bavaria to Austria.

Casket: Ludwig's remains were laid to rest in the Wittelsbach crypt of St. Michael's Church in Munich. However, the Cowled Men (see below) claimed that the casket was empty. To this day, the Wittelsbachs refuse to sanction any forensic investigation of its contents, on the grounds of family piety.

Chloroform: According to one of the many conspiracy theories about the death of Ludwig, chloroform was used as an anesthetic to render him unconscious before he was drowned.

Coat: A coat worn by the king and with two bullet holes in it was apparently in the possession of Countess Josephine von Wrbna-Kaunitz until the 1970s. The countess died in a fire at her apartment in 1973, and since then the coat seems to have disappeared. The shirt worn by the king and showing the bullet entry holes, making it a piece of material evidence, is also said to have been exchanged for another and later destroyed.

Cowled Men: A Bavarian secret society that campaigns to this day for the clarification of what its members, working incognito and disguised by cowls, regard as the murder of King Ludwig. Their legend goes back to the funeral of Frederick Barbarossa, when cowled knights in black habits are said to have followed the funeral procession. There were Cowled Men present at the funeral of Ludwig II in Munich. More about them can be found online at http://www.guglmann.de.

Diary: By his own account, the former chief curator of the Bavarian State Collection of Paintings, Siegfried Wichmann, acquired the diary of the royal physician Dr. Max Schleiss von Loewenfeld in 1987 at an auction. The diary clearly stated that Ludwig II was shot. Witnesses, besides the physician himself, were the painter Hermann Kaulbach (see below), who painted a portrait of the dead king, and the two Hornig brothers (see below). The diary, says Professor Wichmann, was bound in blue velvet adorned with ivory carvings, and the most important documents are currently deposited in archives in the United States and Canada "for reasons of security."

Drowning: The official cause of Ludwig II's death. However, the water of the Starnberger See was only waist-deep at the scene, and Ludwig was a good swimmer. In addition, no water was found in his lungs. All the same, he could have had a heart attack brought on by his agitation, the cold, and the large quantity of alcohol he had drunk with his evening meal.

Dürckheim-Montmartin, Count Eckbrecht von (aka Dürckheim) (1850–1912): Ludwig's adjutant and one of those closest to him. Because he refused to leave his king in Neuschwanstein, he was accused of high treason, but his trial was canceled four weeks later.

Escape: Allegedly, Ludwig's escape from Berg Castle had already been organized. Coaches for the king are said to have been waiting at four places on the Starnberger See (Leoni, Ammerland, Ambach, Seeshaupt) and at the gate of the castle. Boats were also waiting on the lake itself, but they could not come in close to land because the water close to the low-lying banks was so shallow.

Falkenstein: The ruins of Ludwig's fourth castle at Pfronten. The project was never completed because of his early death; the construction work went no farther than laying water pipes and building an access road. The Falkenstein hotel was not built until 1897. It is still standing and was certainly never destroyed by an explosion. A tiny museum there explains the history of the castle ruins to visitors.

Fits of violent rage: According to his servants, Ludwig frequently slapped, kicked, or spat at his subordinates. One servant who committed a minor infraction was permitted, for a full year, to approach him only if wearing a black mask. When the committee members charged with taking Ludwig II into custody at Neuschwanstein Castle (see below) arrived to carry out their mission, the king gave orders for their eyes to be put out and for them to be whipped until their blood ran. His orders were not carried out.

Footprints: According to the notebook of the king's fisherman, Jakob Lidl (see below), footprints were faked at the scene of Ludwig's death with a wooden clog fixed to a pole.

Forgeries: Particularly in Neuschwanstein Castle, cheap materials that appeared magnificent only at first sight were used. What looks like marble is painted stucco, the gleaming gold is really brass, and the "jewels" are colored glass from Lower Bavaria. On closer inspection, the furnishings as a whole give the impression of being a gigantic stage set for a grand opera.

Freyschlag von Freyenstein, Ignaz (1827–1891): Responsible for the operations of the local gendarmerie in Berg. Only two weeks after Ludwig's death, Freyenstein was surprisingly appointed head of the "Prince Regent's Secret Chancellery," known as the "Black Cabinet."

Gudden, Bernhard von (1824–1886): One of the most famous doctors of his time treating the mentally ill. He was commissioned by the ministers to provide an expert medical opinion classifying Ludwig as deranged. However, this medical certificate depended entirely on negative witness statements; the king himself was never interviewed, and positive witness statements were ignored. Gudden died in the Starnberger See with Ludwig. According to many conspiracy theorists, he was either working with Ludwig's enemies or knew too much of the truth for his own good.

Herrenchiemsee: One of Ludwig's three castles, built on an island in the Chiemsee. It is regarded as a tribute to King Louis XIV of France and represents a kind of mini-Versailles.

Hohenschwangau: Castle opposite Neuschwanstein. It belonged to Ludwig's father, Maximilian II, and the Fairy-tale King spent his childhood there.

Holnstein, Count Maximilian Karl Theodor von (1835–1895): Master of the Royal Stables of Bavaria and a playmate of Ludwig in his youth. He was instrumental in arranging the Imperial Letter (see below) and received ten percent commission from the Guelph fund. He played a large part in the later deposition of the king and was to be appointed his guardian. He is quoted as having said, "If I do the king any harm, may I go blind." Holnstein was stone-blind at the time of his death.

Homosexuality: According to the latest research, Ludwig II was homosexual. The fact that many of his modern supporters still regard that as blasphemy says more about their own state of mind than the king's.

Hornig, Richard (1841–1911): Royal equerry and a friend of the king's for many years. In the end, he fell out of favor with him. He had a villa in Allmanshausen on the Starnberger See, and, according to one conspiracy theory, he was one of four witnesses to the murder of Ludwig II, together with his brother, the painter Kaulbach, and the physician Schleiss von Loewenfeld (see below for both).

Imperial Letter: A document drawn up in 1870 by Bismarck (see above) as chancellor of the German Empire, in which Ludwig II ceded the dignity of emperor to the Hohenzollern King Wilhelm I. In his lifetime, the king of Bavaria received some six million marks in gold for this abdication of power. As the money went into his private fortune, a number of historians consider the deal to have been corrupt.

Insanity: Whether Ludwig was insane, and if so to what degree, is a question that can never be entirely settled. However, according to Detlev von Zerssen, professor of psychiatry in Munich, the king suffered from neither paranoia nor schizophrenia (unlike his brother, Otto; see below), but is more likely to have had a schizotypal disorder in combination with an antisocial personality disorder and megalomania, possibly as the result of meningitis contracted when he was a baby. Today he would probably be diagnosed as a borderline case of insanity. In the opinion of Zerssen's colleague, Professor Heinz Häfner, Ludwig II also suffered from a social phobia heightened by his homosexuality. Professor Häfner excludes the possibility of psychosis, in which case the declaration that he was incapacitated and not responsible for his own actions was illegal.

Kainz, Josef (1858–1910): Young actor from Munich whom Ludwig revered, and who went on a journey to Switzerland with him in 1881. The photographs taken of him there with the king were the model for the fictional character of Theodor Marot.

Kaulbach, Hermann (1846–1909): Son of the Munich artist Wilhelm von Kaulbach, and painter of historical subjects. He did five sketches of the ruins of Falkenstein (see above) for Ludwig II. He allegedly painted a picture of the late king on the night of his death, showing blood from Ludwig's lungs at the corner of his mouth (suggesting that he had been shot). According to one theory, he was a witness along with the Hornig brothers (see above) and Dr. Max Schleiss von Loewenfeld (see below) to events on the night of the murder.

Lidl, Jakob (1864–1933): Fisherman to the king, and one of the possible witnesses (see below) to the murder of Ludwig. According to one theory, he was supposed to take the escaping king into his boat, and later wrote down his memories of the night of the murder in a school exercise book that then mysteriously disappeared. Only one page of this journal, which speaks of forged footprints (see above), is still extant.

Linderhof Castle: The smallest of Ludwig's three castles, and the only one to be completed in his lifetime. Famous for the Grotto of Venus and the "magic table" imitating the one in the fairy tale. The linden tree where Ludwig had his tree house can still be seen on the grounds of Linderhof.

Loyal subjects of Ludwig, societies of: There are a number of such organizations in Bavaria, their members devoting themselves to the memory of Ludwig II. They range from serious associations to inveterate monarchists and conspiracy theorists. A memorial service is held annually, on the Sunday after the date of Ludwig's death, in the votive chapel of Berg Castle.

Luitpold of Bavaria (1821–1912): Took over the government of the country after the death of Ludwig II. He was persuaded by John Lutz, president of the Council of Ministers (see below) to carry out a coup d'état, and for some time lived under a cloud with the reputation of having killed the king, but nonetheless ushered in the golden age of Bavaria.

Lutz, Johann Baron von (1826–1890): President of the Bavarian Council of Ministers and regarded by conspiracy theorists as the leading villain instrumental in the assassination of the king. He commissioned Dr. von Gudden (see above) to write a medical report on the king, and convinced Prince Luitpold (see above) to take over as prince regent. If the coup d'état had failed, presumably Lutz would have paid for it with his head.

Neuschwanstein Castle: The most famous of Ludwig's castles, although it was never finished. Confusingly, it was known as Hohenschwangau Castle at the time. It was opened to the public soon after the king's death, with the idea of demonstrating Ludwig's alleged megalomania to the people of Bavaria. To this day it attracts about 1.3 million visitors each year.

Ney, Elisabet (1833–1907): German sculptor whose statue of Ludwig now stands in the Herrenchiemsee museum. There were rumors of an affair between her and the king resulting in an illegitimate child. Ludwig II is also said to have had a son at his Schachen hunting lodge by a chambermaid called Marianna. This legend lies behind the fictional relationship between Ludwig and the maidservant Maria.

Otto von Wittelsbach (1848–1916): Younger brother of Ludwig, officially king of Bavaria after 1886, but incapable of ruling the country because of his mental illness. His illness was presented as part of the evidence that Ludwig's megalomania ran in the family. Their aunt Alexandra Amalie, princess of Bavaria, was also mentally ill and suffered from the obsessive delusion that she had swallowed a glass piano.

Pepys, Samuel (1633–1703): English civil servant known to posterity for his diaries written in shorthand. They provide a graphic picture of London in the late seventeenth century and were not deciphered for the first time until 1825.

Poe, Edgar Allan (1809–1849): Ludwig II was a great fan of the American writer. The king is said to have announced that he would give up his throne for an hour's conversation with the cult author.

Rose Island: Island in the Starnberger See with a villa belonging to the Wittelsbachs, where Ludwig II used to meet his cousin Sisi (see below).

Schachen hunting lodge: The king's house in the Wetterstein mountain range. It has a Turkish room with a fountain, divans, and peacock feathers, where the king played the part of a caliph and regularly celebrated his birthday.

Schleiss von Loewenfeld, Max Joseph (1809–1897): Royal physician first to Maximilian II, later to his son Ludwig II. He was Dr. Gudden's adversary and, after Ludwig's death, he gave his opinion, writing in the Viennese press, that the king had not been insane. However, pressure was put on him to withdraw that statement. According to one conspiracy theory, he was an eyewitness on the night of the murder, together with the Hornig brothers and the painter Hermann Kaulbach (for all three, see above). The diary he is alleged to have kept (see above) provided the basic idea for this crime story.

Shelton, Thomas (circa 1600–1650): English stenographer and inventor of a shorthand much used in the seventeenth and eighteenth centuries. The standard work is his *Tachygraphy*. His shorthand system was also used by Samuel Pepys (see above) in his diaries.

Sisi (Elisabeth) (1837–1889): Empress of Austria-Hungary and Ludwig's cousin. They were friends, and he sometimes met her on Rose Island (see above). It is now thought, even by conspiracy theorists, that Sisi's involvement in Ludwig's failed escape (see above) is improbable. However, she was at Possenhofen Castle on the Starnberger See on the night of her cousin's death.

Tmeicos Ettal: Sometimes also written *Meicost Ettal*, it is an anagram of the saying ascribed to the Sun King, *"L'état, ç'est moi."* It was Ludwig's secret code for the building of Linderhof Castle (see above).

Vigenère cipher: Developed by the French diplomat Blaise de Vigenère (1523–1596), this cipher was cracked only thirty years later by the British mathematician Charles Babbage. A coding and decoding program can be found online at http://einklich.net/etc/vigenere.htm.

Wagner, Richard (1813–1883): Composer revered by Ludwig II. Motifs from his operas are on view everywhere in Neuschwanstein Castle (see above).

Watch: Ludwig's pocket watch stopped at 6:54 P.M., Gudden's not until 8:10 P.M. This circumstance has led to much speculation.

Waxwork figure: When Ludwig II was lying in state on view to the public, his body seemed so artificial that many people suspected it was a waxwork figure in the casket. Ever since, there have been rumors that the king did not die at the time but only, being tired of the business of government, emigrated to an island. However, the waxen look of the face is more likely to have been the result of embalming.

Witnesses: A suspicious number of contemporary witnesses from Berg disappeared, lost their lives, or suddenly seemed to have acquired unusual wealth. A scullion called Gumbiller took his own life, and two servants at the castle were committed to a lunatic asylum, where they died not much later. The bodyguard Ludwig Larose, who apparently "talked too much," soon died as well. Another witness went missing. Of the five gendarmes stationed in Berg, one died in a mysterious accident in the course of his work, and another emigrated to America with a great deal of money. The fisherman Jakob Lidl (see above), not a man of means, who was regarded as one of the key witnesses, came into a considerable fortune, finally rising to be mayor of Berg and a freeman of the town.

Wittelsbach family archive: All the documents on the "Ludwig Case" are in the Wittelsbach family archive, and to this day they are not available to the general public.

XY—unsolved: After the Wittelsbachs had the case investigated again by Wilhelm Wöbking, the former state prosecutor and judge, on the hundredth anniversary of Ludwig II's death, it was officially stated that the king strangled Gudden and then committed suicide in the water. All the same, new conspiracy theories are always being suggested.

JOHN M. CUELENAERE PUBLIC LIBRARY

33292900012661

The Ludwig Conspiracy : a

Stained pages
XIX-10   w/pal
June/14.